Evil _in_

TECHNICOLOR

Evil in TECHNICOLOR

FEATURING

CRAIG LAURANCE GIDNEY · A.C. WISE
NICK MAMATAS · MOLLY TANZER

· STINA LEICHT · BONNIE JO STUFFLEBEAM ·
AND MORE

EDITED BY
JOE M. McDERMOTT

VERNACULAR

EVIL IN TECHNICOLOR

Forgiveness is Warm Like a Tear on the Cheek © 2020 Stina Leicht; *Blue Hole, Red Sea* © 2020 E. Catherine Tobler; *A Thousand Faces Minus One* © 2020 A. C. Wise; *The Maidens of Midnight* © 2020 Rhiannon Rasmussen-Silverstein; *The Ultimate Secret of Magic* © 2020 Adam Gallardo; *The Midnight Feast* © 2020 Haralambi Markov; *Myth and Moor* © 2020 Craig Laurance Gidney; *Hammerville* © 2020 Bonnie Jo Stufflebeam; *Summer Camp Would Have Been a Lot Cheaper* © 2020 Molly Tanzer; *The Thunder, Perfect Mind* © 2020 Nick Mamatas

Cover and interior line art by I L Vinokur

Cover and interior design by ElfElm Publishing LLC

Available as a trade paperback and eBook from Vernacular Books.

ISBN (TPB): 978-1-952283-03-1
ISBN (eBook): 978-1-952283-04-8

Visit us online at **VernacularBooks.com**

TABLE OF CONTENTS

INTRODUCTION

IN THE SPRING OF 2020, we all woke up in a horror movie. Sometime in March or April, all of us slowly realized that the world was trying to kill a lot of us off, and we had to shelter from it. I was working at a community college, and we were leaving for spring break, and I told two of my co-workers that I thought we might be done. I thought that this would be it for the semester, possibly even the college budget for our positions. The campus, at least, was not going to come back after the break. We, in our humble positions, would not be coming back. They were both wiser in the world than I was, and said we would be back in a week, and I was being ridiculous, but then everything we had been trained to think about the way the world works suddenly shifted, and campus closed, and we had to rebuild our entire profession into a virtual workspace. Everything stopped. Everyone started wearing masks everywhere, if we went anywhere, and often gloves, too. Many of the businesses and activities we loved just stopped. We all had to wait, then, and see what would happen, and the only thing we really knew was that we didn't know very much, at all.

One day we went to bed in the world we knew, and then woke up and we were in a horror movie. It wasn't one of the mainstream ones. There was no high concept to discuss. No buildings exploded. It wasn't an invasion of anything constructed by advanced computer graphics. We just had to stay home and wait.

In this new world, some of us over here at Vernacular Books got our heads together and decided to make something. It isn't about this quarantine experience, but it is built inside of it. The many authors I brought in on this project agreed the kind of horror story they wanted to do was the sort of thing that we would expect from old Hammer horror movies, the kind of movies we'd binge watch late at night when we're stuck in the house with nothing else to do. The production company, Hammer Films, still exists, and still produces books and movies, and I'm not talking about their modern iterations and projects. No, I'm talking about the classic era, when these dreams and nightmares were black and white and technicolor. The stories in this anthology are all inspired by these old horrors and thrillers and haunted houses and weird cinema experiences with the unknown.

Experiencing this kind of evil in art is cathartic. It pushes loose feelings pent up and strained by our need to get through horrific things in our own life. Horror invents a language to discuss the visceral gut emotions and experiences, allowing the audience to face and name our collective and individual anxieties. (This isn't *all* horror is, but it is enough of a definition for the purposes of this little introduction.) Often, as well, these visceral experiences are fine entertainment for turning pages in the long, quiet afternoon.

The stories trickled in over eight strange and unsettled weeks in Spring. Some of the stories took their inspiration very directly, and featured vampires and monsters that seem to have walked off the technicolor screens. Others sought the uncanny strangeness that was often an important part of the more psychological films and influences, exploring off corners of the dark psyche. Others turned to the influences of the Weird, where mundane life brushes up against something truly unknown and unknowable. The stage, the book, the song all become the haunted places where the liminal creeps into the world. The houses and castles are haunted. The dreams and nightmares come to beckon even as they threaten. We press on into the unknown future, and use these dreams and nightmares as we will.

On a practical note, I thought it important to do novelettes in this anthology. It's a form uniquely suited to the anthology, with longer, satisfying stories that settle in place and take more time to explore these interesting characters and worlds, while still playing well in concert with other pieces. After seeing it all together, I am pleased with this decision. I hope you will find great pleasure here as well, fair reader.

FORGIVENESS IS WARM LIKE A TEAR ON THE CHEEK
BY STINA LEICHT

SECRETIVE AND BROODING, MAUFRAIS HOUSE squatted atop the hill like a toad within the live oak grove. At night, its windows flickered sickly yellow. Black wrought iron spikes topped the limestone walls ringing the property and its accompanying family cemetery plot. A thirteen-acre parcel of undeveloped land was an unusual feature in Austin—particularly given that it was three blocks east of South Congress Avenue. Like most urban areas, the surrounding neighborhood had seen more diverse, if difficult, times. Many of the original houses—once great Gilded Age ladies—had been condemned and replaced with cheap apartment buildings. The architectural survivors bore the scars of gentrification as ill-conceived renovations. Maufrais was the only exception. An imposing three-story Victorian, it appeared to sneer down at its neighbors in semi-derelict defiance.

The house's history was, for the most part, unclear. But, in 1974, a mentally unstable man broke in and set fire to it, claiming someone inside had possessed him. No evidence of a resident was found. The unfortunate man was taken to Shoal Creek mental hospital for treatment. It wasn't the first time the house had weathered arson.

When located, the absent owners declined to press charges. Soon a swarm of contractors affected repairs. The house began to look whole again. Ten months later, a moving van slowly worked its way up the steep drive and disgorged furnishings. In a vacuum of information, the neighbors speculated for weeks about who would move in. More time passed. Then late one October evening a long black vehicle eased through the iron gate. The next day, the car was still parked in the drive. Like dead men, its heavily tinted windows told no tales.

Again the neighborhood waited, curious. Still, no one emerged to introduce themselves. The only evidence the building was occupied were specters of light in the windows and outside. Every evening at seven o'clock a blue bulb on the back porch snapped on. Sometimes, distant music—a piano or a woman singing—haunted the breeze.

With little ammunition for fresh rumors, the community soon went on about the business of living, working, and dying. Maufrais House became invisible in the way a discarded toy is unseen in an untidy child's bedroom.

Thus, the house and its mysterious tenants were left to dream their dark dreams in peace.

"Screw you and your stupid band!" Andi hurled her beer bottle across the DIY sound-proofed garage. Glass exploded against the wall just missing Jason's new Gibson in its stand. "I quit!"

Jason edged in front of the instrument in case of a second barrage. He knew it was a mistake the instant he said, "You can't quit."

Andi whirled, shoving an accusing finger in his face. "Who the hell are you to tell me what to do?"

Little Sister's drummer, Bud, muttered he needed something from the van and disappeared to the kick-drum beat of a slamming door. Penny, the bass player, rescued her Les Paul before making her own hasty retreat.

"South By Southwest is only a month away. Label reps will be there," Jason said in an attempt to direct Andi's attention to what was important. Even he could detect the pleading tone in his voice.

"No more fucking freebies!" Andi said. She punctuated each word with a poke in his chest.

Certain her sharp nails had left a mark, he backed up in an effort to de-escalate the situation. "You know the deal. Andre let's us practice here. In exchange, we play free gigs. It's a college birthday party. Big Bad Wolf flaked."

"I don't give a shit!" Andi flipped her blond dreadlocks and snatched her leather jacket from the old couch in the corner. "Get yourself another girlfriend and lead singer, limp dick." She flipped him off as she stomped out in a fog of Black Phoenix perfume.

He told himself her leaving again was a good thing—that he'd grown tired of the constant renegotiations. He hoped she'd be gone when he got home. She usually was after one of her tantrums.

You're no prize yourself, he thought. *You get that, right?*

Fishing his phone from his back pocket, he started to dial her cell to ask for his key back. *That'll end it for sure.* But as he watched the beer ooze down the cinder-block wall he reconsidered.

"Well, that went over like the proverbial lead floating thing," Penny said, venturing a cautious return like a campus shooter threat evacuee after the all clear was given. With a relieved sigh, she threw herself onto the sofa and then cradled her bass in her lap. "What are we going to do about tomorrow night?"

"You can sing." Bud flopped down next to her. "You've a great voice."

"I can't." Penny bit her lip and focused on her bass. "I won't."

Her black Theda Bera bob was now an unnatural shade of cotton candy pink blond. She had intense brown eyes that tended to wrinkle at the corners when she laughed. Short with a boyish build, her bass made her look like a waif on stage. Often people—*Male people,* Jason corrected himself—let that first impression form their assessments of her skills. They were dead wrong, of course.

She was a talented bassist, a whirlwind of energy. Raised Roman Catholic, she was uncomfortable with compliments, but Jason often compared her to Flea behind her back. She handled a fiddle with equal skill, having started lessons when she was three. She had a wonderful, clear singing voice too. Unfortunately, she refused to front. It was as if she needed her bass to shield herself from the audience.

Jason had known her for two years and still didn't understand why she wasn't with a better band. *Don't be stupid. You know why.*

Nonetheless, it was good for the band that she wasn't. If she left, that'd be the end. Andre, Penny's uncle, only supported them because of her. Her family was full of savvy bohemians and musicians who supported themselves via real estate. They owned property all over central Austin, including the free practice space.

On the other end of the spectrum, Jason had known Bud since the ninth grade. They'd had many misadventures, starting with sitting detention for causing the emergency evacuation of Mrs. Brennan's fourth period chemistry class—due to a couple of tubes of molten sulfur deposited in the wrong trash can.

"We'll find a sub." Jason began packing his gear. It was late.

The subject of himself or Bud fronting wasn't broached. Little Sister always had a female lead and always would.

"In less than twenty-four hours? Come on, man. No way. We're screwed. Come on. Give her a shot," Bud said.

Jason agreed with Bud on most things—just not Penny.

"Damn it, Bud," Penny said. "You never fucking listen."

"It's okay," Jason interrupted. One screaming match per night is more than enough, he thought. "I'll call my cousin Jolene." Jolene had been the lead singer until a year ago.

Bud groaned. "Oh, man. Why? She's a total bitch."

"And yet, somehow, that doesn't stop you from dating her," Penny said, rolling her eyes.

"Whatever," Bud said.

"It's just one night. We'll post a notice online," Jason said. "Maybe we can start auditions next week." *Unless Andi cools off. Then we won't have to.*

You don't want her back. Remember?

A deep, dull ache in Jason's chest strengthened, making it difficult to breathe. He coughed. "Lock up, will you? I'm going for a walk."

"It's four in the morning," Penny said.

"This is South Congress." Jason refused to call it SoCo. It sounded so pretentious. "What's going to happen? Even the drag rats have called it a night."

Penny abandoned her Les Paul. Lowering her voice, she leaned in close and asked, "You sure you're okay to be alone? That was pretty fucking intense."

He shrugged, shying from her gaze. "You know how she gets." Then he fled before he could change his mind.

Heading north and then turning left on Academy, he ambled to the shabby apartment complex he called home. In the hope that it'd ease the pain, he focused on taking long, slow breaths. When that didn't work he turned his attention to the street with its row of pricey dwellings. It was hard to imagine that any of them had once been a crack house—difficult to imagine for all but one.

Everyone knew about Maufrais House, but no one spoke of it, and to his knowledge no one went up that lonely hill. The closest he ever ventured was the little cemetery. The property was home to a thicket of trees, dewberry canes, and assorted scrub brush between the house and the private family plot. The house was obviously occupied—even if no one knew by who—but he was quiet and respectful. So he figured the owners wouldn't mind his visits. As far as he could tell they rarely tended the graves, so sometimes he left a small bundle of wildflowers. When he returned, he'd take the wilted blooms away along with their chipped mason jar vase—replacing it the next time free flowers were available.

He stopped at the corner and gazed up.

It was said the house was haunted by the ghost of a serial killer. He didn't believe the story, which he was pretty sure was used to scare little kids. He'd heard many like it over the years, so he was pretty good at spotting an urban legend when he heard one.

He wished he knew Maufrais House's real story. No one did. But if anyone had a clue, Penny's family did. The Da Silvas had lived in the Austin area for over a hundred years, having moved up from San Antonio after Texas became a state. They knew all the rumors worth knowing. Unfortunately, Penny's grandma was the only one who talked about such things and, even then, only when she was in the mood.

Jason didn't care about the stories. He liked the place. It too had soldiered on in spite of abuse, and neglect. Although he'd never seen anyone else on the property, he was pretty sure he wasn't the only one who risked trespass laws. Soda cans and booze bottles in paper bags seemed to spontaneously appear. From time to time, he would walk the woods and pick up trash.

A week ago, he'd spied a stray puppy. He wasn't sure of the breed but thought it might be some form of Siberian Husky. The little dog's eyes were pale blue and its fur was brown, black, and silver gray. One day the puppy brought him a red rubber ball. The little beast was enthusiastic about retrieving the toy but never allowed Jason to pet or pick him up. He told himself the puppy had a home. No matter how often Jason tempted him with a treat, the little dog hadn't been hungry.

When Jason was depressed, he'd leave the garbage bag at the gate and perch on one of the worn tombstones. Alone, he'd whisper his troubles to the overgrown graveyard. He'd have done so at the top of the hill, if he could. He imagined he was the only one to empathize with the house's scarred and angry exterior, the only one to understand the broken loneliness beneath, yet, in the year he'd been visiting, he hadn't ventured up the hill—no matter how much he wanted to. Something about Maufrais House forbade it.

The idea of going home was unappealing. He definitely didn't want to see Andi yet.

Largely unlit, the steep slope was a haven for fireflies. The house spent most spring evenings illuminated in magical fairy light. But, it was early February and not quite warm enough—so he assumed. The will o' the wisps appeared to have taken the night off.

Slipping between the wrought iron rods of the graveyard gate, a full moon rode the sky. It had rained earlier, and the shadows under the trees smelled of damp earth. Somewhere a Mountain Laurel had begun to bloom. A hint of not-unpleasant grape-bubble-gum scent clung to the breeze. All was still and quiet. Even the frog chorus from a nearby pond was silent. Something flitted through the branches above his head. He yelped.

It's just a bat. Austin was home to the largest urban bat colony in the world, after all. His short outburst seemed amplified against an eerie vacant backdrop.

Settling on his favorite tombstone—a small worn granite monument dedicated to one Agatha Garcia aged seven, *gone but not forgotten.* He rested his guitar case on his lap. The grass was wet. He laid his hands on top of its leather surface and waited for the tears to come. Frustratingly, the aching lump in the back of his throat refused to permit it. He felt he'd been impaled in the chest like a squirming insect, unable to grieve and unable to ignore the sharp pain.

His life, such as it was, was falling apart. *Again.* He wished the hurting would stop. The need to control something, anything—to heal a wound—almost overwhelmed him. The agony in his chest was unreachable. He needed to create comfort. *Somehow.*

The knife in his pocket sprang to mind. He had even reached for it before another thought stopped him.

Bad idea. You know what happened the last time.

Just one small cut. I have a bandanna. I can bandage it. I need to. Everything is so confused and out of control.

You promised you wouldn't.

And he hadn't. It'd become a point of pride for him. His therapist wouldn't have been happy to know he carried a knife, but this was Texas. Everyone did.

He forced his hand away from his pocket and rested his callused fingertips on top of the guitar case.

"I don't know why anything Andi does or says bothers me." He forced the words past the lump. A faint whisper was the best he could manage. It hurt like hell. "I don't love her. She definitely doesn't love me. She's just... She makes the apartment less... empty."

A low insect buzz inserted itself into the quiet, raising the hair on the backs of his arms, and making him queasy. It wasn't a normal insect sound. It echoed strangely in his head. Anxiety traced a cool finger down his spine. He shuddered. For the first time, he sensed he shouldn't be here. He was intruding. He should leave. *Now. Before—*

He caught a fleeting shadow in the underbrush. It wasn't the puppy. It was too tall. His heart thudded in his ears like a kick drum.

"Is someone there?" His voice cracked.

The question was met with another furtive sign. This time he tracked it to the darkness behind a specific pair of trees.

"Hello?" Fear supplanted grief and the ache in his throat eased.

Silence. Even the hateful buzzing ceased.

He sensed someone stood on the other side of the larger trunk and held their breath. He didn't dare breathe, himself, lest he frighten them away. When nothing happened, he slid off the tombstone and carefully balanced the guitar case on it.

"You don't have to be afraid, you know," he said, keeping his voice gentle. "I'm not here to hurt anyone or anything. I bet you aren't either."

That was when he spotted the woman in white edging from her hiding place.

At first, he took her for a ghost. Her colors were faded like an abandoned watercolor in the rain. Her skin was pale and she was dressed in an old fashioned, puffy-sleeved nightgown. Thick blond hair hung around her shoulders in loose waves. Her long graceful fingers clasped a wrap for warmth.

"Do I know you?" she asked.

He did his best to appear harmless. "I don't think so. I'm Jason. I live in the apartment building off Academy. Who are you?"

She tilted her head to one side. He was about to repeat the question when she spoke. "My name is Miriam Owens. I live here."

"In the cemetery?"

"Don't be silly. Up the hill." She pointed in the direction of Maufrais House without breaking his gaze. Her voice was soft and bore an accent he couldn't quite recognize. It lived somewhere in New England—definitely not Texas. "You said you weren't here to hurt anyone. Why did you lie?"

"I didn't."

"Weren't you thinking of hurting yourself? This really isn't the place for that." She stepped closer. Her feet were bare.

How did she know? And how is she walking in those woods without shoes? It's cold and the ground is covered in thorns, sharp stones, broken glass, and fire ants.

"It isn't safe," she said.

At that moment, he decided he was wrong to think she was afraid of him. Her gaze was an intense coal black in the dimness. *Maybe I should be the one afraid.*

Don't be ridiculous. She a young woman in a nightgown and no shoes. What's she going to do to me?

She seemed to be waiting for him to say something.

"Oh. I'm trespassing. I'm sorry," he said. "But I don't mean any harm. I—I love this place. And I wouldn't—"

"You're the one that leaves the flowers."

"I am."

There was another awkward pause.

"That's thoughtful," she said. "Cousin Agatha likes it. Primroses were her favorite."

It was Jason's turn to be surprised. He knew full well she couldn't be talking about the Agatha memorialized on the tombstone. The last date carved on it was 1924.

The hairs on the back of his neck prickled. Uncomfortable, he mumbled the first thing that sprang to mind. "It's late."

"It is for me," she said in a drifting tone. Her expression was now full of infinite sadness. "Much too late. But maybe not for you." And with that she vanished behind the tree once more.

"Wait!"

He rushed to the edge of the cemetery. He thought he spied her running to the top of the hill. He bolted after her. He was almost to the backyard garden when his toe caught on a root or fallen branch. He pitched forward, smacking his head on a limestone rock with a hollow *bonk*. He felt the blow in the roots of his teeth. The pain was terrific. By the time his head cleared she'd darted inside. He'd heard her footsteps on the porch and the thump of the screen door.

Taking in his surroundings, he wondered at the garden he'd only glimpsed through the trees. He considered stepping onto the gravel path to discover more than flowering plants and the sound of water. Then his eyes were drawn to a dim light in one of the house's attic windows. A bony hand twitched the curtain closed.

Dread shivered down his spine. It occurred to him that perhaps he didn't know Maufrais House as well as he'd thought.

Battling a powerful need to flee, he traced a deliberate path back to the graveyard, retrieved his guitar, and finally stepped onto the sidewalk. He didn't notice the stains on his white t-shirt until he was through the gate. Wiping what he thought was sweat from his eyes, he was shocked when his fingers came away covered in blood.

Damn it. When Penny saw him, she'd demand he go to the clinic. He couldn't afford it, not this month.

Dizzy and sick, he cleaned his hand on his ruined shirt and continued home. The growing lump on his head pounded hot to the beat of his heart. The sky was gray with dawn when he entered the apartment. He found himself hoping Andi would be home after all, but she wasn't. Half-blind he stumbled to the bathroom, washed his face, and dry-swallowed three aspirin tablets. Then he fell asleep with the bitter taste of aspirin in the back of his throat, and a spike of tension wedged between his shoulder blades.

Jason had no recollection of his mother but for a haunting lullaby. He supposed that's why the nightmare inevitably started with a woman singing. After that, the dream faded into another memory—one where he was ten years old. He'd just gotten home from school. He opened the door and noticed the house smelled funny. It didn't feel right either. It felt... empty.

He and his father watched afternoon cartoons together on Wednesdays after school, but today his Daddy wasn't waiting in the living room. *Maybe he's in the bathroom.* Uneasy, Jason went to the kitchen and fixed himself a glass of chocolate milk. When his Daddy still didn't appear, Jason walked through the apartment room by room, calling for him—an indescribable feeling of terror building up inside and threatening to pour down his cheeks.

If the house weren't so silent, he wouldn't have noticed the buzzing. It bunched his skin in cold clumps. Pushing open the door to his Daddy's room, the dread of what might be on the other side slowed him down. Fear made his heart beat faster as if it might run away by itself. He didn't understand what the buzzing meant. He hated the sound and the stale meat stink. As he stepped hesitantly into the room, he spied the bed, the open window, the pile of discarded laundry and the bedside table. The photo of his mother that his father kept there was missing.

The buzzing grew louder, filling his head with impatient anger. It seemed to be coming from the bathroom. He needed to see. *Now.*

"Daddy?"

He spotted the blood first. It painted the pale green bathroom tiles in lumpy splashes of drying crimson. That didn't make sense. It didn't belong. His Daddy was there. *No.* His Daddy didn't take baths with his clothes on. The strange man was dressed in his Daddy's job interview suit. He was also clutching the picture from the nightstand. There was a shotgun lying on his chest. His left hand lay limp in his lap, his Daddy's wedding ring on the fourth finger. The man's mouth hung slack. The back of his head rested in a mass of drying gore and globs of tissue glued to the shattered tile.

The insects broke the spell. Otherwise, Jason might have gaped forever, not comprehending. They were big, black flies, and one of them exited his Daddy's mouth. Another strolled across an open eyeball. The eyes were his Daddy's eyes—eyes that suddenly blinked.

His Daddy sat up. The movement lacked the fluidity of life. His head created a horrible sucking sound as it left its resting place. The mouth hung open, still, but Jason heard buzz saw words—words that seemed to be powered by the angry flies.

"Don't rrrrruunnn."

Jason fled into the hallway. His legs tangled, and he fell. He bit his tongue and then sicked up chocolate milk onto the brown shag carpet. A flickering electric blue-green light illuminated the hallway. Vision blurred with tears, he rolled over and spied his Daddy swaying in the doorway. His neck was now unable to support his head. It rested on his left shoulder.

"Thhheee house. Thheee housssse."

The flies were everywhere. One lit on Jason's arm. His Daddy reached for him. And Jason shrieked and shrieked and shrieked. *Don't touch me! Go away! Don't touch—*

Twenty-three-year old Jason sat upright in bed, his throat sore from screaming, breathing as if he'd just run a marathon. *You left me alone, damn it. I was only a little kid!*

"Fucking dreams," he said, by way of an explanation. But Andi wasn't there to complain. He was glad. He didn't think he had the energy for yet another lie.

Tugging on his jeans, he staggered to the bathroom. The usual anxiety that haunted him after that dream accompanied him down the hall. He probed his forehead with gentle fingers and sensed crusted blood in his hair. Flipping the light switch, the mirror told him how bad it was. It was pretty bad.

Andi's cosmetics and toothbrush were gone.

He finished peeing, washed up, and went to the living room to assess the damage. Afternoon light revealed the television and the DVD player were smashed. Fortunately, he'd been too hurt and exhausted to notice. At least she'd left his stereo, acoustic guitar, and the laptop alone—he assumed because there hadn't been enough time to load her Honda with all of her shoes and then wreck absolutely everything before he showed up.

Numb, he stumbled into the kitchen and made coffee. While the apartment filled with nutty perfume he returned to the bedroom for his cell and punched Penny's number.

"It's four o'clock, loser," Penny said the instant she picked up. "We have to be at the club at six."

"Oh."

"Don't 'oh' me. I called, like, five times. Where have you been?"

"Asleep."

"You didn't call Jolene, did you?"

"Shit."

"Didn't think so," Penny said.

"I'm calling her now. But this short a notice is going to cost."

"Not my problem. I wasn't the one sleeping with the lead singer and then had a screaming break up."

"All right," he said. "Next time *you* sleep with the lead singer."

"Glad we're clear on that. Just remember I like chesty redheads."

"You do?"

Penny snorted. "See you later, shithead."

"You're bi? Seriously? Why didn't I know?" She hung up the phone.

He was right. Convincing Jolene to sub in did cost him.

"I had to give her my favorite leather jacket," Jason said.

"That sucks," Penny said. "But at least it's a standard moto jacket. You can find another."

The aspirin wasn't doing shit. He'd covered the nasty bruise on his forehead with a black bandanna. So far, no one had noticed the bump. Outside of a couple snide comments about his new pirate look, no one gave it much thought.

Penny now sat on the edge of the stage, swinging her feet and knocking back a cold one. He appraised her looks when he didn't think she would notice. She'd told him once that her ancestry was mainly Mexican, American, and Irish. The bleached hair and dark green eyes, made a striking contrast against her tan skin. Tonight, she was wearing a ripped Pogues t-shirt, a black vest, and tight black jeans that were torn at the knees. She'd found time during the day to give her fingernails a fresh coat of black polish. It was already chipped.

Why does she have to look so good?

The jacket wasn't Penny's fault but he was feeling resentful. So, he asked about the one thing he knew would get under her skin. "Why don't you tell me about Maufrais House?"

"What? Why?"

"Come on. I feel like shit. It'll cheer me up."

"I don't know." She looked away. "Grandma Da Silva says it's bad luck to talk about that place. I don't want to jinx the gig."

He knew the real reason she was uncomfortable was because she was embarrassed about her grandma's psychic business—the one she'd been running out of her kitchen since forever. Penny had lived with her hippie grandparents from the time she was twelve when her mother moved to Colorado for a boyfriend.

Jason glanced over at his cousin Jolene and checked an urge to scream. She was flirting with two guys at once. That wouldn't have bothered him. Whom she chose to sleep with was her own damned business. However, Bud was drinking a beer at the bar, merrily pretending not to notice and that *was* a problem. Worse, he'd gone to the trouble of setting his hair into a Mohawk for the gig. That was never a good sign.

"Tell me anyway," Jason said.

"Grandma wouldn't like it," Penny said.

"I won't tell her. Anyway, the bad luck will be mine, won't it? I'm the one who brought it up."

Penny gave him a dirty look. "Only because I hate your guts right now."

"You do not. You adore my guts." He inwardly cursed himself. Now, he was treading too close to lines he shouldn't cross.

"Yeah. Yeah." She focused on picking at her chipped fingernail polish and looked unhappy.

Her discomfort hit him in the gut. He almost told her to forget it but she launched into the story.

"The house was built in 1918 by Hugo Maufrais. He owned a construction company and had buckets of money. Gran says he was a gangster with connections in New York. People who wanted long lives didn't cross him."

"I thought your grandma didn't talk about this."

"Just shut up and let me tell the fucking story, will you?"

"Hurry up," Jason said. "Next set starts in ten, and I have to untangle Jolene's tongue from that guy's tonsils before we start."

Penny rolled her eyes. "Oh, great. Has Bud noticed, yet?"

"The inevitable fist fight hasn't started. So, I assume that's a no."

She sighed. "Hugo Maufrais was into all kinds of evil stuff. Some say even witchcraft."

"You mean like Wicca? Crystals, rainbows, and fluffy bunnies?"

She punched him on the upper arm.

"Ouch!"

"*Anyway*, one night he has this big bash at the mansion. Hookers. Booze. Orgies. This time there was a fire. Lots of people were trapped. He escaped.

"He left town while the house was rebuilt. Went around the world in a yacht. After the place was finished, he shows up with a famous French singer from Paris—a black woman named Melisande Sirene. Pretty soon, people start getting dead around him. Some sort of flu. Suddenly, Maufrais doesn't have so many friends anymore. One day he comes home and finds his girl with his best friend. Maufrais shoots the friend. He's supposed to have buried him behind the house. The girlfriend died too. Drowned in the pool. He loved her so much that he refused to bury her. When Maufrais died in a robbery in 1925 they found her body laid out in a bed on the second floor. He'd been sleeping with her corpse. Pretty sick shit, you know?"

"That's a story, all right," he said, mocking her. "Faulkner's 'A Rose for Emily.' "

"Faulkner doesn't own a copyright on necrophilia, shithead," Penny said. "Anyway, it's a bad place. You stay away from it."

"What if I told you I saw someone who lives there?"

"You're making it up."

"No, I'm not."

She gave him a hard look.

"Oh, come on. You don't really believe that shit, do you?" he asked.

Shifting on the edge of the stage, Penny scanned the partygoers. "Crap."

When Jason spied what Penny had his stomach did a queasy flip. Jolene was in the college kid's lap now and his hand was up her shirt. Bud hadn't noticed—not yet.

"That's you," Penny said. "I'll take care of our rooster."

"On it." Jason rushed over as fast as he could without drawing too much attention. "Show's on."

Jolene arched her back and flipped her hair. "In a minute."

"Not in a minute. *Now*."

The kid with Jolene's tits in his hands glared at him. "Dude. Don't be an asshole."

Jolene glanced Bud's direction as if to check if he was watching. "Don't you vanish on me now," she said, tapping him with a playful slap powerful enough to leave a red print. She got up off him and went to the bathroom.

Jason was relieved when they started up the last set without further incident. Unfortunately, they'd only delayed the inevitable. The moment the show was over Bud busted his knuckles on the college kid's jaw. The whole thing escalated into an embarrassing scene. In the end, Andre stepped in. He promised the college kids a round of free drinks if they went home and forgot about it. After the bar was closed up, Andre informed Jason there would be a long talk in the morning. It didn't take a psychic to understand what it'd be about. Jason hoped he wouldn't be replacing two members instead of one.

Penny waited to crank up the van until everyone had hopped in. Before, Jolene had been dead set on having the college kid take her home. Now she was in the back, sucking Bud's face with an enthusiasm worthy of a porn star. Jason climbed into the front passenger side.

Steering onto Congress, Penny cranked up the radio, leaned over, and whispered, "What the hell does he see in her?"

"Really fantastic sex," Jason said.

"You've got to be kidding."

"Nope. Bud says—"

"I really don't want to know."

Jason shrugged.

Penny dropped Bud and Jolene off first even though Bud lived the farthest from Andre's place.

"Out. Both of you," Penny said. "You're steaming up my windows."

"I'll take care of your kit," Jason said to Bud.

There was an unwritten dude-code when it came to sex, and Bud was his best friend. In exchange, a six pack of beer would show up at the next practice session and Bud was buying.

"Thanks, man." Bud smiled.

Jolene grabbed Bud by the t-shirt front and practically dragged him out of his seat. As Bud tumbled out of the van with Jolene, Jason decided it had better be damned great beer. The two of them had barely made it to the front door of Bud's grubby rental house before Jolene ripped the shirt off him.

"Hey! I loved that shirt," Bud said.

"Stop talking and fuck me," Jolene said.

They practically fell inside. Jason looked away and tried hard not to imagine what would come next.

It was definitely one of those nights.

Penny backed out of the driveway. "Bud is a walking cliché. What is it with men and women like that? She's only going to leave him for someone with more money or a bigger dick. Does it to him every time. God, I don't even know why I'm talking to you. You're just as bad as he is."

"Am not."

She shook her head. "You're going to tell me that underneath it all, Andi was a nice person?"

"Underneath it all… Andi was naked. Really, really naked."

Penny bruised his upper arm again without taking her eyes off the road. "You're a pig."

"Ow! Hey, snot face, that'll leave a mark!"

"Serves you right, shithead."

By the time they'd unloaded at the practice space and locked up, it was three o'clock in the morning. Penny was silent. A thoughtful expression parked itself on her face. Worried, Jason prepared himself for the inevitable difficult chat. He wasn't sure what the subject would be: Bud's lack of self-control or Jason's relationship issues. His money was on the second. Penny could be frighteningly perceptive. He'd been in and out of therapy for years as a kid and hadn't known anyone who saw through him the way Penny could.

He straightened and dropped the key in his pocket. That was when he noticed she was preparing to ask him a question. He decided to avoid the whole thing and turned to the street.

"Get in the van," she said.

"Don't waste the gas. It's not that far. I can walk from here." The words were slurred.

"Not tonight, you're not."

He sighed. "Is this going to be an interrogation?"

"You're drunk. I know exactly what that means," she said. "Andi isn't coming back. So get in the van, or we talk about it here."

All he wanted to do was drink some water, take five or six aspirins, and pass out. His headache was worse than it'd been before the show. He got into the van anyway.

She slammed the driver's side door. "You gonna tell me about it?"

"What's to tell? You were there."

"Come on. You look like hell. Something's got you. Bad. What the fuck did Andi do? Hit you in the head repeatedly with your Fender?" Penny reached for the bandanna.

Wincing, he dodged her. "Damn it. She was going to fucking leave anyway," he said, hating the sound of his voice. "Nobody stays after six months. We both know that. She lasted five and a half. It was time."

Penny harrumphed. "The women you date, that's no surprise."

"Where are we going?"

"My place."

"I'm too tired for computer games. I just want to go home."

"We're not going to play video games, shithead." She was smiling to herself.

"Oh? What are we going to do?"

"We're going to get naked, and then I'm going to do things to you until you scream for mercy," she said. "I may have to gag you. My roommate is home."

"Oh, no we're not."

She paused. "Don't you find me attractive?"

Jason choked and shifted in his seat. If there was one thing he found Penny, it was attractive. At the mere mention of sex he had a terrific boner and she hadn't even touched him. "That's not it. I told you why."

"You don't love me?"

"I care about you more than anyone."

She paused. Her next words came out in a hurt whisper. "But not like that?"

The disappointment in her face made him want to kiss her. Her cheeks were wet and she stared out the windshield as if she were afraid to look at him.

He turned to gaze out the window and said the thing he was afraid to say. "I can't lose you."

The van slowed to a stop. "Jason Findley, you're going to lose me if you don't do something. Maybe not tonight but one day. I don't know what she did to you—"

"Andi didn't—"

Penny slammed her hand against the steering wheel. "I'm not talking about Andi!"

Jason swallowed. "Who, then?"

"Whoever it was that hurt you so bad that you can't ever risk real feelings. God, I hate her. I really do. And you can't even talk about her. That fucking bitch."

"She wasn't a bitch!" He vomited it up before he had time to think about the consequences.

Shocked, Penny turned to him. "Who was she?" Her question was gentle.

He spied Maufrais House in the window beyond Penny's face. His heart raced. The world tilted like a Fun House floor. He squeezed his eyes shut in an attempt to make it stop.

Maybe he could talk to Penny. *Maybe.* This time might be different. Give her one small thing. Buy some time. Maybe she'd stay then? *Women prefer mystery over misery. Right?* "Okay. I'll spill. Just… let me show you something first."

He was wasted and teetering on the edge of an emotional precipice. He might regret jumping later, but he was drunk enough that he decided he didn't care. He was miserable. He had to do something.

He couldn't stand it any more. There was only one place where he'd been able to put his feelings to words.

She parked the van where he told her. The engine ticked as he staggered to the pavement with a simultaneous feeling of hope and terror. He didn't check to see if she followed him to the gate. The gentle breeze was not too cool. The little graveyard was peaceful. Fireflies by the hundreds blinked in and out. It was perfect and beautiful like her.

He slid between the gate's bars.

"Where do you think you're going?" Penny asked. Her feet remained firmly planted on the sidewalk.

"I want to sit here. In the cemetery together." Maybe it was the alcohol, but he decided he'd grown tired of being lonely. The only living person who knew a damned thing about him was Bud—and truth was Bud didn't know all that much.

"After I told you how I feel about this place?"

"You told me how your grandma feels."

Penny shook her head.

"Why not?"

"Because I promised Gran. That's why," Penny said. "Let's go somewhere else. Anywhere else."

"It's here or nowhere. Look. There's no one in that house. And even if they were, they wouldn't care if we sit and talk."

She glared and folded her arms across her chest. "Wasn't it a few hours ago that you said you'd meet someone who said she lived there?"

He felt his cheeks grow hot. "We aren't going up to the house."

"Absolutely not. You just *lied* to me."

"Please?"

Scowling, she said, "If you think stubbornness will wear me down, you're sadly mistaken. I don't break promises to people I care about. You fucking well know better than to ask. I don't lie to people I care about either, even if you do—"

"But—"

"No means no," Penny said. "If you can't handle my having boundaries—particularly about this, then I need to rethink my offer."

"You can't be serious."

"I'm very fucking serious." She stepped backward toward the van. "We're leaving."

He knew she was right on some level, but he was angry about being called on it. "Well, I don't want to go."

"Fine. Suit yourself." Spinning on the ball of her foot, she climbed into the van, slammed the door, and drove off.

One hand wrapped tight around black wrought iron. He watched through the gate's bars like a prisoner as the van's tires left an angry skid at the corner. "What the hell just happened?"

"You were rude and your girlfriend left you."

His heart staggered, cold inside his chest. It was a miracle he didn't scream.

Miriam waited in the woods, one hand on a twisted live oak tree trunk. "I'm sorry. I didn't mean to frighten you."

Laying a hand on his chest, he tried to slow down his breathing. "Well, you fucking did."

Tonight, she wore a pink dress. Based upon the fullness of the skirt and way the waist nipped in, he guessed it was from the 1950s or early 1960s. He'd dated women who were into vintage from that era. As if to complete the look, her hair was pulled back into a conservative ponytail.

She appeared unsure whether staying or vanishing back beneath the trees was the best option. "I am sorry."

It occurred to him that she might have taken extra care on her appearance for him. *Don't be an asshole. Women can dress up for themselves, you know. It doesn't have to be for a man.* Penny had told him that once.

Miriam opted to leave.

"Don't go. I'm the one who should apologize." He went to his usual perch on the little girl's tombstone. *Why is it that every time Miriam shows up, I'm an emotional mess?* "She isn't, you know."

"Who isn't what?"

"Penny isn't my girlfriend."

"Oh." Miriam stepped into the cemetery but hung back in the shadows. "You're drunk."

He shrugged. He hoped she wasn't going to make a big deal about it. "Why?"

"Because I want to be." He muttered it through clenched teeth.

"I see."

"What do you see?"

"You're upset," she said. "Maybe we shouldn't talk." He blinked.

Just then a red rubber ball rolled from the woods into the cemetery. It tapped the toe of his scuffed Doc Marten boot, bounced off, and stopped at Miriam's feet. She bent to pick it up.

"Well, isn't this interesting?" She peered into the moon-shadowed trees.

He slid off the headstone. "Check this out."

When she gave the ball to him her fingertips grazed his palm. Her skin was like ice. He thought to loan her his jacket. And then he remembered he didn't have one anymore. He pressed his lips together. *Let it go.*

He knelt at the edge of the graveyard and held up the ball. "Hey, little guy. Are you out there?" Spying the puppy, he shifted to one knee. "Come here, boy. Come on. There's a good dog."

With a happy yip, the pup darted past him and sat in front of Miriam. She settled onto the grass, sorted her skirts, and then reached out to pet the little dog.

"He won't let you touch him," Jason said.

As if to make a liar out of him, the puppy crawled into her lap. She stroked his fur as if she did it all the time.

"Oh," Jason said. "You know one another."

She smiled. "We do." The puppy leaped up and kissed her chin. "Calm down, silly. You'll muss my dress."

After several quiet minutes of snuggling, the puppy squirmed around to stare intently at the ball in Jason's hand.

"Want to play fetch?" Jason asked. He held up the toy and moved it from side to side, testing the theory. The puppy's ice blue gaze tracked every motion. Jason tossed the ball. The pup chased after it with another series of happy barks.

"You've made a friend," Miriam said, impressed.

He shrugged. "Dogs like me." He joined her on the grass. "Which is good because I like them."

They sat in silence while Jason and the puppy played together. The fireflies winked all around. Soon, the sharp pain in his chest faded into the background ache that was his everyday life.

"How long have you lived in Austin?" Jason asked. It was a safe question—one that everyone asked.

Miriam said, "Ever since I can remember."

"You've never left?"

"Of course, I have," she said. "Mother, Father, Grandma, Grandpa, and I used to drive all around the state. Sometimes we traveled as far as Michigan, California, Florida, or Maine. We had relatives everywhere."

"You're lucky to have a big family. Why did you stop?"

A sad expression settled on her normally cheerful features. "Most of them passed on."

"Why?"

"Old age. Their homes were torn down. Real estate markets have become so volatile."

"House flippers."

"This modern age doesn't care for the undefined, I suppose."

What an odd thing to say. Instead of asking for clarification, he relished the comfortable silence and tossed the ball. Finally, he decided to take the chance he was going to take with Penny. "I... don't have family. I haven't for a long time."

The puppy grew interested in sniffing and wandered off. Jason laid his palm in the soft grass.

"What happened?"

"They died," he said. The backs of his eyeballs stung. His hand curled into a fist.

"I'm so sorry."

With a deep breath, he took the plunge. "My mother left my dad when I was nine. And he killed himself a year later. I found the body."

"That must have been terrible." An odd expression passed over her face. It was almost recognition.

He looked away and tugged at the grass until a clump came up. "He was such a loser." His fingers dug at the dirt again—tore at the roots. "He left me alone."

She laid a chilled hand on his arm. "Don't."

Her touch seemed to suck the warmth out of him. Still, he didn't move away from her fingertips. He let her chill sympathy soothe his fist flat.

"Anyway, you aren't alone," she said.

Before she spoiled the moment by saying something stupid and well meaning, he rushed on. "I'm adopted."

"Me too."

"Really?"

"All my siblings are too."

"Did you go into foster care?"

"No." Her face grew distant as her voice faded away. "It was not that kind."

"You're lucky," he said. "The Findley's adopted me when I was fourteen. Five years later, they died in a car crash. I've been on my own ever since."

"I'm so, so sorry."

"Shit happens." He shrugged again. "At least they left me some money. Not a lot, but enough to take care of myself."

"That's more than the usual amount of tragedy," she said and got to her feet.

He mentally berated himself. *See? You shouldn't have talked. All that is too much to lay on a person you don't even know.*

She held out her pale, cold hand for him to take. "Would you like to meet my family?" Her nails were painted a washed-out robin's egg blue.

I hadn't noticed that before. "I'd like that very much." He rested his hand in hers and shivered. Once again he wished for the missing leather jacket.

"I'm so glad," she said, leading him through the woods.

The fireflies seemed to follow as she led him up a dirt path he hadn't noticed before. It was steep and he was out of breath by the time they reached the limestone border dividing the woods from the garden. Pea gravel created a pathway around a swimming pool-sized pond. Flowering plants, trees, and bushes grew all along the perimeter: honeysuckle along the fence, mountain laurel, oleander, magnolia, jasmine... they all blended together in a riot of perfume. Positioned in the center of the circular lily pond was a beautiful, black marble statue of a mermaid. It was clear by her profile that she was a black woman. Her hair had been sculpted in long braids and a necklace of cowrie shells hung about her neck. She was top-less and unlike the Disney mermaid, immodest about it. Her arms were stretched wide as if she were dancing in the water. Her tail was bifurcated.

Not a mermaid, a siren.

He dropped Miriam's hand and wandered up to the short limestone wall surrounding the pond. Moonlight reflected off the water where broad leaves didn't float. The lilies were blooming. That was weird. Even in central Texas, February was too soon for such a thing. In the dark, he couldn't tell if the blooms were blue or purple. He stepped closer. Beneath the water something slid a graceful arc sending rip-ples through the pond—something with scales and fins. *Something big and dark.*

For some reason an unwelcome image of *The Creature From the Black Lagoon* sprang to mind.

"Not so close," Miriam said, grabbing his outstretched arm. "The water is much deeper and more dangerous than you think."

"It's so beautiful." He stepped back. "Did I see fish in there?"

Miriam smiled. "Yes. It's my sister's pool." She looked over her shoulder. "Ethan is here. Let me introduce you to my little brother. Ethan, this is Jason."

Jason reluctantly turned his back on whatever swam in the pond's murky depths. A small boy stood on the gravel path. His dark hair was a bit mussed. He was dressed in short pants and a white shirt with a wide ruffled collar. The outfit looked like a costume from a museum painting.

Does everyone in her family wear vintage clothes? Jason thought.

Ethan held the red rubber ball in one hand. "Hello. It's nice to meet you." He gave him a quick smile.

Jason thought he spied a flash of pointed canine teeth.

"And on the porch over there is my little sister Agatha," Miriam said.

Agatha appeared to be a little girl age seven or eight. Her black hair was braided into long pigtails. She wore an embroidered peasant dress and old fashioned ankle boots. Both were more modern than Ethan's costume. Her head was bent at an odd angle such that her ear almost rested on her left shoulder.

She gave Jason the creeps. That was when he remembered the girl in his fifth grade class. *She has scoliosis. But if that's what that is, it's the worst case I've ever seen.*

"Mother was just wondering where you'd gone," Agatha said in a formal tone. "She wants to talk to you. You know why."

"Of course," Miriam said. "I was gone rather a long time." She spoke to Jason. "I must go now. Why don't you come back? You can meet the rest of the family."

"Sure." Unnerved, he said goodbye and headed down the hill. He was almost to the cemetery when he realized it was five o'clock in the morning. *Why were the children awake so late? Isn't it a school night?*

Homeschooled. They're probably homeschooled.

Shrugging, he decided it wasn't any of his business. He slipped through the wrought iron bars of the cemetery gate and walked to Academy. When he reached the corner he saw an old woman standing on the sidewalk in front of Maufrais House. It took him a moment to recognize her. It was Penny's grandmother. She was staring up at the house with an unreadable expression.

I thought she hated this place? She seemed to be looking up at one of the ground floor windows. A shadow shaped like Agatha was there.

The curtains swung back in place and she was gone.

Mrs. Da Silva took in a breath that might have been a sob.

He waited, thinking maybe he shouldn't disturb her grief. At the same time, it'd be difficult to walk across the street without her noticing. He couldn't go the long way around—he didn't like the idea of going past the cemetery again. She smoothed her hair to steady herself. The bun at the base of her neck was coming undone. She was so intent on the house that she didn't notice him until he spoke.

"Mrs. Da Silva," he said. "Partying late tonight?"

An old grief swelled in her eyes as she spun to face him. With a blink, it was replaced with a friendly expression. "Jason? Is that you?" She sniffed and patted her face dry.

"It is."

"What are you doing here?"

"Walking home from Andre's place." Jason lifted his guitar case to back up his assertion. "My apartment is three blocks from here. Didn't Penny tell you we had a gig tonight?"

"Oh. Right. I remember now. Do you often walk home this late?"

He shrugged. "Sometimes."

"Don't you have a car?"

"Sadly no." Mostly he walked and when he couldn't, Penny drove him—if he paid for the gas. "Parking spaces are hard to get around here, anyway."

She nodded. "Walk an old lady to the corner?"

"It's only a block out of my way," he said with a smile. "Why not?"

"The cheek on you." She returned his good humor. After a few steps, she changed the subject. "You should stay away from that house."

"Penny told you?" He yawned. He was suddenly very tired.

"She did," Mrs. Da Silva said. "It's not a place for you."

"Houses aren't evil. That's just made up shit from movies and books." He caught her frown and assumed she didn't like his language. "Sorry. I meant stuff from movies and books."

"Have you ever noticed that an empty house will only stand for so long? With no one living inside, they fall apart more quickly. The paint peels faster. Windows break. Wood splits. Plumbing fails."

"The owners spot the need for repairs before it gets bad, that's all."

"Houses hold on to love and joy and laughter—even grief and rage. They're like sponges. They absorb emotional energy from the people who live inside them. Over time, those emotions become a part of the house, like the wallpaper. Particularly, strong emotions."

"Do they?"

"Haven't you been in a place where you felt comfortable all at once? Or holy? Particularly a spot that has seen long use in a specific capacity?" she asked. "Old churches, old buildings… graveyards?"

He blinked.

"Some houses feed off of bad things. Bad *memories*. It makes them dangerous for some people," she said. She stopped as they had reached the corner. "*Sensitive* people. Please listen. Penny loves you." Then she laid a hand on his arm. "I don't want any harm to come to…"

He felt a tiny electrical spark—as if Mrs. Da Silva had recently dragged her feet across a static-filled rug. Shock registered in her face. Then she lifted her hand and glanced back the way they'd come.

"How did I not see this before?" She swallowed and nodded. "You're haunted. That is why it calls you." She gave him a comforting hug.

It wasn't the first time. He'd eaten many dinners with Penny's family. He'd even spent holidays with them because Penny had insisted he not be alone. The fact that Mrs. Da Silva was genuinely concerned disturbed him.

He hugged her back.

"Please. Be careful. Sometimes in our rush to shed pain we abandon too much." And then she continued on her way.

Stunned and confused, he watched her go. The next two weeks passed in a blur and he didn't go back.

A slap stung Jason's cheek and rocked his head back. Bleary, he blinked up at Penny and Bud, wondering what the hell just happened. They'd finished practicing one of Jolene's favorite songs—an old Dolly Parton number. One minute, Penny, Bud, and Jolene were talking about SXSW set plans and the next he was flat on his back, stretched out on the sofa. He'd only shut his eyes for a second.

"Jason, wake the fuck up," Penny said, frightened.

"I'm fine. Just exhausted." Jason hadn't been sleeping. Each attempt resulted in too many dreams, none of them good. "Maybe I'll take a nap. Y'all practice without me."

"Dude, you fainted," Bud said. "If Jolene hadn't grabbed your new guitar it would've have smacked into the concrete."

By the feel of his head, no one had thought to catch him. Still, he was glad the guitar had been saved. "Thanks, Jolene."

Jolene stayed back, an expression of concern hanging awkwardly on her face.

Two weeks had passed since Bud had begged him to let her back into the band. Reluctantly, Penny had agreed. Jolene swore they wouldn't regret it. So far, she'd kept her word. It was easy to see Bud was happy.

Maybe I misjudged her, Jason thought. She'd been Little Sister's lead back when the band first formed but they'd had to replace her due to all the drama. *People can change.*

"Jason!" When he didn't open his eyes Penny grabbed his arm.

He winced. She yanked up his sleeve.

"What's this?" she asked.

He struggled against the weight of his eyelids. There was a new gauze bandage around his scarred left forearm. *That's weird.*

Penny's tan face darkened and her eyebrows pinched together. "You promised you wouldn't do that any more."

"I didn't," Jason said.

"Then explain the bandage," she said. "Because that looks a lot like a fresh cut."

"I don't remember doing it," he muttered. "Just let me sleep."

Lowering her voice, Penny said, "It's that house. Isn't it? I told you to stay away from it."

He wanted to argue that he hadn't been there in two weeks—that her grandmother visited the house too—but he didn't have the energy. "I feel sick. Play the gig without me."

Jolene answered the knock on the door. Cool night air drifted in along with Mrs. Da Silva. A long, full, dark blue skirt, a baggy white t-shirt, and a brown cardigan hung on her heavy frame. An old, paisley scarf was tucked around her neck. She rested a cloth grocery bag on the floor.

"Do you have water?" Mrs. Da Silva asked.

"It's over there," Penny said. "There's a hot plate too. On the counter."

Penny's hand felt cool on Jason's forehead. "I don't think he has a fever. Did you bring a thermometer?"

Mrs. Da Silva said, "I think I know what is wrong. It isn't fever."

Bud said, "Let me get that for you." He grabbed the heavy cloth bag and carried it to what served as the practice space's kitchen area.

"Set everything on the counter, if you don't mind," Mrs. Da Silva said. She moved to the sofa and bent close. "How long has he been like this?"

Jason said, "I need a nap. That's all."

"He hasn't been himself," Bud said from across the room. "Spends all his time sleeping."

"South By is in a couple of weeks," Jolene said. "And he doesn't seem to care. That isn't like him at all."

"It's odd that *you* do," Jason muttered with his eyes closed. "What's up with that?"

"You really have been out of it. You're only just noticing?" Penny asked.

"You're defending her?" Jason asked. The power of his verbal indignation was more intense than he actually felt. *What is wrong with me?*

"Yes," Penny said and folded her arms across her chest. "Yes, I am."

Mrs. Da Silva left his side. "Stop bickering. It won't help." She poured water into the tin saucepan that Bud kept on the counter for heating soup and turned on the hotplate. Then she hummed to herself as she mixed various herbs.

"What is she doing?" Jason asked.

Penny said, "Making tea."

Soon, an evil smelling concoction was shoved under his nose.

"Drink," Mrs. Da Silva said.

"What if I don't want to?" Jason asked.

Mrs. Da Silva's eyes narrowed. "Then I will pinch your nose until you open your mouth. Don't tempt me."

He gulped it down. It tasted as bad as it smelled, but he managed to keep it down. Bud took Penny's place at his side while Penny and her grandma had a quiet discussion in the corner. Jolene hovered near by—making herself useful by soaking a bandanna with cool water so Bud could place it on Jason's bruised forehead. The cloth felt nice. It wasn't long before he had the energy to sit up.

"How about that?" Bud asked. "It lives."

Jason moved to get to his feet but Bud pushed him back onto the couch.

"Not until Mrs. D says it's okay," Bud said.

Slumping in the cushions, Jason sighed. "It's not that big a deal."

"How's your head?" Bud asked. "That bruise looks bad. Is that why you've been feeling dizzy? A concussion? Did Andi clobber you with something heavy?"

"Why does everyone assume it was her?" Jason asked.

"Well, was it?" Bud asked.

"I slipped and fell on a trail, if you must know," Jason said. "Hit my head on a rock."

"Since when do you hike?" Bud asked.

"Feeling better?" Mrs. Da Silva asked. Her gaze grew serious while she searched his face for some sign.

Jason asked, "Can I get up now?" He felt more alert than he had in a long time.

"We must go for a short walk," Mrs. Da Silva said. "If you're ready."

Jolene and Bud stayed behind to lock up. Everyone said their good-nights and then the three of them headed over to Maufrais House. The night air was chilly and the moon was a thin sliver. Street lights and neon store signs lit the way. It was midnight, but The Continental Club would remain open until two in the morning. The sidewalks and parking spaces were full. By the time they'd reached their turn, they'd left the foot traffic behind.

Mrs. Da Silva waited until they were on Academy. "When I was a little girl my parents worked for the man that built that house."

Jason didn't ask which house. He knew.

"My father was the gardener and my mother was the cook. When we weren't in school, my sister and I would help. Mr. Maufrais traveled often and brought home artifacts and treasures. One day he returned with a mummy from Egypt. That was when bad things started happening. Mr. Maufrais's friends began dying. It all ended when my sister fell down the stairs." Mrs. Da Silva stared straight ahead as she walked.

Jason got the impression she wasn't seeing the present.

"She died. After that, my parents wouldn't let me near the house. Father found other work. Mother remained until the night of the fire. She never spoke of it until the day she died." Mrs. Da Silva took a deep breath. "My sister's name was—"

"Agatha," Jason said.

Mrs. Da Silva nodded.

They continued in silence until they reached the cemetery gate. That was when Mrs. Da Silva handed him a heavy duty flashlight.

"This is dangerous, but it's too late. The house has a hold on you," she said. "You must do this or be consumed as others have been before you."

The fireflies were back, drifting among the weathered tombstones. Jason reached out for the gate. It swung open with a high-pitched creak.

"It seems they're ready for you. Go," Mrs. Da Silva said. "Penny and I will meet you on the front sidewalk. Good luck." She turned and walked away.

"Well, this is it," Penny said. She looked terrified.

Jason hesitated. "I—I need to say something." He gathered up his courage. "I love you."

"Oh."

"That's all you have to say?"

Penny smiled. "I love you too, shithead. Now, get your ass up there so you can come back to me." She leaned in and kissed him. "For luck." Her lips were warm and soft.

Tugging his flannel shirt tight around him, he was happy to have that warmth with him as he braved the chill under trees smelling faintly of decaying leaves. He carefully picked his way up the path. It wasn't long before he stood on the flat limestone rock garden border with his heart hammering in his ears.

You can do this.

Miriam, Agatha, and Ethan were waiting beside the pond. Others looked on from the porch—two tall, thin young men holding hands, a Black soldier dressed in WWII fatigues, three somber toddlers, a mummy whose dark skull peeked out from wraps that had begun to unravel...

In front of the ghostly crowd stood a beautiful woman. Her long black hair had a gray streak. A dark choker circled her graceful neck and she wore a filmy gown the color of moonlight. At her side lurked an athletic, broad-shouldered man built like a professional football player. His skin was mottled with blue, black, and green patches like a two-week-old corpse. White flecks of mold dotted the corners of his mouth and his eyes were a glazed over white.

"We were hoping you'd return," Miriam said. "Come. Meet my parents."

Jason hesitated. Little Agatha smiled encouragement up at him. That was when he noticed the family resemblance. *Penny has her chin and cheekbones.* It was clear to him now that Agatha's neck was broken. *I don't know why I thought that was scoliosis.*

"They're ghosts," he whispered.

Miriam laid a chill hand on his shoulder. Her touch seeped cold through his flannel and t-shirt.

"Not exactly," Miriam said. "But close enough." She led him up the three short steps to the porch. "Mother, Father, this is the young man I told you about."

Jason wondered what was expected from him when the woman in the filmy dress spoke.

"Welcome. You may call me Luna." The accent was eastern European. Her teeth were sharp like Ethan's.

Of course they are, Jason thought. The unreality of the situation made Jason feel as if he were in a trance or dreaming.

"Please. Give me your hand." Luna's voice was soothing, melodic.

He complied without giving it a thought. Unlike Miriam, Luna's skin was warm. Her light-colored eyes narrowed, seeming to stare right through him.

I'm so cold.

"It's time to let him go," Miriam said.

Who?

He felt a shift deep inside his chest. Luna traced signs over his hand. A ghostly mist began to congeal over his forearm. It slowly contracted until it became the image of an arm clad in a stained suit sleeve.

Jason blinked.

"Don't speak," Luna said. "The process is delicate. I must concentrate."

His mouth snapped shut and this time her long, needle-like nails dug into his arm. She began to pinch and pull at something inside. The scab on his arm parted. He began to bleed. His scars burned like fresh cuts. A buzzing sound, hardly noticeable at first, grew in volume. Dull agony flared up in his chest and suddenly he knew it for what it was—the grief and anger that he'd been desperately attempting to carve out of himself for most of his life. In a flash, he didn't see his father as a small boy did, a failed hero-god. He saw him as another adult, a sympathetic human being whose heart had been broken beyond repair.

The backs of Jason's eyeballs stung and his vision blurred. The painful lump in his throat materialized. All at once, he comprehended the enormous strength it'd taken to stay alive each and every day. The energy taking care of a small child as a single parent had required.

The deep love.

And in that moment, Jason forgave his father.

"It is time for you to leave." And with that, Luna made a coaxing motion. "This will be your new home. Your new family. Do not worry. You will not be forgotten by your old one."

The pain intensified and then Jason felt something snap. The buzzing was silenced. A ghostly image of his father floated next to him.

Luna clasped the ghost father's hand now. "Welcome." She guided his father's ghost toward the house.

The others gathered around in a circle, enveloping him. His father turned around to look at him one last time. Jason thought he saw tears in his eyes.

Goodbye, Dad, Jason thought. *I know you did your best.*

His father nodded once and then the others gathered in tight like a hug. Then the back door opened and all but Ethan, Agatha, and Miriam went inside. Jason looked on with wet cheeks while feelings tangled themselves inside his mind. It hadn't been until the pain in his chest was gone that he understood how heavy it'd been—how much grief's gravity had warped his life.

Ethan and Agatha paused at the door and Miriam appeared at his side.

"Go and never come back," Miriam said. "Let your father stay with us."

Jason had many questions but decided that it would be best to leave them unasked. He was warm for the first time in days and felt lighter and freer than he had in his whole life. "Thank you."

"Goodbye, Jason. Live a good life." She smiled before joining Ethan and Agatha.

Jason walked around the house and down the hill. Penny and her grandmother were waiting for him.

Stina Leicht writes science fiction, horror, and fantasy. Her next novels, *Persephone Station* and *Loki's Ring* are Feminist Space Operas scheduled for publication in January 2021 and 2022 by Saga Press. She was a finalist for the Crawford Award in 2011 and the Astounding Award for Best New Writer in 2011 and 2012. She has also written four Fantasy novels: *Cold Iron*, *Blackthorne*, *Of Blood and Honey*, and *Blue Skies from Pain*.

BLUE HOLE, RED SEA
BY E. CATHERINE TOBLER

IT WAS NEVER NOT HOT in Alexandria, but beneath the sea, everything was cool and quiet, and Helen Dane thought she would like to stay forever. Submerged in the Mediterranean, Helen made an adjustment to the alidade before her, focusing in on the angle of the fallen, algae-coated obelisk in the distance. The black granite looked like a long finger, pointing her down the length of the ruin they were documenting. Through the sea, the obelisk was ephemeral, there and gone when a school of golden fish wavered past. Helen focused again and the sea moved without aid of the fish, expanding into a strange darkness beyond the obelisk. She imagined a tunnel, an arch, extending forever into black. The space held mysteries—bones and fragments of other lives lived—until it opened into a new sea.

The new sea was warmer, saltier. The water was like silk across her skin—bare skin, her wetsuit stripped away as if it had never existed. The salt water buoyed her up and up, as if she were in a balloon, and when she surfaced, it was an unfamiliar landscape that greeted her. She knew she was beneath the Mediterranean, safely wrapped in diving gear, and yet her eyes told her otherwise, for the land rose and fell in sandy, caramel hues everywhere. The sea around her was perfectly still, not shot through with fish. Before her in the sea spread a great darkness, a hole that bored into the water itself and vanished.

And beneath the water, a whisper. A word she couldn't quite make out.

As Helen blinked to clear her vision, her diving watch beeped three times, telling her it was past time to resurface. Three times? Helen looked at the watch face with concern. Her oxygen gauge confirmed that she was late, that her air was growing in short supply. She glanced once more to the obelisk, to see the black hole it was pointing to had gone, then adjusted her life jacket, dropping weight to help her kick back for the surface.

The *Lotus* awaited her, a cacophony of worried Arabic greeting her when she surfaced. Grasping hands pulled her from the sea and into the bed of the boat, water streaming every which way. Habit had Helen reaching to check that she'd clipped her underwater camera to her waistband, and she only relaxed at the feel of its plastic curves beneath her pruned fingers. It was cumbersome outside of the water, the size of a melon, but she couldn't lose it.

"What were you thinking?"

The boat crew took a step back at the harsh question. Helen spat the breather from her mouth, and reached for her mask, but it was removed before she could touch it. Her guardian, professor and Egyptologist Frank Dane, pulled it up her face and off, his glare replacing the sea that still hung in her mind's eye. She tried to turn from him, but his hand wrapped her upper arm and held her firm. Through her rubber dive suit, she could feel his fingers pressing hard and harder.

"You weren't thinking," he said before she could reply. When he released her, he gave her a little shove, as if to set her at a distance. He strode away, to the other divers who'd come up on time, to see what they had learned. Snatches of their conversations came back to her— did the men know of the rumored lighthouse? The mighty Pharos who overlooked the sea and her sailors? Many knew the rumors, but rumors of monsters, too—of gods protecting what the sea had taken.

Helen raked her hair from her eyes. She was shaking and didn't dare stand. She sat for a moment, thinking of the obelisk, of the space it had seemingly pointed toward. A tunnel, she had thought, but maybe a colonnade? Had they found the queen's palace after all? But it was something more than that, because there had been a landscape, a landscape they didn't presently inhabit, and she could not explain it. She had felt the wind against her wet hair, had seen the spreading black in the sea around her. And beneath the water, a whisper.

Her heart hammered to think of it—the strangeness she could not explain, but also the idea of a submerged palace. She'd been diving for four years now, Roman shipwrecks mostly, but this—this was Alexandria, Egypt. This was a civilization swallowed by the sea, reaching a hand from the past to clasp their own now.

She stood and moved to the edge of the boat, looking into the water. From the surface, nothing of the ruin could be seen. But she had seen the columns, the obelisks, and the sea-sunk sphinx, and could not forget them. People had lived here. She wanted to touch every stone they'd left behind before Frank could sully them.

"Here."

A sun-warm towel was pressed into her hands and she looked at the familiar figure standing beside her. Frank called the boy Alex, but only because they had hired him in this city and not another. Helen took the towel and pressed her face into it. The warmth eased the chill of the water on her, and Alex set to helping her remove the rest of her gear.

Helen scrubbed the towel across her hair and looked at her guardian. Frank was gathered with the others—three divers, and an assembly of young Egyptian men who would do anything for payment. The divers were telling Frank what they'd seen and measured—they thought it was the queen's palace, too—and the Egyptian men chattered excitedly. A palace meant riches.

She had not cared about riches—at least not at first. Shipwrecks were thrilling all on their own. Cautionary tales, to be sure, but thrilling too. Imagining the people who crewed them, where they had dreamed of going, and how they ended up at the bottom of the sea. Helen knew she would risk the danger. The bottom of the sea was worth it.

"They are fools," Alex said softly, but before Helen could ask what he meant, Frank called him and Alex scampered to his side, tending whatever needed tending.

Evening saw them back on dry land, ensconced in the Cecil Hotel, where belly dancers roamed the Monty Bar to entertain the gathered men. Helen kept to herself, but not for long, because Gary Lawrence slid into the chair beside hers, reeking of cigarette smoke and Egyptian beer. In another life, perhaps she would have liked him. He was beautiful, as golden as any Egyptian statue, but his regard for her seemed specific, physical and wholly disinterested in her skills as a diver or an archaeologist. She certainly couldn't claim that last position as her own—it was a dream, though, for it would allow her to see the world.

"Did you see the palace?" he asked, and offered Helen a cigarette from his case.

She took one, and leaned in when he offered to light it. She did not care for cigarettes, but it gave her something to hold on to. She pinched a fleck of tobacco from the tip of her tongue and nodded, the belly dancers whirling in a blur of color between the tables and stools.

"I think so," she said, her mind drawn back to the pointing finger of the obelisk. She needed to photograph it. "Did you? Did you dive today?" She could not recall that point of business, but would've been surprised had he said no.

"I did," Gary said, and leaned an elbow upon the table to crowd her space. "Perhaps tomorrow I can borrow you and your camera, and I can figure out what else I saw down there."

Helen's gaze slid away from the dancers, to focus with more certainty on him. He really was attractive, eyes brown and reflective, the bridge of his wide nose scarred, no doubt from some terrifically heroic adventure. His lips enclosed the end of his cigarette and for a moment, Helen imagined she was that cigarette, being drawn on and blown out.

"What *else* you saw?" she asked. Her heart was already beating like a hammer. "What else could you have possibly seen? A shark?" A shark seemed less dangerous than a looming void.

"I keep telling myself it was just the ocean—and you know the ocean, you've been on so many dives." He leaned away from the table now, back in his chair so he could cross his long legs. His cigarette dangled between his fingers, momentarily forgotten. "So much depends on the light, what we can see and what remains hidden."

Helen tried not to squirm in her chair. What had come over her? Had he just acknowledged her work—the many dives she had been on? Had she mistaken his interest in her?

"It's true," she said carefully, praying her voice didn't waver. "On my last dive, everyone was convinced the ship they'd found was Mycenean, but when the light brightened the waters, the ship could only be Phoenician because—"

"When the light brightened the waters," Gary echoed. He nodded and took another drag from his cigarette. He held the smoke, then slowly released it. "Yesterday, you also dove—did you see the darkness? At the end of the obelisk? Ah—you did."

Helen had never played cards, because she knew her expression gave away too much. So it was here, when he mentioned the darkness at the end of the obelisk. She remembered what it was like in that moment, skin prickling as the void beckoned.

"It could be a colonnade," Helen said quickly, offering the easiest explanation to see what Gary would do with it. What he would make of it.

Gary tapped the ash from his cigarette into the ashtray. "Of course I thought the same thing when I first saw it, but there was a... feeling? It was something more than an ordinary shadow in the water, Helen, and your face tells me you felt it, too."

Warmth bloomed along the back of her neck. "It is an extraordinary site," she said, again careful to keep her voice even. She didn't want to hope they'd found something no one else had before. Something that might explain an ancient culture in ways no one had anticipated? Something that would change the field forever—the *world* forever—and that was arrogance. She didn't want to be that person, but she felt it in her gut that she already was that person. That she didn't want to only explore wrecks, she wanted to discover and revolutionize and—Women didn't do such things, let alone archaeologists.

"Feelings should be kept out of it," she finished.

Gary's golden eyebrows arched. "Oh? Do you think Carter kept his feelings out of it when he gazed upon the golden wonders of Tutankhamun's tomb? If we have found the queen's palace, we've every right to feel every thing—but that is not what I am talking about, and I think you know it."

The ash plummeted from the end of Helen's cigarette, and she set the entire thing aside in the ashtray to look at Gary through the curling smoke. She hadn't met him before this dive, but she had heard of him and his work. His professional reputation was a good one, though he tended to fall into bed with those he worked alongside. Helen could not deny that kind of attraction, but she couldn't allow herself to get distracted. Women didn't have that luxury, especially young women.

His hand, still balancing the cigarette, covered hers, smoke twining between them. He was as warm as the air around them, as warm as Egypt.

"Dive with me tomorrow," he said. "I need your camera, but more so your eye. Do not tell me it wasn't you who determined that ship was Phoenician and not Mycenean. You may place that credit elsewhere, but I know how good you are—how good women are not supposed to be, eh?"

Helen's skin prickled. "Frank won't like—"

"I don't give a damn what Frank likes," Gary said. "He brought you. On some level he knows how good you are, so why not put your mind to work." He lifted his hand from hers, but the ghost warmth of him lingered. Now, he discarded the cigarette in the ashtray. "There is always someone else ready to take that credit and run off into the newspaper headlines—but not this time. Tomorrow we go down together, Frank or no."

When Gary left the table, he wandered through the other workers, to find Frank at a table surrounded by dancers. They moved in such ways that their gauzy costumes trailed in whispers against the men's cheeks. Gary laughed and joked with Frank as if he'd never spoken with Helen and she didn't know what to think—was the jokester real, or was the man who'd acknowledged her ability?

She pushed away from the table and left the bar, supposing both could be true of him. She had played the vixen in order to acquire access to a dive. She had slept with men in order to further her own career, which was no career at all yet. She had traded the one thing she believed she had—her body—to access her ability. She had fallen in love and lost that love all in the course of one excavation. Had carried a child within her body for three months, until it too was taken from her, because Frank didn't believe she needed the distraction. *The distraction.* What would Gary ask of her before all was said and done? If they discovered something beneath the waters, would he claim it for himself after all?

The opportunity was worth the risk, because it called to her even now. The hotel overlooked the Alexandrian waterfront and from her room, through the narrow doors that opened onto an even narrower balcony, she stared into the waters, as if willing herself to see the hole, if it were such a thing. It was foolish—she could see nothing of where they'd dived today, but she felt it, as if a heart beat under the water, thrumming through her entire body.

When she was at last able to pull herself away from the view, she took that feeling to bed with her. Or, perhaps it was more precise to say the feeling followed her. Helen curled into a ball, clasping the sensation to her belly as she fell into a deep and dreamless sleep.

On waking, she couldn't remember if she'd slept—how she had slept. She sat on the edge of the bed, keenly aware of an absence, but unable to pinpoint it. She dragged a hand down her body, to rest it on her belly where nothing at all hummed anymore. It wasn't *that* absence, it was…

Out the window, Alexandria and its waters awaited, and Helen did not linger long before them, getting dressed and leaving her room so she could be in both the city and its waters, because Gary was waiting. At the sunrise-spangled harbor, it wasn't the *Lotus* Gary was on; she found him on a smaller boat entirely. *The Crane at Dawn* had only one crew member, a young boy Helen didn't know. Helen's skin prickled, but she wasn't sure if it was anticipation or fear. She'd never dived without a crew.

"We don't need anyone else for this," Gary said. "Not yet."

Least of all Frank, Helen thought. Frank wouldn't like it. It was his dive, his excavation. They all dreamed of sunken Pharos, the lighthouse that had been swallowed by the sea, but only Frank had organized and funded the exploratory dives. He was in control and in charge, and the idea that Gary was eliminating Frank from the discoveries they might make was—

Insulting?

Thrilling.

It would have been a lie to say otherwise. Frank was well connected and funded, but he wanted his hands on everything. It had been so when she'd been young; it would be so when she was old. As his ward and to reach the places she had, she'd had to endure his control. Orphaned at an early age, her father's will placed her in Frank's care, Frank having been like a brother to him. She had respected that relationship all her life, but the older she grew, the more cracks she saw. She wanted her own life, unbeholden.

Gary extended a hand to her, helping her into the boat. He was as warm as he'd been the night before, and some of her worry leached out, but the closer they sailed to the dive, the more worry and anticipation mingled and made her feel like throwing up. Getting into her gear made her nerves settle though, and once they were beneath the water, they vanished entirely. This was the world she knew, the blue and the black at the bottom of it all.

They sank in silence. Ribbons of bubbles spiraled to the surface in their wake, the young boy but a shadow watching them descend. This close to sunrise, the water was still draped in black, but Helen could see it was already beginning to brighten the deeper they sank. It felt backwards, the brightening, because the bottom of the ocean was where the void gathered—

And a whisper she could not entirely make out.

Helen pushed away the memory, and pulled her camera into position, wanting to capture the ruin as they came upon it.

It was to be a thirty-minute dive, to photograph the obelisk and the presumed colonnade, and she didn't want to waste a minute of the time. When the obelisk reared out of the dark, the first rays of morning light reaching down to its granite length, she was ready. Gary and Frank and everything else fell away. There was only the sea and the wonders it held.

It reminded her of the obelisk that had been given to Paris in exchange for a mechanical clock, seventy-five feet tall at the very least. Unlike that obelisk, the one before her didn't appear engraved. Helen swam closer, to photograph the algae-coated stone, and couldn't resist touching it. The algae was slick, but beneath that, the stone was firm and cold, and she slid her fingers against it, searching for markings of any kind. When the smooth granite dipped beneath her fingertips, she thought it was the beginning of a mark, a letter.

Gary touched her shoulder and gestured that they should continue on. Helen nodded, reminding herself that this was only a scouting run, to see if the colonnade existed, and if it did not—to scout the darkness? Helen pushed herself onward, following Gary's path through the ruin, past fallen columns and algae-coated sphinx. She photographed everything she could along the way, only realizing the light had begun to fade when shadow swallowed half a sphinx. She paddled backwards, but Gary swam on, into the black.

A glance behind her showed her only the tip of the obelisk, but the obelisk plainly pointed her forward. Into the shadow that had swallowed Gary whole. She couldn't even see his lights, and the lights she carried didn't do much to pierce the dark on their own. Drawing on her breather, she kicked onward. The water was warmer than she expected, as salty and slick as her dream.

She imagined the space as a colonnade, columns on either side, but the deeper she swam, the more it seemed the colonnade existed. The columns made niches, and in each niche sat the statue of an ancient god. They were old, algae-smothered, eyes vacant as Helen's camera passed over them. Hathor, Isis, Sekhmet. She captured what images she could, until the camera clicked empty.

Helen clipped the camera line to her belt and swam on. Ahead, there was only black, no sign of Gary at all. The niches alongside held more gods and they were all female. Helen couldn't remember seeing that before. The final niche on the right side was empty. The palace wall—if it were the palace—had tumbled to the sea floor. Helen angled her light down, but there was no floor, palace or sea. It was only darkness here.

Darkness and a low murmur that sounded like a whispering cat.

When she looked back, she could no longer see the obelisk, nor the tunnel she had passed through. It was only the looming forms of the Egyptian statues. She reached for the compass dangling from her belt and made certain of her position before she pushed on into the dark after Gary. He could not be far. The murk couldn't go on forever.

The longer she swam, the less she believed herself. Had she gone the wrong way? Had she taken a branching corridor in the absolute gloom? Once, Helen swam into a wall, thick with algae and nearly invisible even under the sweep of her light. She pushed away from it, and swam with strong strokes, ever forward.

That whisper again. Insistent the deeper she went. It felt like she needed to clear her throat, like she needed to spit, and then surely the sound would stop, but it didn't. The sound seemed to run over her bare skin, encouraging her to swim faster, harder, so that when she suddenly broke the surface of the water, she was crazed with it, clawing at her arms, at the breather that seemed likely to choke her.

With a cry, Helen kicked away from the sound, to find her hands curling into a wet sand shore, where Gary sat laughing. Helen flung herself down to stare at the sky—the evening sky that was bisected by the sharp line of a temple roof. She tried to form words, but her throat was raw, as if she'd been screaming.

"Just breathe," Gary said, "and then look."

It was the shore she'd dreamed of earlier, cliffs of caramel stone jutting against the sky. Wedged into the cliffs, a beautiful temple with limestone ramps leading up to colonnades, where statues of she knew not who stood weathered but not damaged, surveying the sea beyond. The sea, with its gaping blue hole.

There were tracks in the sand where Gary had dragged himself up and out of the water, his gear thrown about as if he'd also been clawing at himself. Helen didn't ask if he'd heard the whisper, the sound, only got to her knees and cursed.

"The camera is empty," she said when Gary looked her way. "I shot everything in the passage. I didn't imagine…"

"Everything in the passage?" Gary got to his feet, glancing back at the water, but then to her. "The passage was empty."

Helen unclipped her gear from her belt, setting the large camera carefully aside. Had she dreamed the statues? She could not believe that for one minute, but in the end, the film would tell them the story of their journey.

"All right," she said, and managed to come to her feet, heading for the temple. "Have you been inside? We should—"

He didn't answer her and she didn't finish her sentence. The temple was astonishing, rearing large against the cliffs from which it seemed to have been carved. The statues were like none she'd seen before. Gods they had not known before? Kings and queens? Helen stumbled toward it, feeling clumsy in her wetsuit but not caring. Her heart was stuck in her throat and she cursed herself for having spent all her film, but how could they have known?

There were four statues on either side of the entry—no courtyard, only the ramp to the entry and the temple itself. Simpler, perhaps from an earlier time? How much earlier, Helen could not yet say. Inside the temple, Helen stopped in her tracks, the floor gritty with blown sand. Gary strode past her, deeper into the hypostyle hall and into the sanctuary.

She forced herself to follow, because it was all overwhelming. She had no film, no paper, only her mind to remember what they were seeing. Could they come back with proper equipment and the entire crew? Could they—She realized she didn't even know what body of water they had emerged into. Was it the Red Sea? How could that be—they'd been in Alexandria!

"Helen."

The sound of Gary's voice was startling, but Helen moved toward him, where he stood before a limestone statue. The statue was unknown to her—a face that was neither male nor female, gazing tranquilly on the sanctuary before them. A child had been carved near the statue's right leg, an infant with softly curling hair not yet pared back into the sidelock Egyptian children wore. Helen felt a jolt at the sight of an infant, an echoing emptiness inside her.

None of the offerings at the statue were new; collected at the statue's bare feet were the skeletal remains of palm leaves and fish. Recent enough to have not entirely withered, but Helen couldn't sort it once the other offerings caught her attention. Stones had been piled to one side, but more than just stones. Gems. She reached for a pearl that could have filled her entire palm, but then drew her hand back before touching it.

"We shouldn't touch anything," she said. She took a step back.

"For God's sake, how did I shoot all my film?" The despairing edge of her voice sounded so unlike her, it caught her off guard. "We should... Oh God." She rubbed her fingers across her temple, a headache coming on. "We should go back." Gary shot her a disagreeing look. "We should go and return with proper gear. With—" She swallowed hard. "With Frank."

"With Frank." Gary spat the words out. He turned from the altar and strode back toward the entry. "I cannot believe you! All of this." Gary gestured to the temple around them, with its perfect walls and their perfect undamaged artworks. Helen was torn between studying them and paying attention to Gary's anger. "All of this is ours—I brought you here because I believed in you and you want to bring *Frank*."

She didn't understand the anger at first—nor the idea that he had brought her here, because she had seen the darkness on her own, had felt its pull and the certainty that more lay just beyond. She'd thought Gary only wanted one thing from her. Perhaps his praise of her abilities had been meant to bend her will, to get her into the sack, but it felt deeper than that now. Maybe he'd also suspected this place existed and needed her knowledge. But she needed Frank's. He'd been at this his whole life, and might know what they were looking at, better than she ever would. It wasn't sex Gary was after—but he wasn't adverse to using it to get what he really wanted: professional recognition. A find like this would seal his fate—hers too, but he'd not have Frank taking the spotlight.

Gary left the temple and Helen exhaled. She didn't want to leave, but they had to—they had no gear for a find like this, and even if they didn't bring Frank, they'd have to make a return trip. She had to smooth the waters with Gary, make the trip back to Alexandria, and then... Then they could figure out how to handle all of this. She crouched before the unknown statue, and touched the carefully carved feet. The stone felt warm, still holding the warmth of the day's sun, but it also felt horribly ancient. Wholly removed from the modern world. Artifacts had always struck her as such, but this one felt older somehow.

Helen stepped back into the night. She didn't want to leave. She didn't want to—The sight of Gary striding into the water startled her. He meant to leave without her. He'd clipped her camera to his belt, and he was going.

She called his name, but he did not turn.

Helen ran for the rest of her gear: her oxygen, her mask, her breather. He'd left her exactly what she needed to get back, but he'd taken her camera. He'd taken her evidence of the passage here.

"You goddamned man," she growled as she geared up. "I need your camera but more so your eye. What a crock! You needed my camera, all right." If he reached the boat before she did—Helen didn't want to think he would leave her behind in the ocean, but if he wanted to stake rights to the claim, he just might. Her legs grew weak at the idea, but she launched herself toward the ocean once more, a glance of regret thrown to the temple as she did. She didn't want to leave.

But she did leave, sinking into the hole the way they'd come. She could see Gary by his dive lights, ahead of her and not quite a pin-prick yet. She swam harder, intent on keeping him in her sights this time, and not losing him the way she had before. She had always been a strong swimmer, but as the black crept up around them, she felt her energy waning. It had been a long swim the first time, so long they'd emerged to night skies. She knew that was impossible, but she felt as though it had taken an entire day. Felt as though she needed a nap, or a snack, or—

The water surged around her, pushing her deeper into what she thought of as the tunnel. It wasn't that the water was helping her—the very idea was amusing, as if the water gave a damn—but that something else had passed through the water nearby. The wake made swimming harder. Gary's lights moved farther away as she lagged. Helen blew out an annoyed breath, and then Gary's lights went out.

She thought at first that she was mistaken, that he'd just gotten far enough ahead of her again. That perhaps he'd moved around one of those algae-caked walls and had gotten out of sight. But his light didn't reappear. Helen pressed on, swimming hard though her arms and legs screamed at her to stop. She kept on, until her dive light swept across Gary's oxygen tank. She reached for him, for where his arm should be, but blood clouded the water between them.

Some distance away, her light found his arm, floating free and away from his body. When she focused again on Gary's face, he was trying not to scream around his breather, still conscious, his eyes wide and wild behind his mask. He had the presence of mind to gesture with his other hand—the gesture for "danger, that way," his fist thrusting into the bloody water, indicating the water behind her. Helen grabbed him by the straps holding his oxygen tank to his body and continued swimming.

Her body screamed to stop. Even in the water, Gary was a heavy weight, and the idea that a shark was down here with them was—Troubling?

That word was too small for the feeling that filled her.

Swimming with one arm and holding onto Gary with the other, Helen could not think about a shark or anything else. She could not—until the water surged around them again, and something tugged on Gary. Helen held on as tightly as she could, tugging in the opposite direction. But the second tug was harder than she could counter and Gary was ripped from her hold. Helen tumbled in the churning water, having no idea where Gary was, or what had taken him. Clouds of blood bloomed in the water, the statues in their niches gazing impassively at her.

She paddled into the blood, but there was no sign of Gary, or anything else. Helen hung there, hearing once again the whisper. Like a cat, a low *mmm* sound that rattled her bones. She kicked backward to get away from it, but the sound got louder and closer, and something touched her shoulder. Helen spun around, flailing arms and legs, but the thing she struck repeatedly with her fists was her camera, floating in the water behind her alongside Gary's dry sack. She grabbed both and held them to her chest.

She couldn't say how long she floated, waiting for Gary, waiting for *something*, but nothing returned. No Gary. No shark. The water around her calmed, the blood thinned, and Helen clipped the camera and sack to her belt. Her compass was there too, and she checked her heading, swimming and swimming. Time ceased to matter beneath the water; when she surfaced, the sky above her was the pale pink of a new morning. *The Crane at Dawn* floated nearby, the young boy still peering from its edge.

The boy helped Helen into the boat, and she couldn't get her arms or legs to work properly. She lay like a landed fish, feeling the power of whatever had taken Gary from her hold. Her shoulder and arm ached from the wrench. The boy peered over the edge of the boat again and Helen closed her eyes.

"He's not coming," she said, having no idea if the boy spoke English.

The boy lingered, but not long, and then he picked up the oars and set himself to rowing. He rowed with a distinct destination, which made Helen think he'd been told what to do in case the worst happened. The boat crossed the morning-calm water, until they met up with the *Lotus*, and Frank, and the entire crew.

Helen didn't want to be there, but couldn't think how to leave. Her shoulder throbbed, fingers clutching her camera, hauling it into her lap now that she'd finally managed to sit up. At the sight of her, Frank leaped into the *Crane*, because of course he hadn't gone down with his men. He waited up top, dry and ready to take credit for their discoveries.

"Where is Gary?" Frank asked.

"Something—" Helen tried to put it into words, but couldn't. She pulled her gaze from the water, to look at Frank. He wasn't angry, not yet. Concern creased his face, but she wasn't sure what concerned him most. A diving accident wouldn't look good. Authorities would want to be involved, would want to investigate.

"Helen."

Frank raised a hand, and she flinched, but he didn't strike her. He dragged his fingers along her cheek and when he pulled them back, they were bloody. Helen became aware of a throbbing in her cheek too. Something had struck her. The thing that had taken Gary?

"There was…" She closed her eyes, pushing nausea back. "Gary asked me to come out early—wanted me to photograph the obelisk." She could feel the hieroglyphs beneath her fingers. A warning maybe? "There was a shark."

It was the easiest explanation.

Frank came swiftly to his feet, leaping back to the *Lotus*, where he directed his men in sharp Arabic. Helen looked down at her camera, its bulk cradled against her belly. She knew only one thing with certainty: she needed a darkroom.

If there was one thing Frank was good at—and Helen supposed there was more than one, really—it was the control of a dig site. Or a dive site. He rounded up his men and said they would come back the following day. If there were a shark in the waters, they needed to be careful, they could not lose anyone else. The loss of Gary was horrific—Frank looked genuinely shaken, his color only returning after he'd taken two shots of whiskey back at the Cecil. He did not stray far from Helen's side, but left her alone long enough that she could develop the photographs she'd taken that morning.

The hotel concierge helped her find a small and isolated closet in the employee corridors, and helped her set up the necessary materials. All the while, Frank lingered in the hallway. Helen pictured him pacing and smoking the way an anxious father might as he awaited the arrival of a child. As she carefully hung each image up to allow them to dry, she stared in wonder at the passageway recreated on film around her.

Gary had said the passage was empty, but it was as she remembered, lined with nooks. Each and every one held a statue. Eventhe end nook she remembered as empty held a statue—Nephthys, she thought, given her headdress of house and basket—but in the last snapped image of the passage, Nephthys was gone, as if she'd leaped from her position to—

To what?

Helen's mind stuttered. She stared at the empty niche and then at the image before, where it was not empty and she could not breathe. Nephthys had been worshipped as a goddess of rivers—they'd certainly still been in the sea?—but also of childbirth. Helen thought back to the temple they had found, the statue with the infant. The offerings.

A knock at the door made Helen jump and she closed her eyes, trying to calm her heart. "Almost done," she called, and carefully pinned the photos up to dry, but in a way that concealed the photograph of the empty niche from casual view.

When she had finished, she left the closet, drawing the door closed behind her. Frank stared down at her, the concierge nearby. Helen looked at the concierge.

"The photos need to dry and must not be disturbed," she said. "I'll be back in an hour—let no one else in."

The concierge brandished a key, locked the door, and offered the key to Helen when he had finished. "Your realm, madam," he said, and made a swift bow before leaving.

Helen slid the key into her pocket and looked at Frank, who looked better than he had when they'd arrived. She'd never seen him quite so upset, but then didn't know if he'd ever lost someone on an excavation.

"How do they look?" Frank asked. "The photographs. Is—did you get any of Gary? The shark?"

Helen shook her head. "I was out of film on the return swim," she said, because it was true. "But I photographed the length of passage we took, and it's… it's full of wonders." Her smile was genuine; the entire thing was an incredible find. She was certain that they would make sense of where the passage led in the days to come, because that's what they did as archaeologists.

"Do you think it is the queen's palace?" Frank asked.

Helen didn't know, but she kept to honesty. "It is unlike anything I've ever seen. The passage is lined with a collection of statuary, but each and every god there is female. I have never seen such a display. Perhaps it was a corridor within the palace. A deliberate collection of female deities. But…"

The idea that it was a palace corridor did not sit well with her, because it led somewhere entirely else. It led to the blue hole on a strange shore, where a perfect temple held offerings to an unknown god.

"But?" Frank pressed.

"I don't know. There are too many unknowns here." She thought of the last photograph, the empty niche. "Did you notify authorities about Gary's death?"

"No," Frank said without hesitation. "I will, just not yet. If they close the waters to us, we won't be able to dive again. We'll go prepared for sharks, but we're still going. I want to see what you saw. I want to dive it with you."

Helen knew she could not deny him. He was a good diver—always in control of everything—even if he preferred to have others do the work for him. So when they went out the following morning, Helen said nothing, only watched him suit up. Three other divers were coming with them, each carrying harpoon guns. She didn't like the idea of the guns, wondered if the weapons would do any good at all against whatever had killed Gary, but she didn't say a word. Frank offered her a sizable knife, one that could gut a shark surely, and she strapped it to her thigh, within easy reach.

She loaded the underwater camera and packed extra film in her dry sack, in case they reached the temple again. Each and every man had dry sacks strapped to their bodies, and they were empty, and the idea bothered Helen. For all of archaeology's discoveries, there was all of the history that had been carried away.

"Helen's got lead," Frank told the divers, checking everyone's lights, everyone's tanks. "You follow her. We stay close. You see anything amiss, use the signals I taught you." He nodded at Helen after he'd finished checking the gear.

"It's weird down there," she said. "Pitch black, until it's not. You might hear…" She didn't want to call it a whisper. "Noises. Makes me wonder if there's a shipwreck down there somewhere, wood creaking?" She shrugged, wishing she hadn't brought up noises at all. "It's pretty straightforward. In case anyone wanders, you'll be on a southeast heading. Once you're in the tunnel, it's straight through until you see the light, then it's up."

She and Frank had talked about belting everyone together, but they both felt it increased the danger. If they were beset by a shark—or something else—they didn't want to risk everyone being hauled away together. Going individually had its own dangers, but in the end they decided it was better. The safer danger.

Beneath the water, Helen felt more at ease. It was strange. She expected to feel uneasy, and maybe that would come when she reached the place Gary had been taken, but diving down to the ruin was only placid, calm. It was everything she wanted to do. She swam strongly down, trusting the men would follow. She looked back every now and then, but mostly kept her focus on the looming ruins, on the pointing obelisk.

When they reached the obelisk, she indicated that she wanted to pause. She smoothed some of the algae from the surface of the granite. Dug her fingers back in until she found the marks within the stone. The hieroglyphs were small, would have looked even smaller from the ground, had the obelisk been standing.

She angled her light and her camera to capture the writing, but didn't like what she thought it said. She stared at it long enough that Frank tapped her arm and gestured that they should continue on. Helen nodded, pushing from the obelisk and into the yawning void it pointed toward. The obelisk was marked with something that appeared to say *beautiful tongue*, and Helen didn't know what it meant, but she thought of Gary and how he'd been ripped away, his arm torn clean off. By a mouth? By a beautiful tongue?

The tunnel awaited them as it had earlier, shadowed and statue-filled. They swam slower here, allowing Frank to explore as he would. He took the camera to capture some images, and Helen watched for dangers, but the water was calm, not surging the way it had on the earlier trip.

That, she reminded herself, had only been on the journey out. Not the journey in.

And then, the whisper again. The need to clear her throat, but the inability to do so with the breather lodged in her mouth. Helen gestured that they should continue, and she let Frank keep the camera strapped to his belt, because she couldn't get the whisper out of her head.

She tapped her right ear to ask if Frank could hear it too, but he shook his head. None of the others seemed able to hear it. Helen tried to focus on something else, but as it had before, the sound overtook her, until it grew clearer, and she could hear the word being said. Mama, it said. *Mama. Mama. Maaama.*

The final niche in the wall was occupied this time—Nephthys gazing impassively at the arched ceiling above her—and Helen told herself she must have remembered it wrong. That her photograph hadn't been of this niche, but of another. Helen swallowed down the bile that wanted to rise, and kicked hard. She guided the men out of the tunnel and into the brightening waters at its other end. As before, she came out of the water wanting to claw her skin off. She spat the breather out and bent double on the strange shore, overcome. Frank and the others were there, but she couldn't stop them from running to the temple, given the whisper in her mind.

Mama.

It was vile; she pushed it away. She unstrapped her tanks and left her gear at the shore, walking on unsteady legs up to the temple where the men already gaped in wonder. Frank gestured for her to come, that he needed another roll of film, and she gave him one from her dry sack.

"Do you recognize any of it?" she asked him.

"None of it—none of them. My God, Helen. This is unprecedented." He gently touched her shoulder and leapt back toward the temple with her camera. It was perfectly functional above water, too, so she had no doubt they would bring some quality images back this time.

She sat for a long while, under the once-again nighttime sky, as Frank explored the temple. The men inside exclaimed and laughed from time to time. She wanted to get up, wanted to walk inside, but she felt frozen outside.

Mama, come.

The whisper would not leave her. She shook it away, annoyed. She was not a mother. Might have been, had Frank not... Nephthys was a mother, was a protector of mothers, and when this idea occurred to Helen, she stood, striding toward the temple. Inside, the air was cool, lit by the diving lights the men wore. The statue she had seen on her first visit here, however, was gone. Statue and infant both, though the offerings remained. Helen didn't understand.

"This is amazing," Frank whispered, still photographing as he moved through the temple. "Do you have more film, Helen?" He moved toward his workers, speaking to them in low Arabic, gesturing to the piled offerings, to the gems and golden coins.

Helen had one last roll of film and offered it to Frank, allowing him to work. She could not stop starting at the empty statuary base.

"There must have been a statue here. See these marks, as if feet?" Frank said. He photographed the empty stone, the offerings, and then casually palmed the massive pearl. Like a magician with a coin, he slipped it into his dry sack.

She noticed other things had been taken, too—the sacks the men wore now bulging with artifacts. They were busy making rubbings from the markings on the wall now, but they'd taken everything they perceived as valuable first. Helen leaned against the nearest wall. It was their way—it was Frank's way—and he had photographed it *in situ* first. This was how she explained it away. This was how it was all done, she told herself. They had to record it, they had to preserve it, lest it crumble to dust.

Did they?

"Frank, we shouldn't—"

Frank laughed, pressing the camera back into Helen's hands. "I've shot all there is—be good and sure this comes back with us." He dropped a kiss on her forehead and then went back to his men, animatedly discussing the temple around them.

Be good and sure. Helen cradled the camera and paced out of the temple. She sat on the ramp, the stone still warm from the sun, though she had never seen the sun this side of the hole. This side of the hole where a figure that was not a man or a woman frolicked on the wet beach with a child.

Their appearance startled Helen. She thought for certain she was dreaming them. They were the color of the granite they had been carved from, strong but clumsy in the ways they moved, because they hadn't been jointed properly.

"Mama, come!"

Helen felt herself moving, drawn to the child as it scampered, clapped its hands, shrieked in delight at the sight of her approaching. It was not her child—she knew it in her bones—and yet she could not stop herself from walking toward it. From scooping the small body into her arms and hugging it tight. This was what Nephthys was protecting, Helen thought. This was what should have never been found. If they went back into the tunnel—

"Helen!"

Frank's sharp call made her turn. Her arms were empty now, but she could still feel the weight of the small body within them. She did not question what had happened—Frank had no right to see this, because he would take it as he took everything. She moved toward him, toward the other men who were gearing up to leave.

"We need to return with more supplies," Frank said when she was near enough. "We need to understand this place—where it is, and why it is, and what these figures are."

When he gestured to the temple, Helen followed his motion. Two of the eight statues were gone now. Had Frank noticed? Had anyone?

"We can't," she said softly. How could any of them ever begin to understand? This space was sacred and should be protected at all costs. If Frank came back...

She thought of the blood in the water, of Gary vanishing into the dark.

"Understanding is what we do," Frank said, and he turned from her to swing his oxygen tank back on. "Helen, come—guide us back."

Helen hesitated. "You can't. This..." She looked back at the temple to see another statue had gone. Was it all evaporating, or was Nephthys assembling her army? Her protection. "We can't take this place apart, Frank. You... Empty your sacks, all of you. None of this can be taken. None of it." But taking was what they did. Always taking.

Frank's laugh was as sure as it had ever been. "This is what we do," he repeated. "Do you think other men won't come to this place and take it apart?"

He kept to honesty, just as she had. If it wasn't them, it would be someone else. It would be everyone else. If she could keep it to these four...

"All right," she said softly. It was not a solution, but she didn't know what was.

Beneath the water, she found the same solace she always had. Helen sank into it, the weight of the camera at her side becoming as the weight of the child on the shore had been. It was a comfort, but more than that, it was hers. No other could take it this time, for it was wrapped around her and she around it.

She imagined the child diving with them, showing her the way. Into the darkness where the algae bloomed in unseen corridors. Helen imagined herself taking this child's hand, and swimming with them, away from the water when it surged once more.

At the press of the water, Helen knew what was coming. She turned in time to see Frank's contorted face, his mask and tank ripped away. She felt her diving knife in her own hand, but told herself it was not so. Frank was pale in the water, in the explosion of blood that followed. He knew he was dying all the while he died, hands scrabbling helplessly, trying to reach Helen, trying to reach anything he might hold to.

Helen felt the knife in her hand, but swam to the nearest wall, anchoring herself against the statue of Bastet, where she watched as Nephthys—as *something*—untethered from her niche once more, ripped through the water and the men. The water ran with blood, so thick Helen's light did not pierce it. She was aware of the child at her side, curled hard into her neck with its face pressed away. A warm weight in the darkness. A whisper.

Mama, come.

One by one, the bodies came apart. Helen, pulled by that small weighted hand, swam away from the furor, northwest the way they'd come, and the whisper no longer made her want to claw her skin off, because she understood it. I am yours, the whisper said, and no other. Around her, the ruin began to crumble, walls and statues crumbling to dust, swallowing the men, and their dry sacks full of looted offerings. Helen couldn't see, the water had grown so murky, but she felt the strike of a stone, and then another, her body and gear battered as she swam her way free.

Helen broke the surface of the ocean and pulled herself onto the boat, heaving and gasping for air. She reached for the small presence that had been with her, but it was gone. The voice that had urged her out of the crumbling ruin was silent. She lay looking at the sunrise sky, pale and fragile, for there was no eternal night here—only the breaking of a new day above the sea. Helen reached for her camera, but it was no longer clipped to her belt. Lost in the collapse. The only evidence of what they had found. What she had found. What she had defended. The knife was gone, too. Blood beaded on her skin.

Back on dry land, Helen tied the boat to the dock, startled by a voice at her side.

"Here."

A sun-warm towel was pressed into her hands and she looked at the familiar figure standing beside her. Frank called the boy Alex, but only because they had hired him in this city and not another.

Helen pressed her face into the warm towel and exhaled. "Sharks," Helen murmured, though Alex had not asked why she had returned alone. Someone would, surely.

"They were fools," Alex said, and helped Helen gather her gear.

There would be questions to answer, but back at the Cecil Hotel, Helen got herself cleaned up and dressed, and headed for her closet darkroom. Your realm, the concierge had said, and she unlocked the door with the key he had given her. But inside, the closet was only a closet, boxes of supplies having replaced her pans, chemicals, and photographs. The line she had strung to hang drying prints from was gone, and so too the prints.

Helen stepped into the corridor, standing in shock. When she forced herself to move once more, she sought the concierge, but at his desk stood a man she did not recognize, a man who knew nothing of her photographs, but took the closet key nonetheless. Helen walked through the lobby in a daze, joining Alex at the hotel entry. She shook her head at the boy, because everything she had brought from the dive, but for the memory, was gone, simply gone.

Across the road, the sea beckoned, green and blue, and somewhere, Helen thought, red. And beneath the darkness, a whisper—

Mama, come.

E. Catherine Tobler dreams of Egypt. Among others, her short fiction has appeared in *Clarkesworld, Lightspeed,* and *Apex Magazine.* She edited the World Fantasy and Hugo-finalist *Shimmer Magazine,* and co-edited the World Fantasy Award finalist anthology, *Sword & Sonnet.* Follow her on Twitter @ECthetwit or her website, www.ecatherine.com.

A THOUSAND FACES MINUS ONE
BY A.C. WISE

DONOVAN DREAMS OF A MAN without a face.

Or rather, the man has a face, but Donovan can't see it. It's hidden under a black hood, like a criminal in an old movie might wear as he's about to hang. The man doesn't do anything other than stand in the corner, but somehow that simple act induces a sense of dread. The man has a message, or there's something important Donovan has forgotten. The man has come to take away something Donovan loves.

Donovan wishes the man would get it over with, but he only stands there, breathing, and the cloth over his mouth goes in and out, in and out.

He shouldn't be thinking about Paris—he promised himself he wouldn't, but how can he avoid it when Notre Dame is burning? The footage is horrifying, the towers going up in flame, and the skeletal remains of the building afterward. He watches the videos over and over, unable stop, and he thinks about Henry.

It's been over two years since he stood atop the cathedral, gazing out at the city spread below. Bright sunlight stretched shadows across the courtyard, flattening the people they belonged to into dots. Then Henry had put a hand on the small of Donovan's back, whispering in his ear, and warmth spread like fire across Donovan's skin.

Their "chance" meeting had been pre-arranged, but that didn't lessen the thrill. Donovan felt like a spy, slipping into a role Henry designed for him, pretending to be someone else and leaving his own failure of a life behind. In the instant before turning to see Henry for the first time, he'd been swept by the vertiginous feeling of doing something incredibly dangerous, and yet being incredibly safe at the same time.

When we meet, I want you to pretend we're strangers.

Henry had sent the message while Donovan waited at the airport, brand new passport clutched in his hand. He'd never flown internationally before, couldn't afford it. But Henry had paid for everything, flying Donovan—a complete stranger—seven and a half hours across the ocean to meet him at the top of Notre Dame.

We *are* strangers, Donovan had texted back, tacking on a smiley face. He'd stopped just short of using the eggplant emoji, even though they both knew they were meeting up explicitly for sex. It felt too forward, like a cartoon vegetable implied an intimacy he hadn't earned.

That's not what I mean. Pretend you're not you. Pretend to be somebody else.

In that moment, Donovan had almost gotten cold feet and backed out. Henry had picked his dating profile out of hundreds, and contacted him, but now he wanted him to be someone else. And who could blame him? Donovan was barely able to afford his shitty one room apartment, working shifts at two different restaurants, and ready to give up on ever having a music career. He was a loser.

Whereas Henry seemed too good to be true. Older, smart, funny, a foodie, a world traveler, and he had the kind of money required to fly a stranger to a whole other continent based solely on a handful of messages exchanged through a dating app.

Donovan put his nerves aside. What did he have to lose, really? And when would he ever get an opportunity like that again?

So he'd flown to Paris, gone to the top of Notre Dame as instructed, and nervously waited. Then Henry's hand rested on his back, and his lips brushed Donovan's ear. Donovan's mind had gone completely blank. Henry could have whispered anything—a comment about the view, a request—a *demand*—to fuck him. All Donovan registered was a dizzy sensation of lust, as though he was falling from the top of the cathedral.

Donovan wishes he could remember Henry's words. He would have something to hold onto now. As it is, he doesn't even have pictures. Henry made him promise not to take any, and Donovan had obeyed, like he'd obeyed all of Henry's other rules, except one.

He'd spent a week in Paris pretending to be someone else, ordering what Henry told him to order, visiting the places Henry wanted to visit. Donovan let himself become someone for whom it was perfectly natural to dine in fine restaurants and drink expensive champagne. Ride to the top of the Eiffel Tower, watch the city dissolve in a smear of light below. Visit the catacombs under the city, walk through the galleries of the Louvre, find a quiet, shadowed corner along the banks of the Seine, and go down on his knees to take Henry's cock in his mouth while tourists sailed by, oblivious to their presence.

When he came home, he *was* somebody different. Within a week, his life had transformed; he'd gotten an offer from a producer based on the demo recording he'd made, just when he'd been ready to give up. Like Henry choosing him out of all the profiles on the dating app, it was another impossibility, the offer he'd always dreamed of. And he'd been almost too heart-broken to take it, until his best friend Mel all but slapped him upside the head and forced him to accept.

Now, if he wanted to, Donovan could afford to fly to Paris on his own, stay in the same hotel he stayed in with Henry, eat at all the same restaurants. Only Notre Dame is gone and it wouldn't be the same. It will never be *his* Notre Dame again, the exact place he stood with

Henry's hand on his back, telling himself over and over it would just be another hookup. Telling himself over and over not to fall in love.

Except even then, at the top of the cathedral, it had already been too late. He'd broken Henry's rule before he'd even delivered it. Donovan had lied to himself, told himself it would be fine. But at the end of the week, Henry had kissed Donovan perfunctorily, a brief touch of lip against lip, and put him in a cab.

Exhausted and jetlagged, Donovan messaged Henry when he landed. Another promise he'd broken, but one message to say he'd arrived home safely didn't seem too out of line. The message bounced; Henry had blocked him. Donovan never heard from him again.

The problem with pretending to be someone else, Donovan had discovered, is that somewhere along the line he'd convinced himself he was actually the person Henry wanted him to be. The night before Donovan flew home, he'd woken to soft light spilling from under the bathroom door in their expensive hotel room. He'd heard what sounded like crying, then the shower came on, drowning out the noise.

Henry had left his laptop open, and Donovan crept over to take a peek, thinking he might find a clue to Henry's sorrow, or the way to unlock his heart. A web browser was open, page displaying a news story from a few years back, showing a man who looked enough like Donovan that they could be brothers smiling into the camera. The man had been killed in a car accident. Looking at the picture, a leap of intuition clicked everything into place. Henry had loved the man in the picture; they'd spent a week in Paris together, and now he'd essentially hired Donovan to take his place.

Before he'd been able to read any further, the shower stopped, and Donovan dived back into bed. The bathroom light clicked off. The mattress sank, and Donovan smelled heat and soap and water from Henry's skin. He touched Donovan's arm lightly, a question.

Donovan froze and pretended to be asleep. Henry rolled away, and Donovan immediately regretted his choice. It would have been so easy to play the role Henry wanted. Maybe he would have found a way to transmute that into real affection, even love. But in that moment, he'd been overtaken with resentment; Henry didn't want him, he wanted someone else, and for that Donovan chose to punish him.

Donovan watches yet another video of Notre Dame burning. If he'd rolled into Henry's touch that night, would things have been different? Henry had told him over and over again that their week in Paris meant nothing, but what if that was only armor, defense against his fear of falling in love again?

No. Nothing would have changed, no matter what he'd done. Their relationship had always been on rails, destined to run in only one direction. Some wounds can't be healed; some loves are irreplaceable.

"Kate Bush," Donovan says when Richard answers the phone. "Meg Myers."

He's practically bouncing on his toes, pacing around his apartment. He'd woken up before the sun, struck with a bolt of inspiration. Unable to sleep again, he'd gone for an early morning run, now his entire body buzzes with creative energy and post-workout endorphins.

"What?" Richard, on the other hand, sounds like he just woke up.

"Meg Myers, her cover of 'Running Up That Hill,' that's what I want to do for my next song. I'll build the whole album around it. I've even got the video figured out and everything."

"You want to redo what Meg Myers just did, and you expect it to be successful." It's not really a question.

Donovan pictures Richard rolling out of bed in loose pants, shirtless, and gathering his just-starting-to-grey hair into a ponytail before wandering barefoot into his kitchen to make coffee.

"Not 'Running Up That Hill,' another song." Donovan grins, even though Richard can't see him. "'Hammer Horror.'"

"What the fuck are you talking about?"

Donovan hears the coffee machine grumble to life. He pictures his producer's immaculate kitchen, every surface white or stainless steel, everything shining.

"'Hammer Horror,'" Donovan continues, undaunted by Richard's lack of enthusiasm. "It was Kate Bush's first single from *Lionheart*."

In the background, he hears Richard typing. A moment later, the strains of Kate Bush come through the phone. The faint echoing quality tells Donovan that Richard has put him on speaker phone.

"What the fuck am I watching?" Richard's question doesn't seem to be directed entirely at Donovan, but he answers anyway.

"It's a song all about replacing someone else—an actor haunted by the ghost of his friend, whose role he took on after his friend died. The song was inspired by James Cagney playing Lon Chaney playing the Hunchback of Notre Dame. When I do it, it'll be a song playing the role of another song—it's meta, meta, meta-textual."

"It doesn't even make sense. Hammer Films never made a version of Hunchback."

"That isn't the point. It's about the roles we play in life, the masks we wear. It's about feeling replaceable, and being haunted by the past. I'm thinking I'll do it down tempo, almost like a love song."

"Don—"

Donovan interrupts before Richard can even get out his name. "Hear it before you say no."

Richard is close enough to the phone that Donovan hears him sigh.

"Fine," Richard says. "I'll get you in the studio, but I can't make any promises. We don't even know if we can get the rights."

"We'll get them." Chords run through Donovan's head; he already sees the music video unfolding. He'll recreate Kate Bush's choreography, but instead of her and a masked dancer in front of a black backdrop, he'll get someone who looks like him to dance through the streets of a city. Paris. Maybe he'll even be able to get permission to film part of it in Notre Dame before they begin reconstruction. It's going to be brilliant.

Donovan dances with the faceless man.

They recreate Kate Bush's video for "Hammer Horror," hands lifting Donovan, turning him, positioning him like a doll. His limbs trail ghosts every time he moves.

And his limbs are ghosts, fitting into spaces other limbs occupied just moments before. He's following in someone else's footsteps, trying desperately to catch up. The faceless man dips him, splays a hand across Donovan's throat, and bends to whisper something in his ear. But the cloth gets in the way and the words are lost.

Donovan wakes kicking off the covers. A lingering sense of unease follows him from the dream, the feeling of having disappointed someone, of having forgotten something important. The more he chases it though, the further it slips away, even though he can still feel it—just out of sight, just behind him, or just around the next corner up ahead.

Dawn pinks the sky. Donovan goes for a run, pushing himself to work up a sweat, pushing until his legs ache and his lungs burn. As he completes the second loop, coming back within sight of his building, he gets the sudden, unshakable sense that someone is following him.

Lots of people jog this route, but this feels specific, targeted. The person behind him matches his pace; if he sidesteps a crack or an uneven bit of pavement, they do the same at the exact same time.

Donovan twists around hoping to catch the person and loses his footing. He strikes the ground hard, pain jolting up to his shoulder as he tries to stop his fall.

"Are you okay, man?"

A man in a highlighter-yellow athletic shirt pulls earbuds from his ear. The man breathes hard, definitely not the sleek shadow he'd been so certain was following him. Embarrassment tightens his skin, replacing the fear.

"Yeah, my ankle just went out. Old injury." Donovan offers a reassuring smile with the lie.

He lets the man help him up, scanning the early morning dog-walkers and commuters, people minding their own business, going about their days. There's no one skulking off into the shadows, no one threatening or mysterious. He's sure that someone was about to touch his shoulder though. Could he have a stalker?

Donovan thanks the man in yellow again, and quick-walks the rest of the way home. Being out on the street makes him feel watched, exposed. His ankle isn't even sore; it's his hand that smarts and throbs. As he waits for the elevator in his building's lobby, a faint pressure brushes against the base of Donovan's spine and he jumps.

There's no one there, but for a moment, he could swear Henry's hand rested on his back. The skin of his ear even tingles in anticipation of whispered words, and he rubs at it vigorously, scrubbing the sensation away. The elevator dings and Donovan steps in, tense until the doors close.

After Paris, he tried to find Henry. It didn't occur to him until later that everything Henry told him about himself—including his name—might have been a lie. Even the article left conveniently open on his laptop could have been for show. Henry had projected sorrow, but maybe it was all an act for Donovan's benefit. It had certainly worked, making Donovan trust him—God help him—making Donovan want to save him. But what if the whole time Henry had simply been manipulating him, an emotional predator set on draining him dry?

Donovan double and triple checks the locks on his apartment door before taking a shower. He stays under the sluicing water until his skin turns bright pink. Once he's dried off and dressed, he calls Mel. She can bring her guitar, they can try out different arrangements, he can lose himself in the music the way he couldn't lose himself in the run, and he can put the thought of faceless men following him out of his head.

"Do you believe in ghosts?" Donovan asks.

He breathes out a lungful of smoke. Along with her guitar, Mel brought weed. Startled, Mel drops the joint as he passes it between them. She swears and brushes at invisible flecks of ash, frowning.

"What do you mean, ghosts?" There's a strange edge to Mel's voice, and Donovan gets the sense that she's asking more than just the question he hears.

"I dunno. Like earlier, I was sure someone was following me, but there was nobody there. Then in the lobby, I thought I felt..." Donovan shakes his head. "Never mind."

"Being followed by invisible people. Got it. I'm sure this will help." Mel holds up the joint, but softens her words with a smile.

"Hey, I've got an idea." Mel leans forward. Her eyes shine, and Donovan can't help feeling she's trying to distract him, get him onto a different subject. Or maybe the weed really is making him paranoid.

"Viral marketing," Mel says. "You could start some kind of weird urban legend about the original Kate Bush "Hammer Horror" video, like the suicidal munchkin in the *Wizard of Oz*, or the ghost boy in *Three Men and a Baby*. People love hidden histories and conspiracy theories."

"Okay, so what's our story?" Donovan sits up straighter. The skin at the base of his spine prickles, not like the touch he felt earlier, more like the anticipation of a touch that never comes.

"Here's something," Mel says after a moment of looking at her phone. "This says Kate Bush never met the dancer in her video before she started working with him, so we start with a grain of truth. Maybe he shows up on the set already wearing a black hood over his head. The whole time they're working together, she never sees his face..."

"Then after the video comes out, she finds out that the dancer she actually hired never made it to set." Donovan picks up the thread of Mel's narrative, grinning. "The guy who showed up had been obsessed with her for years, he'd been planning to kill her so no one else could have her, but he lost his nerve. The whole time, Kate was dancing with her would-be killer, and she never knew."

"Love it!" Mel flops back into her chair, arms spread. "I mean, we'll never get away with it. You'll get sued for slander or something, but I love it."

"Yeah." Donovan leans back, closing his eyes, letting his mind drift. There's something there. A haunted mask, a shadowy figure, an important message from beyond the grave, one person taking another's place. He just has to put it all together.

Donovan watches Kate Bush's video of "Hammer Horror" for the dozenth time, this time without sound. He focuses on the masked dancer, on the way he touches Kate's body, on the way he moves. He's always found something a little creepy about her songs, like there's a secret song-within-a-song just under the surface. It's the same with this video; there's nothing overtly threatening about it—it's a little cheesy actually—but he's still unsettled in a way he can't quite define.

Did Henry introduce him to Kate Bush's music? He can't remember.

Donovan pauses just before the video ends, freezing on the image of the dancer's hand splayed across Kate's throat as she hangs upside down. It's the most Hammer horror thing about the video, about the whole song, really. The way the dancer's fingers splay makes Donovan think of Christopher Lee touching Melissa Stribling's face, holding his hand at Veronica Carlson's throat, touching Caroline Munroe's shoulder. The implied sexuality, the implied threat—violence and seduction and desire all tied into one.

By Kate Bush's own admission, "Hammer Horror" isn't really about Hammer horror films, but the more Donovan watches, the more he convinces himself the connection is there.

Memories are ghosts we make for ourselves. The thought pops into Donovan's mind unbidden.

And like horror movie monsters, once memories are unleashed, you can't banish them again without extreme measures. They keep rising, like Dracula being played by new actors, recreated for new screens. Immortal. Eternal.

Donovan is the man in the mask.

He watches himself sleep. It's an eerie feeling, seeing himself from across the room, feeling the fabric of the mask going in and out over his mouth as he breathes, being in two places at once. He tries to untie the string holding the mask in place, so he can look in a mirror, be sure he's really himself. But the string is too tight, he can't get it undone. He breathes faster, and the fabric sucks into his mouth, suffocating him.

He wakes trying to claw the hood free and finds his pillowcase freed from the pillow and twisted around his face, as though he tried to strangle himself in his sleep.

"You're still set on this 'Hammer Horror' thing?" Richard asks as Donovan slides a thumb drive across the countertop.

He could have sent the files without coming in person, but he wanted to get out of his apartment. As much as he's excited about it, this project, this idea, is eating him up inside. He's on edge.

On the way over to Richard's, he'd once again been convinced someone was following him. He'd even caught a glimpse, reflected in a window—black windbreaker, black baseball cap, black sunglasses wrapped around a face hidden behind some kind of scarf or high collar. When he turned around, whoever it was had already slipped out of sight. Or was never there.

Now, instead of a stalker, he wonders if he has a spy. Could Henry have hired someone to find him? What if he'd watched the same footage of Notre Dame burning that Donovan had, and it had surfaced his own regrets. He could have paid someone to track Donovan down, learn his routines, so he could arrange a chance meeting, sidle up beside Donovan, lay a hand against the base of Donovan's spine— dangerous and seductive—and whisper in Donovan's ear.

This time, Donovan would remember the words, and fix them in his memory forever.

It's an absurd fantasy. Donovan knows he needs to let Henry go. He needs to let Paris go, but he can't. Maybe the ghost haunting him is Henry's lost lover, seeking revenge for Donovan taking his place. Or maybe he's planning to possess Donovan, slip into his skin and go walking around looking just like him. The thought is as absurd as the idea of Henry hiring someone to follow him, but Donovan can't stop himself.

All of this has to mean something—the sudden impulse to cover Kate Bush's song and recreate her video, his dreams of the masked man, Paris burning. It's a message just for him. He just has to decode it.

Richard plugs the drive into his laptop, opening the first of Donovan's files. Donovan busies himself moving around Richard's apartment, looking at the photographs and awards on his shelves, the books arranged artfully on his coffee table. The cuts he brought with him are all rough, Donovan playing around with different sounds, waiting for something to spark. Now that he's hearing them aloud, he's suddenly embarrassed.

One version ends and Richard moves on to the next one. Donovan is about to tell him to stop when he catches sight of Richard's expression. He's frowning, but it isn't displeasure. He's concentrating, considering, picking the song apart but not to destroy it. Donovan catches his breath.

He and Richard slept together once, and only once. They'd both been drunk, and Richard had invited Donovan back to his apartment. It was soon after Henry, and Donovan had wanted to erase the memory of him—a little bit of sorrow, a little bit of spite. It hadn't been a producer extorting sex in exchange for promises of making Donovan a star. Richard never promised him anything. He'd simply been alone, they both had, and they'd tried to find solace in each other. The sex was full of longing, but not for each other. The next day, they'd both admitted it was a mistake, and they'd both agreed it would never happen again. Ever since, their relationship has been purely professional.

Donovan finds himself flushed with that longing again now, like a memory of a memory. It was unfair, trying to replace Henry with Richard, even for one night. What if he'd tried to see Richard on his own terms, as just himself? Donovan pushes the thought out of his mind, arranging his expression into something carefully neutral.

"What do you think?"

"I like the third version," Richard says after a moment. "It needs a lot of work, but there's something there you can build on."

"I was afraid you'd hate it." Donovan feels a genuine rush of gratitude, and realizes he's been holding himself tense.

When he looks up again, Richard is watching him, and his expression catches Donovan off guard. There's something almost puzzled in his expression, or worried, like Richard can't quite place him. It lasts only a second, but in the instant before he looks away, Donovan is convinced that Richard's gaze shifts to a point just beyond Donovan's shoulder, like he's looking at someone else entirely, a shadow haunting him.

Donovan trolls dating apps, looking for dancers. Inevitably, every profile he clicks on reminds him of Henry. It isn't healthy. He should go through professional networks; he should leave casting up to Richard. He hasn't even recorded the song yet, and it's too early to be thinking about a video. On the other hand, it doesn't hurt to look, does it? He's not going to contact any of the men. This is just to gather inspiration, just for fun.

He'd seen a therapist for a while after returning from Paris. That time in his life is hazy—the rush of sudden success, the launch of a new career, his broken heart healing all at once. Donovan remembers his life before Paris sharply, then the dreamy blur of the city of lights, then picking up the thread of his life sometime later. The time in-between though, it's as though it happened to someone else entirely.

A thought strikes him—what if he never came home at all? What if he's an imposter and Donovan, the real Donovan, is the faceless man haunting him, lying in wait to reclaim his life?

His skin prickles, a sudden and visceral reaction. Instead of dissipating, the sensation only grows. He isn't alone. There's someone in the apartment with him.

Donovan sets his phone down, getting to his feet as quietly as he can. He grabs the lamp from his bedside table, feeling slightly foolish for doing so, yet comforted by the weight in his palm. He creeps out of the bedroom and into the hall.

Donovan's muscles actually ache, he's holding himself so tense. He springs around the corner and into the open sitting room and kitchen, as if he'll catch his intruder by surprise. The curtains pulled over the balcony doors taunt him. They're undisturbed, but some-one could be hiding behind them. Donovan snatches them aside. Nothing but the city shining brightly beyond the glass. He checks the hall closet and the bathroom, feeling more ridiculous with every moment. Of course there's no one in his apartment. The lamp grows heavy, dragging at his arm.

As he steps back into the bedroom, a shadowy figure steps toward him and Donovan hurls the lamp, an animal reaction. Glass shatters as the lamp strikes the full-length mirror beside his closet, raining shards all over the floor.

"Shit!"

Donovan covers his face with his hands, emitting a sound between a laugh and a sob. His pulse hammers. He's cracking up. He bends to carefully pick up one of the pieces of broken mirror, catching a sliver of his face reflected. No wonder he freaked out; he doesn't even look like himself anymore.

I'm worried about you, Van. You've been doing so well this past year, I thought you'd finally turned a corner, making new music, moving on. But the video you sent me? Honestly, you kinda freaked me out. I think you should talk to someone, even if it isn't me. Promise me you will? And call me when you get this so I know you're okay?

Donovan listens to Mel's message a second time, but it still doesn't make sense. He didn't email her anything, not that he can recall. Why would she be worried about him?

Donovan checks his email sent folder to set his mind at ease, and there is the email to Mel, complete with attachment. Farther down the page are five emails sent to names he doesn't recognize. Has he been hacked?

Donovan hesitates, then opens an email addressed to someone named Thomas. A creeping feeling washes over him, like there's someone, some*thing*, else occupying his skin. He almost remembers typing the email, late at night, sending it out along with the other four. It's brief, asking about dance and movement experience, asking for a resume and a sample of past work. The next email, to a man named Joseph, is almost word for word the same, and so is the one addressed to Adam.

Donovan doesn't bother checking the last two. The names— Thomas, Joseph, Adam—they're all profiles he looked at on dating apps, all dancers who reminded him in some way of Henry. But it had only been an idle thought, he hadn't actually… Donovan grabs his phone, opening one of the apps to check his message log.

Messages exchanged with Thomas, Joseph, and Adam, along with a handful of other men, stare him in the face. His whole body itches. It's like he's two people, one inhabiting his body, one watching himself from outside, the two constantly switching places.

Panic claws at him, his heart racing, skin clammy. There has to be a reasonable explanation. He returns to the message he sent to Mel and opens the video.

Kate Bush's "Hammer Horror" plays in the background as a man in a black mask dances with a man who looks like Henry. It's Kate Bush's video almost exactly—the same choreography, the same effect that makes it look like the masked man's limbs are trailing ghosts—only it's all backward. The masked man is in front, and the unmasked dancer is behind, lifting the masked man, moving him, placing a hand on the small of his back as his body bends with improbable grace.

Donovan isn't a dancer. He couldn't possibly be the masked man, but who else could it be? There's a faint soreness, the lingering effects of muscles moving in unaccustomed ways. The backdrop behind the dancers—it's his apartment. No wonder the video freaked Mel out. Donovan is freaked out too.

A wave of dizziness sweeps through him. Donovan pushes away from his desk, stumbling into the bedroom and wrenching open his closet. Below the neatly hung shirts and pants, where he normally throws dirty laundry, are two crumpled pieces of black fabric—a dancer's leotard and a mask, a hood really, just like the one in the video.

He doesn't remember shooting the video. He doesn't remember the man who looks like Henry coming to his apartment. But he does. Numbness creeps through his fingers, leaving them cold. His hands are very far away from the rest of his body, belonging to someone else. He is very far away from his body, watching himself lean back against his bed.

And Donovan is in his body, leaning back against his bed, holding the mask by its top corners. It's scarcely more than a cloth bag really, but he can feel it staring at him. He turns it, holding it by the opening. He remembers wearing it, but how can that be true?

He slips the mask over his head. The fabric blurs the room. Donovan breathes in. Breathes out again. The fabric moves with each breath, growing moist with condensation. It's almost comforting, safe where he expected to feel claustrophobic. It's familiar. And at the same time, terrifying.

He rises, moving carefully, arms out in front of him so he doesn't bang into anything. Back down the hallway into the sitting area, the kitchen. Everything is transformed, strange. He's surrounded by his furniture, but it's not his. It's his life, but it belongs to someone else. There's something missing, something he cannot see.

There. A blurred shape. Donovan turns his head slowly. A figure stands beside the window, pressed into the corner. Donovan's breath catches, his pulse catches, the world spins. The light makes the figure indistinct, the mask more so. He can't see any features, just a tall, elongated blot of shadow. The man might even be masked, too. Donovan steps forward. His shin barks against the coffee table. He expects the figure to swear at the pain, to move when he moves, but it remains still. Another step and the figure resolves into a guitar case resting atop an amp, leaning up against the wall.

A strange, broken sound ticks at the edges of his consciousness. It's coming from the corner. No, it's coming from him—a dry, hitching click in his throat. It hurts, and he can't tell whether it's laughter, or whether he's crying.

Donovan is afraid to sleep. He's afraid of what he'll do, and he's afraid of what he'll dream. Some other version of himself might slip in through the window like a vampire and go walking around in his skin. He can't trust himself. But he can't trust anyone else either.

Mel's message—she said something about him turning a corner. She said she was worried, but not why. There's something she isn't telling him. There's something no one is telling him.

Donovan turns on the TV. He rarely watches it these days, but he needs a distraction, and he needs to stay awake. On screen, Notre Dame is burning. He freezes, unable to look away. The news cycle had almost moved on, because that's the way the world works these days—one disaster, one outrage after another, swallowing up 24-hour coverage for days on end, and then gone, subsumed by the next thing.

Everything is replaceable, even the news.

Flames rise up the tower, smoke pouring into the sky. For a moment, Donovan thinks he catches sight of a figure caught against the flame, a crooked shape swinging through the bell tower. He blinks, and the image is gone. Victor Hugo's poor unloved orphan becoming Lon Chaney becoming James Cagney. Donovan scrubs at his eyes, banishing them all.

He's surprised to find the stinging persists, tears building behind his lids. He thinks of Paris, Notre Dame, and the last time he was truly happy.

He flips the channel, hitting the buttons on the remote with more force than necessary.

"…return to our Hammer horror marathon with *The Devil Rides Out.*"

Laughter catches in his throat, replacing the tears. He's being haunted in more ways than one. He's about to change the channel again, then stops. He might as well watch. The rest of *The Devil Rides Out* slides into *The Two Faces of Dr. Jekyll*, then *Hands of the Ripper*. He makes popcorn and drinks iced coffee to stay awake. But despite himself, he drifts off somewhere in-between *The Curse of the Mummy's Tomb* and *The Mummy's Shroud*.

He wakes with no sense of the time. It's dark outside—still dark, or already dark again he isn't sure. He squints as the words THE SOMNAMBULIST, STARRING LON CHANEY, JR drift in wavy, ghostly font across the screen.

Donovan watches a figure in ragged clothing stagger through the fog—dry ice pumped from unseen machines. His gait is stiff, awkward, and when the camera zooms in on his face, his eyes are glassy and wide. He's asleep.

Donovan wonders if he's asleep too. He struggles to sit upright, but everything is heavy. His eyes don't want to open all the way and his head feels thick and muzzy. He tries to go the other way, letting himself sink back into true sleep and away from the feeling of being trapped in-between. But fragments of the movie keep rising to the surface of his mind, glimpsed and then vanishing, like the man in the fog.

Lon Chaney Jr. plays multiple roles, wearing different faces, like his father would. Something about a kidnapping, or maybe a murder, or both. The actor's eyes widen, shock, as if he's coming awake all at once. His mouth opens painfully wide in a silent scream, and he drops to his knees, burying his face in his hands.

When Donovan wakes again, two men sit opposite each other in director's chairs against a blank backdrop, discussing Hammer Films' catalogue of thrillers, and the sun is up outside. A headache pounds behind Donovan's eyes. He feels sleep drunk. He stumbles up, half listening as he makes coffee. The titles bounce back and forth between the two men—*Maniac, Paranoiac, Fanatic, Hysteria.* There's no mention of *The Somnambulist.*

He's suddenly overwhelmed by the desire to talk to Henry. It's not just because Donovan misses him; Henry was a font of all kinds of obscure knowledge. If anyone would know about *The Somnambulist,* Donovan is sure it would be him. If he could just find Henry, talk to him one last time, everything would make sense. If he could talk to Henry, he would say he was sorry. He would find a way to make everything right again.

He leaves the TV on, volume turned low, as he looks up *The Somnambulist.* There are two hits on IMDb, a movie from 1903 and one from 2014, but nothing made by Hammer Films or starring Lon Chaney Jr. Behind him, the two men on TV continue discussing Hammer Films' thrillers—people in disguise, people pretending to be other people, plots to get revenge or to trick the guilty into confessing to murder. There are amnesiacs, people traumatized by their past into forgetting some horrific incident, lost loves, faked deaths and real ones. There are monsters, but they are the human kind. Donovan is starting to feel like he's caught in one of those movies.

Donovan pushes the thought away, and with it the itching in his nose presaging tears, scrolling until he hits a site called ScreenLegendz purporting to share the real truth about all the supposedly discredited urban legends of film. See? He doesn't need Henry after all. A sense of déjà vu hits him as he scans the articles on the site—the Hanged Munchkin, the Three Men and a Baby Ghost, the Poltergeist Curse, the Superman Curse. He talked about them all with Mel. Partway down the page there's one he hasn't heard of: Hammer Productions' Lost Film.

In 1967, Hammer Films produced a movie that despite being completed was never released. *The Somnambulist* starring Lon Chaney Jr., directed by Freddie Francis, and written by Jimmy Sangster, follows the story of Norman Hastings, played by Chaney, who becomes convinced he has an evil twin after friends tell him they've seen him in places he doesn't remember being, behaving strangely.

When a friend mentions seeing Norman's fiancée, Elizabeta, on one of these occasions as well, Norman decides his doppleganger must be out to steal her. He grows increasingly paranoid, obsessed, until it is revealed that Norman is a sleepwalker. He is his own doppelganger.

In the penultimate scene, he finds a note in his own handwriting, asking Elizabeta to meet him at the lighthouse, promising to explain everything, and he rushes to her. In the final scene, we see only Elizabeta's reaction to Norman, so there's no way of knowing whether he's awake or asleep when he finds her. Her eyes widen in terror, she opens her mouth to scream, throws her hands up to shield her face, and backs into the railing, falling to the rocks below. The movie ends as it began with Chaney wandering lost in the fog, a sleepwalker waking from a terrible dream. He discovers Elizabeta's broken body. He has accidentally killed the woman he loves.

Donovan is cold. He tries to match the description with the fragments he remembers from last night. There's no date on the article. Maybe the lost film has been found, and that's what he saw. He continues reading.

The Somnambulist was screened only once, but the studio pulled the film prior to release due to the tragic death of Chaney's co-star, Mary Alston. Rumors swirled around her death—from drug abuse to foul play, and whispers that someone from the studio might have been involved. Collectors have long sought a copy of the film or even the script, but they remain among the holy grails of memorabilia. Every few years, a claim that either script or movie has been found will surface, but inevitably there are debunked as fake.

Donovan types then deletes several versions of an email to Mel. Finally he settles for pasting the link and simply writing—something weird is happening to me and hits send. How could he have dreamed the movie without knowing it existed? And if he'd seen the real thing, wouldn't there be more than just one article about it on a questionable website? There's something else, something nagging at the back of Donovan's mind, like a dream he can't quite remember.

His phone lights up with Mel's number not fifteen minutes later.

"You actually published it?" Mel says instead of hello.

"What?" It isn't what he was expecting, and Donovan scrambles to catch up.

"Van, you—"

"You're talking about the link I sent, right? The conspiracy site article?"

"The story you wrote." Mel's voice is tight, angry, or maybe scared.

"No, I—"

"Van, you sent me that story last week. You wrote it up and sent it over asking if I thought it would work as viral marketing. I thought it was a joke. Jesus, I didn't think you were actually going to try to get it published."

The floor drops out from under Donovan, his stomach swooping. Again the phantom sensation of sitting at his computer, typing the story, sending it to Mel. Pins and needles prickle his fingertips, and he shakes his hands out, squeezing his fingers as if to return blood flow. He remembers the screen blurred through the black fabric of the mask, chuckling to himself as he typed. As someone typed, but surely not him.

"I don't—"

"I'm coming over," Mel says. "Stay there. Don't do anything."

What does she think he's going to do? Donovan stares at his phone. Mel has already hung up. He drops back onto the couch. He shuts off the TV. None of this makes sense.

The buzzer for his apartment makes Donovan jump. Mel. He'd already forgotten. How did she get here so quickly? Donovan glances at his phone. Half an hour, it's been half an hour since Mel called. But he only just sat down.

"Van? Donovan—okay?" Mel's words cut in and out, and Donovan starts. Her hand is on his arm; she's peering at him, her expression one of deep concern. He doesn't remember opening the door.

"I need to find Henry." The words come out of his mouth before he's had time to think them through.

Mel's entire face changes; it's like watching a structure crumble, like watching Notre Dame burn. He doesn't understand the expression left in its place—pity, sorrow—and so Donovan plows on, rushing through his thoughts before she can stop him.

"I know it's a bad idea, but look. Last time I didn't have any money, but I do now. I could hire a private investigator. I just want to talk to him, that's all, just talk, and then I can finally move on. That's a good thing, right? Closure?"

Donovan is breathing hard, as if he's run a race. There's something, someone behind him, a shadowy figure he's trying to outrun. The man in the black mask, following him and reaching for his shoulder. His own private ghost.

"Donovan, you have to stop." Mel's voice is firm, that same mixture of anger and fear he heard from her on the phone.

She guides him to the couch, her hand tightening on his arm. She almost pushes him into a sitting position, then takes a seat beside him. Her eyes are shiny, on the verge of tears, but Donovan has no idea why.

"I talked to Richard. I... we both agreed." Mel takes a shuddering breath. "I need to tell you something. You're not going to like it, and you probably shouldn't hear it from me, but I don't know what else to do because I think you need to know this now before you go too far."

Mel reaches into her bag and draws out an over-stuffed eight by ten envelope. She sets it on her lap, doubt playing across her face as she fidgets with its edges.

"You gave me this after... You didn't want it in your apartment, anywhere it would remind you. You were moving on, you were doing so much better, and Dr. Rosen agreed it was a good idea, healthy even, but I think..."

Mel hands the envelope over, turning her face away from Donovan. He holds it, uncertain what to do with it. It's heavy in his hands. Part of him knows what's inside, but if he doesn't open it, then it can't become real.

"Nobody blames you but yourself. It was an accident. What you were doing wasn't healthy, but…" Mel's words fade in an out again as Donovan slides the contents of the envelope onto his lap.

The folded paper on top of the pile is a program from a funeral. There's a picture above the date—Henry's face.

Donovan looks at the next item in the pile, a small article clipped from a newspaper. The words blur. He already knows what they say. Another version of him read them a thousand times, a lifetime ago. The article describes a car accident, describes a man swerving to avoid a pedestrian who suddenly leapt into the road, colliding head-on with a bus that instantly killed him.

Donovan remembers, after months of searching, finally finding Henry. He remembers traveling, watching for days—unseen—planning the timing and route of his run to intersect with Henry's morning commute. He remembers stepping into the road and reaching out his hand as if to stop Henry's car by force of will. Then the screech of tires, the tortured sound of metal twisting and the pop of shattered glass.

Mel is saying his name from somewhere far away. He sets the newspaper clipping aside, turning his attention to the photographs. He'd printed them out just to have something physical and tangible to hold after Henry blocked him. He remembers, Henry had been sick. He knew he was dying. He wanted to see Paris one more time, as he had when he was young, and he didn't want to see it alone. He wasn't looking for a relationship, or a long-term attachment, just a moment—he'd said—just something beautiful before saying goodbye.

Donovan looks through the pictures, the ones he promised not to take, then promised to delete. Donovan and Henry at the Eiffel Tower, on a boat on the Seine, Notre Dame, whole and unburned.

"Dissociative amnesia," Mel says, and Donovan's head snaps up, focusing on her as the photographs and clippings slide from his lap to the floor. It's hard to breathe. Grief and guilt all at once, his body shaking from the dual impact, muscles aching as they fight between motion and stillness.

"I killed him."

Mel reaches to pick up the fallen papers and pictures, but Donovan catches her wrist.

"Van, it was an accident. You didn't—"

"No." His fingers tighten and Mel winces, but he doesn't let go. She blurs in his vision, tears overwhelming his eyes and spilling from them. He hears himself make a terrible noise, half a gasp for air, half a sob. The sound breaks open the hollow space inside him. It hurts. Everything hurts. He's never felt anything like this in his life before. Except he has.

"I tracked him down. I stalked him. I caused the accident, so I killed him."

"The cancer was already doing that. He knew that, before he even met you."

Tears wet Mel's cheeks now too. Donovan's fingers spring open, releasing her wrist. She pulls back, wiping at her face.

He remembers Henry's hand on the small of his back, the electric thrill spreading through his entire body from one simple touch. He'd never felt anything so warm, so loving, so erotic. He hadn't even turned to see Henry's face yet, felt only that hand and heard his words, the timbre of his voice, and he'd already been in love.

"Paris is so beautiful from up here," Henry says in his mind. "I wanted to see it one last time, and I wanted someone beautiful to see it with as I say goodbye."

He feels dizzy. He's at the top of Notre Dame, falling. Henry knew he was dying. He'd told Donovan as much. He'd chosen Donovan as someone to whom Paris would all be brand new, to recreate it afresh through different eyes.

"It hurts." Donovan shudders, doubling over. Mel touches his shoulder. He knows she's talking, comforting words, but he can't hear them through the ringing in his skull.

"Please, leave me alone." He hears his own voice from far away and hears Mel's protest. Maybe he yells at her. She tells him she's calling Richard, and Dr. Rosen, and he tells her he doesn't care, and she leaves.

Good. He doesn't deserve a friend like her. When Richard comes, when Dr. Rosen comes, he'll lock the door and keep them all out. Donovan staggers to his feet, kicking at fallen photographs and papers, chasing them under the couch. It isn't real. None of it is real.

He goes into his bedroom, into his closet. The black leotard and mask are still there, crumpled beneath his other clothes. He puts them on, and returns to the main room. The fabric of the mask is already damp from his tears. His breath dampens it further, so it clings to him, a feeling like suffocation, like drowning, like a comforting hand. In the corner, the guitar case propped on the amp becomes his dark twin again, and the presence is reassuring.

Donovan opens his laptop. He feels the smooth casing under his fingers as he does it, and he feels nothing at all, watching someone who looks like him from very far away. He can just barely see the screen through the mask. He can't tell whether he's awake or asleep, but it doesn't matter. Kate Bush's song is already cued up in an open tab. Donovan finds the mini tripod for his phone and sets it up, pointing it at the empty space between his couch and the window. He hits record, then on the laptop, he hits play.

Kate Bush singing "Hammer Horror" fills his apartment. Donovan steps into the camera's view and moves, bending and contorting his body in impossible poses. He doesn't so much dance as he lets himself be shaped and guided. There are other hands there, touching his body, lifting him. They trail ghosts behind them, just as he trails ghosts, a thousand versions of himself expanding and collapsing backward into one with every motion. When he watches the video later, he'll see the truth he knows down deep in his bones.

Henry is there, a hand on the small of his back, guiding him, keeping him safe, keeping him from falling. The warmth of that hand, steering him into the role he was hired to play, feels like love.

Donovan sinks into the touch, letting himself be led so he doesn't have to think, doesn't have to feel. He's safe. Everything is okay. He is loved.

Inside the mask, faceless, Donovan smiles.

A.C. Wise's fiction has appeared in publications such as Uncanny, Tor.com, and several Year's Best anthologies. She has two collections published with Lethe Press, and a novella published with Broken Eye Books. Her work has won the Sunburst Award for Excellence in Canadian Literature of the Fantastic, as well as twice more being a finalist for the award, twice being a finalist for the Nebula Award, and being a finalist for the Lambda Literary Award. Her debut novel, *Wendy, Darling*, is forthcoming from Titan Books in June 2021, and a new collection, *The Ghost Sequences* is forthcoming from Undertow in August 2021. Find her online at www.acwise.net.

THE MAIDENS OF MIDNIGHT
BY RHIANNON RASMUSSEN

The film begins abruptly, crimson text emblazoned
over the dark stones of a castle wall. The
boldness suggests brassy accompaniment, but the
film was never scored. As is common on cheap film,
the red is too bright. In silence it wobbles and
bleeds into the shadows. The title is tacky. The
silence is ominous.

Despite everything, I do think *The Maidens of Midnight* would have
been my most interesting film. Not that there was much to measure
up against. I remember sitting in this shitty van rattling through
the mountain roads, reading this slapped-together script composed
on a typewriter so cheap that the ink smudged on my hands and
thinking about how I'd finally gotten a billing role—and it was, of
course, with the hounds of bankruptcy breathing their wet breath
down our necks. Before I'd boarded the plane, I'd threatened to find
another studio—actually, my agent had already been looking, not that
I told Paul that. But this one, Paul swore, this one would make it.
Paul Pellou, he was the director, still thinking he could make another
The Curse of the Blood Swamp of Mars (Terror! In Technicolor!). He was a

sleazeball, but he had a good eye for talent and a way with words, and our cinematographer—Del, he was driving—he had just won some kind of award for his last movie, though Paul was the one who kept bringing it up.

I'm not sure I believed Paul about this supposed surefire success of *Maidens*. As far as we could tell he was a one-hit wonder, although at this point, we'd done eight films together, each more desperate than the last. Lower budgets, lower ratings, lower returns. In the end, it was only three weeks of my life, and even in the woods in the back of a van where I could see the road through the floor, I remember thinking that the script wasn't half bad. Some of my scenes with Joelle were pretty hot. Room for improvement, sure, but improvements I could make. I couldn't act if I had nothing to work with.

The truth was, my agent hadn't gotten any leads, either. Horror was out, comedy and thrillers in. No one wanted to work with a second-rate horror actress getting on the older side. Older, bullshit—I was in my prime. But that's film for you.

I'll admit the other reason I agreed was that Paul promised I'd finally get to play a monster. A monster and a lesbian. That was the big third act shocker, though I'm sure it would have ended up on the poster. I don't remember who wrote the script—maybe he did. It didn't have a name on it. Anyway, at some point that mandate had been handed down. The virginal sacrifice wanted to be a monster all along.

And there's a visceral appeal to monsters, a thrill at hauntings, at the power they hold to take your breath and your life and, perhaps, your desire. I'd only been menaced by them so far, which was sexy in its own way, being frightened and desirable and certainly not *intending* to be ravished, but there was a sharp hot jealousy that ran through me any time I saw our famous villain in his makeup, pacing back and forth, muttering Shakespeare under his breath to warm up, and sweeping his cape. An electric sort of energy. I wanted it. I wanted to be it—the shadow that held the room.

Half my life I'd told myself I was interested in men. I was only interested in their power.

What Paul didn't say was that he wanted me on the film because our other big star, the famous monster man, had quit the series. Paul didn't have to say it; I knew I was playing second string.

"Couldn't have written it better myself," I said by way of half-assed compliment, shuffling the script back together. I had a nightmare of sheets flying out the window, lost in the grim pines of a tiny backwater country in Eastern Europe. Then it would be all-hands-on-deck recreating the thing from memory; or worse, improvising. My personal policy was to have as little to do with writing as possible. In high school, one time I'd tried to pay another student to finish an essay for me. I was almost suspended because the essay was "above my level." Acting had saved me.

Paul was sitting next to me, staring out the window, smoking—it helped his motion sickness, he claimed. Del hated it, but he hated puke more, so he put up with it.

"Yeah," Paul said. That was all. Isn't bad. Conversation over. I had no idea how he'd ever gotten a position as director. Whatever he was looking at, it was far beyond the trees.

We didn't speak again until we arrived at the castle gates.

```
Pan up a muddy road so desaturated the film
could be mistaken for black and white if not
for the garish smear of the title moments
before. Twisted pines reach towards the iron-
riveted castle gates, shut against the forest.
The camera lingers, uncomfortably. Shadows
shift in the toss of branches to either side
of the road. It is easy to imagine a person
standing in the thick, hidden.
    The gate is shoved open, and a blonde woman
stumbles out, dressed in a sheer nightgown, her
```

hair wild. The courtyard is black behind her;
what she is running from, unseen.

When we finally reached the castle, long after I'd decided that we were hopelessly lost, the gates were shut and, despite shoving, locked or barred from the inside. After we'd given up on yanking on them and idled outside while Paul and his assistant-cum-financial-yes man Michael argued for a good twenty minutes, Paul jumped back out of the van and shouted up at the ramparts while Del rapped his fingers on the steering wheel. The night made a beautifully framed picture—our manic director pacing back and forth, veins standing out on his head through his buzzcut from the stress of not having a smoke for several minutes, his stooping shadow blown out by the yellow headlights over massive gates that must have been a hundred years old at the newest.

I slid up into Paul's abandoned seat. The cool air was refreshing on my face, pine-scented and free of stale secondhand smoke, sharpened with a hint of gasoline. God, I needed to wash my hair.

"You oughta shoot this," I said, leaning around Del's seat to watch. In the passenger seat Joelle was either asleep or pretending to be, smart lady, and Hoyt—lead actor and Mr. Top Billing himself, heroic slayer of vampires—was passed out and snoring, which is why I felt safe shit-talking Paul. Hoyt liked to act magnanimous, but we all knew he was a narc.

The second van sat behind us, framing Del's greasy mustache in the dancing light of unwashed windshield. The hair twitched when he frowned. "It'd come out garbage. And who the hell'd pay to see *his* mug on screen?"

"It is a horror movie."

"Oh, shut up, Maxine, you're gonna get us some trouble."

Del was the only one on the crew who called me Maxine—I was Maxie to everyone else, and the billing on the posters—Maxie Madison. Picked the name myself. Liked how it rolled off the tongue. Intriguing—a little spicy, even.

I laughed. "I've got a question. Aren't castles supposed to overlook villages? For the lords to feel superior about their lot, not like those dirty peasants, or whatever? Why make them so damn inaccessible?"

"Beats me. At this point I think Paul just picks locations to make my life hard."

"Yeah, sounds like him. Do you think we're even supposed to be here? Suppose Paul just found some abandoned castle in an atlas and drags out all our asses—"

Del groaned. Hoyt stirred beside me with a rattling snore, ending our conversation. At the same time, Paul paused in front of the gates. I didn't hear anything, and there was no movement from above as far as I could see, but there was a terrible shriek of metal and the gates yawed open, inwards. Heavy, monstrous things. It was easy to imagine them repelling a siege.

Paul climbed back in, face red, about into my lap, and slammed the door shut. "About fucking time," he growled. "Assholes. Tibor knew we were coming today and he pulls this shit." Tee-bor was how he said it. New name to me, but you met all kinds in film.

I looked back to the gates as our sad little procession lurched through, but there was no one there.

It really was a classical sort of castle—a grand tower in the middle, barely visible against the starry night save for the light burning from a single window, tiers of parapets like jagged teeth studding the mossy stone walls, a moldering stable that clearly hadn't seen a horse in it for decades even in the sickly headlights of our vans. I wasn't sure there was electricity—certainly the courtyard had no lights. Even so, it was a sight—like the bones of a dragon. Impressive even in death. I'm an American girl, I'd never seen one up close before, but I didn't want to seem like some naïve broad, regardless of what Paul said, so I kept my excitement to myself.

The rest of the crew didn't have reservations about sounding naïve—or at least expletives were, I'd learned, how they expressed all sorts of disbelief. They piled out of the second van, hauling the equipment out, swearing and sweating. First the sullen grip, big ol' Linder; then our resident open queer and self-professed "wardrobe mistress," Reid; then poor Enoch. Enoch was the youngest of us. You could tell from how his face lit up when he talked about art. He had a foul mouth, too, but something about it wasn't sincere. I suspected he'd cultivated it to keep people from asking him how Mormon he was.

"Where's the lights?" Del asked.

"Doesn't have any, Del, it's a fucking castle."

"Are you serious? It's fucking 1660 in here?"

"What, you think we bought a generator for fun?" Hoyt piped in.

"Go back to sleep, Hoyt, I don't pay you to start talking until tomorrow." That was Paul.

I didn't want to stick around for another round of this, so I shoved the door open and pushed myself over Paul, into the courtyard.

"You okay, doll?" he asked, followed shortly by: "Christ, don't I keep telling you to lose some damn weight?"

Mud and straw stuck to my shoes—hopefully not horseshit, based on the state of the stable. I grimaced and plodded across the courtyard until I could barely hear Hoyt and Paul arguing. Boy, I missed those few hours he'd been asleep. The wind picked up and reminded me that I'd kill a man for a shower. My hair was so greasy it was sticking to my greaseless foundation, which was extra impressive because I'd bleached it to hell for this shoot. I was the endangered virginal blonde this time, Joelle the black-haired seductress. At least until the end, which, I assumed, involved a wig. Evil darkens the hair.

I suppose of all the crew, I miss Joelle the most. She was lovely to work with. You wouldn't think it from the movies.

Free from the van, my eyes were already adjusting to the murk. The sky was completely clear, not black but a rich dark blue sparkled with stars. I could even see the belt of the Milky Way, shimmering down until it was cut off by the sharp silhouettes of the pines. I stood there, stretching my arms and listening to my shoulders crack while I took a moment to just drink that sky in.

In a series of shots intercut with aggressive zoom, the woman in white stumbles frantically through the forest, her eyes sunken, her expression one of shock. Her pursuers are hooded in black, indistinct among the trees, blurred by motion and the constant twisting of the camera. It is unclear whether the woman falls or is pushed; either way, her pursuers surround her as she sobs among the leaves.

A last hooded figure pushes through the others, pausing to gaze down at the fallen woman. This figure pulls down her own hood, revealing striking beauty, eyes lined in kohl, her expression one of pity. She leans close, stroking the fallen woman's cheek; her lips move, forming the phrase oh, my sister, though it is clear that there is no familial intent. The woman calms. Her face grows vacant. She stands. Her movements are limp, unnatural.

The hooded figures flank her, and together they return to the castle. The woman in black pauses at the gate and pulls down her hood, looking back down the empty road, her hair black and sleek, her lips curled into a self-satisfied smile.

Someone inhaled, to my left, and I was suddenly aware of how far from the two vans I was, and that I was outside of the pool of light. I stepped back and my hand balled into a fist, though I was kidding myself if I thought I could put up a fight. What was the name of the landlord? Tibor? I took a breath, myself. To scream, maybe.

"It's beautiful, isn't it?" They spoke in a soft murmur, as if they'd heard my panic. As if to reassure me—it was a woman, a woman with a velvet voice with a hint of a rich accent that I couldn't place. And it did reassure me—just hearing the voice, a calmness washed through me. Paul knew the guy, right? So, of course other people lived here. Weirdos, probably, out in the woods in the middle of nowhere, surrounded by the USSR. But harmless weirdos, right?

She stepped out of the shadows, just into our circle of light. I thought it was strange I hadn't seen her earlier, because she was dressed all in white. And she was so pale it was hard to tell where her collared dress began against her neck. Her face was serene, with rosepetal lips and black eyes and black hair curled and cut into a loose bob around her face.

"Yeah, it's something," I said. "You live here?"

"I do. You are the film crew?"

"Yes."

A hint of a smile curled her red, red lips. "I am Vreka. Your name...?"

"Maxine Madison." I don't know what possessed me to tell her my full name. "But everyone calls me Maxie."

"Maxine," she repeated, syllable by syllable. Savoring it. "The pleasure is mine."

"Nah, it's, uh, mine," I said, but stumbling over the words a little, just like a schoolgirl. Vreka's smile didn't change. She probably had that effect on everyone. She had the kind of presence that made it seem like every mote of dust caught in the circle of headlights was drawn to her.

"I have heard you are staying with us for a month."

"More or less. Three weeks. Hell of a schedule."

"I see. I look forward to learning more. The business of film, it is fascinating to me." She paused at the edge of the exhale, as if waiting for me, then continued just as I thought of some halfway intelligent reply. "But you must be tired after all that long way here. I must let you go for now, but—Maxine, will you do me one small favor?"

"Sure," I said, still so mesmerized by her voice, her deep and sincere gaze, the way her lips moved as she talked, the way that slight smile crinkled the edges of her eyes, that my brain was just now catching up with her words.

"Do not go into the upper halls of the castle," Vreka said. Her smile didn't change. "It is not safe. It is not part of the agreement."

The night turned cold, breeze slipping a sudden chill down my body. I took a breath to respond, but the boys' argument hit a pitch that drew Vreka's attention away from me. Her expression was so quizzical that it was almost a relief from that subtle smile.

Her gaze flicked back to mine, as if I could explain what Paul was on about at any given moment. I shrugged, apologetically, and followed her gaze back to the crew. It didn't look like anyone was about to come to blows, so I figured I didn't need to get involved.

When I looked back, Vreka was gone.

Fair enough. I'd tried to flee the scene myself, after all, but this was my job. Vreka just lived here. I grimaced and started toward the light, just in time to hear Michael yell "For fuck's sake, Paul! You blew *how much* for us to fucking sleep *outside?*"

Foolish me. I thought we'd packed tents in case it rained during filming. Maybe the upper floors were rotting. I'd heard that was a problem in historic buildings. Adding eight people and a bunch of thirty-pound cameras and lighting rigs on top of that seemed like a recipe for disaster.

Yet, a solitary lamp burned at the top window of the tower.

```
The hero removes his fedora as he steps through
the threshold of the castle, into the foyer. He
glances around the vaulted room, his handsome
face in sharp relief to the dark surroundings.
He looks out of place with his more modern
dress, with his bashful mannerisms. It is the
famous monster who greets him, who fills the
screen, as much a presence as the looming
```

castle itself. She is elegant, much more poised
than the shuffling hero; but the hero's sloped
shoulders betray a readiness, not a defeat.

The monster is gracious, pleasant,
condescending. She bides her time; she plays.
What you are looking for will not be found
here, she laughs; but the hero presses on, his
back now to the screen. He does not seem to
understand that he is in danger. In an awkward,
lingering shot, he is passed off to a robed
figure, masked in featureless white, strands of
blonde hair just visible under the hood. By
this figure he is led to a guest bedroom draped
in moldering tapestries of wolves and deer
locked in mortal combat.

Joelle's first act playing the villain was to get debilitating diarrhea as
soon as we started shooting the introduction scene. I didn't blame
her, what with our whole rotten tarp-tent sleeping and drinking
boiled well-water situation—Paul did, of course, but that bastard
brought his own bourbon to inhale between takes—but I also didn't
care to hear about any of the details except in that I wanted to avoid
whatever she'd been eating. Bad enough that our shit pit was within
smelling distance of the gate, where we were shooting the first scene.
I was standing around in a white negligee and bare feet, arms folded
over my tits, shivering and fantasizing about shooting inside, where I
didn't smell the film crew's shit. I didn't mind nudity—I minded cold
and stench.

Most embarrassingly the man who owned this whole castle, Mr.
Tibor himself, had come down from his high tower to watch. You'd
think they'd never heard of film in Eastern Europe from how he
examined the gear—or maybe the circus had never paid *him* to host
a show before.

All of this scrutiny would have been fine if he hadn't had the same completely stone-cold face as Vreka. He kept a significant distance away, and it was impossible to tell what he thought about the whole thing other than maybe some mild disappointment. Trying to film in a sheer gown under the stern gaze of this European landlord felt like trying to be titillating at church—it just made me nervous. Paul kept trying to be well-behaved in front of him, too—more or less—which was downright unnatural.

Despite Paul's constant wheedling—or maybe because of it—Tibor wouldn't even let us film anywhere above the ground floor of the castle. Ground floor, courtyard, forest. That was it. Couldn't even sleep inside. Couldn't put a camera on the walls. If you wanted privacy, why invite a movie crew?

"We're not behind schedule, Paul, it's the first day," Michael was saying, running his hands through his floppy ginger hair like he could find God's hidden patience in there. "Just give Joelle a few more minutes."

"A few minutes here, a few minutes there, boom, time's up and we'll be skittering back to the US with half a goddamned film! What are you gonna do about it, Michael? We can't shoot the scene without Joelle! There's no damn appeal if it's just Maxie thrashing around on the ground!"

Flattering.

"What about that other woman hanging around?" Enoch said, trepidatiously, from behind Linder and Linder's massive trunk of tape reels. Since the camera and rig was in place, and there was only one line of dialogue for the scene, Linder had chosen to take this minute to smoke. Enoch was practicing being a good boom operator—as invisible as humanly possible.

"What other woman?" Paul snapped. "You got some kinda hot ticket you've been hiding from me?"

"No, I mean—you know, that black-haired lady. I saw her lurking around in the courtyard while we were setting up, I think she lives in the castle? She's got pretty good presence. Creeped me the hell out, anyway."

"You think she speaks English?" Hoyt said, with a derisive sneer. He was being snooty because big shot billing hero Hoyt had been tapped in as an extra for this scene, one of the masked and hooded cultists—never mind that the script had originally specified the cultists were all women. A personal insult, obviously, which somehow only Reid and Linder were able to bear with dignity.

I kept my mouth shut. So did Del, his face carefully wooden behind the camera, but he kept shooting looks over his shoulder toward the latrine every fifteen seconds.

Paul's expression shifted immediately, to a new one—just as intense as every other expression he made, but rather than disgust, righteousness, or whatever sad dominance trip he was on at the moment, it looked like a guarded fear. I'd never seen him make that face before, and certainly not over a woman.

Then Paul glanced back at Tibor, and I got it. Tibor wasn't even looking at us, just staring out into the woods, but I would have bet Vreka was his daughter, and Paul'd run his nasty mouth in front of the guy before. All Mr. Tibor had to do is threaten to kick us all out and Paul would scrape and kowtow.

"Stay the hell away from her if you know what's good for you," Paul said, and that was that. In the end, we decided, since we had a few wigs, we'd do miserable Joelle up as me and me up as Joelle, and since our makeup guy was a wizard with wigs despite—or maybe because of—being bald himself, we did a pretty damn good job. Joelle soldiered through it, too, without a word, though she looked sick and crampy the entire time.

"It's great," Paul said. "Great take. Sells that she's scared."

After that Joelle got to sleep for an hour or two while we set up for the next scene, heroic Hoyt arriving looking for his missing sister—that was me, a relationship upgrade I'd insisted on over being his fiancée *again*—only to be greeted by a highly suspicious Joelle. It went smoothly, considering. Joelle, even on her hour nap, was marvelous, chewing her lines with such aplomb even Paul cheered up a little.

We even snuck in a second scene ahead of schedule, a nice relaxing one where Hoyt, thinking he was hallucinating, saw me flitting through the corridor in my negligee. As the kidnapping victims of vampire cultists are wont to do.

When I'd flitted to the other end of the corridor, I saw the far door was open, and through the sliver of the frame there was a pale face with shadows for eyes—I put my hand to my chest right when my brain caught up with my gasp. A normal face. A pretty one, even—it was Vreka, watching me from one of the rooms, her hand on the doorframe. As soon as she noticed me noticing her, she yanked her hand back like it'd been stung and shut the door, so softly and so quickly I thought I might have been imagining things.

Del, at the threshold between the corridor and the foyer, pulled his head up from behind the camera to stare at me. Not at the door where Vreka had vanished into—at me.

"That's the woman Paul's worried about?" he asked.

"Guess so," I said. I didn't want to tell him I'd talked to her, that she did speak English—any of that. I liked Del and all, but I felt like everything on this set would get back to Paul somehow.

"Seems a bit starstruck," Del said.

I snorted. "By who?"

"You." I didn't like how serious his tone was.

"What are you, a professional apple-polisher? Her father probably just told her to stay the hell away from our national treasure, Paul."

Del chewed his mustache for a moment, then got a decisive set to his mouth.

"Well, fuck Paul. She can hang around and watch the filming if she wants, as long as she stays out of the shots. If her old man does, I don't see why she can't. And if Paul tries anything, I swear to God I'll deck him."

Bless Del's sweet heart—he never assumed Vreka was anything but Tibor's reticent daughter.

I borrowed some of Paul's bourbon after we wrapped for the day, warm in a glass—no ice, and much stronger than I preferred, but I figured it'd help me sleep. I was cold, and tired, and wired in the bad way from our late afternoon shoot, some kind of Satanic garbage with a rooster sacrifice. I just kept telling myself that the whole thing didn't seem to bother Joelle. Not like we'd ever had American Humane on our sets. But didn't people get sued over this kind of shit?

Well, the rooster would be soup stock tomorrow, Michael promised, and I accepted that as moral absolution. Wasn't every meal with meat in it a sacrifice?

What I really wanted wasn't bourbon but a long, hot shower. I wandered across the courtyard with the glass, avoiding conversation until I found Joelle chewing on an unlit cigarette, perched next to Del in the floodlight we'd used for the courtyard shots from the morning.

"Paul's gonna flip his lid when he sees this," Joelle said. "Don't they insure that shit?"

Del shook his head. He was frowning and coiling and uncoiling the same foot of reel over and over again, squinting at it frame by frame. "Film fucks up all the time. I'll just give Paul a different take. He doesn't give a shit anymore, and he'll be too drunk in the morning to notice." Del squinted up at me. "Sorry, Maxine. The best take's fucked up."

I sat down next to him and offered him the glass. He looked like he needed it more than I did. He turned it down. "Fucked up how?"

"It... I dunno. It melted. This better be the only fucking reel with the problem or..."

"Or we'll have to pack up and go home early?"

Joelle chuckled. "Here's hoping. Look, it's fine, Del. I'm not gonna tell anyone, Maxie's not gonna tell anyone, you're not gonna show Paul, and the rest of the film will be fine. Hell, it looks spooky, doesn't it? It's a horror movie. Who cares?"

"Who cares," Del echoed.

I sipped the bourbon. "Lemme see."

Del handed the film over with the disdain of a professor dumping out lecture slides at the end of the day. I had to squint to see, and hold the tiny print up to the light. There I was, all right—I recognized the take, the one Vreka'd been spying on. But where she would have been standing, if she'd stood outside the door, there was a smear.

It didn't look like much to me. Just a smear across the door. But the way it shifted from frame to frame, like oil—like the film refused to take on the image. *It melted,* Del'd said.

The film looked fine. It was the picture that was wrong.

"Hey!" Michael shouted, from across the yard. I closed my mouth. Joelle rolled her eyes.

"What'd you think Paul did now?" she muttered. Del pretended not to hear her, but I smothered my laugh into a cough, and she smiled at me. She had crow's feet around her eyes—one of those strange little details you notice sometimes. They lended a dignity to her, a realness the ethereal characters she played never had.

But Michael wasn't talking to Paul. He ran up to us, face red, puffing. I shoved the dailies into my lap and tried to think of some kind of excuse for him not to look at them, but he looked straight past it, right to us, especially to Del.

"Hey, Del. Ladies. Any of you seen Enoch since wrap?" he asked. We all shook our heads.

"God dammit," Michael muttered. "If that dumb kid went AWOL on the first damn day I'll—"

We never found out what Michael was gonna do, because a scream broke the night, so sudden and shrill I thought for a second it was one of those mountain lions from back home.

It was Hoyt.

The screen fades in to a windowless room hewn
from stone, bathed in lurid red. Four hooded

figures stand, hands clasped, each poised at one of the four base points of a pentagram painted sloppily across the floor. At the fifth point the black-haired woman stands, her hair loose and wild, her breasts and torso bare, arms raised to the sky. In her left hand she holds a rooster; in her right, a knife.

The rooster struggles. If it is a prop, it is a clever one. In the center of the array the woman in white is curled, naked, her hands over her head.

The black-haired woman's mouth moves. She slits the rooster's throat. Blood sprays over the pentagram, over the naked woman's side. It is tarry and dark.

Enoch was alive, but he didn't look it. Hoyt had been the one to find the poor boy, but it took Reid and Linder to drag Enoch out, and Hoyt with him. He was screaming enough for all four of them.

I understood why when I got close. Whatever had happened to Enoch, his whole scalp was hanging off, just peeled right off his head like a grapefruit, hair and all, from forehead to neck. He was covered in blood, shoulders hanging limp. By then Hoyt had stopped screaming and was rambling about armor and the floor and an axe and an accident or something, on and on until I was surprised that he didn't pass out from lack of oxygen.

Reid bundled up his shirt and wrapped it around Enoch's head and neck. "We have to get him to a hospital," he was saying. He was so pale I'd have believed it if someone had told me the blood came from him. Linder seemed to be faring better, but not by much—he just kept nodding.

Paul exploded. "Where the fuck was he? What the fuck did I tell you? I told you one thing, just one goddamn thing, not to go upstairs!"

I didn't really want to get involved. I hovered from several feet away, silently, thinking about how there had to be something I could do, but everyone else seemed to have a handle on Enoch's condition. What could I do? Bring another sheet? Cry? It's not like I knew him well. But hell, I could at least try to handle Paul.

I approached him with my hands out like he was a bear. "Hey, Paul," I started. "This is pretty bad—"

He wheeled on me. "*Pretty bad?* Does the camera look like it's rolling to you, Maxie? This isn't special effects shit! He's dead!"

"I just think we need to stay calm and find out where the nearest hospital is," I said. Paul's eyes were so wide they seemed like they were all whites. Any wider and they might pop out of his head.

"I'm not paying you for your fucking opinions!"

I looked around Paul. The whole crew was gathered around now, between the lights. I remembered I was still holding that bourbon, and I drained the glass. The burn helped a little.

"We passed a town on the way up, right? An hour away?" Linder asked Del. Del was shaking his head. Joelle was crouched next to Enoch.

"We're all shocked, I just don't think right now is the time to play the blame game." I felt like I was talking from a million miles away. "Paul, please, I'm begging you. Can you find Mr. Tibor and see if he knows a doctor?"

Paul ground his teeth. He turned on his heel.

Tibor was already there. I hadn't seen him arrive, heard that ancient door creak open, anything, though I don't think anyone would have in these circumstances. He wore the same all-black outfit from that morning and an expression of mild concern. Vreka trailed behind him, head cast down. Our eyes met, and she quirked an eyebrow in my direction. I shook my head.

"Mr. Pellou? Has there been an accident?" Tibor asked. He overlooked the chaos with a regal air, like a lord disappointed with his peons. Linder was sitting with his arm around Enoch's shoulder, the front of his shirt pink with blood. He was a big man, way bigger than

Enoch, with the emotional display of a boulder. He looked like he was about to cry.

"This dumb sonova—" Paul seemed to realize who he was speaking to, and straightened up. "Guess Hoyt found him over the foyer. Armor fell on him."

Tibor tsked, shallow between his teeth. "Yes, the castle is dangerous in places. A shame."

I shoved in. "Where's the nearest hospital? There a doctor in town? He's lost a lot of blood." I didn't know anything about blood, but it sounded good. People said that a lot on television.

Tibor looked at me for the first time, directly at me. He had the same jet-black eyes as his daughter.

"There's no hospital," he said. "No doctor. The nearest phone is over three hour's drive away, Miss Madison. On Monday the truck comes in with our delivery. Their route is along the city. It is best if you send your man along with them then."

"It's Friday," I said, stupidly. "He's not gonna live three days. Is he?"

"His life is in God's hands," Tibor said. "Perhaps you should pray."

In the ritual room, the black-haired woman
is flanked by two slouching, heavy suits of
knight's armor, each propped on their own
stands, filthy glaives tilted in their lifeless
gauntlets as if to suggest they might cross
behind the woman's back. The hooded cloaks are
black; the woman's sheer skirts and the armors'
tabards may be red or white, but in the harsh
light it is impossible to tell. The armor on
the left bears more stains.

The camera travels. Behind the armor is the
door to the room; through the open crack in
the door is shadow. The hero is crouched there
in the shadow, light only cast on his eyes as

he watches the ritual unfold. The shadows twist sickeningly behind him. They are always being watched.

Del made the drive, and Joelle and I went with him. Enoch stayed at the castle. We didn't want to move him too much, or something, I don't remember. It was a weird, tense drive, and when we got to town it must have been three in the morning. We banged on every door and ended up in the lobby of a little house converted to some kind of cheap motel. Then we couldn't figure out who to call; the proprietor just stood there and smoked. He didn't seem to understand a word we said, just that we were upset and there was blood. Maybe he thought we were American criminals.

Del ended up ringing the emergency line for the embassy from the next country over. I guess he'd written it down, since this country didn't have one—we'd basically snuck in. Supposedly the Soviets were going to annex this place any day now. That hadn't seemed like a real issue until now. Now we were in the middle of nowhere, surrounded by enemies.

As soon as the proprietor saw the number he started shouting at Del. International charges, I guessed—I grabbed some money off Del and shoved bills at the guy until he calmed down and Del hung up the phone. He turned back to us, his face a dark red—anger.

"They want to know how we got our visas," he said.

"Are they sending help?"

"No. Fuck."

We got back at sunrise. I didn't think anyone had slept. Paul was the first one we saw when our van trundled through the gate. He was dragging lights around and swearing.

Del leaned out the driver's side window. "The fuck are you doing?" he shouted.

"Picture's not gonna film itself!" Paul shouted back.

"You're filming the fucking picture while Enoch is dying?"

"You think he'd just be sitting on his ass right now? That kid had a work ethic! Look, all we can do is wait, so may as well get something done!"

Joelle ran her hand over her face. "Christ," she muttered.

No, I got it. I wanted something to keep my mind off the night. Work was what I knew how to do. Horror was supposed to be cathartic, right?

"Why the hell not?" was what I said out loud. "Either of you got anything better to do than film or wait?"

I don't know why they listened to me, sitting there sleepless and agreeing with Paul, but they did. I guess we were all in shock. That's the only way I can explain how we started filming again.

```
The woman in white dances by herself in the
courtyard. She spins in a partnerless waltz,
her head tilted up in bliss. Her gown is
splattered with blood. The hero approaches her,
but she does not acknowledge him. He speaks
first, then shouts, then pleads. He is frantic.
    When he seizes her, crying out at her, she
pushes him away.
```

It was kind of funny; filming all of Saturday went fine, like the set was an old god that just wanted one little blood sacrifice so it'd behave. A couple of people took shifts sitting with Enoch during the day, mostly Michael, Linder, and Joelle.

On Sunday I got up my nerve enough to take one shift. I lasted about fifteen minutes, right up to the time where Enoch shifted and I remembered I was supposed to squeeze water into his mouth with the towel by the mat. When I pressed the towel to his dry mouth, Enoch opened his eyes and looked at me and a long grating noise came out of his throat. The skin up by his forehead flapped. His whole body rolled like he was going to throw up.

I was going to throw up. I jumped back, left the whole towel on his face, folded my hands against my chest, and ducked out the tent. My hands were shaking so badly I couldn't close the flap behind me.

Vreka was standing outside, holding a glass pitcher full of water. She held it out to me. She was even paler in the sun. No wonder she stayed inside.

"I gotta get someone else," I said. "I'm no good at this. Man, I never even broke a bone as a kid."

"It is difficult," she said, kindly. "I'm surprised he has survived so long."

Morbid. Blunt.

"Me too." I cleared my throat. "Can you—can't you come down to town with us? Translate? Call the hospital?"

"No. We have delivery from another village. This one does not deal with us." Her smile was gentle. "Our family ruled here for a long time. Now such roles are abolished and my brother and I, we are tolerated so long as we ask nothing."

"Your brother?" I said, seizing on the part of that which made sense to my American sensibilities. "I, uh, I thought he was your dad."

Vreka blinked, and then laughed. "No, no. We are quite close in age."

"Huh," I said, and then, "Oh, fuck. Enoch. I'm so sorry. Listen, I'm sorry to ask, but can you get Michael? Or stay here? I can get Michael. As long as he's not alone."

"You go," Vreka said, and inclined her head. "I'll wait."

Enoch died a few hours later, with Michael sitting next to him. He didn't tell us until we'd wrapped the scene; then he just kind of announced it, without fanfare, and immediately pulled Paul aside. Joelle started crying.

I walked off set, out to the gate, and stared out at the pines. Another funny thing—out of everyone, the whole crew, it was Vreka who came out and joined me. We just stood there for a bit. I was wishing I had some more of that bourbon, or a smoke, or something to do with my hands. I was picking at my face instead, mascara getting all chunky and itchy around my eyes like I was back in high school.

"What is this film about?" Vreka asked.

"What?"

"The film. Here, come sit. Perhaps it will be a distraction." She swept her skirts out and sat. She was wearing laced-up boots. They looked Victorian. I went ahead and sat next to her, feeling stupid.

"It's just really fucked up," I said. I wiped my face and the side of my hand came off smeared with mascara. They always advertised this shit as waterproof.

"It is an accident. These things happen. Tell me, what is the film about?"

"God, I don't even remember." How long ago had I read the script? Felt like months. "There's this girl who goes missing, this guy goes looking for her, turns out she got abducted by vampires. But then, I don't know, she likes it. She just saw people die. She wants to live forever. And she falls in love with the woman who abducted her. So she tries to kill the guy who came to save her, even though he's her brother, and he has to kill her too."

"You are the girl, or the vampire?" Vreka asked.

"I'm the girl. Joelle's the vampire." I was watching the grass. Ants were crawling in it. Black ants, back and forth. "Well, I'm the vampire at the end, I guess. Nervous about it, honestly. The girl in danger, that's what I'm used to playing. But a change would have been good."

"I would imagine so," Vreka said. She placed her hand over mine. I lifted my head to stare at her, study her face, what she was after, but all I saw was sincerity. Like she just wanted to talk to me. Like she was worried about me. "I know you are upset. Humor me. It is art; isn't it worth finishing?"

"I don't know," I said. "I'm not even sure it's art. Entertainment, sure."

"What is entertaining about vampires?"

"They're sexy, you know. Intimate. Like you want this seductive woman in your bed, even if it kills you. Even if you throw out your whole family for it." That's how I'd felt reading the script, knowing it was Joelle in the scenes with me. "But it's kind of funny, right? Vamps don't have souls, they're invisible in mirrors and pictures, but they're big in film." I think it was so funny at the time because of stress, like I was just seizing on anything absurd. "Imagine if I were a vampire— it'd end my career. Maybe I could do radio."

Something shifted in Vreka's face, something I couldn't place, and I didn't like it. "Then, if you were the girl, what would you do?" she asked.

"What?"

"In the face of death, knowing that cost. If it were offered to you. Would you decide to live forever?"

I thought about Enoch's face. I thought about how his eyes had looked when they tried to fix on mine, desperate, bloodshot. The rattling noise. I squeezed Vreka's hand, just to feel it. Her hand was colder than mine.

Wasn't that why I got into film in the first place? You could be everywhere at once, reflected in every window, remembered for your beautiful face and your beautiful voice and everything else was just gravy.

I lied.

I said no.

The man who arrived at the castle intending
to be a hero sits in the foyer, framed by the
rotting banisters of the stairs. He is slumped,
his head in his hands, his hat fallen unnoticed
to the floor. Perhaps in his imagination, the
woman in white and the blackhaired woman dance
beside him as though he is not there. Her steps
mirror that of her dance alone.

The black-haired woman leans in, limbs entwined, her face close to the other woman's, their eyes meeting, their lips close. She dips her head as if to kiss her dancing partner, and sinks pointed teeth into the neck of the woman in white. When she steps out of the next turn of the waltz, the front of her white gown is soaked in garish blood. She smiles.

The man breaks wood from the banister and takes a pocketknife to the shorn edges.

Joelle, Linder, and Tibor bundled Enoch up in garbage bags and buried him in a box outside the castle wall. For preservation, Tibor said, since it wasn't like we were just going to leave him here. Kept the body colder. Slowed decay.

Decay made me think of the shape in the film, contorted, distorted, destroyed.

I didn't ask how he knew.

Then we filmed Joelle and I flirting and waltzing in the foyer. I also didn't ask her what handling a dead body felt like, and she didn't volunteer the information, just put the finishing touches on her lipstick after Reid moved on to doing my makeup, examined herself in the mirror like she hadn't just buried a coworker. She seemed so at ease with the whole thing, slipping right back into her femme fatale persona, shrugging it over herself like a second skin. I got caught up in the scene, her hands on mine. When she leaned in to nip me, her breath was hot—eager—dizzying.

I almost fainted. Joelle helped me down.

"You all right?" she asked, and just like that the act was gone.

"Keep thinking about Enoch," I muttered.

"Yeah, me too," Joelle said. "Try to stay distracted. We're stuck here. Let's just do the fucking job."

After the foyer dance, since we had to ruin the main nightgown,

Reid said we should go ahead and shoot the climax, where Hoyt killed me. I wasn't sure I was up for it, but Paul seized on that idea like he was drowning and Reid had just handed him a can of air.

Paul was such a shithead.

We mixed a ton of blood for the climax scene—not a literal ton, maybe twenty gallons in all, but it felt like it. It was surreal. I'd never really thought about it before, but the stuff didn't look like real blood at all. Corn syrup, starch, fungicide, film wetter, food dye. It smelled like taffy from hell.

Looking down at my chest, doused in poison-apple candy, I honestly didn't think of Enoch at all. It was too lurid. That whole shoot was a blur. It was in the foyer, lots of tarps, black drapes, big lumps on the floor I assumed were starch bags dressed up in the cultist cloaks. Linder ran back and forth between lights and sound like he was possessed, and never saying a word.

"It's fine," Del kept saying. "We can just dub over. It doesn't matter, man. Just get the shots."

I remember at some point Tibor came in, saw the tarps and the lumps and the liberal spatters of syrup blood. He exchanged words with Paul, and stalked off—I don't think Paul'd let him know what we were going to do to his foyer.

"It's detergent!" Paul shouted after him. "Don't be such a tight-ass!" Hoyt laughed. He and Paul were hitting the bourbon between every take, and Hoyt was getting sloppy. He'd never been an angel to work with. Now he was a devil.

Hoyt shouted a lot, too, in character and out, a little at Paul but mostly at me. I was in his way, I was hogging the light, I was botching my lines, I was talking over him. Paul threw out the script and made us shoot improvisations. Joelle died at my feet; then she died across the room from me, then Paul decided she shouldn't be onscreen at all and should have her own death scene, so she sat on the side and ate a bowl of soup with her hair plastered to her scalp, only her hands and face washed of crimson goop.

Then it was my turn. I started crouched, my front drenched in blood. I stood, I rolled my head back, boneless, I bared my fangs, I spread my hands, languid. While the camera was rolling the scene was mine. Was this how Joelle felt?

Hoyt retreated as his character realized his sister had given in to the embrace of the vampire. Perhaps she had been in on the workings of the cult the entire time, her abduction a ploy. She was a Satan-worshipper. A lesbian, even! His rescue became a trap, and now—his grave—!

That was my line. It was heady. I stepped toward Hoyt, toward the black eye of the camera, toward the light to catch the line of my cheekbone, my gown, my claws. If there was an opposite of radiance, a seeping darkness, it was what I felt there.

Hoyt staggered backwards, grasping for something to keep me away—a cross, a stake—but he was helpless as I approached. His lips lifted into a sneer.

"Didn't expect you to get off on being a man-hating bitch like Joelle does," Hoyt mouthed. Del couldn't see his face through his back, and Paul didn't give a shit. He knew it.

Normally there's a space between a thought and an action, the space where the thought becomes a commitment. At Hoyt's sneer that space shriveled right up, and something in me snapped. *I'm going to kill him,* I thought, crystal-clear, and realized I was already lunging.

I was *supposed* to bite him. Yeah, I was going to bite him—not the gentle nip Joelle had given me, no. I was going to maul him. I'd chew through his windpipe, split his jugular between my sharpened teeth. I'd claw and strangle him. I'd bury him next to our best boy. I didn't give a shit.

It wasn't even about me. He knew what Joelle had just been through and he still said that. My expression must have scared him—more than the lunge, maybe—because his face went white and he stumbled back. His heel caught on the hem of the cloaked bag behind him and he tripped backwards, right on his ass. In his flailing the cloak flipped up over Hoyt's legs. While trying to fight this big black flappy cloth off, he rolled right into the legs of the camera.

I would have laughed. I would have, but I screamed.

It was Michael. The cloak had been wrapped around Michael's corpse, limp, eyes open. His head lolled like his neck had been broken—his face was all one pallid clay color. There was an open gash on his neck, but there wasn't any blood.

I staggered back. "There's no blood," I said, stupidly. "Not on his skin, not on his clothes." Hoyt was screaming, tangled in the cloth. Every flailing move he made caught him up in it worse.

I don't remember much of what happened next. I got lightheaded. Reid caught me, Linder caught Hoyt, and Joelle checked Michael's pulse. I told her that was stupid because he was obviously fucking dead. She ignored me. She ignored Paul and Del too, and Hoyt screaming about how there was a neck wound and no blood and that meant there was a vampire.

"That's a postmortem injury," Joelle said. I remember that because she was so calm. "It's normal. When someone's been dead for a while, blood congeals. Wounds don't bleed."

"How the fuck do you know that?"

I wish Hoyt'd been the one to say that, but no. It was me.

"You've done enough horror movie shit; you should know blood. I used to be an emergency dispatcher," Joelle said, gently. Much more gently than I deserved. "You know, 9-1-1."

"How long has he been dead?" That was Paul. He lit a cigarette with shaking hands. "What of?"

"Do you think I'm a coroner, Paul? How am I supposed to know?"

"Well, I'm a fucking film director!"

They decided he'd probably climbed into one of the hoods, gotten wrapped in it or something, suffocated, and then the camera rolled on him and broke his neck—that was the gash—and I guess none of us noticed.

They—I mean Paul, Joelle, and Tibor—buried Michael outside,

next to Enoch, while Del and I went through the dailies and Linder threw together some kind of dinner. It wasn't even dark yet.

In the dailies, I looked fantastic. I looked terrifying, fearless, unhinged, murderous, blood on my mouth and my hands. Beautiful, wild-haired, deep lined eyes. I kept wondering which frame Michael croaked in. Del kept muttering about a curse while the projector sputtered. I didn't feel like I was sitting there with him at all. I was someone else, somewhere else, watching me go through the scenes from a distance. I really did look great. Did it matter?

"Can I show Vreka?" I asked Del.

"What? Why?"

"She was asking me about film the other day. How the sausage gets made. You know."

"Sure. I guess. Just let her know this isn't the final. Some of that weird shit's on the end of a couple takes. I'm thinking the developer's bad. Man, I don't even care anymore. I just wanna get out of here."

I stood—more or less, though I had to stoop in this stupid tent so that my hair wouldn't get caught in the fraying tarp. "Thanks, Del."

Del paused. "Hey, if you see that handheld while you're looking for Vreka, let me know."

"Handheld?"

"Camera."

"We have one?"

"Yeah. Well, no, I brought my own. Shoulda written my name on it so they didn't think it was studio... or I'll ask Michael for reimburse..."

I didn't have anything left to add. I nodded and left him there, sitting in the tent with his hand on his face, staring out past my washed out, hissing face being played back at 1.5x speed.

I hadn't been in the castle by myself before—none of us had, except maybe Enoch, and someone, probably Tibor, had carefully delineated which areas we were and weren't allowed into—occasionally with padlocks. I had that in mind when I tried the door.

It wasn't locked, but it didn't open easily. I shoved it with a protesting groan—mine, or the door's, I wasn't entirely sure.

I stepped into the dark and silent foyer. May as well have been a cave. I thought I saw movement as my eyes struggled to adjust.

"Vreka?" I called. No answer. Gooseflesh crawled up my arms. It was cold, like an icebox. Colder than the breezy courtyard.

I shouldn't have come in here. I called her name again, my hand still on the door.

On the stairs, something rustled.

"Maxine?" Vreka said, curious, soft. Behind me. I whipped around. She was standing in the courtyard, in the dimming late afternoon sunlight, dressed in black with her eyes crinkled into an easy smile.

"Do you need something?"

"Oh, I uh…" God, I felt stupid. "Did you hear about Michael?"

"Yes. I am sorry to hear it. A terrible accident, and so soon after the first."

"Yeah. Accident." Everyone but Hoyt agreed, and Hoyt was drunk. "You met him, right? Or…" Who had I seen her talking to? Was it just me? Her brother, and me?

Maybe Del was right about that crush.

"You introduced us when you brought him to watch the boy who died. Enoch?"

"Oh. Yeah." I sure had. Way to go, Maxie. "Uh. Do you want to see what we shot today?" I stepped back outside. Vreka ducked around me, to close the door, and my face flushed. I'd barely slept. My mind felt like it was swaddled in cloth. Like it was drowning.

"More than anything," Vreka said. She smiled again, the sun darkening her lips with shadow. I studied her teeth—normal. A little crooked, even, two teeth on the top overlapping. Guess she'd never had braces. "I would love to."

There is a room of masks. The woman in white
lounges back on a loveseat covered in a white

sheet. The black-haired woman straddles her, touching her face, her neck. The wound is clear. They are speaking, but too distantly for words to be distinguished.

Beside them, the door shudders.

Del had a keener sense for interpersonal relations than I did, and vacated the tent when Vreka and I arrived. He'd wound the reel back for us and everything, not that it was very long. She was fascinated. Entranced. I was flattered, honestly. It was just work to me, and this had all the flubs, the many cuts, Hoyt flubbing his line and rolling his eyes because he was drunk, but she wanted to see it all, even the mistakes.

I asked if she'd seen movies before and Vreka laughed.

"Of course. But it looks so perfect on the screen, all together. As though it happened all at once, without rehearsal, without tricks. As though it is the truth. Here it seems… so human, I think. Before the mistakes are removed. You see the play as it is, the way the false-hood is constructed. It is charming."

"Charming, huh?" I said. I was tired of seeing my face shrieking. I wanted to look at Vreka instead, so I did. The flickering light sharp-ened her features, made her face impish, her curls dance when she moved her head. And she did move her head; to look at me.

"You look beautiful on the screen, but moreso next to me," Vreka said. I felt that flush creep up my neck again, the same way it did when Joelle said that kind of thing. At least with Joelle it just seemed like professional flirting, so I could shrug it off. Everyone did that in film. And anyway, I was pretty sure she was with Del.

The way Vreka leaned forward made it very clear that she was here for me. I felt like I was going to catch on fire. Well, fuck it. Why not? Every relationship I'd ever had was shitty, destructive, secret, and here was Vreka bravely coming on to me in a country I vaguely remembered as having a reputation for executing accused lesbians. I don't remember what I said out loud—I hope to hell it wasn't that—but it made Vreka laugh, and that was good enough for me. As for who started—maybe I did. I twined her curls around my fingers. Her lips were cool, her breath hot. She pulled me against her like she was starving, started to pull down my collar.

I was barely aware of the reel emptying and sputtering, blank, beside us, until Paul started screaming. I yanked my jacket back on and stumbled out of the tent. Vreka trailed behind me, hand lightly over her mouth.

Paul wasn't dead. There wasn't any blood. He was holding a bottle of bourbon and his megaphone and shrieking. Del, Joelle, Linder, and Reid were already outside, Reid shoveling a bowl of soup into his face like it was going to be his last meal.

"What the fuck?" I wiped my face, limp with equal parts relief and exhaustion. "I thought someone died."

Paul swiveled to point the butt of the bourbon at me. "We're shooting!" he boomed.

"What?" I said.

"You fucking heard me! Don't try to weasel out of your fucking contract!"

Del cupped his hands over his mouth. "We're leaving tomorrow," he shouted. "We're doing the scene and then we're packing up and leaving with that truck tomorrow."

I looked back for Vreka, but she'd slipped away—back into the tent, I thought. I saw an odd shadow in there, flickering with the reel. Fine—not like we were dating. Paul boomed again. "Move your ass! We're shooting!"

I winced and covered my ears and inched toward Paul, who lowered the megaphone. "Why aren't we just leaving now?"

"The vans are dead!"

"Michael just died. You're a lunatic!" I don't know if I was talking to Del or Paul. Joelle shook her head. She was smoking, too. She looked like she hadn't slept in a week. All of us did. Some fucking movie.

"Yeah? You want all this to go to fucking waste? What d'ya think the investors are gonna say? Well, that fuckin' sucks but where's the goddamn film? You got morals starring in a titty horror flick suddenly? Not filming going to rightously resurrect Michael and Enoch from their graves like Jesus fucking Christ? You wanna be able to afford airmailing their fucking bodies back to their families? Huh, Maxie?"

I think I went white. I stepped back. Paul was only as loud as the pounding in my head. I couldn't tell if I was about to hit him or pass out. Linder reached out and steadied me.

"Just—" Del gestured at Paul. He looked like he was about to have a stroke. I could see the veins on his scalp, the corners of his mouth flecked with spittle. "We can figure out what to do about the studio after we're back in the states and everyone calms down."

Linder nodded along. Reid didn't say shit; his mouth was full of his soup and his expression indicated that he'd said everything he cared to say while I'd been messing around with Vreka in the tent.

"As if there's a studio without Michael," Joelle muttered. Her breath was a cloud of smoke.

"Just give up, Joelle. Whatever Paul wants, he gets," Linder said.

The man who would be a hero takes a hammer to
the door until it splinters. He steps through
the dust. In his hands he holds the hammer; his
arms strain from the weight of it. At his belt
hangs a roughly hewn stake. His hair is wild.
Both women roll from the lounge. Both hiss,
bearing their fangs. The black-haired woman is
catlike in how her back arches, how she prowls.
She holds her hand out to gesture the other
woman back, behind her. Back, where she may
be safe.

The hero lunges. They wrestle with the stake
and hammer; there is blood, the set crumbling

in on itself unnoticed behind them. The film
stutters as it snaps from cut to cut.

The scene was still pretty much set up as we'd left it when we discovered Michael's body. We just moved the lights a bit and hung a sheet for a false wall. Reid set out the rest of the fake blood and filled a more or less flesh-colored bag with it. He kept asking Joelle if she was all right with this, since everyone was tired, and she kept saying it wasn't dangerous, the stake wasn't anywhere near her, and she just wanted the whole thing over with.

My role was to cower behind the furniture and hiss. That was about as much as I felt up to doing. The lights and the sounds and everything made my head throb. I wanted to sit in the dark. If I were going to get specific, I wanted to sit in the dark, quietly, with Vreka's hands in my hair, and also never have to hear Paul's sputtering voice ever again.

It was a pretty simple scene, and pivotal, so I understood why Paul wanted it. Hoyt lifted the hammer—stone mallet, actually—they'd cut to his raised hand, and then they'd cut to the blood gushing up through the punctured bag. Getting the bag shot was easy, but Hoyt kept fucking up the wrestling Joelle to the ground. He was shaking so badly I thought he was going to break his foot dropping the mallet on it. Linder gave up maybe forty-five minutes in and went to start packing up. We kept shooting without him.

Paul had smoked through a carton of cigarettes by the time we got a take of Hoyt knocking her down that he deemed acceptable.

Joelle started to get up, and Paul shooed her down. She rolled her eyes.

"Just stay down!" Paul flung his hand out at Hoyt like a curse. "Hoyt, what—just fucking—lift the goddamn hammer!"

Hoyt stared at Paul, his hair stringy, eyes as wide as Paul's, and yanked the hammer up. It slipped out of his trembling grip.

I didn't see it from behind the couch, but I heard the noise when it hit Joelle's skull. She didn't make a sound. Hoyt did. He flung himself backwards with a wail.

The set was dead silent. Not a breath, not a step. Not even Del made a noise from behind the camera. I could hear it running.

I leaned over the couch and looked at Joelle's head. She didn't look as bad as Enoch. There was blood all over her face and under her head—no idea how much of it was fake or real. It was all bright red. Part of her skull was knocked in. I thought I saw bone, maybe some grey. I'd like to say I did something heroic, leapt into action, checked her pulse, but I just... felt dizzy, and sat down.

I didn't even know if she was dead or not. I didn't know how to tell. I remembered how long it had taken Enoch to die, and that you weren't supposed to move someone with a head wound. I wondered if we were going to use this in the final cut of the film.

That was it: the beat of silence before everyone sprung to life, so to speak. Del made the worst cry I'd ever heard a human make, like a shot rabbit. Hoyt was dragging himself away from the scene like if he got far enough away he was free from what he'd done. Reid was the one who actually went to Joelle's side. Del went for Paul's throat. I'd seen a few fistfights before. This was probably the saddest.

"It's my fault," Hoyt was yelling.

"Turn off the camera," Reid told me. Yeah, that made sense. I shoved my numb body to its feet and stumbled over and hit the switch. Del and Paul were still fighting, Del clawing at Paul's face. "It was an accident," Paul was yelling.

I wish I'd passed out. Instead I just sunk down again and sat there like an idiot while Reid pulled Del off Paul and steered him outside.

Hoyt was in the same state of shell shock as I was, his head in his hands, mumbling "I can't believe it" in this cartoon high-pitched voice, over and over.

Paul pulled a cigarette out of his pocket and lit it with a click of his lighter. He puffed a few times. Del had got him good in the side of his head a few times; his lip was puffing up, and his forehead was bloody.

"It was an accident, Hoyt," Paul said. "Forget about it. We'll burn the footage. No one will know. Help me get her outside."

Neither of them knew how to carry a body. It was almost comedic.

I just sat there, willing myself to have the strength to move, willing Joelle to get up and come check on me, or Del, or whoever, trying to figure out if I was just in shock or maybe it was because I hadn't eaten in who knew how long and now the one woman I'd ever looked up to had died in front of me. Died? Been killed?

Vreka sat next to me. She arched an eyebrow, and touched my shoulder. "Are you all right?" she asked.

"No," I said. "I think Joelle's dead."

"Ah, well. A dangerous industry, isn't it, this horror film business?" I looked over at her. She was still smiling, just like when I'd last seen her; looking at me with the same amused flirtatiousness. There was even a bit of a pink flush to her cheeks. She was holding the camcorder in her lap, easily, casually, like it wasn't a fifteen-pound shoulder-mounted chrome monstrosity.

When she moved, she was reflected in the case—or something was. My own face was warped in the familiar funhouse ways, but Vreka was featureless. Her reflection crawled, pulled in upon itself, eyeless, mouthless, curling like smoke.

I recognized it.

"Here," Vreka said. "I do like you, you know. And I believe you were looking for this?"

Del and Reid both came running when they heard me screaming, but Vreka was long gone by then. They looked about as good as I felt.

"Oh thank fuck, you're alive," Reid said. He leaned against the legs of the camera, ashen.

"Where's Joelle?" Del asked.

"Paul and Hoyt took her."

"Fuck them!" He kicked the base of the camera. Then he seemed to finally see the camera in my lap. Reid patrolled the foyer. "Where the hell did you find that?"

I almost lied, like I could protect her if I claimed I'd tripped on it in the cloaks. "Vreka. Vreka gave it to me. No idea where she found it. Where's Linder?"

"He's dead."

"What? He was just here." Wasn't he? Had I been sitting here for... how long? I stuck my hand out and grabbed Del's sleeve. He felt real. Kind of grimy. Smelled kind of grimy too. I felt like I was going crazy, that Del's B.O. was the most grounding thing I'd noticed in days. "How do you know?"

Del shook his head.

"C'mon, stand up, Maxie." Reid slipped his arm behind me and helped me up. "We're sticking together from now on."

"What happened to Linder?" I asked again.

Neither of them answered me.

A man with red hair stands in front of a tent in the middle of the afternoon, his hand on his forehead. He's staring away from the screen, at the wall of the castle. The edges of the screen warp, liquify; something slips behind him, up to him, roiling, pulling the earth and the sky and the stone along with it. It embraces the man, pushes his head aside, pulls him down. He grasps at his neck, opens his mouth, then goes limp.

The blur smears across the screen, to another man, another time of day. It is night. He leans against a wall, next to a small hole designed for scaffolding. The camera wobbles, unsteady, amateur. The man lifts his head, speaks, rubbing the butt of his cigarette out on the stones he leans against. The camera is set down. The man says something, his eyebrows furrowing into puzzlement before they blossom into fear. He is smashed against the wall, forced into the hole, cracking and compressing until there is no difference between man and meat.

We ended up huddling in one of the rotting stable stalls all night instead of going back to the tents. More walls between us and everything else was my logic. Our light was a little penlight Del had; with it he determined the camera had been used since he'd last seen it. I thought he was just examining the thing because we didn't have anything better to do, but then he started to talk about going to his portable darkroom and developing the footage right now. Reid and I convinced him that was delirium talking. The truck was coming in the morning, we could get out, he could develop the film later. Or hand it over to the police, or whatever. Sure, it was important. It was evidence from a crime scene now.

At one point he really did duck out, and I got up to follow him, but Reid stopped me with a hand on my leg.

"Just because Del's a dumbass doesn't mean you have to be," he said. Fair point.

Del got back all right, a duffel bulging with reel cans. He emptied out the camera and shoved those reels in too.

"Did you see Hoyt or Paul?"

"No. Do you think it was a setup?"

"I think Enoch was an accident, then everyone's gone crazy. You too. Is that the whole damn movie?" Reid asked him.

"No," Del said. I only had a second to see before he zipped the duffel back up, but it looked like the date and scene scrawled on one can indicated one of the shots Joelle had been in.

"What are you going to do with that? There's not a fucking movie anymore, Del."

"It's my job," Del said.

"It's not Joelle," I said. Reid rubbed his face and stared out across the courtyard.

"I know," Del said. Then he asked me where Hoyt and Paul had taken Joelle's body for the umpeenth time. I said they'd taken her to bury her, but I had no idea. I hoped that was true. What the hell else would they do with it? Anyway, I didn't care. Joelle was dead. The body wasn't her. The film cans weren't her. Even if you assembled them, they were barely her shadow. Her reflection. Looking at Del's lumpy olive duffel all I could think of was the three dozen times either of us had posed ourselves thrown back along the ground, in a coffin, in repose on a bed, willing our eyes to stay shut, our faces smooth, fake blood sticky on our exposed skin, willing ourselves to be the most beautiful corpse.

I dozed off a few times, trying to listen for Vreka or Tibor or, more likely, Paul and Hoyt. Whatever Vreka and Tibor wanted, I didn't think we could stop them.

At some point I heard one of them going through the tents. Don't know what they were looking for or if they found it. The whole night went like that while we pretended we weren't cowering in century-old horse shit. Morning crept in, sickly, with the crackling calls of birds, with that suffusion of twilight so slow it doesn't seem to happen at all.

We heard the rumble of a truck over the wall, a slam, footsteps. A voice barking in an unfamiliar language. Reid and I exchanged looks, and we both got up.

Del stayed put, arms around the duffel. In the grey light, staring at the wall, he looked as much like a dead man as Michael's body had.

"I'll be right after you," Del said.

"Sure," I muttered. I didn't believe him.

Reid and I crept out into the courtyard.

The gate was barred shut from the inside. The bar was padlocked. I don't know why we assumed no one else had figured out where we were, or that we were so smart for hiding all night. Of course they could just lock us in. They knew we didn't know any other way in or out.

Tibor was standing in front of the gate, looking at his wrist. A wristwatch. How mundane. He'd ostentatiously hung a key from his coat, just in case we didn't get the hint.

He looked up from his watch, directly at us, smoothed down his cuff. I couldn't read his expression from where I was standing, but I thought it was a dour Eastern European attempt at a hospitable smile. I stumbled and grabbed Reid's arm.

"I expect you would like to leave," Tibor said. He did not seem to cast a shadow against the gate.

"We are leaving," Reid said, in a brooks-no-argument tone that I'd heard even make Paul back down. Tibor was unmoved.

"Are you?" Tibor nodded at something behind us. I glanced back. The tents had been thrown together, the vans emptied and gutted. Behind the gate, sounds of packages being unloaded. The scrape of metal on dirt. The thrum of a diesel engine, idling. "What you Yankees do with yourself isn't my concern, but it seems there is quite a bit of the film missing. Give it to me, and I will open the gate."

"What do you mean, missing?" I said.

"That's all of it. Why the hell would we want it?"

Tibor frowned. His eyes narrowed, flicked from me to the tent. I could tell he didn't know how much film there was, or even how to be sure a reel was used or not. And for some reason, he needed to be sure. "I understand there is a missing camera," he said.

"I think he's fighting with his sister," I muttered to Reid.

"What?"

"Vreka's his sister. She gave me the camera. That's what he wants. Evidence on it, I guess."

"Sure. Fuck. Paul hired a fucking castle from the mafia." Reid swallowed and raised his voice. "I'm not bargaining with a murderer."

Tibor sighed. "I should think the gesture that I am willing to let you go is enough to show I am not a murderer. The truck is leaving in fifteen minutes. You may turn over the film to me and go with it, or you may keep your film and remain here. I don't care which."

"Paul has it," I said, grasping at straws.

"Good day, Maxine. If you make up your mind, call for me. I have a shipment to oversee."

Just like that, he walked away. Reid and I ran up to the gate; Reid pulled his penknife and started jimmying at the keyhole. Hope swelled in my chest, so full and desperate a feeling that it hurt.

"Do you know how to pick a lock?" I asked him.

"No, but we've got ten fucking minutes to figure out how."

I glanced around, looking for a bar or something to help with. I was pretty sure you needed two tools for a lockpick, not just one knife. I didn't see anything, but I did see Vreka, standing in the shadow of the tower, watching us. Silent. The blade snapped in the lock and Reid swore and threw the penknife down.

Reid slammed his hand against the wood, shook the padlock, screamed. "Del! You motherfucker, just give him the fucking film! Hell, I'm just going to tell him—"

"Shut up!" I kicked Reid, grabbed his jacket. "Shut up, he'll kill Del. Vreka!" I let go of Reid and stumbled a step or two toward her. "Vreka, help. Please."

She put a finger to her mouth, glanced behind her—checking for her brother, I thought—and then was beside me, though I could have sworn I only saw her take a single step. She drew a keyring from her dress and jangled it playfully. "Do you have the camera?" she asked.

All that painful hope in me evaporated.

"No," I said, stupidly.

Vreka tsked. Reid stepped forward; I could tell he was about to assault her. I didn't think that would end well for him, so I held his arm again. The rough denim was comforting, too. Anything with texture helped anchor my lightheadedness. When was the last time I'd eaten or drank anything? Twelve hours? Sixteen?

"Tibor's going to burn the whole thing, which would be a shame," Vreka said, as though this were a reasonable concern at this hour. "I would like you to leave with some, but also, I would like to keep some.

As a memento. Do you know where the segment is you showed me?"

"I think Paul has it," I said, lamely. Reid rested his head against the iron bar. His chest was shaking.

"Del has it," Reid said.

"And he is in the stables?"

"I'm here," Del said. He sounded exhausted, raspy. He limped out from behind one of the vans. I guess he'd been trying to spy-flick his way from cover to cover. Vreka brightened; that lovely smile touched her lips again. Reid and I did an awkward shuffle where we both tried to shove each other out of the way to grab at Del and his bag at the same time, ending in a lot of dust and nothing. Del unzipped the duffel and threw one of the cans at Vreka. I honestly wasn't sure he even checked which one, or if he'd just been sitting in the stables counting them and listening to us argue with Tibor over his bullshit or what.

"Thank you." Vreka picked up the can with a little curtsy, testing its weight. Satisfied, she jangled the keys again and shooed us a step back. I leaned harder on Reid while she unlocked the gate; I felt Del's hand on my back, and I tensed up. I wanted to trust him, but I expected a knife between my ribs more than any comfort.

Vreka tossed the padlock aside and shoved the bar over until it covered only one door. I stepped back again, into Del, pretty sure the gate opened inward and we'd need to be out of its way. She hooked her hand around the ring of the gate, and then her head snapped up, focused on something behind us. She shouted something in that harsh language. I couldn't make out a word of it, or a name, but I didn't need to. Tibor was here. Del shoved me forward.

The hinges shrieked as Vreka yanked the gate open. There was just enough space for a person to squeeze through. Reid pushed past me and Del to run for it. In the span of one shocked blink Tibor had appeared beside us, ripped him from the gap, and slammed him back against the gate hard enough for the wood to splinter between the iron bars; Reid crumpled to the ground with his limbs at all the wrong angles.

My mind went blank. I'm not sure what I intended to accomplish—maybe nothing. Maybe it was just the same animal instinct that had seized me when Hoyt called Joelle a bitch, all anger, no thoughts, no care for survival. I threw myself at Tibor, got a fistful of his jacket and his hair. It wasn't much; he shook me off, snarling, kicked me to the ground. It didn't need to be, though—it was enough. Enough for Del to throw the duffel through and squeeze past after. And Vreka threw herself between me and snarling Tibor. The way his face twisted, he looked like an animal, pupils slits and fangs extended out behind his teeth like a viper.

For Vreka and not for me he straightened up, closing his mouth, smoothing his face and his black coat back down to stony blandness at the same time. They exchanged words while I struggled back up to sitting, hand pressed to my side, trying to figure out if I'd heard my own ribcage break or some other kind of crunch when I'd landed.

Vreka closed the gate. There were voices; broken English, and Del, and then the truck's idle thrum kicked up into a roar and pulled away, down the road.

It was over. Reid lay unmoving. Tibor and Vreka kept talking, in lowered voices this time, Tibor snappish, punctuating his words with sharp gestures and Vreka unhurried, shrugging. Arguing over me, I thought, or maybe over the film, or why not both?

I looked up at the tower, at the window where I remembered seeing the solitary light when we'd pulled our sad little caravan in. I thought I saw a camera lens pushed to the glass, and Paul, leering. I looked away.

```
In the room where masks line the walls, the
hero stands, panting, over the corpse of
the black-haired woman, the hammer a crooked
counterweight in his hands. The woman in white
hisses at him. She lunges.
    It is too late. He is ready.
```

Tibor replaced the padlock and Vreka helped me up, my arm over her shoulder, and walked me inside, past the mess we'd made of their old foyer, up the stairs, into one of the doors Tibor had so carefully labeled NO TRESPASSING.

They were really normal rooms, if a bit old-fashioned, everything hand-carved and lacquered and upholstered sometime in the 1800s. Lots of red and gold and snarling lion faces. I don't know why it was such a big deal. I guess they kept the coffins they slept in up here, although I'd always assumed vampires slept in tombs and basements, right? Closer to the grave.

Vreka sat me down on one of the chairs. "Wait here," she said, and patted me on the shoulder and smiled. I thought that was an odd way to treat a sandwich. She came back with a glass of water.

"Will he finish the movie?" Vreka asked me.

It took me a second for my mind to catch up with her words. Del, right, with the film. "I don't know. If he gets back to the States, maybe. I don't think he'll be able to get distribution for it, though."

"Ah, good. That is what I told Tibor. There is no danger, because it will not be in the cinema. But it's enough that the mystery exists, don't you think? Of course, we will have to move for a while. Don't you have such a saying? Curiosity killed the cat?"

"Sure," I said, around the lip of the glass of water. "So, you just wanted to see what you looked like in a movie?"

"The satisfaction brought them back." Vreka leaned forward, her chin resting on her hand, that same charming smile on her face. Mischievous. As if people hadn't died on her whim. "The cat, of course. Not many others are so lucky. Have you thought again about what you would do if you were the girl in the film? If someone came to you, and asked if you would live forever?"

"You knew who I was when we arrived."

Vreka shrugged. "No more than one knows a picture. But you may like a picture without knowing it."

Here I was, sitting and conversing with the viper. I thought about

Enoch, Michael. Joelle. Linder, wherever he'd gone. Reid, if he was still laying down in the dirt in the courtyard. Maybe Tibor had moved him by now. Del, with his duffel full of everything he could save of Joelle.

My whole body ached, everything except my throat, now wetted with gratitude at that little glass of water. That kept my voice from breaking. "No, Vreka. I don't want to live forever." Wasn't it enough to live in film? A hundred reflections, imperfect, but preserved.

"Ah, well. That means you are going to die, you know."

I looked in the depth of the glass. My face looked back, rippling, distorted. What did Vreka see when she looked in a mirror? In a glass? "Yeah. I know. Hey, uh… Paul. What are you doing with him and Hoyt? Are they still alive?"

Vreka looked thoughtful. "The deal was Paul would have the movie. Now that it's out, I'll have to ask Tibor." Without so much as a good-bye, she got up and left. As soon as she was gone, I thought of a bunch of questions I could have asked her, about sunlight, crosses, garlic, and silver. The clichés. Was that why they bent and twisted light around them on film? The silver?

I stood up, slowly, and hobbled to the window. The view was pretty good—the entire courtyard was visible, stable and all, and the walls and their parapets and out into the pine forest. Dawn crept over the courtyard, the upended tents, the rusty white vans, their contents spilled over the ground like entrails. Reid's body was gone. The truck was gone, too, and the graves seemed to have been freshly turned.

The door creaked heavily behind me. I turned around, expecting Vreka. What greeted me was Hoyt, with one of the utility knives we used to cut gaffer tape clutched white-knuckled in his dominant hand, blade fully extended. Paul stood behind him with Del's camera on his shoulder, leaning against the door. He was already filming.

"The thing is," Paul was saying, "if it's lurid enough, no one can tell if it's real or not. That's art. We all know blood is red, right? But what color red?"

"Shut the fuck up, Paul," Hoyt hissed. "I'm just doing this so we can leave. Then I fucking quit." His eyes fixed on mine. I didn't see Hoyt in there. Well, that wasn't entirely true—I'd seen him high on coke a few times, eyes so dilated they were a different color from his natural watery blue. Now it was desperation that flushed his features.

I wondered what I looked like. If it was similar. I wasn't scared, though; I guess I'd moved beyond that. I braced myself against the windowsill, waiting for Hoyt to charge me. He was hanging back, though, hesitating.

"Sorry, Maxie," Hoyt said, approaching me with one hand up, palm open, the tip of the knife pointed at my neck. "Gotta finish shooting. Film needs a climax."

Calm. That was the emotion I felt, so calm that it muted the ache and the pounding in my chest. This must have been how Joelle felt, I thought. I understood now. There was a threshold of crisis that your body just had to get used to, and then this calm kicked in. I stepped to the side while Hoyt sidled at me, clearly pulling on every last little detail his body could remember from fight choreography. I just wanted to get the chair between him and me.

Maybe I didn't want to live forever, but I sure as hell didn't want to die for Paul.

"C'mon, Hoyt," I said. "You don't have to do what Paul says."

"It's not Paul. It's the fucking monsters he made a bargain with. You didn't see what they did to Enoch and Linder. But they want a film, so they're getting a film. I'm not fucking dying in this pig shit country."

"I saw what they did to Enoch," I said, hands out, up, to cover my chest, trying to remember anything I'd heard about knife fights. I'd mostly planned to not get in any. Hoyt had noticed there was a chair between us, and he was calculating how many steps it would take him to get around it, how fast he thought he was. He scrunched up his nose like he was trying to remember if I'd seen Enoch or not. Figured. He'd been pretty drunk for the last couple days.

"You didn't see Linder," he said, his big gotcha, and lunged, full on scrambling over the chair. I shoved it out from under him, the knife blade nicking me across the cheek. It probably hurt—I couldn't tell, but I felt the skin part, the wet on my jaw. He tumbled onto the floor, arms out to catch himself. I stomped on his wrist; he screamed, and in that heartbeat, I was on him, my knee in his chest, trying to scratch the knife out of his palms.

"Get her, idiot," Paul shouted. "We already filmed the last scene! She's dead!"

Hoyt got his hand around my neck and I clamped my teeth around his wrist until his fingers spasmed and he dropped the knife. I snatched it up by the blade and shoved it into his neck as far as it would go, until it scraped floor or spine. Blood didn't spray. It barely welled. But Hoyt gurgled and his hand tightened around my windpipe and then just as black stars constricted my vision he went limp.

I put all my weight on the handle as I stood.

Paul lowered the camera and stared at me. The reel clicked, empty. He didn't bother shutting it off.

"Well, hell, girl," he said. There was actual awe in his voice. "I didn't think you had it in you. Guess we'll film a new finale."

I leaned down and dug my hand into Hoyt's neck. The knife came out with a pop, and finally that spurt of blood. The smell made me sick, oily and wet. Paul wasn't stupid. He backed up a step, carefully shifted the weight of the camera to his shoulder while he went for something at his belt. He still spoke easily, too easily.

"Unexpected ending, but I think audiences are ready for it," he said. "The hero dead, the monster triumphant. Why not, you know? Surprised I didn't think of it myself. It's a new world."

I didn't have shit to say to him. I went for his throat. I got him, in the chest, my moment of triumph, but the knife was slick and he was ready for me, flipping the switchblade on his belt open and sliding it up between my ribs. He knew what he was doing. He didn't even drop the fucking camera.

I couldn't breathe. I fell to my knees, then to the floor. I wondered why it didn't hurt. Paul had the nerve to look a little apologetic, and he opened his fucking mouth again—and then a hand seized him and blood bloomed from the arc of his neck and shoulder. The camera hit the floor with a crunch. I hoped it broke.

Vreka leaned over me, hand resting lightly on my forehead. Her skin felt cool, clean. She sat next to me, shifting my head so it rested on her lap while she examined the wound in my chest. It seemed like such a little wound in comparison. I heard Paul's body drop to the floor beside me, and Tibor's voice, staccato, from the corridor.

"A shame," Vreka said, her face a featureless smear, her voice kind. "But not so long now."

I was drowning. My chest wouldn't move—my lungs wouldn't fill. I was never going to wake up. I brushed Vreka's hand with mine, but my fingers would not close.

"Take me with you," I said.

Vreka's mouth opened to a smile so wide I could see it even through the haze. Her fingers tightened around mine. With her other hand she slit open the corner of her mouth, brighter than her red lips, brighter than the light outside, and pressed her lips to mine, searching, deeply.

I tasted blood—cold, and copper.

```
The castle gate has been wrenched wide, the
courtyard dark and empty through the open doors.
The hero walks—strides—out onto the dirt road.
His overcoat is buttoned against the wind, his
hat pressed to his chest in solemn thought. The
confidence in his gait is marred only by the bow
of his head, the lines of his face.
    Behind him, lingering on the threshold of
the gate, the two remaining cultists remove
their featureless masks, pull down their black
```

hoods. One is a large man, broad-shouldered, his expression a tired line; the other is slim, bald, swaying in confusion. They both look out, exhausted, bewildered, into the light of the rising sun.

Rhiannon Rasmussen is a nonbinary lesbian illustrator, writer, and print consultant preoccupied with monstrosity. For more writing & art, visit rhiannonrs.com. For shitposts & conversation, visit @charibdys on Twitter.

THE ULTIMATE SECRET OF MAGIC
BY ADAM GALLARDO

THE GIRL SITTING ON MY front porch didn't say hello. To introduce herself, she said, "I saw you do magic once."

She was young, Asian, and pretty in that thin, boyish way girls are pretty before they transform into women and come fully into themselves. I thought she must be a fan who had managed to track down my home address—it's happened before, believe it or not—but she didn't give off that vibe. For one thing, she wasn't smiling.

"I do my show all over town, all over the country," I said. "I bet that dozens, maybe *hundreds* of people have seen me do magic."

She continued not to smile at my little joke. "Not that kind of magic," she said. "Real magic."

That stopped me.

"I don't know what you mean."

"Of course you do," she said, and she waved her hand in front of her face like she was shooing away my inept lie. "I was back stage at a performance you gave and I saw you do some *real* magic. Maybe you should invite me inside."

"I think we'll stay out here for the time being. Who are you and what do you want?"

She nodded to herself, as if the conversation had finally gotten where she wanted it to go.

"It was Sergio the Great's command performance," she said. "You were having trouble doing the Mad Hatter's Revenge and I was standing back stage. You didn't know I was there, obviously. You did something with your hands." Here she pantomimed a complicated hand gesture that actually looked pretty close to what I must have done on the stage. "And then poof! It worked."

I studied her for a long time, trying desperately to figure out who she might be. A memory hovered just out of reach, but nothing concrete.

"Yeah," I said finally, "that trick never did work for me the way it was supposed to. Maybe I should invite you inside, after all."

And for the first time, she smiled.

At the time this happened, I still lived in my little one-bedroom house in Portland's Lents neighborhood. The area was just beginning to be gentrified so it was still something of a shithole, but at least I could afford my property tax. And I didn't mind the rundown condition of the place. I'd grown up nearby, so it was at least familiar.

I had just started to make a name for myself as a close-up magician, even though I'd been playing clubs around the city, and across the country since I was a teenager. But here's the thing. The girl had my number. I was a real, honest to God magician—a sorcerer or wizard, whatever the hell you want to call it. I hid that fact behind the facade of a not-too-successful stage magician. At least, I thought I'd been hiding that fact. This girl showing up on my doorstep in this way was unwelcome proof to the contrary.

I winced when I turned on the light. My place, while never being filthy, has never really been clean, either. Piles of books were augmented by the occasional dirty dish and bit of worn clothing.

Apparatuses from my stage act sat in various stages of completion on most flat surfaces. And the shelves that should have held books were crammed with occult knickknacks like skulls and fetuses in jars, all of them fake. I keep the real stuff locked up in my basement. And on top of it all, a vague smell of mildew and cooking oil. I motioned for her to come in behind me and I noticed how she surveyed the room, her nose wrinkled in mild disgust.

"Sorry," I said, "I don't get many women in here." Then, realizing how that sounded, I followed up with, "Visitors. Many visitors." She didn't seem to hear any of it.

"Want a drink?" I asked. "It might help the décor."

"I'm not old enough to drink."

"Anything?" I asked. She looked, I guess the word is *petulant?* Arms crossed on her chest, one hip cocked, she looked younger just then than she had on the front step. "Water? Soda? I might have some milk in the fridge that hasn't turned to cheese yet."

"Nothing." She lifted some books out of an old wing back chair and shifted them to another pile. She waited a moment to make sure the wobbling structure was sound. Then she sat down and watched while I mixed myself a drink. It was just gin and tonic, but helped take the edge off the heat. Unfortunately, my place had no air conditioning. After I had taken an initial sip and found the drink bearable, I sat across from her on my loveseat. A small stack of books collapsed as I changed the integrity of the cushions. I didn't bother picking them up.

"Maybe we should start with who you are," I said.

"I'm surprised you don't remember me. We've met."

"Back at Sergio's gig? That was, what, nine or ten years ago."

"More recently than that. My dad asked you over for dinner. But maybe I should forgive you for not remembering. I was so afraid of you; I didn't speak through the whole meal."

I stared at her and started matching up what she'd just said with some physical cues in her face and her body.

"You favor your mother," I finally said. "Which is lucky for you since old Sergio is not the handsomest man on the planet."

"I never thought he was ugly," she said. "And his name isn't—"

"I know that," I said, "but that was the name he chose for himself so it's good enough for me." I took a drink. For some reason, she was making me uncomfortable. Her name, I couldn't remember her name. I took another swig as I thought. "Helena," I said, happy that it had come to me. "After Madame Blavatsky."

"Only because my mom wouldn't let him name me Hecate," she said. "Hello, Mr. Dark."

"Oh, God. Not that. Call me Christopher. Or Chris, make it Chris."

"Thank you, Christopher."

"So, now that we've got introductions out of the way, what can I do for you?"

"I want you to teach me magic."

I thanked God I hadn't just taken a drink, because I would have gagged on it or spit it in her face.

"Helena," I said, "I can think of few things more horrific. For either of us."

"Why?" she demanded.

"Listen," I said, as I found a spot on the table next to me for my drink. I sat forward. "Ask anyone in the magic community: I can barely do a French pass. Hell, your dad is one of the finest stage magicians I've ever seen. Ask him to teach you. I'm sure he'd be thrilled.

"And if you don't want to learn from him, I can offer you a short list of people who'd be happy to take on an assistant-slash-apprentice with your family's background."

The set of her jaw and her arms crossed against her chest told me I'd missed the mark.

"I think we should use terms to, um, to *differentiate* between illusions and real, you know, *arcane* magic," she said

"Let's keep things simple, then," I said. I didn't like where this was going. "Let's just say 'illusions' and 'magic.' "

"Great. I don't want to learn *illusions*. What I want to learn is *magic*."

I killed off my drink and stood up. "Helena, it was nice of you to stop by, but I think you should be going."

"Why won't you help me?"

"For a number of reasons," I said, "but the biggest reason is that your father would kill me if I taught you."

"Call him."

"What?"

"Call him and talk to him," she said. Her veneer of calm eroded before my eyes. She sat forward and her voice took on a near-panicked edge. I tried to tell if her eyes were dilated, but couldn't be sure. "After you talk to him, if you still don't want to teach me, I'll drop it."

I wanted to tell her to drop it right now—there was no way in hell I was going to take her on as some sort of apprentice. But I wanted to ease her into that fact so that she'd maybe leave me in peace.

"Listen, I'll call your father—"

"Call him right now."

"I'll call him," I said, "but not right now." I put my hand up to stop her when she started to protest. "It's late, I'll call him tomorrow, and then I'll call you. That's the best I can do."

She thought about that for a while and then she dug into her purse for a pencil and a pad of paper. She scratched on it for a second, tore out a sheet, and handed it to me. "That's my cell phone number," she said. "You can call me anytime and you'll be able to get a hold of me."

"I know how they work," I said, and took the paper. I folded it and stuffed it into my breast pocket.

She stood, hesitated, and said, "I really wish you'd call him now."

"All I'm doing right now is brushing my teeth and going to bed."

She opened her mouth to say something, closed it again, and then turned and walked out the door. She closed it softly behind her and I sat in my chair staring after her for a long time.

Helena's dad, Sergio, was a funny old man. I met him when I first started haunting the clubs where I'd eventually begin to hone my magic, my *illusionist* act. I was around eighteen at the time. He'd seemed ancient even then, but I guess he was probably forty-five at the oldest. A few years after I met him, he married a bartender and sometime dancer about twenty years younger than him and they seemed happy. Then they had Helena and their happiness seemed to go off the charts. But life never lets you be just happy. Around the time Helena turned fifteen, her mom got breast cancer and died. It seemed to happen just that fast. Sergio was never himself after that.

He knew about the kind of magic I did, but he was never interested in it. He liked being an illusionist. As I sat in my chair staring at the door through which his daughter had just exited, I remembered a story he told me once.

We sat back stage at a little bar. He'd come to see my act and we were sharing a drink afterward. He hadn't been performing for years by that time. His wife was still alive. I asked him why he'd never done real magic.

"*Real* magic," he said and waved his hand in front of his face like I'd just passed gas. "I'll tell you why I never got into *real magic.*" He took a slow sip of his drink—something with fruit floating in it and umbrellas all around the rim. "You used to read comic books, right?"

"Still do," I said.

"Still do! You're like a twenty-year-old kid." I was younger than that, but I didn't correct him. "When I was your age, I was supporting my family at a slaughterhouse."

"And you had to walk three miles through the snow to get there," I said.

Sergio stifled a grin. He enjoyed the back and forth, but I knew he had a lesson to impart.

"I took a horse-drawn cart, Christopher; the technology had been invented by then. Anyway, you know the comics writer Alan Moore?" he asked.

"Of course I do," I said. Besides being a famous comic book writer—and maybe my favorite comic book writer—Alan Moore was also a practicing magician. My type of magic. *Real* magic. And the really weird thing? He wasn't the only comic book writer who was.

"You do," Sergio said. "Great. So here's the story. Alan Moore is in a bar or something one night."

"How do *you* know who he is?"

"Oh, one of those punks you hang out with told me this story. Lemming, or Joe, or one of the others. It's not important. You want to hear this?" I agreed that I did. "So he's in a bar. Who does he find standing next to him? One of his own characters! A magician!"

"That must be John Constantine. Do you mean he found himself standing next to someone who *looked like* John Constantine?"

"Did I say that? No, he looks up and there is the character he created. In real life. This, what did you say, Constantine? Constantine says to Alan Moore, 'I'll tell you the ultimate secret of magic.' Do you know what he says?"

"I have no idea."

"He says, 'Any cunt can do it.' "

I burst out laughing. Not so much because the story was that funny, but because Sergio never swore. He was a bit of a prude, his choice of bride notwithstanding, and he didn't like vulgar language. So, to hear him pull out a big gun like that was just hilarious.

After my laughter died down, Sergio went on. "But that's why I never liked your so-called real magic. Anyone can do it. Any jerk with a beef and the lack of common sense can do it. But my magic, *stage* magic? There aren't many people on the planet who can do what I do. And there are maybe two dozen who can do it as well as I could when I was at my best. Dedication, hard work, practice—those things are the real magic."

He had a point, of course. I'd seen backwood, meth-head, alcoholic hillbillies who could conjure a demon. These people couldn't balance a check book, but they could work a summoning. What I learned in the time since then was that to do real magic correctly, so that no one got hurt, so that no one died or was permanently scarred, that required a lot of hard work, too. It was just that a lot of folks weren't interested in putting the work in. I like to fool myself that I'm one of those few.

I told Sergio how right he was, and I bought him another awful drink. And then we sat there and shot the shit late into the night.

That was probably the last time I saw him happy.

It was that memory more than anything else that made me pick up the phone and call Sergio. I hunted through the drawers of my desk and found my battered old address book. After several deep breaths, I dialed his number.

He picked up after the second ring. "Hello?"

"Hello, Sergio, it's Christopher. Christopher Dark."

"Chrissy. You waited long enough to call."

Chrissy? No one ever called me that.

I squirmed in my chair a little. "I know, and I'm sorry about that. How have you been?"

"Not too well, to be honest."

I leaned forward in my seat and grimaced. "I'm sorry to hear that, Sergio. Is there any way I can help?" The only answer I got was a short, barking laugh. This was going worse than I imagined it would.

"Everyone's so sorry," he sighed.

"Listen," I said after a moment, "the reason I'm calling is that your daughter came to visit me this evening."

"That little whore. What'd she say?"

I held the phone away from my ear and looked at it. What I'd just heard had to be my imagination or a technical glitch. Sergio would never say that, especially not about Helena. I put the phone back to my ear.

"What did you say?"

"You heard me, *Chrissy*. Or have you suddenly gone fucking deaf?"

"Sergio, are you all right?"

"Sergio is very far indeed from 'all right', son."

"What's going on?"

"And where were you when his wife, flax-wench that she was, lay dying?"

"Why are you talking in the third person, Sergio?"

There was more of that barking laughter, but this time it went on for a long time.

"You were never a clever one, were you, you dipshit? Sussed that out, have you? It'll do you no good. The next time you see that daughter, that tasty morsel, send her home. We're hungry, Mr. Dark, and she's just what we desire. If you catch our meaning." And the line went dead.

I sat there for what felt like a long time. My skin tingly and tight. I didn't like this at all. I swallowed the rest of my drink and then dialed the phone again.

Helena answered on the first ring.

"Did you call him?" she asked by way of hello.

"How'd you know it was me?"

"My phone has caller ID." I nearly heard the sound of her eyes rolling. "What did you get when you called him?"

"It didn't sound like him." I paused, wondering how to say this next part. There was really no way to break it to her easily. "Helena, I think your father is... *possessed*."

"No shit, Sherlock."

There was a knock at my door. I asked Helena to hold on a second and, stretching the phone cord as long as it would go, I peered through the peephole in my front door. She stood on the front porch with her cell phone to her ear.

"Open the stupid door, Christopher," she said.

I hung up the phone and opened the door like she'd asked.

"Have you been out there the whole time?"

"Of course. I knew you were going to call as soon as I left. What do we do?"

"We?"

She shot me a look that didn't really invite an opposing opinion. Since it was obvious that she had some idea what was going on with her dad, I wasn't really in a position to disagree.

"Okay," I said. "You can drive us to your dad's place. But when we get there, I go in alone."

"That's fine for now," she said.

"And we go tomorrow."

"No fucking way." She started for the door.

I didn't want to put my hands on her so I stood between her and the door, my hands spread pleadingly. I was afraid that if I couldn't convince her, she'd try to do something dumb without me.

"Listen," I said, "we don't know what we're dealing with here. Let me ask you some questions, do a little research, then we can go in the morning. Informed. Okay?"

She glared at me as she thought, her arms crossed. She looked like she wanted to punch me, and I braced myself for it, but she finally relaxed.

"Okay," she said.

I felt my shoulders relax. "Great. Go have a seat, and I'll get us a drink."

"I don't want a drink."

"Well, I do." I saw her sour look. "Some coffee," I said.

Helena sat in my favorite arm chair again—the only flat surface not taken up by books—arms and legs crossed, frowning and glaring.

"Do you have creamer?"

"I have milk."

"Fine," she said.

A few minutes later, we both sat with coffee in front of us. It was almost civilized.

"Tell me about your dad."

"What about him?"

"What's he's been like? What made you think something was wrong enough to come see me?"

She took a deep breath and then started talking—slowly at first, but then it came in a steady stream. She told me how her father had been devastated by the illness and then the death of her mother. I squirmed in my seat as she told me this. She said that after her mother's funeral, Sergio wandered restlessly through the house. She would find him in different rooms either standing and staring silently, or he'd be muttering to himself, arguing with himself. I wondered if it had been himself he'd been arguing with, but I didn't say anything out loud, I didn't want to interrupt her story.

"He was like that for about a year," she said. Her eyes distant, clouded with memory. "Until about six months ago."

"What happened six months ago?" I asked after she fell silent. I thought she might not go on.

"He started buying books and reading them like crazy."

"Books?"

"You know how he feels about… about the kind of magic you do, right?"

I nodded. He'd never made a secret of his feelings. She went on to tell me that he spent more and more of his time tracking down and studying books about magic. He was always in his office, reading and making notes. And the muttering intensified. Even when they were at the dinner table together, Sergio would conduct conversations with himself rather than speak to his daughter.

"And then, about a month ago, he installed these heavy locks on his study door."

I perked up at hearing this. "Do you know why?"

"Not then," she said. He spent more and more time there. She started taking his meals to him there, but she had to leave the trays for him outside the door. He would only open it once she went away.

"Then, about a week ago, he was back to normal."

"What do you mean?"

"I guess I should say he *seemed* normal."

She told me how one day she woke up and found her dad sitting at the dining table and he was coherent, engaged, *there*. She felt a wave of relief sitting across from him as they talked and ate together. But that relief only lasted through that first meal. After that his behavior became more and more erratic. She always had the sense that he was watching her. *Leering* at her. A couple of times he brushed up against her when it wasn't necessary—*touched* her. And then he started swearing.

"Swearing?"

"You know my dad doesn't cuss, right?"

I thought of his story about magic. "Well, hardly ever."

"Yeah, well, he started cussing like a fucking sailor." I nodded.

"There's not much else to say, except..." She paused and drove for a bit. "Except that when I look at him, I don't feel like it's him anymore."

"He looks different?"

"No," she said. "He looks the same as always but there's a look behind his eyes that's different. He's different, if it's still him."

I knew what she meant, but didn't say anything. Her dad wasn't her dad anymore.

I took a sip of my coffee more to have something to do than because I wanted any.

"Is there anything else you can remember about your dad's behavior over the last few days?"

"Like what?"

"Like anything," I said. I downed the last of my coffee and set the cup down. "Anything he might have said. Weird marks on his body. A smell?" I shrugged.

A light turned on in her eyes.

"He does smell," she said. "Like, bad."

"Bad in what way?"

"Like unwashed, but even worse." She blushed and looked away. "You know how people smell when they've been on the streets? Like, body odor and pee, and... stuff?"

"Yeah," I said.

"Like that, but concentrated," she said. "I couldn't stand to be in the same room the last few days. Is that anything?"

"Maybe," I said, trying to appear more confident than I felt. "I'll spend some time downstairs looking things up. I'll see what I can turn up."

"And what should I do?"

"I'm going to make up a bed on the couch here," I said, "so you can at least rest."

Her body stiffened and her mouth drew into a line.

"We should wait until morning to do anything," I said. "Most likely, whatever we're talking about will be weaker in the daytime. And the best thing you can do with that time is to gather your energy.

"I'm going to do the same once I'm done downstairs."

An icy silence fell between us and I saw Helena wanting so badly to reject my offer. Finally the tension in her shoulders relaxed. She didn't say she agreed, but I let it slide. I didn't want to press her.

I stood up and started to clear things off the couch.

"This is a lot more comfortable than it looks," I said and she gave me a thin smile. "Once I'm done here, I'll show you the bathroom."

After Helena was situated on the couch, I said goodnight and headed downstairs to my basement workroom.

Two heavy bolt locks keep out the uninvited. The bolts, plus some heavy-duty charms, I should say. I'd almost feel sorry for anyone breaking into the basement, but since it's where I keep all of my truly dangerous magic items, it needs to be protected.

The least dangerous, but probably most useful, thing I keep in the basement is a worn Army great coat. It used to be green, but it's now faded to gray. A number of protective charms have been sewn into the lining, and the pockets are filled with magical odds and ends that have come in handy over the years. I took the coat off the peg where it hangs and checked its various pockets. Everything was where I remembered it. I put the coat back where I'd gotten it, then went to a locked gun cabinet at the foot of the stairs. I actually keep guns in it. They often do the trick when a spell takes too long. I chose a snub nosed .38 revolver. It fit easily into the outside pocket of the coat.

That done, I started perusing the books that line the shelves taking up the west wall of the basement. You might be picturing something like musty old tomes collected over the centuries, but the reality is a lot less picturesque. They're mostly musty old paperbacks found in secondhand shops and esoteric bookstores and head shops. Real or genuine books of magic are few and far between, so you make do with what's readily available.

I chose a book at random, a dog-eared copy of Guiley's *Encyclopedia of Demons and Demonology*. I started to leaf through it to see if anything caught my eye. It wasn't a lot to go on; a bad smell. Demons weren't exactly known for their adherence to personal hygiene.

I heard footsteps above me. Probably just Helena getting up to use the bathroom or get a drink. I went back to browsing the book. But then I heard the front door open. My heart thudded heavy in my chest and I closed the Guiley.

"Helena?" I called, and got no answer.

The door closed and I threw the book down and made for the stairs, calling her name again.

I'd just entered the kitchen when I saw headlights strafing the house and heard a motor revving.

I shouted out her name again, though I knew it was useless. Her little car was pulling away as I ran out the door. I stood in the street and watched the taillights recede, feeling like a total jackass. All I could do now was go inside, grab my coat, and call a fucking cab.

Sergio lived in a modest house in Lake Oswego, just about fifteen or twenty minutes south of Portland. It's a nice town, but sort of culturally dead. Maybe that's why he liked it. The house is a one story job, spread out on a quarter-acre lot; built around an interior courtyard. It looks like something Frank Lloyd Wright's little brother might have designed. As the Radio Cab pulled up to the curb, I saw Helena's beat-up, used commuter car sitting in the driveway.

I paid and tipped the cabbie. I stepped out into the cool evening air. The cab pulled away.

I'd been to the house a few times over the years, and I knew from experience that Sergio's study was in the back of the house. I was pretty sure that's where he'd be, and I could sneak my way in there. First, though, I wanted to find Helena. I hoped to find her before anything too bad happened to her.

I crept up the walk, glancing around to make sure no one was watching me. The front door stood ajar, so I pushed it open and stepped inside.

The living room was trashed. The sliding glass doors that led into the central courtyard had been smashed out. The other doors leading to the courtyard had been similarly destroyed. Stuffing from the slashed furniture lay in tufts on the floor. Bookshelves lay on the floor, the books ripped apart. The walls sported holes here and there. Had Sergio, or whatever he'd become, been looking for something? Or was this just mindless destruction? I scanned the room and saw Sergio wasn't there. I let out a breath I hadn't realized I'd been holding.

That's when I noticed a smell just below the surface. It was the too-sweet smell of food left out to rot; faint enough that it could have been my imagination, but I knew I needed to pay attention to it.

I reached into one of my coat's many pockets and pulled out a tiny fetish I'd made several years ago. I'd once tracked down a little girl who'd been abducted by her estranged father. Found and returned her to her mother before the cult she'd been delivered to was able to carry out any of its plans for her. Her mother had been so grateful that she barely batted an eye when I asked for a lock of the little girl's hair as part of my payment. The baby tooth was a harder sell.

Now I held the fetish I'd constructed with those materials in front of my mouth and breathed onto it.

"Find her," I said, and I immediately felt the thing tugging toward the back of the house. Before I followed its prompt, I made sure that a vial I'd need later was in the pocket it was meant to be. That done, I headed down the hallway.

Since I wasn't really looking to run into Sergio before I had to, I didn't bother with any of the closed doors along the way. I just made my way to where the fetish seemed to be leading me... his study. The walls along the way had been torn up just like in the living room. Holes exposed sheet rock, studs, and wiring.

My heart thudded in my chest and I had a metallic taste in my mouth. Fear responses that I did my best to ignore. I also felt something that's harder to describe. A pressure in the back of my head like a building headache, but it was deeper than that. I could feel it all up and down my spine, too, and in my balls. Magic always leaves residue and that's what I was picking up on. I paid attention to this. Since all of the feelings were painful or uncomfortable, I knew it was some bad fucking juju. The rotted meat smell got stronger as I walked toward the back of the house.

What did you do here, Sergio? I wondered

I reached the door to his study and stopped. Hand on the door-knob, I tried to collect myself. All of the responses, the fear and the magic, were screaming off the charts now, feeding off one another.

I wished Helena had stayed put, that I could have formulated some sort of plan besides rushing in like an asshole. Because of my fear, I wanted so badly to reach into my pocket and grasp my pistol, but some part of me said that would be a bad idea. Besides, Sergio was still my friend and there was no way I was going to draw down on him without knowing for sure it was necessary. I took a deep breath and opened the door.

The room looked empty. And, as far as I'd seen, it was the only room in the house that hadn't been tossed. Built-in bookshelves lined the walls, and the shelves were crammed with books and things I recognized as occult paraphernalia. A human skull, a black candle, and a fucking crystal ball—talismans and trinkets. The Sergio I knew never had any use for this stuff. But I was beginning to think that the Sergio I knew had been gone for a while.

Everything in the room had been pushed back against the walls to clear a space in the middle of the floor. Three concentric circles had been drawn on the floor in chalk, symbols and words filled the spaces between the circles. A large heptagram, a seven-pointed star, filled the center. It looked like someone had taken their finger and deliberately run it through the circles so that none of them were complete anymore. That was a bad sign. In magic, circles are usually used to contain something, but they only work if they're complete, unbroken.

The fetish told me that Helena was still in this room somewhere, and I needed to find her, make sure she was alive.

"Helena," I called as loudly as I dared. "Can you hear me?" Nothing.

Stepping carefully around the circles on the floor, I began to look behind the furniture pushed against the wall.

She lay behind the large desk, unconscious and breathing in a shallow rasp.

"Helena," I whispered. "Wake up." Again, she didn't react. But now I knew where she was and that she was alive, I could move on to the next bit of business.

I looked at the desk and other furniture against the walls, but quickly decided that I'd never find what I was looking for there. Instead, I went through the pockets of my coat as fast as I could until I found what I needed. A piece of chalk.

I got down on my hands and knees and, as carefully as I could, I redrew the lines of the circles so that they were complete. I stood up to admire my handiwork and dusted my hands. That's when I became aware that someone stood in the doorway.

Sergio stood there, but it wasn't really Sergio. Where I had never seen Sergio anything but impeccably dressed, the thing wearing his skin had on a suit that was stained and torn. And I could smell him from where he stood—he was the source of the rotting smell. I swallowed hard to keep from gagging. He smiled at me. It made me think of monkeys smiling at one another in threat.

"Can I help you, Chris? Looking for something?"

"I'm not here to talk to you."

"No?"

I ignored him. I backed away from the door, careful to not step into the circles on the floor, and looked for another way out of the room. There was a good chance I'd want to leave quickly.

"I suppose I should be used to that," the thing wearing Sergio said. "I mean, there were all those years when you weren't here to talk to me."

I was sizing up the window, but it had bars across it. I might know a word that could blow the casing out of the wall, but I doubted I'd have time to say it if things got hairy.

Sergio's face stretched into a horrible frown.

"All those months when Silvia was dying—rotting on the inside—and I could have used a friend. But you were too busy being a self-absorbed piece of shit to reach out to me. So fucking selfish that you kept your distance while I sat by her side and listened to her scream."

"Just stop," I said. "This whole guilt trip thing? It only works if what you're saying is news to me. I've got to tell you, I'm well aware

I'm a shitty friend, and I wasn't there when Sergio needed me."

It narrowed its eyes at me. "And you think that absolves you?"

"So, let me guess," I said, ignoring its latest jibe, "Sergio misses his wife so much he starts researching ways to bring her back or, at least, to communicate with her wherever she is."

"She's roasting on a spit in Hell. When she's not being passed around by demons, that is." The frown was gone and had been replaced by that monkey grin again.

"Whether or not that's true doesn't matter," I said. "And you have to know I'm not taking anything you say at face value.

"Anyway, while doing his research, he runs across you—whoever you are. Don't bother telling me you won't reveal your name. I understand how this works."

The fucking thing gave me a little *bow*. I rolled my eyes, playing it cooler than I really was.

"You're smarter than you look," it said. "But then, you do look like a mouth-breathing asshole."

"Done with the insults?"

"Not by a long shot." It wagged its finger at me. "And I want you to stop looking for a way out. It's really *fucking* annoying."

I froze in my tracks. I didn't want to anger this thing until I needed to.

"How did you convince Sergio to step into the circle once he'd summoned you?"

"Told him it was necessary to communicate with his wife in the great beyond, *et cetera*. When he hesitated, I told him Crowley did the same thing. Magicians can't stand to be upstaged."

Goddamned Aleister Crowley! That old fake had more than one evil to answer for.

"My turn now," it said. "I felt you repair the circle. How did you imagine you'd get me to step into it?"

I snaked my left hand into my coat pocket and wrapped my hand around a vial I found there. I took a deep breath and prepared to do what I had to.

"Well, I guess I figured I'd *distract you*!" I whipped my hand out of my pocket and thumbed open the vial I held in my hand. I threw the contents at Sergio's body. Holy water splashed him in the face and ran down his chest. The thing immediately clutched at its face and convulsed in pain. It screamed loud enough to set my head ringing. I rushed forward and grabbed the thing by the shoulders and tried to give it a shove. It didn't budge, but its screams stopped and the convulsions suddenly ended. Very slowly it lifted its head and it smiled up at me.

"You are a stupid asshole, aren't you?" it asked. Then, faster than I thought possible, it straightened and grabbed me by my shoulders. It squeezed my upper arms in its vicelike grip and lifted me off the floor. I cursed myself. Holy water would have worked on a lesser demon. My bad luck that whatever had taken over Sergio was a heavy hitter. The thing squeezed my arms and the pain shooting up my body cut off all thought.

"You just wasted holy water to get your friend's body wet. You shit-smeared afterbirth. I'm inside him, deep inside. Wherever it is his tiny, black soul resides, that's where I lie. Just try and get that wet!"

He threw me across the room. I smashed into the glass doors of a bookshelf on the opposite wall. My coat took most of the damage, but the glass cut into my cheek and my hands. I felt warm blood course down my face.

I hit the floor and tried to get my feet under me, but that thing was too fast. Strong hands gripped my face on either side and lifted me to my feet. My head felt like it would collapse under the pressure. I screamed. It waited for me to stop and open my eyes. I looked right into that goddammed smile. It opened its mouth and its tongue snaked out, licking me.

"Mmm-mmm," it moaned. "The taste of damnation adds savor, did you know? And let me tell you, whore-son, you are heavily spiced." It drew me close and licked me again. Its breath smelled of rot and I gagged at it. Then it released me and I started to collapse. But before

I hit the floor, unseen hands grabbed me and threw me again.

I landed on top of the desk against the wall. Boxes and pieces of office furniture gave way underneath me. I screamed again as something in my back gave way. I writhed in pain. The thing stalked toward me. I tried my best to kick away from it, but my legs barely worked. It stood over me and placed its hand on my chest and pinned me to the desk like a bug. Behind me, I heard Helena moan.

"Where are you going, sweetness? We're just getting started." It chuckled. "I don't think he'd want to admit it, but I'm pretty sure that Sergio is going to like watching this from his hiding place." *Hiding place?* "There's a lot of resentment in the old poof over how you abandoned him, you know?"

I struggled to get out from under its grip. Its hand lay in the middle of my chest and pressed down until it felt like my sternum would give way. Nothing I did budged that hand. When I kicked it with my knees it barely noticed. The whole time I struggled, the damned thing ignored me and looked over the refuse on top of the desk. It looked calm and detached as it did and, for some reason, that scared me more than anything. After a minute, it whistled low and then smiled. It rummaged around over my head and then held up what it had found.

An old-fashioned letter spike caught the light. The type of thing that hasn't sat on an office desk in fifty years, but of course Sergio had one. The creature that wore Sergio smiled down at me.

I grabbed the hand with the spike and did everything I could to stop it, but it was no good. Slowly it placed the tip of the spike against my shoulder. And then, just as slowly, it pushed. I screamed as the spike popped through my skin. My whole world seemed to be focused on that one point in my shoulder. By fractions, the demon that wore Sergio like a suit pushed the spike through skin and muscle and sinew. Occasionally it met resistance, but it just pushed a little harder. Every time the thing moved, I screamed again. I redoubled my efforts to get the creature off me, but it just seemed to grow stronger.

Finally, the spike was all the way through my shoulder and there was still a good half-inch left exposed. The creature considered this for a moment and then it exerted itself once again. The spike penetrated the solid wood of the desk. By this time I had no voice left. A thin gasp was all that escaped me.

It took its hand off my chest and regarded me. I couldn't have moved if I'd wanted to—I was pinned to the desk.

"Well," it said as it looked over its handiwork, "that's a good start. Let's see what else we can find." It looked over its choices like a housewife choosing oranges at the market. "The old man must have a letter opener around. Maybe even some pushpins. How's that sound?"

I had my hand on the base of the spike. I counted to three and pulled for all I was worth—and nearly blacked out. Black dots swam in front of my vision. The pain in my shoulder was a white hot presence that stole my breath. I lay back and prayed I'd just hurry up and go into shock.

"Dad?" a voice from the desk called. "Mr. Dark?"

"Sweet cheeks!" the demon smiled broadly. It pushed the desk, with me pinned to the top, out of the way as if it weighed nothing. "Me and Christopher were just working some things out. But now that *you're* awake, I think we can let him stew for a while, don't you?"

I took a deep breath and did my best to calm myself. I tried to separate myself from the pain in my shoulder. This was something that my mentor showed me a long time ago during my first initiation. I still have the scars of that lesson all over my body. When the pain was a distant rumor of sensation, I quickly reached across my body with my right hand, took hold of the paper spike, and pulled for all I was worth.

The pain was enormous. Even with the self-hypnosis it felt like the whole left side of my body had caught fire. I was immediately drenched in sweat and I screamed out. My body writhed uncontrollably. It took all my powers to start shutting down the agonizing pain that radiated through me. I knew that I had to get a handle on it or

Helena was dead. I made sure and left the spike in my arm since I didn't think I'd be able to control the hemorrhaging that would result from removing it.

After what felt like hours, I sat up on the desk and swung my feet to the floor. Across the room, the creature stood before Helena. One hand gripped her shoulder; the other stroked her cheek. Helena struggled to get out of his grip, but there was no escaping those vice-like fingers. Tears welled up in her eyes. Blood flowed from a blow she'd taken in her scalp.

"So much fun," the demon said. "Now that you're awake, we're going to have so much fun. I was just waiting for Christopher to arrive before I got started."

"Don't do this," she pleaded, her voice slurred, but the thing inside her father just laughed.

"Get away from her," I said as I stood up.

It turned and smiled at me. "I'll get back to you later," it said, and then I flew across the room and landed in a heap on top of a pile of books. I struggled to my feet.

"It's time to be a good girl," I heard it say. "Time to do what daddy asks."

"Dad, if you're in there, make this stop!"

"I'm your daddy now, you stupid little slag! And I'm telling you what to do."

I looked through the detritus on the office floor and looked for anything that could be used as a weapon. Nothing. Sergio's disdain for the occult meant that he'd collected nothing that could be of use right then. I considered ripping the spike out of my shoulder and using that.

"Daddy," Helena said, more calm than I could have imagined possible. "You need to fight this thing. You need to take control. Please."

"Baby, it is too late for that. Papa Bear went away and left me in charge. Now let's get down to it…" The thing reached down and with its free hand started to fumble with its belt. I decided that the spike was my best bet and reached up to grab it.

"Don't do this, Dad!"

And the thing *stopped*. It's fly undone, it stood there, unsteady, swaying. It seemed to deflate right in front of us.

I let my hand fall from the spike, waiting to see what was going to happen.

The thing looked up into Helena's face and tears flowed down its cheeks. "Oh, love, I'm so sorry."

"Sergio?" I asked and my old friend turned to me.

"Thank you so much for helping my daughter," he said. I gestured wordlessly at the spike in my shoulder. *I haven't done much*, I thought, but I didn't say it.

And then his body convulsed. He stood up straight and renewed his grip on Helena's arm.

"No you don't, old man," the thing said as it regained control. "No Indian-giving, you old queen."

It tried to pull Helena closer to itself but it lost control again. It looked like a toy whose batteries had run down. It screamed wordlessly and gnashed its teeth. It bit its tongue in the process and spit blood. Helena wrenched her arm free and ran deeper into the room away from it.

"Fight it, Dad," she yelled. "You can beat it!"

"She's right, Sergio," I said.

Slowly it began to move toward the circle in the middle of the floor. Its legs bent in ways no human body was ever meant to. The whole time it moved, the thing inside him cursed and spat blood. It told him the things it would do to me and Helena once it was free. The things it would do to everyone he ever cared about. But still Sergio wrestled the demon to the edge of the circle. Sweat poured down his face and his eyes bulged, but despite the old man's best efforts, he couldn't get the demon to step into the circle.

"Dad," Helena said, "get rid of it."

"Get into the circle," I hissed, and slumped against the desk. "You can do it."

Sergio shook his head wearily. "I can't. Maybe I could have once, but I'm too weak now."

"That's right, cocksucker," the thing spat at me. The transitions between Sergio and the thing controlling the body were sickening to watch. How long could Sergio hold it in check?

"Don't listen to him," I said. "Take another step, Sergio."

"Too weak," Sergio said as he gained control once more and his body slumped down. "I can't do it. You came here to help, Christopher. Finish this."

I rushed forward, trying to push the demon into the circle. Even though it wasn't in control, it still wouldn't move.

"I don't have time to work up something to make it move."

"You've got everything you need in your coat pocket," he said. "I can see the bulge from here."

I looked down at my pocket, then I reached inside it and wrapped my hand around my pistol. When I pulled it out, Helena gasped.

"No, there's got to be another way!"

"There isn't. Helena, please," her father said, "I can't hold this thing much longer. I'm so tired. Know that I love you, and I'm sorry I was so weak. I just missed your mother so much."

The thing inside him took control and cursed at me in a language I couldn't identify let alone understand. At the same time that it had greater control of his mouth, it also seemed to be gaining more control over his body. His arms and torso twitched, and it took one shuffling step away from the edge of the circle. It had to be now.

"Sergio," I said as I lifted the pistol and aimed it at his face. He turned to look at me and he nodded, telling me to do what I had to.

"No!" Helena screamed and ran at me.

I pulled the trigger.

The blast filled the room and made my head ring. I staggered backward from the recoil, but I didn't fall down.

The bullet caught him in the forehead and threw his head back.

His whole body arched backward, falling into the circle. Helena buried her face in her hands. The body stopped just before it toppled over backward. Slowly it stood straight once more. His eyes opened and he smiled at me as blood trickled from the pencil-sized hole in his head. Helena took her hands from her eyes and saw this and she edged closer to me.

"This isn't over, Dark," the thing said to me. "Not by a long shot. I have all the time in the world to find a way back to this world and fuck you good. Hell, I have more than that. And I'll spend every moment it takes to get back planning what to do to you. You bought yourself four deaths and still have three coming. When you cash in your last chip, I'll be there, you waste of spunk."

It paused and smiled more broadly.

"And I know I'm not the only denizen of Hell who's gunning for you. Gader'el asked me to give you his regards. Enjoy what little time you have left."

And the body crumpled to the floor, falling into the circle. The stench in the room intensified and the body convulsed once. There was the sound of cracking bones, and then it lay still.

My legs decided supporting me was no longer a good idea and I fell to the floor. I lay there for a minute, trying to catalog the various injuries that thing had inflicted on me. I really should have been getting up and heading to a doctor, but it felt good down there on the floor. There was a period of blackness, then I heard Helena approach. She knelt down beside me and hissed through her teeth.

"You look like hell, Christopher." Her voice wavered, her throat raw from sobbing.

"We need to get you out of here," she said, and she started to tug me to my feet. I tried my best to help her, but I'm afraid she did most of the heavy lifting. The best I could offer was to not fight her every time pain surged through my shoulder. Once I was on my feet, she steered me out of the room and down the hall. I hoped that none of the neighbors had heard the gunshot and that they weren't peeking at us through their blinds. I didn't have it in me to be sneaky, and I certainly couldn't muster the strength to fog their memories. If anyone saw us limping out of the house, they'd be able to give an excellent description to the police.

More blackness. When I became aware again, Helena dragged me to the car and got me inside. It was then that I noticed I was no longer holding my revolver. "We have to go back for my gun," I said.

"Jesus," she said. "You gave it to me back in the house and said I had to throw it in the river. You don't remember?"

I didn't.

"You went on for a while about how sorry it made you to get rid of it. It was a gift from someone named Liza."

"I said all of that?"

"Yeah, and more, but I couldn't understand everything."

"I think I'm going into shock here, Helena."

She didn't answer, just swung my legs into the car and then ran around to the driver's side. She fired up the car and swung out into the street.

"We need to get you to a hospital," she said.

"No hospital," I said as loud as I could. "They'll report my injuries to the police." I gave her the address of a doctor I know that sees patients after hours and who doesn't ask questions.

"What was that thing saying about you having four deaths?" she asked.

I knew exactly what she was talking about, but there was no way I was gonna talk about it just then. "It was gibberish," I said. "Half the shit those things say is designed to confuse you." Answering her questions left me exhausted.

"Don't be freaked out," I told her, "but I'm going to close my eyes for a while."

She said something back to me. It sounded like a protest, but I didn't catch it all. My vision was already tunneling down into blackness and I gladly followed it.

I came to in a bed with clean, white gauze wrapped around my shoulder, bandages on my face. A thin blanket covered me and I pulled it up under my chin. I shivered from the cold. Helena sat next to me on a folding chair. She bent at the waist and rested her upper body and arms on the bed. I think she was asleep.

I looked around the room. It was small with dark wood paneling. Posters advertising Budweiser and the Portland Trail Blazers adorned the walls. A small TV was bolted to the wall. I smelled stale beer. This was someone's den. I realized then that the bed I was on was a hide-a-bed. The bar lay right in the small of my back and was making my legs numb. I tried to shift my weight to get more comfortable and grunted as pain shot through my shoulder.

Helena sat up and frowned at me.

"The doctor said you have to lay still or you'll tear your stitches."

"Did he say anything about losing the use of my legs because of this fucking bed?"

"He said you'd complain and to not be a baby." She frowned at me but she stood and bent over me. Together we were able to find a new position on the bed. My butt and legs started to tingle as blood began to circulate again.

"How long have I been out?"

"More than a day," she said. "The doctor said that none of your wounds were too serious, but you lost a lot of blood. He won't tell me his name."

Thank God for that, I thought. "You stayed here the whole time I was out?" She was still wearing the same clothes.

"I left to get rid of..." she trailed off and gave me a look. I let her know I got what she meant. "Other than that, yeah, I've been here."

"You're a good kid," I said.

"When are you going to teach me magic, Christopher?"

"What? I thought that was just because of—you know, your dad."

"I still want to learn."

I could think of a million reasons not to teach her anything, but if she was determined, she'd just go find someone else to teach her. And I was no saint, but there were a lot of people in the magic world who were a whole lot worse than me.

"I need to get better," I said. "To heal."

"I can wait," she said, and she smiled again. "For a while."

"And if you ever lie to me, or go against one of my orders…"

She nodded. I couldn't be all that angry at her, despite the thrashing I'd just been handed. She was trying to save her dad.

"I've never had an apprentice," I told her. "We'll see if I can keep from fucking it up too bad."

"As long as you're not teaching me manners, I think we'll be fine." She smiled sardonically at me and she looked so much like her father then. Her father who had been such a prude and who had disliked magic. And who had normally hated foul language.

I chuckled, but the pain in my shoulder brought that to an abrupt end.

"What's so funny?"

"Listen," I said, "we won't start your training for a while yet, but let me tell you something." She sat up straight, so eager, and I had a moment of doubt. She had no idea what a life in magic would mean—the heartbreak, the terrors, but the joys, too. I had been even younger than her when I started my journey and no matter how bad things got, I'd never regretted what I'd done.

"This is something your dad told me about magic," I said. "Magic's ultimate secret."

And there, in that cramped little nondescript room, wrapped in bandages, I began her formal education.

Adam Gallardo is the author of two novels, *Zomburbia* and *Zombified*, and a handful of comic books: *Star Wars*, *100 Girls*, *Gear School*, and others. He is a bookseller who lives with his family in Oregon.

THE MIDNIGHT FEAST
By Haralambi Markov

IT WAS A TIME FOR hauntings, close to midnight in early November. A time the House on the Hill anticipated. Its body crowded massive on the land and from afar resembled the dried carapace of a giant beast. On its side, like a gash through its belly, kitchen windows bled light and conversation disturbed its characteristic sullenness. They had named it the House on the Hill even though it was hardly a house but a mansion—now a B&B—and sat not on a hill but in the dense forests of Maine.

It had been meant as a home once, but had lost all its hospitality. They might have repainted, rebuilt, and refurbished, but there was little to do to remove ill will from its foundations. Gabriel loved the house exactly for its refusal to be loved. He had fallen in love with the oppression in the walls, and how willingly it conspired to terrify its guests—each one of them in search of a fright and eager to pay Gabriel and his husband a handsome booking fee to stay in a "haunted house".

Tonight would begin their most important booking to date. One assignment would determine the trajectory of their business. He found something thrilling in the dramatic stakes, so he channeled his giddiness into meal prep. The following two days would be nothing but sandwiches, energy drinks, and protein bars, while they entertained the rich, old woman who'd booked the entire B&B for a bespoke haunting.

Bernadette. That's all he knew about her. The sound of a name.

He slathered slices of bread with homemade tuna spread, tiled slices of pickles on top, and assembled each sandwich with a satisfying smack. Gianna sat to his left on the kitchen table and ladled the last of the *olla de carne* he'd made for dinner into Tupperware bowls. The after-warmth of gas cooktops undercut the chill inside.

"Seconds?" Bryan asked as he brought his plate across the table in one of his massive palms.

"It's thirds, man. Haven't you eaten enough?" Gianna said, ignoring his plate altogether.

"Come on, G. I'm starved. I've earned my thirds!"

"Questionable," she shot back, but relented and poured him a ladlefull.

Bryan grinned and set out to devour the stew. The way the boy ate reminded Gabriel of a starved dog—in greedy bites that distended his throat in order to accommodate so much food at once. He ate with his entire body, back hunched over and jaw working furiously. He wrestled with the spoon and made the round muscles of his arms jump. They strained against the white fabric of his uniforms' shirt, drawing the eye instantly to his forearms. Those great big arms reminded Gabriel of a particular boyfriend from his rebellious days. The memories made him blush. It was the intended effect. Hire young, beautiful people as servants, and complement the terror of Thanatos with the desire of Eros. Disarm with flirtation, then scare half to death. It never failed, though this haunting didn't call for seduction.

Once Bryan scraped the last drop of soup clean, he heaved demonstratively and pulled out his Juul. Sugar tufts of smoke pistoned out of his nostrils and ruffled around his neck like a collar.

"And stop smoking that piece of shit. The smoke is nauseating," Gianna admonished as she proceeded to close the containers.

"Yeah, yeah."

"One more puff and you'll have that thing far up your ass."

Bryan puffed out another cloud of smoke. "I hear butt stuff feels really good. Right, Mr. Corsaro?"

Gabriel snorted in surprise, and let out a belly laugh at Gianna frozen in place. Her complexion turned a bright red, which only intensified the shine of her bleached buzz cut.

"My sex life is for the bedroom, Bryan, and stop calling me Mr. Corsaro, when it's just us. I am yet to become my father." It was his husband's rule to deepen the clients' immersion. *Always be in character. Our guests pay a lot to be scared. Address us by last name even if there is no one to hear.*

"You might not be your father, Gabe, but you're my dad now," Bryan said and tapped his chest with a closed fist.

"Very funny, Bri. You're grounded, young man." Gabriel earned a few chuckles and then he checked his watch just in case—a little before eleven pm. Good, though Kalle should be here already. "Is Kalle still in HQ?"

"Yeah, testing the video and sound equipment. Do I go tell him to come?" Bryan offered.

"No need." They still had time. Kalle had a one-track mind and try as he might to make him slow down, the closest Gabriel had come to get him to take care of himself was to force feed him on the go like a temperamental child.

"All right."

They resumed their work. Gabriel packed provisions in a basket, while Brian busied himself with his black bowtie. Gianna turned her attention to a wig stand to her left. Nimble fingers ruffled the black bangs and combed through the strands of human hair with care. Once satisfied with the result, she removed the wig from its stand and eclipsed her golden head with it. The gesture lasted no more than a few seconds, but fully erased her face and redrew her features. The addition of long hair softened her expression and imbued her with a shallow layer of sweetness that told guests all they thought they knew about a person like her without looking into her eyes. She looked herself over in her phone camera. "How to become a racist stereotype of Asian women in one step," she said.

"I think you're forgetting step two—"

"Finish that sentence, and I'll skin you alive."

"Only if you wear me as a coat after."

"That gives me ideas about the attic. Garment bags with skin suits," Gabriel said in hopes to nip the conflict before it escalated. Confrontation sat ill with him, and he didn't want to start a job feeling like he couldn't find his calm in his stomach.

Mercifully, Kalle chose that moment to saunter into the kitchen with an unenthusiastic "Hello" and beelined straight to the moka pot, diffusing the tension.

"What do we think about good old Bernadette? Other than, you know, she has a death wish," Gianna asked.

"You know what I know. The client is a woman and she's travelling with a companion," Kalle answered, dry as ever, and prepared his coffee with great tenderness.

"Probably a recluse. Old money. Not really all there. Really messed up in the head," Bryan added, and he had a point. The level of detail in her request for a bespoke haunting had raised eyebrows, and Gabriel was curious to meet the woman, who had specified her arrival time as simply "midnight". The only reason they knew her first name at all was because she'd submitted a line-by-line script for the ghost call she'd requested in her room. "But she pays well. I've bought a new washing machine and stove for my momma for Thanksgiving with the advance."

"The money is really good…" Gianna joined in, hands busy rubbing off her black nail polish. *Almost too good*, Gabriel read on her face. "My parents had a meltdown when I showed them the tickets to Korea. We're spending Thanksgiving with some uncles and aunts they haven't seen since they were kids."

If the advance was generous, the pay upon completion was astronomical. Sufficient enough to close the B&B until January and take off with Kalle to Costa Rica, where they'd spend the whole of December with relatives in Heredia. Once back, Mr. Pavich—their benefactor—would sign over the House on the Hill in their name and they'd run it as they wanted. No more bespoke requests from oddball ultra-rich clients Mr. Pavich dragged their way every so often.

Gabriel appreciated the technical challenge. It kept his imagination alive to reimagine the house's soundscape and invoke new horrors. But he was past the point where he needed to prove himself. He preferred the natural stream of guests as it ebbed and flowed.

"All we have to do is live through this and we'll collect the rest of the payment," Kalle said. He sat himself next to Gabriel, a steaming mug of coffee in his hand. They kissed and Gabriel tasted the hints of bitter mint.

"Kal, you're kissing me with snus in your mouth again."

"Right. Sorry," Kalle reached his spider-leg fingers into his mouth, and dislodged the worn out packet of tobacco from the inside of his cheek, then wrapped it carefully in a paper napkin.

"Boss, that's gross." Bryan made a face. Kalle glanced at the Juul in Brian's hand, and looked back at the boy to make his point.

"You all look in order. Where's Jodie?"

"Somewhere on the upper floor. She told me she wanted to practice walking in her dress some more, but she's ready. The prosthetics on her face turned out great."

"Then it seems we're as ready as we'll ever be."

Then they went over the brief one final time. As far as bespoke hauntings went, this one required meticulous timing. The woman would stay a total of two nights, counting her arrival, and remain entirely in the house. The brief mentioned nothing about dietary requests, which further increased speculation about the client. The ultra-rich always indulged in weird foods. *It's like they use eccentricity to separate themselves from those who can't afford it*, Gianna had once said.

Gabriel knew food and he doubted any of the bizarre stuff he'd seen guests eat tasted good, or that they enjoyed them whatsoever. To Gabriel it all felt like character work. A performance of wealth.

The client was to be woken up by heavy knocks and loud breathing shortly after falling asleep, then have the ghost—"Arlene"—call her room and threaten her. The script had a rigid frame, and only a few spots where Jodie could improvise. Hang up, cue the smoke machines and have Arlene enter the bedroom. Easy enough to do as most rooms were connected to each other through sliding panels in the wardrobes. At this stage, it was vital for Arlene to lift her veil and show her face to the client. The dialogue didn't matter as much as the act of unveiling.

Another oddity of the brief—the client hadn't specified any details during daytime. Here they allowed themselves improvisation, and instructed Jodie to follow the client during the day, and finish off with a poltergeist scene in the salon. They had strict instructions only after sunset. Arlene would chase the client to the basement near midnight and the haunting would culminate in a feast. Eight chairs around a table set with candles, three seats reserved for the client, her companion, and Arlene, and six for the lifelike corpses. As the centerpiece on the table—an unborn fetus served in a large baking dish.

"We're absolutely sure we'll hit every single point as written?" Kalle asked for the third time.

"It'll all work out. We've done this before." Gabriel soothed his husband and stood to massage his shoulders. That was the others' cue leave with the provisions to HQ. In the newfound silence, the house engaged in its nightly chorus of creaks and groans, settling for tonight's work. Once the knots in Kalle's shoulders gave in, Gabriel rested his chin on his husband's fine brown hair.

"You're winding yourself up," he said.

"I'm fine, I promise," Kalle replied, and gulped down the rest of his coffee.

"That's what you always say, and then you're half-dead the next day from exhaustion."

"It's our heads on the line, Gabe."

"All the more reason to save your strength. We've done enough. You've done more than enough. Rest and let things follow their course. I'm invoking the agreement."

He felt Kalle smile. They'd jokingly made the agreement early on in their relationship some thirteen years ago, and it had stuck. It was obvious right from the start Kalle needed someone to hit the breaks for him lest he burn out, and Gabriel felt the metaphorical flames now.

"If my love insists."

"I insist."

"Then I don't have a choice, do I?" Kalle joked and clasped his hand over Gabriel's giving it a soft squeeze. He stayed in the kitchen, while Gabriel prepared lime and mint tea for himself. It was a habit he'd picked up from his aunt Marcela, who'd brew mint tea before any important moment in life, and he enjoyed the little ritual ever since he was a boy.

Both stayed still and quiet, each lost in their thoughts, and didn't hear the heavy rustle of fabric approach from down the hallway, until a veiled woman dressed in dirty white materialized at the threshold, startling the pair for a second. She moved at a halting pace and gesticulated with gloved hands. She stopped in the middle of the room and cheerfully asked, "Are you scared?"

"Terrified," Gabriel answered and sipped on his tea.

"How are you getting on in your costume, Jodie?" Kalle asked.

"This dress is... something. The skirt catches on my shoes all the time, but I've gotten the hang of it more or less. Do I really have to wear the veil at all times?" Jodie staggered to the table, and flipped over the off-color tulle. Beneath the thick fabric stared out a grisly face. Torn lips, exposed muscle, sunken eyes and rot all over.

"The prosthetics look like the real thing. Gianna has really outdone herself. How do they feel on your face?" Gabriel asked as he leaned over to inspect the elimorph plastic teeth.

"They're really comfortable. I can move my mouth without any pull at the corners, so talking's not going to be difficult."

"You only have to wear them for the unveiling tonight, and then you can take them off. Gianna can re-apply them tomorrow for the feast," Kalle said, returning his mug to the sink and stretching in the process.

"Good, cause I don't know how long I can wear them even in this chill before they start peeling. Man, is it just me or is it colder than usual? I can feel the cold even through my thermal underwear."

"Well, the forecast said we're bound for a drop in temperature," Gabriel answered and checked his watch. Right, the moment of truth was almost upon them. "But I can promise you a hot cocoa later."

"You are the best, work dad!" Jodie smiled. With the yellowed prosthetic teeth in her mouth, it came off as disgusting rather than endearing.

"Stop coddling the employees, Gabe."

"It's called incentivizing, and we ought to get in positions." Gabriel finished the last of his tea. The warmth of the mug lingered on his hands, and he felt a wave of calm roll down his entire body once he stood up. He smiled in anticipation of closing a chapter in their life in Maine.

Ten to midnight, the staff—all in uniform—gathered in the foyer to greet the client. Bryan and Gianna in all black with the exception of Gianna's white apron. Kalle and Gabriel in wool suits; hair and beards sculpted to perfection.

Kalle kept his eyes glued on the grandfather clock and said, "Your phones better be in HQ. Only walkie-talkies from now on and use them sparingly."

"Do we still have to go through this? You know by now we're professional," Gianna retorted.

"Protocol is protocol," Kalle and Bryan recited in unison, the young man more to tease Gianna than any affection for the rules.

Gabriel watched the glazed doors leading into the foyer and focused his ear on the night winds outside. The conversation around him dimmed as if he'd turned down the volume on a radio and the sound of winds colliding with the house grew clear. He straightened his back, squared his shoulders and willed himself against the cold though he swore this year felt worse. Wherever he turned, he either entered a cold spot or stepped in front of a draft, which stabbed through his layers of wool and thermal undergarments.

As proprietors of the House on the Hill, the husbands functioned as extensions of the fantasy, unmoored in time by their formal clothing and attempts at a trans-Atlantic accent that came off as hammy, but guests adored nonetheless.

"They're here," Gabriel announced. He could hear tires on the gravel road for some time, and now the car pulled up outside, and the the engine's purr reverberated through the glass panels.

"Show time," Kalle said and assumed his position right next to his husband. The brief said not to head out and greet the client, but rather stay inside. So they did.

The inner doors swung open and the oddest pair entered. Bernadette was an old woman. Late in her seventies. Bird-like in stature and mannerisms. She kept her white hair chopped short and slicked back, and it glowed radiant against her thick, green suit that wrapped around her like armor. Life had evaporated from her like steam, leaving little padding between skin and bone. Watery eyes, robbed of their color, if they'd had any to begin with, landed straight onto Gabriel.

Instead of looking around in awe like every other guest who entered the Second Empire Victorian monstrosity, her gaze pierced him with the ease of a pin pushed through a butterfly's thorax. Even celebrities stopped in their tracks, awed by its grandeur. It was the house they met and greeted first. The staff waited to be uncovered like the ghost's guests paid to scare themselves with. But *she* looked at him.

Behind her followed her companion: a bald, muscular woman dressed in the non-descript black suit bodyguards wore. She had large sunglasses pushed back on her nose and her skin was marked red with acne. Something in the way she held her jaw clamped instilled absolute terror.

"Welcome to the House on the Hill. The most haunted B&B in America!" Kalle welcomed the duo with his usual pep, which always reminded Gabriel of a circus ringmaster. For a brief moment, his melodious voice gained momentum and burst forth.

"I am your host, Kalle Hård. This is my partner, Gabriel Corsaro, and behind me are our service members—Gianna and Bryan—available to you at your leisure." At each introduction they bowed their head and offered a 'Hello'. They'd done this so many times, Gabriel did not hear his cue as much as felt it come. "On behalf of us all, I wish you a frightful stay and hope you find our efforts to your satisfaction."

The old woman slowly regarded each face, and spoke in a voice laced with opium. Word followed word in textured calm as clouds on a windless sky. "Pleasure to make your acquaintance. I am Bernadette Clemens; I do apologize for the inconvenience of my late check-in. Hopefully, you understand that some things have to happen precisely as they are meant to. Is this the entire crew on the premises?"

"Yes, with the exception of the ghost, of course."

"Of course." The old woman's arched the edges of her mouth upward just shy of a smile.

"We always begin bespoke hauntings with a disclosure," Kalle continued. "Given your specific requests, we have installed cameras in your bedroom. The cameras are for logistical purposes only; I want to assure you no footage will be recorded, unless otherwise requested."

"Mr. Pavich instructed me regarding your practices. Do what you must do for my experience."

"Excellent!" Kalle exclaimed. "Shall we take your luggage to your rooms then." He signaled to Bryan and they relieved the bodyguard of the suitcases she'd walked in with. "I've had the Rose Red Room prepared for you, and your companion will stay in the Yellow Room just across."

The stairs groaned under their weight as the four climbed up the staircase and Gabriel waited for the tell-tale cutoff when they stepped on the carpet to exhale.

Just then Gianna squeezed his arm with both hands, "Holy shit! Bernadette Clemens is in our house!" Her voice was barely below a full-on yell and Gabriel had to shush her before turning on his walkie-talkie.

"Jodie, the guests have arrived. Look alive. Over," he said into the mic and signed Gianna to start walking. They moved toward the conservatory at the back of the house.

Automatic lights clicked on and illuminated demure pastels and polished hardwood. They kept the ground floor uncarpeted so they'd have a better environment to create sounds late in the night and deliver them to the rooms above through concealed vents. It had become Gabriel's favorite feature, because if he stopped still long enough he'd hear the whole house breathe.

"Jodie?" he called again when he received no answer. "Do you copy? Over!"

"Sorry, it's hard working this thing with gloves on. Yes, I'm in position."

"Good, Kalle and Bryan should be down shortly. We'll call you when it's time. Over."

"Got it. Over."

"So now… who's Bernadette Clemens?" Gabriel asked Gianna.

"An absolute legend in modern art. She was huge in the seventies and eighties, then one day vanished. Not just from the art world. She packed her bags and left overnight. They found a single note in her home—'It's been a ball, but I'll be leaving now. XO.' Nobody knew where she'd gone or what she looks like today. Many think she's dead."

They turned left by the kitchen and down a hallway overcrowded with massive portraits. Each face more severe and sour than the last. The spectator had to endure a barrage of condemnation to reach their destination, which distracted them from one particular section of the wall shaped like a door. Nor could they see the lever on the inside of the picture frame Gabriel pulled to open the door to HQ.

"She's dressed really well for a dead woman," Gabriel said. "Is she worth a lot?"

"Millions! A lot, considering she draws torture porn."

"Torture porn? You're messing with me." The woman he'd met was the last person he'd ever consider drawing graphic torture, and how did her work cost millions?

HQ, their workshop, had been the indoor swimming pool. A later edition to the house that was ostentatious with its high ceiling and arches. Blue tiles reflected an eerie aquamarine from the monitors before he flipped the lights on. The first thing a person saw upon entering was the ten-foot tall mosaic of a Gorgon head, taking over the entire back wall. They'd built over the pool to increase floor space, and three rows of workstations with tools, molds, and stands ran the full length of the room.

"No, it's true, let me show you." Giana booted up her laptop by a pile of distressed clothing and googled furiously, showing him a stream of paintings and sketches of gruesome torture and body horror. Some he'd seen in passing in horror movies he'd done Foley work for. Her work lent itself to horror production design well. The one image she clicked on showed an oil painting—red on black—of a flayed woman, crawling out of another, identical one. A form of birth. But with the mother quartered and pulled until her body resembled a hoop where only strings of flesh and skin connected the rest together.

"That's supposed to be a self-portrait? I can't imagine hanging this at home or paying millions for the nightmares." Gabriel had a high tolerance for gore, and he found something special in that aspect of horror, but he lacked the backbone to see this every single day.

"She's a bit too much for me, too."

"How do you even know about her?"

"I used to date a guy who wouldn't fucking stop talking about her." Gianna closed her laptop and started distressing a pair of pants. "He also made me watch a tedious documentary: 'Finding Bernadette Clemens—the Mother of Torment'. What I'm saying is, she's going to be a tough customer."

Gabriel thought about that. What could scare a person who sees this in their mind's eye and what motivated her to book this stay? Was it inspiration or self-flagellation?

Shortly after one thirty, the monitors showed Madam Clemens—as they'd come to call her—asleep. Bryan and Kalle manned the control panel and monitor while Gabriel and Gianna sat by the mic stand set up below the highest point in the ceiling. Gabriel preferred how the acoustics here imbued sounds with a faraway, otherworldly texture.

There were inherent risks to subjecting a person as old as her to intense stress, so they aimed for a balance between the desired effect and not giving the client a heart attack.

Kalle flipped on the mic connected to wireless speakers hidden atop the wardrobe in Clemens's room and gestured—*begin*. Gabriel picked a thick piece of lacquered wood and rasped twice with his knuckles. Then gradually he increased the number of knocks and their intensity until he punched the wood in earnest. He stopped once his knuckles bruised red.

On the monitor, Madam Clemens startled awake, but otherwise didn't move. At Kalle's signal, Gianna leaned over and breathed into the mic. Deep rasping inhales and exhales. These were the heaving breaths of a person struggling to breathe. Of life migrating from the lungs. She finished with a sharp gasp, then Kalle cut off the mic.

"Right. So far so good. Time for the phone call," Kalle said.

"Jodie? Are you by the telephone?" Bryan asked on his walkie-talkie.

"Yes…" The single syllable slithered out of the receiver. "I am ready for my heart-to-heart," Jodie said and her voice ran instant chills down Gabriel's spine. He wouldn't recognize her without knowing beforehand it was her.

"That's so good, Jodie! The old broad is going to piss herself." To which Kalle slapped on the table and scolded, "Hey, hey! Language!"

"Thank you," Jodie simply said, and that was that.

Although the House on the Hill had no connection to the outside, Kalle had insisted on a private telephone system for all rooms and the investment had been worth it. Jodie dialed Clemens's room, while Bryan brought up the wiretap feed from the receiver. During the late-night hours, the phone's ringing bordered on hysteria. Gabriel mellowed at the sound as it had taken him a long time to find a vintage phone model with the right quality of ring. He couldn't stop his smile at seeing his effort pay off. Anyone would be distressed by its tone. It took four rings for Madam Clemens to answer.

"Hello?" She sounded collected. Disoriented, but not like someone who was scared witless.

"Bernadette… It has been a long, long time since we last occupied the same space."

"Many years, yes," Madam Clemens agreed.

"Fifty years to the day I died. That's half a century. Do you hear it? Half. A. Century. Exhausts me to even say it. This density of time separates us and it's not right. Twins should not be apart."

"Isn't this why I've returned? You want to reunite; I'm here to fulfill your will."

"During all the years you've stolen from me, you failed to outgrow that nasty habit of yours to spin everything. Your visit is *not* voluntary."

"It doesn't matter in the end. But I would volunteer if I had a choice. Would you?"

"No, but I never had one either. I didn't choose to die so you'd live a delicious life. I'm here to remind you that you can't pay for anything with what you don't own."

"You've taken half my life already. That should be enough."

"I decide what's enough. There's no mercy for you! Not while you live. Not after. I'm going to get you, Bernadette!"

The abrupt silence startled the four of them in HQ. They hadn't caught the click as Jodie hung up. Gabriel's pulse throbbed at his Adam's apple and a thin layer of sweat slicked his palms. On paper, the script sounded childish and pedestrian, but to hear it... Gabriel shuddered at its rawness. The two voices—echoes of each other—captivated. Allowed for nothing other than to listen.

"I'm in position," Jodie rasped on the walkie-talkie, sending another jolt of surprise through the room. The fuzz of the static shook off any lingering trance from the call, and they remembered they had a job to do. Bryan turned on the two smoke machines.

"We've turned on the smoke machines." Kalle cleared his throat. "You were spectacular back there. That's exactly the performance we need tonight. Keep it up."

"I didn't rise from the dead to be meek."

"Yes, stay in character. We're waiting for visual confirmation on the smoke."

"That woman has nerves of steel. I'd be pissing myself in bed," Gianna said, and gulped loudly. Her eyes had grown large and she dared not blink.

"The proof is in the sheets." Kalle laughed at his joke, but his laugh warbled and shook. No one else joined in.

On the monitors, thick smoke rolled from under the bed and wardrobe, close to the floor. The two waves met in the middle and fused upward into a wall. Madam Clemens rose from bed and walked to where the smoke rose in front of the wardrobe. Kalle switched the camera from the one overlooking the bed to the one pointed at the wardrobe.

"That's your cue, Jodie," Kalle said into his walkie-talkie, and instructed Bryan, "Cut the smoke."

There was no response. Instead the door to the wardrobe opened just a fraction and Jodie's hand grabbed hold of the edge controlling, the speed at which she revealed herself. She commanded time itself, and her manifestation into the room generated quiet dread. They'd opted not to install a mic in the room. *We don't want to invade her privacy any more than necessary*, Kalle had insisted and now the scene played out in a vacuum empty of sound.

"What are they doing?" Gianna asked. The two women just stood there face to face. "Are they talking? I can't see anything."

"Bryan, kill the smoke." Kalle repeated, now impatient.

"I did," Bryan said. "I don't know what's happening. The machines are supposed to be off," he explained and pointed at his screen.

"Well, they're not! Shit!" Kalle swore and hit the keys several times with the same result. Smoke continued to billow out and fill the room. "To hell and all!"

Gianna jumped off her chair and paced back and forth. "Reboot the system?" she suggested.

Eyes trained on the feed, Gabriel said, "Look." The moment of the unveiling arrived, though little could be seen. The only way he could tell Jodie flipped over her veil was by the rush of smoke the movement created. Her face wasn't visible but Madam Clemens's reaction was. Her whole body quaked and her shoulders rocked as if she were sobbing. Right then she flung her body at the door of her room, but it didn't open.

"This is a fucking disaster! Go open the door! Now!" Kalle ordered Bryan and Gianna, who ran out of HQ almost knocking over a prop rack.

The smoke grew so thick it covered the entire screen in white, and Gabriel lost himself in it. Faint lines undulated on the screen, suggesting movement and contours of a face watching back, though he wasn't sure what he saw. A part of him wished that it was a face, that the house had lost its shyness and revealed its spirits in earnest, rather than hide them in its walls. All he knew was that he became so light.

"Gabriel!" Kalle's yell snapped him to his body. "Move it! Cut the power in Clemens's room."

Gabriel apologized and ran to the breakers, while Kalle rebooted the system. The adrenaline from the incident blurred what happened next, but he knew it had taken hours before he fell asleep. No one could figure out why both smoke machines malfunctioned, nor why the door was locked one minute and wasn't when Bryan and Gianna arrived. They aired the room and helped Madam Clemens into bed with the help of her ever mute bodyguard, who seated herself by her employer's bed for the remainder of the night.

Jodie had excused herself so as to not traumatize Madam Clemens any further, and it was decided Gabriel would speak to her in the morning. He had no idea what to say to the woman after all this, but he closed his eyes now in his own bed and emptied his mind. Tonight he'd let himself feel the tension from the haunting. Tomorrow he'd assess the damage.

Halfway awake the next morning, Gabriel headed out to smooth things with Madam Clemens over a cup of tea. He found her in the conservatory. She stood erect and unmoving, blending with the greenery if not for her long-sleeved, red dress, then for the stillness in her being. She faced the sun, weak in the sky, and in profile her body appeared rail thin. She was a paper doll—fold her one more time and she'd disappear like she was never really there to begin with. Ready to leave no trace behind like the condensation on the glass panes. She was not alone as her bodyguard hung in the back, her bald head red and glistening with sweat.

"Oh, I'm sorry. I only brought one cup of tea. It's a personal blend. Thought you'd need to calm your nerves from the commotion last night. I can go make another?" he offered as he extended the tray to her.

"No. Lydia… has a specific regimen when at work, but I'll gladly accept." She pinned him with her gaze again as she spoke. Deep circles sagged under her eyes, but her voice was awake.

The cup traded hands and she silently drank. Her movements flowed in smooth lines and all sound disappeared around her. Gabriel loved the texture of silence and its depth, but hers was something else. Like the thin air on top of a mountain. He couldn't hear her swallow, nor did she make a noise as the scalding liquid touched her lips. He could not even hear her breathe and he strained his ear to the point he heard not only his own heartbeat, but Lydia's even breathing.

She turned sideways again with the same fluid grace and continued to pull all sounds to her until they disappeared. Where? Gabriel didn't know. His hand held the empty tray until he remembered why he was there in the first place. Between him and Kalle, Gabriel was regarded as inviting. Early on, they had realized how people saw them and what they expected. Pale and wiry, Kalle had that Scandinavian air of reservation and people mistook his demeanor as impenetrable authority. Gabriel, though, became the guests' confidante. They trusted his smile lines and sought his low, warm voice as he relayed stories and crafted narratives of ghosts and grisly murders. Kalle set the boundaries and Gabriel clued them in. If someone were to restore faith in them after last night's fiasco, it would be him. He took a deep breath and launched into it. No attempt at an official apology. It had to be from the heart, if it were to work.

"I want to apologize on behalf of everyone, Madam Clemens. Last night did not go according to plan and I can't offer a good excuse. We take our work very seriously—"

"There's no need to placate me," she cut him off. "I'm aware of the risks associated with what I paid for, Mr. Corsaro."

"Of course, Madam Clemens."

"You—" and there was no doubt that she meant only him—"may call me Bernadette."

"Then, I'm Gabriel."

She smiled, the first smile he'd seen from her, and looked out the window again. This was going better than expected, but he had to be absolutely sure she was satisfied.

"I don't usually do this, but we've prepared a scene in the parlor today. Should we scrap it and leave only the program for tonight?"

"It seems you've had difficult guests in the past."

Gabriel smiled apologetically, but withheld any opinion regarding their rich guests. Any remark—even the most harmless—had a way of trickling back to the wrong ears.

"I won't be difficult. In all honesty, I had to see the house one more time. I enjoy what you've done with it. I nearly missed where you've hidden the entrance to the pool. I wish I could see it, but I imagine you're using it for something else."

Gabriel nodded, dumbfounded at what he heard.

"You've been here before," he repeated, not so much to ask, but to confirm what she told him.

"The house belonged to my family for sixty years before we sold it. I grew up here, relatively speaking. Mostly summers and a few holidays."

"I'm so sorry to hear this. It must have been heartbreaking to lose your home."

"Hardly. This house stopped being a home when Arlene died. You don't know this, but you've put me in her old room."

Gabriel bit his tongue to stop himself from swearing. Arlene was a real person and this woman paid to be tormented by her own twin. Who did that?

"We always fought, her and I," she continued. "Neither of us believed we'd have a full life with the other as a living shadow. Imagine it. Two people, one face, half a life. We did a lot of cruel things to each other and I'm ashamed at how I behaved during my youth. She died young and she's never forgiven me."

"I'm sure she did."

"Sisters know. She's just as relentless as I am, and she doesn't forgive. The past has stayed with me for a long time. It's only right to face my ugliness. Confront her and myself."

"I'd never be able to do something like that. I'm sorry you feel you need to do this in order to let go of the past."

"You're a kind man. Perhaps I'm not able to do this either. The past has decided to not let go." She smiled genuinely and clasped her free hand over his. He was surprised at how cool her skin felt. "Some things once set in motion are inevitable. They must come to pass. I regret a lot in my life, what happened to her most of all."

"Thank you, dear Bernadette. The sentiment warms my heart, but you've withheld crucial information."

Jodie startled the pair with her interjection. In the commotion to spot where she was, Gabriel knocked the cup out of Bernadette's hands and it shattered. Scalding liquid splashed on the skirt and opened wet wounds of crimson on the fabric.

"Care to give Mr. Corsaro the full story?"

Jodie, veil in place, stood next to Lydia—who'd not moved even an iota—framed by the croton shrubs that bent at the ceiling. Her fingers massaged a meaty leaf.

"Jesus Christ, Jo—" he caught himself in time, and apologized profusely as he picked up the pieces. How had he not heard her come in? "Tisk, tisk. You ought to be more careful, Mr. Corsaro."

"I'm so sorry," he stammered, uncertain whether he was apologizing to Bernadette or the ghost, then realized how absurd this whole situation was. He'd let his sleep-deprived brain trick him and even now he refused to look sideways at Jodie. "I ruined your dress."

"The dress is inconsequential."

Gabriel observed Madam Clemens for a reaction. She had been startled. He saw her tremble for a second, then compose herself. For someone who wished to be scared, Bernadette denied herself the release fear offered. He'd heard it last night on the phone, her bracing herself. Now she coiled her muscles. So as to not let slip her real reaction.

"Right... I still need to clean this up." Bernadette nodded and he felt dismissed.

Turning to exit, he saw Jodie's absence. Just like that, in the seconds it took to place the shattered cup on the tray, she'd slipped away. This stopped him in his tracks until his brain confirmed she wasn't hiding somewhere else. Jodie was really giving this part her all and channeled a darkness that raised the hairs on his arms. His heart beat hard again, and he barely concealed his grin as he exited.

"The good news is she says everything's fine and she's not mad about last night," Gabriel announced at entering HQ and went to pour himself a cup of coffee. There were only two people in the workshop—Gianna and Kalle—and they finished the final set pieces for the feast. Gianna labored over the foam fetus with a small brush, while Kalle—sitting across from her—painted blood around the inside of the severed head's mouth.

"Tell me the bad news," Kalle said as he dipped his brush in fake blood and applied it.

"There's always a catch with these people," Gianna added.

"I don't know if it's bad news per se, but it might mean we'll have to be a lot more careful from now on." Gabriel didn't know how to formulate what he'd learned.

"You're stalling, love."

Both looked at him expectantly as he walked to Kalle. "It's tough to sum up. Her script..." Gabriel pulled on his beard in thought. There was no right way to say this, so he shrugged. "It's real. She had a sister named Arlene and she died in this house." He went to explain everything to their amazement. Gianna had to sit down, and Kalle's mouth hung slack.

"You're joking me," Kalle said finally after Gabriel had finished.

"That's all sorts of fucked up," Gianna added. "Could she be lying?"

"I doubt it. She knew about the pool and how we've masked it."

Kalle stared at the Gorgon with a faraway expression. "The fact Mr. Pavich didn't disclose this means there's a reason to it. The question is why."

"It doesn't make much of a difference," Gabriel said. He shrugged, sipping on his coffee.

"But it does. Are we supposed to know or not? Did she expect us to know? It makes all the difference in how we're supposed to treat her. How did she tell you this?"

"I don't know. She was just sharing her life. Insisted I call her Bernadette. I think it's therapeutic for her."

"I'd stick to therapy," Gianna retorted and went back to work.

"What does this mean for today?" Kalle asked.

"She wants us to continue as planned. No cancellations. Jodie nearly gave me a heart attack, and she barely flinched. I say give her what she wants. She can handle it."

"Either that or she'll croak," Gianna concluded and conversation naturally died down.

Gabriel gathered his strength for later on a rickety swivel chair that squeaked any time he took as much as a deeper breath and closed his eyes. He rested. The warmth of the coffee mug against his palms. The tongue-laps of brushed on silicone in his ears. His thoughts circled round Bernadette and the fury of their wings chased any rest away.

He'd lied to Kalle when he said it didn't matter this was her house—her truth. It mattered, because until this point, they were the ones telling the story. They shaped the narrative and knew the conclusion. Now that power transferred to Bernadette. They were now props to arrange as she was the story.

At some point Gianna announced she was done with the fetus and needed a nap in her room. Now alone, Gabriel reheated some stew on the solitary hot plate in the corner and they had lunch.

"Did you manage to sleep at all?" Gabriel asked. "I didn't feel you come to bed."

"Couldn't go to bed. I still feel the adrenaline."

"Now that it's the two of us—" Gabriel smiled, waving a spoon.

"Three," Kalle corrected and pointed at the severed head, whose blond curls matted on its forehead. "Don't forget Thomas."

"I'm pretty sure Thomas can keep a secret."

"I don't know, but I can blackmail him into silence. He died in a bench-pressing accident. The guy lifted so much weight that when his elbow gave out the bar decapitated him."

Gabriel laughed and the blood rushed to his face. He loved the silly backgrounds Kalle always made for every creative and prop he made. The silliness brought him some much needed energy.

"Don't distract me. I'm asking a question here." Kalle raised his hands in defeat. "Were you scared?"

"Of course! Terrified! That's the most important client in our lives! We can't have her die."

"That's not what I mean. I'm talking about the haunting. Exactly when things went off script, didn't you get that moment where the rational part of your brain didn't click on and for a second you thought—'it's all real'?"

Kalle chuckled, "You are way too excited at the possibility of a real ghost!"

"Admit it! It was great! You thought it was real, too!"

Kalle only let an enigmatic smile cross his face and pulled on his husband's beard. "I'll certainly remember it for some time."

"Maybe it's the lack of sleep, but I dare say the rest of our lives, babe."

As a compromise for last night, Kalle and Gabriel agreed for the parlor scene to have a more informal feeling to it. No narrative structure. They'd just talk with Madam Clemens casually over a macaron and at some point, Bryan would fiddle with the lights and project Jodie onto the mirror for a brief conversation. They'd scrapped another in-person appearance as well as other possible effects. No need to overkill a B-scene.

That's how Kalle and Gabriel found themselves seated across from Madam Clemens in the parlor with a seven-tiered serving stand crowned with macarons placed as a barrier between them. The parlor was the culmination of several lengthy antique hunts, where they'd collected authentic and period-accurate ornaments and decorations, building this vast bric-a-brac ecosystem. By late afternoon, the sun had already set and under the chandelier's glow the tchotchkes swelled in size so the parlor resembled more of a matchbox than a room.

Bernadette occupied the settee and delicately nibbled on a macaron, while Lydia—ever present and ever silent—shadowed her one step behind. This was the only time Gabriel had seen Bernadette eat anything and she prolonged the process needlessly. Her teeth grazed a little at the end and she'd let the bit melt in her mouth before repeating.

The husbands exchanged nervous glances. Kalle inclined his head as if to say, *What in the hell is she doing?* and Gabriel gesticulated, *Why are you asking me?*

"Are you enjoying the macaron?" Gabriel braved to break the ice first, to which Bernadette let out a peck of a smile.

"It's delicious, thank you. I've not eaten sugar since I don't remember, so the taste is intense."

Kalle shook his head at his husband—definitely the wrong topic—and jumped in, "Gabriel tells me you're familiar with the house?"

"My great-great-grandfather built this house. I'm told he had a strong ambition to have a family with many children. He left personal notes on who'd live in the rooms in the original blueprints for the house. I think they should still be around somewhere."

"Really? Then you must know of any stories about the house."

"You mean ghost stories," she answered and took another minis-cule bite. "Not any real ones. Arlene and I used to scare each other with ghost stories, but they were all made up."

"Is this how you got into art?" Gabriel changed the subject away from the dead sister and shot Kalle a dirty look, *Why are you even going there?*

"You're familiar with my work?" Bernadette focused intently on both of them now.

"Yes," Kalle joined in for the double approach. Divide and con-quer with politeness was his motto. "Your paintings have been so influential in horror cinema. Frankly, you're iconic."

"I didn't know that," she said, her macaron pinched between thumb and forefinger. Not a dessert but an entomological specimen to be catalogued. The tinge of disappointment was palpable.

"How can you not?" Kalle prodded, even though Gabriel signed, *Abort! Abort!*

"Rights and sales are handled by others. I haven't been involved with such matters for decades. Tell me about you. How did you become involved with—" she waved the macaron around the parlor—"all of this?"

"The story isn't that interesting." Gabriel hadn't thought of his life any harder than he had to. He loved it, of course, and it had brought him fulfillment and peace, but he never regarded it as a story worth the time of an eccentric millionaire.

"But I think it is, Gabriel. I insist." All it took was one look from her to loosen his tongue.

"We met on the set of a cheap independent movie," he began.

He reached over to hold Kalle's hand, who added, "It was a pas-sion project of a friend of mine, so it paid terribly."

"Yes. A shoestring budget and we had to work these incredibly long hours, where you have to talk with the people around you or you'd fall asleep standing from the exhaustion," Gabriel went on, smiling at the moment he realized Kalle was meant to be in his life. "Kalle was the best conversation I had on that set—and off it for that matter." They squeezed hands.

"Since then, we've done all there is to do professionally. Eleven years in the industry is a long time and we wanted a new challenge." Kalle bit into a macaron.

"We both love Halloween and scaring people, so this B&B was the natural next step."

Bernadette nodded at the story the whole time, then asked, "In that time have you ever seen a real ghost?"

"I'm sorry. No. I don't believe ghosts are real." Kalle shrugged apologetically.

"Let's put a pin in that thought now, shall we," a ghostly voice spoke, startling the party, and the chandelier flickered on and off. *We've started finally*, Gabriel thought, shielding his eyes. Simultaneously, paintings on the walls trembled and rotated on their heads. The veiled silhouette of Jodie materialized in the mirror.

"How's that for real?" she asked. The image in the mirror was so realistic Gabriel chanced a second look to see whether Jodie hadn't snuck into the room like in the conservatory. But no. She was only a live stream on the ultra-thin LCD screen Bryan had applied on top of the mirror. He sighed in relief and turned his attention to Bernadette. This interaction was meant for Kalle, so he wanted to observe her reaction. Through the bells and whistles, Bernadette maintained a stoic face, but Gabriel noticed how the macaron had disintegrated into crumbs in her fist.

Finally, some results, Gabriel thought.

"Do you think that's enough to scare me?" Kalle boasted. Although they didn't have a set plan on how to interact, Kalle insisted on playing the brave sceptic who'd stand up to Arlene.

"You will be once I'm done with you!" Arlene threatened and the chandelier died, leaving her spectral form in the mirror as the sole illumination.

"Leave now, spirit. You're not welcome here."

Gabriel contained his chuckle at how politely Kalle banished the ghost.

"You're not the one who makes the rules, pompous deviant! The feast is drawing near, my dear sister, and these people will be meat."

Jodie disappeared in the mirror and the chandelier lit up again. Gabriel and Kalle sat stunned in their armchairs. She had threatened them, and even though it was for the benefit of the haunting, Gabriel sat with disquiet and tension. She'd triggered something primal in him and his body had seized up. Kalle didn't fare any better.

Surprisingly, Bernadette had gone through it the worst. Her already pale skin drained further of color and the veins in her neck pulled through to the surface. Twin strands of tears streaked down her hollow cheeks. Breath rattled in her chest. Without so much as a prompt, Lydia leaned over and assisted her employer in standing.

"I apologize, but I will retire to my room until midnight." She excused herself and let Lydia lead her out of the parlor. This happened so quickly neither of them could react in time to say anything.

"It's not precisely fear, but it's an emotion," Gabriel tried his hand at lightening the mood.

Kalle simply cupped his face in both hands and rubbed it. "We can't fuck up the feast, Gabe. We can't fuck it up or else we'll lose everything."

"We won't," Gabriel reassured him, but he didn't know anymore. He wanted for the feast to come and go, so he'd sleep in and process this godawful visit.

As it was, there was still work to do. The midnight feast approached as Jodie had said.

Gabriel disliked working in the basement. The space repelled human presence with its constant chill even at the height of summer. The world above didn't exist and the basement drifted into a realm of its own. The banquet table had been set for the midnight feast and Gabriel had to sound check the prerecorded infant screams that would play once Gianna lifted the cloche off the fetus.

His breath misted and hung in the air where he circled the table careful not to snag on the red tablecloth. Under the naked lightbulbs the cutlery and metal plates cast a faint glow. Where a beam slid at a particular angle on the metal, light danced on the bloodied corpse dummies and from the corner of the eye one could mistake them for real. Unlit candles littered the surface and Gabriel was glad he'd not have to light them.

He played the wailing for a few seconds from the hidden speakers mounted at various points in the basement to gauge the volume and sound quality. The cry unnerved him when he mixed the clip, but on the scene it instilled primal fear. *Good*, he pushed through his unease. This was what the brief called for and he'd delivered. Horror was his life; this is what he breathed, but he couldn't stand the pain of a child. He wanted to cradle the imaginary baby and sing it to sleep.

"The crying is absolutely blood-curdling. I can hear it through the door."

Gabriel hadn't heard Jodie enter the basement. His whole body spasmed and he almost bit his tongue in surprise. Jodie stood motionless halfway down the staircase. Veil still over her face and in the weak light she looked almost translucent.

"Jesus, Jodie! We don't scare each other in the middle of a job."

"I thought you had a stomach for scares."

"Do you think this is funny? Because I don't. Not when I haven't slept for more than four hours. I understand you want to do a good job, but there's a line. I don't appreciate this just as much I didn't appreciate you threatening me and Kalle. You don't do that even as part of the role."

"I apologize, Gabriel. I am staying in my character for this important performance." She spaced out the words, mindful to let each word echo into a whisper before saying the next. He felt a sudden urge to leave the basement as soon as possible, but he couldn't bring himself to approach Jodie. Instead he busied himself with the collar of a corpse.

"Well, you can stop now! After this is done we're going to talk about appropriate workplace behavior, if you want to stay on with us."

"As you wish. I wanted to see how you'd set up the stage. There's no denying your artistry. My sister will absolutely loathe this."

"Yes, of course. Your sister. Next you'll tell me you're buried in the basement." He rolled with whatever she tossed his way, but he didn't like where this conversation was heading.

"Yes—a very astute guess. I was buried in the wine cellar."

Gabriel had enough. It was late. No amount of coffee or tea could get him up and running, and it was the combination of lack of sleep and strained nerves that fueled a kind of stupid anger that held no regard for personal safety.

"Just shut the fuck up, Jodie! I've been really lax with you. I'm up for having fun as much as everyone else, but I'm pissed off, and this is too important for us to lose control!" he yelled and the basement rang long with his raw emotion. He'd even flinched at his own loudness.

"Well?" he asked when Jodie remained still, regarding him through her veil. There was no way for him to know this, but he did none the less. Her eyes were twin hooks lodged into his cheeks.

"We have both known for some time that you lost control of the situation the moment Bernadette arrived," she answered at last. "You have convinced yourself otherwise. Just as you have convinced yourself I'm Jodie."

She placed her hands on her belly and laced her fingers in a cradle, and now Gabriel noticed how emaciated they were. Wrists and knuckles bulged and her digits dangled longer than they should. A red crescent formed right beneath the cradle and a thick redness trailed down, down to the very hem of her dress. In the taut silence, Gabriel heard heavy drip-drop. By instinct he balled his hands into fists, nails digging into his palms, and he accidentally pressed the remote. The wailing started anew.

"It sounds just like my baby. It's been decades, but a mother remembers the cries of her child. I only heard it once when my sister carved my daughter out of me. You pity her. Think her a frail, remorseful woman." Her voice was calm, yet cut clear through the wailing directly played to his mind. She wailed, too. Wailed until the clip ended and then punched herself in the belly with both hands.

The lights flickered and the whole table shook. Gabriel dared not move. He'd seen enough films to know not to piss of an already angered ghost.

"That cunt sacrificed me and my baby to a demon! Not just so she'd be the only one alive, but to have all the glory in the world! Did you know that you can stay alive for a good stretch of time cut open before succumbing to blood loss? I lived long enough to see Bernadette pluck my little girl out of me and bite into her head!"

The instant she said it, he imagined it, and the vomit rushed out of his mouth all over the floor.

"That's the proper reaction right there!"

"Why are you telling me this?" Gabriel asked through secondary retches. He steadied himself against an empty chair and wiped his mouth on his sleeve.

"Because she took a liking to you!" The table shook on its legs at her scream and the cutlery rattled against each other. The entire thing dragged over the floor in an abrupt lurch and slammed him against the wall. The first thing he felt was the sharp pressure at his groin. *Fucked. I'm so fucked!* he thought. *I'm going to die here.*

"I can't have you think well of her without knowing the truth. Now listen," she commanded—poised and collected once more, to which Gabriel nodded.

"She got the demon, got her wish—fifty years of extraordinary living, but it didn't work out quite like she thought. Turns out the dying can strike a deal, too, and I took my half. I've been planning her damnation for half her life and I expect nothing short of perfection for tonight's festivities."

She sighed. An outlandish noise to hear from a ghost, that threw Gabriel out of the moment for a second. Like this wasn't real, but staged. An elaborate prank? But soon the same sinking feeling returned to the pit of his stomach and there was no doubt in his mind.

"Excuse me. I lost composure. I need to put my energy elsewhere for the moment. I'll help your staff get ready. You're all my distinguished guests. Stay put now," she instructed, glided up the stairs, and disappeared through the closed door.

Gabriel couldn't tell how long he stood rooted in his spot with the taste of stomach acid on his tongue before the loud thunder of something heavy hitting the floor broke his trance.

Kalle! His first pure thought in ages kick-started his body and Gabriel threw his entire being against the table, pushing it out of his way. He rushed the stairs and hurtled into the door. The wood shook, but didn't budge. He jiggled the handle—locked. He shouldered against it in desperation until his right arm and shoulder went numb.

Unlock the door, he thought. *I have to unlock the door, then save my husband and my friends from a ghost.* A real ghost. That's what ate him— ghosts were real. He'd roomed with one so long without knowing and what was he going to do? He'd wished it was real, but now that it was, what could anyone do?

He scanned the basement for a fitting tool and improvised. Threw a chair into the door with no damage to either. Jammed a knife into the lock. Pushed a shovel where door and case met. Nothing worked, and it had grown quiet again. Too quiet.

Think! He sat on the stairs in Arlene's blood, heaving from the effort. He spotted the open door to the wine cellar and epiphany struck. *The dumbwaiter shaft!*

They'd expanded and converted the dumbwaiter into a vertical ladder so "ghosts" could move around undetected between floors and that's what he'd do. The metal door in the cellar gave in after the second pull and he flipped the lights on. It was a tight fit, but he forced his shoulders in the shaft and climbed, scraping his arms on the freezing walls. The climb felt painfully slow, but he pushed himself through the exit in the parlor all sweaty and clothes dirty from the shaft. The silence was all consuming.

"Kalle!" he kept yelling, but no one answered. He passed through the dining room—the kitchen—the reception. Nothing. Everything was in place. There was nothing to suggest violence or even a struggle. "Where is everybody?"

But he knew where: with Bernadette, on the upper level. As he took the stairs—three steps at a time—Gabriel realized with absolute certainty how he played into Arlene's script. She'd been planning everything for decades. She'd confessed as much, so them working in this house in the first place was no coincidence.

"Kalle!" he yelled once he cleared the landing and rushed into the hallway. Light stained the carpeting from Bernadette's open door, and Gabriel caught the faintest murmurs from inside.

The very first thing he gazed upon entering the room were Bernadette's eyes, two glass marbles set deep into her eye sockets, but this time he searched in them for that cruelty. He wanted to find the woman Arlene had described. Do ghosts lie? But he found nothing. Just emptiness. The sight of her exerted its own gravitational force.

Bernadette sat nude on her bed. He finally witnessed the extent of her thinness: the definition of her ribcage, the depth of shadows between the ridges of her ribs, and the near-vanished abdomen like a magician's trick gone wrong. Her legs were stripped of muscle and Gabriel wondered, *Jesus, how did she support her own weight?* Her body glistened, martyred in blood, shoulders shrouded in something slick and wet. It took seconds to see this, but wore him out like a lifetime.

"Help me," Gianna called and Gabriel realized there were others in the room. He saw the rest.

Gianna, swollen-eyed and split-lipped, hunched over the woman and worked a bloody needle through the material and the flesh beneath. At her back, Lydia kept a firm hold on the back of her head and held her there to do her work. But why? Why would she act against her own employer? Was she possessed?

"It's rude to interrupt a lady during her toilette." Gabriel heard Arlene but could not see her in the room. "You should have remained in the basement, Mr. Corsaro," the disembodied voice said right beside his ear.

Gabriel gulped on air, choking on the thick smell of blood in the room.

There's blood and Gianna is sewing something onto Bernadette. Gabriel observed this, but the elements didn't connect until he noticed the flap on Bernadette's left breast sported a mop of blond hair still waxed into an immaculate swoop.

"Bryan," Gabriel whispered and covered his mouth. He'd seen this all before. Watched all the classic splatter films and knew enough to piece the clues even if he didn't see a body. Hell, he'd made movies like this, so he knew what was real and what artificial. How the latter had been sewn onto the subsumed reality. Here there was no seam. He didn't smell the sweetness of corn syrup. Only copper. The taste of sucking on a quarter. An acrid smell of piss and shit. Bryan was really dead and his skin was being sewn onto Bernadette.

"You've skinned Bryan…" Gabriel gagged again and he couldn't hold it in.

He fell on his knees and emptied his stomach a second time. A blind instinct to flee drove him to crawl on all fours into the hallway just so he'd not smell death, all the while Gianna begged him not to leave. He had to act now and his choices were shit. Fight off Lydia in this weak, panicked state or flee to HQ and call 911, but leave Gianna alone. All the while it became harder and harder to breathe and his arms and legs trembled uncontrollably. *Move*, he pleaded with his body, but it didn't comply.

"Kalle…" He croaked the name as a prayer that he'd appear from thin air and swoop him away.

"You wish to see your husband? I can help." Arlene manifested in front of him, but he only saw a pair of rotting, bare feet and a torn dress skirt. "He's behind this door."

The door to the Yellow Room creaked open and Gabriel resisted the pull to look. He could muster the strength to peek inside, but he didn't want to. It had to be goading. A trick.

"Want to see what I've done to him?" Gabriel started crying and he couldn't stop himself. He didn't have time to waste, and he sobbed until his whole face swelled.

"Maybe later when you've had a chance to calm yourself. Lydia, please ensure Mr. Corsaro is properly seated downstairs," Arlene ordered.

"No!" Gabriel yelled and rolled away toward the staircase. He refused to end like this—waiting to be put out of his misery. He crawled to the wall and pushed himself upward, but Lydia proved herself faster. Her strong hands clamped on his shoulders and then she threw him on his back in one swift pull, knocking the air out of his chest.

Gasping for breath, Gabriel dragged himself away, but still found himself pinned under Lydia, who wrapped her meaty hands around his neck and squeezed. While he still could, he kicked and flailed to no effect. Lydia tightened her grip and his vision blurred.

"Fuck you," he cursed through his teeth and threw one last punch right into her temples, which knocked the shades off her face, but it didn't knock *her* out. Instead it revealed two hollow sockets where her eyes should have been.

"What are you?" he asked, but received no answer.

Those dark holes bore into his mind as he lost consciousness.

"Look at how marvelous you look, Bernadette. A true vision."

"You're gloating a little too much as ever."

The voices trickled into Gabriel's ear from afar and slowly grew clearer. At first he didn't understand what was happening, but knew one thing—he was alive. A deep chill bit at his nose and the rest of his body was so numb it might not be there at all.

"Not much room for character growth in death, dear."

"But rotting, however…"

"There goes that tongue of yours again. I put in so much effort the past twenty-five years to make your life a living hell; I still could never break your spirit."

As he listened, more and more sensations flickered on. His head throbbed and there was a chink in his neck from lying on his left shoulder, but he didn't move. Not even a twitch. He didn't want to give himself away. The plan was simple—play dead until he had an idea of how to escape. He peaked through one eye to assess where he was and recognized the basement floor. The lightbulbs were on and he saw he was tied to one of the dining chairs.

"It's the only difference between us, dear." He recognized Bernadette, though now he discerned a malicious edge to her voice, erasing any difference between her and her sister. "Explains why I'm alive and you died."

"Ah, so you've finally dropped the act?"

"You've determined to end me. I could be the next Virgin Mary and you'd still drag me to Hell."

The ghostly laugh bounced off the walls and startled Gabriel out of his pretend sleep.

"Our guest is awake," Arlene said from beside his right ear. The very sound of her words gave him a freezer burn. "No reason to pretend, Mr. Corsaro. There's no miraculous rescue. This coffin is airtight."

Gabriel complied and blinked against the swarm of lit candles running the length of the table. Even their faint light hurt his eyes. On the other end of the table facing him sat Bernadette. To his left was propped the flayed Bryan and to the right, Gianna with her throat slashed and one chair further the real Jodie with strangulation marks around her neck. He was so close to them he heard the stillness of their death. A stillness he'd heard only a handful of times at funerals and recognized at an instant. Tears streamed down his face. He'd lost them. They were like a family to him and he'd seen them dead.

"You give me an opinion," Arlene addressed him as she floated around the table. "You've set a lot of tables in your life. It's exquisite, isn't it?"

His breath came in short bursts and he couldn't even breathe deep enough to sob.

"I'll give you some time to compose yourself, then," she said as she glided to her sister's side.

Unable to stare further into their faces, Gabriel focused the table. Though that wasn't any better. Arlene had made certain changes. On his own plate sat a lump covered with a cloth. Thickly packed in between the candles were arranged platters of tiny carcasses. Pig fetuses braided together by their umbilical cords. Unhatched chicks served in their eggshells, now liquid graves. An infant in its intact placenta. Meat and viscera. So much meat. Gabriel retched at the sight.

"At least someone is giving me my due," Arlene said and clapped her ghostly hands together.

"You did what you could," Bernadette responded, cold and unimpressed. How could she be face to face with all of this and not even tremble?

"It is smaller than what you're used to, but who needs princes and dignitaries when you have family. Your twin sister… your loving daughter Lydia."

Gabriel whipped his head back and stared at Lydia seated at the far end of the table. This giant of a woman bore no resemblance to Bernadette, but the old woman grimaced nonetheless.

"Lydia appears to be a sore subject? Then I must have pierced through that exterior at least a little. I made her better, you have to admit.

"You'll find this irresistible gossip." Arlene addressed Gabriel. "Lydia was once a beauty and she was an exceptional classical singer. *Once* being the key word. As soon as my half of the deal started, I gave her a much needed makeover. Took her tongue and removed her eyes. Injected her with every single steroid on the market. Lydia is now the perfect servant—efficient and silent."

"You're sick... Your whole family is monsters!" Gabriel yelled. He didn't mean to speak. The words just tumbled out.

"Said the man who scares others for a job. Shouldn't you be giddy you're seeing the real thing. There's no artifice here, but if you are disrespectful, you won't meet your lover."

"*Kalle?!*" Gabriel searched in the room, but saw no sign of his husband. All eight chairs were occupied: three for his friends, two for Lydia and Arlene, two for himself and Bernadette, and one for a skeleton in a tattered dress.

"Mr. Hård was the odd man out, so he's not seated, but we have incorporated him into the feast so you didn't feel alone." Arlene pointed at his plate and the cloth on the lump crawled off on its own accord.

Gabriel didn't want to see. Didn't want to believe. He knew as soon as he first saw the lump. It was so obvious. The foreshadowing a slap to the face, but while it was hidden, he could ignore it. He could hope for some other horror. His hope wrenched out of his chest at the first lock of auburn hair peeking underneath the rim of the cloth. The hair he'd woken to so many times before, nuzzled and rubbed the stress away.

The wail he gave battered the walls and unspooled out of his mouth for minutes. The cloth fell off and Gabriel locked eyes with the vacant face of his husband. He pleaded and begged for it to be fake. Anything but reality! He pushed against his chair. Pulled his head down toward Kalle's. Almost close enough to touch foreheads, but a sliver of air remained between the two. No matter how hard he threw his weight forward, Gabriel couldn't bridge this distance. This intangible border between life and death.

"Do something! Help him!" he yelled at Bernadette, who observed calmly with hands on the plate in front of her. Of course, he realized he was talking nonsense. He repeated the script of other movies, of other victims when there was nothing left to yell about and they understood there was no way to undo this. He wasn't going to survive. But he also refused to beg for his life.

"Gabriel. I'm unbound, but my hands are tied. As I told you in the conservatory—there are things that must happen, and we're solely there to see them through."

From above a bell *rang*... The sound reverberated through the entire basement.

"It's beginning! Finally!" Arlene exclaimed and took her seat opposite Lydia. "Now, niece, help your mother eat," she commanded. Lydia forced the contents of one egg into her mouth. Without breaking eye contact with Gabriel, Bernadette chewed. He heard the initial crunch, then the bell rang out a *second* time. Not a bell, but the strike of a clock. *It's midnight*, Gabriel thought.

Three. Four. Five.

The further the clock counted the louder the sound grew and the basement hummed.

Six.

The placenta ripped and the fetus inside cried as if it were being born. Candles toppled over. Patches of fire poured alive onto the fabric.

Seven.

Debris rained from the ceiling. Gabriel snapped his jaws shut over his tongue, severing the tip, and blood gushed out of his mouth.

Lydia fed Bernadette another baby chick.

Eight.

"As above so below," Arlene chanted and spread her arms to the ceiling. Next to her, the skeletal remains mirrored her gesture.

Nine.

"Blood sings to blood," she cried. Lydia held a pig fetus to Bernadette's mouth, who bit off its entire head and chomped on it.

Ten.

"The sweet of the vine for the pit of the earth!" Kalle's head rolled off the table and landed in Gabriel's lap. Blood dripped onto his open eyes like tears.

Eleven.

"The halves of the mirror are once more whole." The chairs shook so wildly the bodies of his friends rolled onto the ground or face planted onto the table. Gianna's hair caught on fire.

Twelve.

The twelfth strike ripped the ground apart and a voice spoke from deep below, "Let's begin the midnight feast." Bernadette regarded Gabriel, the pig fetus halfway into her mouth. In the center of the table, the human stillborn wiggled blue fists.

"You are about to witness something truly transcendent," Arlene said and then lifted her veil.

Haralambi Markov was the first ever Bulgarian to be accepted to attend the Clarion Writers' Workshop in 2014. His fiction blends speculative genres and literary writing, but always returns to myths and folklore as well as the weird tradition. His short story "The Language of Knives" was long-listed for the Nebula award for Best Short Story. His work has appeared in TOR. com, *Uncanny Magazine*, Weird Fiction Review, Apex Book of SF and *Stories for Chip*—tribute anthology to Samuel Delany. Markov functioned as the submissions' editor for the successful horror podcast *Tales to Terrify* for forty-two consecutive shows and co-edited the volume of best stories *Tales to Terrify, Volume 1* with Tony C. Smith and Lawrence Santoro that came out in 2012. His reviews and literary profiles have appeared on TOR. com and SF Signal.

MYTH AND MOOR
BY CRAIG LAURANCE GIDNEY

I'VE LOST MY WAY.

Emily heard the small voice beneath the rustle of the morning winds. It was a child's voice, high as a piccolo, full of distress.

I've lost my way.

She turned in her bed, faced the bedroom window. It was still dark outside though the horizon was bleeding at the edge. She was in her dressing gown and her hair was coiled up in a braid under her bonnet. The floor was chill beneath her bare feet, but Emily didn't bother to put on slippers.

She saw him at the window, beneath a shrub. A young boy in tattered dull clothing. He had blond hair under a cap and the chubby cheeks of a cherub. His skin was as thin as tracing paper. She could see things beneath its surface. Moth wings, curled ferns, as if he were a stuffed doll. And his eyes were a pale turquoise blue that glowed.

The moor was full of ghosts. She had seen them many times during her long walks, men and women and children with translucent skin, earth-colored clothes and bewildered expressions. They wandered the windy grasslands, drifting here and there like scattered dandelion fluff. They never seemed to see her, appearing to be preoccupied by some private matters. Emily ignored them and for the most part, they ignored her. A couple of times, one of them might follow her for a brief spell or tried to get her attention. Eventually they would dissolve like mist. The ghosts moved their mouths, but no sound issued forth.

This young boy was the only one who could hear. That must have meant something.

"Who are you?" Emily asked.

The child reached through the fogged glass and touched her hand. The fingers on her flesh felt like icicles made of feathers. They tickled her; gooseflesh rose in response.

I've lost my way.

The refrain echoed in her brain. She knew that voice, that angelic boy soprano that resounded throughout the church nave. Then, she recalled the face.

"Heath Linton," Emily said.

He'd gone missing a little over a year ago. Vanished. Had he been kidnapped? Beset by highwaymen? Or fallen down some hidden hole on the moor, in pain and in the dark? Heath was like Emily in that he loved the countryside. She'd even gone on a few walks with him.

Why was he there, outside of her window? And why could she *hear* him?

Emily's late mother could hear the spirits of the departed.

"I hear my babies in the wind," she told Emily on her deathbed. "They're saying 'We've come home, Mama! Let us in!'" Her mother was referring to her two sisters, taken from them by consumption. Just like her mother had been, in a cruel twist of fate.

Papa and Charlotte and the attending physician had believed that Mama was in the throes of delirium and that the phantoms she saw were induced by the fever that raged in her frail body. Emily knew otherwise. Because she could see them. Her sisters, pale and faintly luminescent in their calico pinafores were standing outside the window, waiting patiently for their Mama to join them.

Emily didn't tell anyone that she could see the dead, not even Anne, her closest sibling, nor Bran, even though he adored dark stories. Now, she could hear them. Or, at least, Heath.

He faded as the sun rose over the moor, melting into dew. Soon he was a cutout made of green grass and purple heather.

Isobel Linton, Heath's mother, dropped by the parsonage that afternoon. She was a husk of the woman she had been before her child went missing. Her vitality had been robbed by grief and a reliance on laudanum. She had never been a beauty; her face was too sharp and angular, her body stout. But she did love fashionable dresses in bright, gay colors. Now everything she wore was black as coal. Her brown hair was messily hidden under her bonnet, and she emitted a rank odor, as if she had given up on hygiene.

"I would like to see your father," she said, slurring her words ever so slightly.

"I'm afraid that he's visiting Jane Berkshire. She asked him to pray over her husband Innocent. He's in a bad way."

Mrs. Linton's eyes were widely dilated as she stood in the foyer, and Emily thought she saw her wavering.

"I have no idea when he'll return," Emily said. She knew that she should invite the woman in, offer her some tea. She wanted to comfort the woman, and tell her that she'd seen Heath this morning. But she knew that Mrs. Linton was in a fragile state, that she should keep her abilities to herself. Besides, there was an erratic air about the woman. Madness radiated off her person.

"I'll tell Papa that you stopped by."

"Will you now," Mrs. Linton said. "Which one are you? Charlotte, or Anne? I get you mixed up." Emily said her name.

"Oh yes. The wild one. The one who prowls the moor with a huge black dog like some fey thing. Some folk say that you're peculiar.

Wandering the wilderness with no escort." Mrs. Linton narrowed her eyes.

"I like to take the air," Emily said. "What of it?"

Isobel Linton eyed her suspiciously. "You must know that things live out there. Unnatural things. Wicked creatures. Heath never learned that. He just blithely went hither and yon."

Her brother Bran entered the house, interrupting this odd conversation. His bright orange hair was in disarray, as usual. He paused, sensing the tension in the air. This sudden appearance seemed to calm Isobel Linton, her wild eyes losing their focus.

"I should be off," Mrs. Linton said. Then she grasped Emily's arm in a vicelike grip. "The land is beautiful, but it is also treacherous. Please be careful. I would not want you to suffer the same fate as my little lamb."

"What was she on about," Branwell asked Emily after Isobel Linton left.

"I think she believes that someone—some *thing*—is responsible for Heath's disappearance."

"Some *thing*?" Branwell replied. "Such as what? A boggart or hobgoblin? Jenny Greenteeth? Or maybe Black Shuck came and carried the child off in his jaws."

"Bran!" Emily said, batting at him. "It is tragic to lose one's own child. I won't have you laugh at her misfortune."

Branwell sucked his teeth. "It is tragic, I agree. She is addlebrained due to grief. But she has four other children and a husband that she must stay steadfast for. Her idle speculation won't see their needs met."

"Maybe not," Emily said. "There before the grace of God, go I."

Heath appeared to Emily during the next few days. Sometimes in the morning, sometimes at dusk. Always when she was alone or with Keeper, her tall mastiff. He always said the same thing, over and over.

A litany or a plea. Maybe that was all he could say. He was trapped in some nether land between life and death. Emily assumed that he would go to Heaven. Surely, the Lord would want such a pure, innocent soul as that little boy.

For a week, Emily ignored the revenant. Her talent for seeing the dead was a secret she closely guarded. Papa, being a man of the cloth, frowned upon superstition, considering them coarse and sinister. But she and her siblings loved the supernatural and the uncanny. The four of them dreamed up worlds full of romance and dark intrigue, and all of them wrote poetry and stories filled with magical occurrences. But this was not a fairy story or a gothic novel.

There was some reason that Heath manifested, some message he wanted to impart to her.

I've lost my way. I've lost my way.

One Wednesday morning, before the sun rose, Emily took Keeper and her walking stick and stood outside, waiting for the boy's spirit to materialize. She waited in the chilly, damp meadow while Keeper sniffed the ground. In the dim light, he could have been the demon hound of the moors. He was an imposing dog and many people were frightened of him.

She heard Heath before she saw him. His plaintive chant sounded in her brain, drowning out the chorus of early morning birds. Then he formed. First, a floating face. Then hands and torso. The rest of him, the legs and feet, were invisible. His spirit was faded and unfinished, just the impression of a child of six.

He said his piece.

She replied, speaking aloud to the shimmering boy: "What do you want to tell me? How can I help you?"

He melted into mist. Then, maybe a yard away, his face reappeared. A face made of moss, bracken and heather with milky blue eyes.

…my way…. The words echoed in Emily's brain.

She followed him out onto the moors.

The sky was grey and white, much like Keeper's coat.

Keeper bounded ahead of her, flushing out an ornery grouse that took to the air with reluctance. The mastiff expressed his excitement with barking and a kind of canine acrobatics, standing on his hind legs. Emily laughed, then whistled for him to follow her.

The day was chilly, and the grass still wet from the morning dew. Her older sister would certainly chastise her. She could hear Charlotte now: "You'll catch your death out there. Consumption or the flu." Maybe so, but there was a small part of her that believed that she was invincible. That she was part fairy, an elemental changeling burdened with a human form. Papa would frown on such supernatural whimsies and sternly remind her that the Christian soul had no room for competition with nonsense.

At first, Emily thought he was leading her to the Linton farm. They raised a meager flock of goats and sold milk and cheese. But they breezed right past the farm. Emily shivered, thinking about the ominous behavior of Isobel Linton. *The land is beautiful, but treacherous...* Heath led her deeper and deeper into the moors, past fields embroidered with newly emerged flowers. Sometimes, he was fully materialized, a boy of seven, gamboling in the fields like a lamb. Other times, he was wan impression, thin as tracing paper. They skirted the edges of farms, past pens full of sheep and chicken coops.

This is madness, Emily thought. Emily knew she had a reputation as an odd duck, and that Papa's parishioners thought she was queer and unladylike strolling through the heather and gorse unaccompanied, but she didn't care. The wide open grasslands, clad in green, yellow, and purple, were sacred to Emily, holier than the cold stone and hard pews of the church. Here, where she could have been the only person for miles, was where the Lord's awesome powers of creation were on display. God lived in the wild, and not in the staid, ritualized confines of Man's civilization. It was here, in Nature's church, that she felt like herself. Not the little sister, or the vicar's daughter, or the household chatelaine. Here, in the sea of grass, she was a poetess. Words and images drifted to the top of her head. The fluttering moths, the darting mice, the slinking lizards all demanded to be captured somehow. Ballads, odes, and couplets danced around her head during these solitary constitutionals. Chasing the ghost of a child was exhilarating.

A few hours later, Emily found herself in a relatively sparse area, a place where the grasslands gave way to coarse, shrubby vegetation and bizarre large rocks exploded from the land. Mottled grey and brown outcroppings that seemed to have materialized out of nowhere, they belonged in a land of volcanoes, not in the English countryside. She could easily imagine some ancient monstrous lizard walking around there. Heath's outline had faded to a mere disturbance in the air, his voice silent in her mind.

A single, stunted tree burst out of the ground. It was a tough, wizened looking thing, with grasping spindly branches, nude of any leaf. There was something about the outline of the tree that reminded her of a human figure frozen in time. The branches grasped at the air. She saw that the branches were hung with tiny, bizarre ornaments. Spiky little things strung up with wire that rattled in the wind, making a strange percussive sound.

Then she saw the severed leg. A haunch of some animal, probably a goat, lay in front of an opening in one of the rocks. The black-and-white hair of the leg was matted with blood and seething with flies. The top of the leg was gnawed on, with strips of glistening red raw meat surrounding a yellowish bone.

It looked out of place in that barren space. Nature's cruelty in a naked display. It looked freshly severed. Emily loved all the creatures of God's creation, and her first emotion was one of horrified sorrow. She could almost feel the terror and pain of the hoofed creature as it was rent by—by what? Wolves were unheard of in this part of the country. Wolves were creatures of the forest, not the wide open grasslands. Maybe one of them had wandered there. Could it have been a bear? Whatever had killed the poor goat had done so with much violence, and furthermore, had devoured the rest of the animal.

She saw some movement near the dismembered leg—

"Keeper!" she called. He had been nosing near the carnage. He perked up his ears. Then he lay flat on the stony ground, his ears lay back, and bared his fangs. She heard him snarl at someone—something that lurked in that crevice. Fear chilled her as she ran to her beloved mastiff. He was formidable, but no match against the ravening creature hiding within that slice of darkness. Emily ignored the hampering of her muslin dress as she moved from grass to stone.

When she reached his taut, alert body she smelled the stench of rotting flesh. It was so nauseating, the smell, that she was dizzy. The smell was layered, the foul and sweet mingled together, and so overpowering that she began to gag. But the smell did not just come from the severed limb. It came from within the crevice. That mouth-like opening. It was the perfume of Hell, gaseous and putrefying. Death himself would be taken aback.

Then she felt the tingle of being seen by something unseen. Eyes were in the dark. Feral eyes, measuring her and Keeper, considering the meat they would provide. The thing that ate the goat could easily dispatch her.

Then she heard something stir in the shallow cave. A rasp of some rough fabric, like burlap, against stone floors. She recognized that sound; after all, she was a genius at needlework and knew all of the qualities of various fabrics. That's when Emily knew that whatever lived in that depression was human.

Keeper growled, low and guttural. Emily gripped her walking stick so tightly that her knuckles became as white as snow. A sudden gust of wind came off the moors, bending seed heads and blossoms. And something moved in the dark. Emily knew that she should run. She took far too many risks, and laughed off her siblings' concerns about stray highwaymen or gypsies looking to do harm to her person. Now, their hectoring concern came back to her, tenfold. Fey girls could get their throats slashed. And Keeper, as ferocious as he looked, was daft and was just as likely to abandon her as he was to protect her.

A cowled figure, garbed in a dun-colored monk's robe, emerged from the crevice. The person was grotesquely thin. The hands that emerged from the voluminous sleeves had long fingers, longer than was natural, and the nails were untrimmed and sharp. They reminded Emily of the bare switches of some shrub. The person had to bend in order to leave the overhanging rock, and unfolded itself with insect-like maneuvers to its full height. The elongation of the limbs suggested some illness that caused deformity. A sliver of Christian charity underscored the tumult of fear wreaking havoc in her mind.

"The meat is mine! It is not thine!" the cowled figure said. The voice was high and reedy. "I have killed the beast and alone I shall feast. Away with thee!"

"Gentle sir, I meant no offense," Emily said. She was intensely aware of the space between them, and the heft of her walking stick. Her long skirt would impede a hasty retreat. "I will be on my way."

The figure observed her for a moment, then threw back the hood of the cowl. At first, Emily couldn't make sense of the face that was revealed.

The skin was blue, the color of the woad dye that ancient Celts used in battle. The blue was not just on the face, it was also on the neck. A mane of hair, white as flour, erupted from the scalp, some of it braided and haphazardly entwined with objects, such as the skull of a field mouse or a bird. The sharp features suggested that this was a female figure, and now that she thought that, Emily could perceive a womanly shape beneath that rough cloth. The slight protrusion of breasts, the curved hips. It was the sharp glitter of the nails that caught her eye. They were more like claws. And they were iron in shade. Tiny knives, embedded in wizened hands.

This was no human thing. It—she—the dweller in the rocks—was some nightmare creature, belched forth by the bowels of Hell. Emily lifted her skirts, and began running. Then she stopped.

Isobel Linton's drug-addled warning surfaced in Emily's brain. *Keeper! Where was he?*

Emily spun around, scanning the grasses. Then she saw that her beloved mastiff was at the feet of the blue-skinned hag. Her iron-like nails hovered above his snout. She found herself heading back to the rocky plateau.

"If you harm him, you fiend, I shall—" she gasped out.

The blue hag calmly glanced in Emily's direction. Her iron claws clacked together over the dog's head. Keeper, fool that he was, sat on his haunches and stupidly wagged his tail.

"No harm shall come to the hound," the hag said. "I have no quarrel with him."

"Good day, madam," Emily said. "We will leave you to your... repast, and trouble you no further."

"I have no particular quarrel with you either, sylph. The rest of your kind, alas! They call me hag, witch. Black Agnes, Black Annis. Never 'madam.' All I want is a bed of earth to lay down, a bit of meat for my pot."

"Miss Agnes, is it?" Emily said. "I cannot apologize on behalf of my brethren. We can be a rude people, nasty to those whose looks and beliefs lay outside of Christendom. Once, in Brussels, I saw a group of men say horrible things to people whose only difference was that their skin was dark."

"Skin as dark as mine?" The blue woman seemed to be amused at the thought.

"No," Emily replied. "Even darker than yours! And with hair of wool that they can craft into elaborate sculptures."

"How curious," the hag said, and bent to stroke the underside of Keeper's jowls with her metallic fingers. He closed his eyes in pleasure while Agnes muttered, "You're a sweet one, aren't you?"

A gust of wind seemed to whirl up from nowhere. It chilled Emily to the bone, even though she wore a bonnet and had a shawl wrapped around her shoulders. She glanced up into the sky, saw grey and white clouds creeping across, obscuring the wild blue sky and the yellow sun. They were as thick as clotted cream.

"I really should be going," Emily said.

Black Agnes stopped stroking the dog, casting a glance up at the sky.

"You'll be caught in the rain," she said.

"Not if I hurry," Emily said. "Here, Keeper!"

"It'll be a wild one, that storm will," said the blue woman. "It will wash the likes of you away. Trust me, child. I have lived in this wilderness for many an aeon."

"Yes, Miss Agnes," Emily said, trying to quash the note of anxiety that crept into her voice. Keeper looked up to her, his deep brown eyes wide with concern. No doubt, he could sense her unease.

"You are afraid of me, child." Black Agnes stated this as a fact. "As I said before, I have no quarrel with you or your hound." She flashed Emily a gummy smile. It reminded Emily of dolmen pillars sprouting from black earth.

Nature conspired against Emily with a squall of air followed by the icy pinpricks of rain.

"Come, and be warm around my fire," Black Agnes said. "The rain shan't last too long." The blue-faced, iron clawed figure beckoned from the opening.

Emily knew that she should leave this ominous place and walk to the parsonage through the driving rain. She'd done so many, many times. She would be in front of the fire in two hours, three at most, and Anne or Charlotte could warm her up with a cup of tea. That would be the sensible thing to do. She thought of Heath Linton Surely, he had led her here for some reason. There was no doubt that this blue monstrosity was responsible for his disappearance.

But she wasn't just the minister's daughter. There was another, less proper Emily in her heart. An Emily that loved adventure, a young woman enthralled with the macabre and the numinous. *That* Emily wanted—even *needed*—to follow this eldritch figure into the Stygian darkness. And it was this feral part of her nature that led her and her dog to follow the hag beneath the earth.

Agnes had gathered the bloody shank of meat and stood in the rocky lobby of the cave when Emily and the dog entered. The rain came down in full force. The sky turned crow-black and the moorlands became a sodden swirl of purple heather, yellow gorse, green grass and brown mud. The storm was violent and stunning, the Lord displaying his awesome power. A crack of lightning, purple-white, razored the air.

"It's a wutherin' deluge," Black Agnes said. Emily turned to see the woman with the haunch of bloody meat in her glittering claws. Drops of blood flew in the wind, landing on stones and in her hair and on the rough-spun robe she wore. The woman didn't care that she was being baptized with liquid offal.

"Come on, then," the witch said and continued walking. Emily paused, both exhilarated and terrified in equal measure. She was leaving the above-world, full of light, family, civilization, and Christian doctrine for a sojourn in a lightless, lawless place.

What wonders will I see here? she thought. *What terrors?*

She turned from the dripping curtain at the cave's mouth to follow Black Agnes. Keeper followed at her heels.

It wasn't hard to follow Agnes. While it was dim, Agnes cast a kind of soft lambent light. Her blue skin illuminated the rock walls, bounced off of molds and lichen that clung to the stones. The ground under their feet sloped ever so slightly.

"Agnes," Emily said after a few minutes of walking, "how long have you lived here?"

Agnes paused, as if considering the question. Then she strode on through the darkness.

"The measure of time is a concern of mortals," she finally said.

"Many days, many nights. Before you, or your grandmother were born. Before your kind set up stone buildings to live in, before your kind tamed the earth and the animals that roamed it."

"Do you have parents? Sisters? Brothers?"

"No," she replied harshly. "I have always been the same. No birth. No death. I just am. Things like me don't have families. I assume you have one. A family."

Emily stayed silent, because it seemed that the witch-woman was peeved. They passed down one path, turned into another. The air here was cool and a damp musky smell rose from the dirt floor. There were no animals underground. No insects, bats, or lizards. No badgers or voles. Maybe Agnes had eaten them all.

"I do have a family," Emily said, if only to fill the awkward silence. "My mother died when I was young. Papa never remarried. I have two sisters and a brother. There were two other sisters, but they both died of consumption."

She thought of them now. She and her siblings had created imaginary countries full of intrigue and romance. She could hardly wait to tell Anne and Bran about her encounter with Agnes. Outright sorcery wasn't a part of the Gondal canon, but since Anne had a taste for the gothic, Agnes would surely enflame her imagination. And Bran could paint a magnificent portrait of the blue-skinned witch. As they walked through chambers, Emily forgot her fear momentarily. Her excitement at this adventure drowned it out. It was as if she had been suddenly transported into *The Castle of Otranto* or one of Lord Byron's more fanciful poems.

So taken away with these fanciful thoughts, she dawdled a little behind Agnes. For a moment, the glowing blue figure was a mere dot. That's when the chill returned.

There's no way the caves beneath the moors are this extensive, she thought The close ceiling of the crevice opening had expanded until the ceiling was as high as any cathedral's. The parsonage could fit in this chamber. In fact, the entire population of Haworth could fit inside.

Glancing up, she saw stalactites dripping down from the ceiling like monstrous candles. There was a world beneath the windy grasslands. A hollow earth, a deep place where things like Agnes lived. She thought of the fairy mounds in the stories her late mother told her, of how their architecture did not obey the laws of nature. Those things were full of endless hallways and confusing mazes.

She and Keeper rushed to catch up with Black Agnes. Emily heard her shoes and Keeper's claws echo throughout the large cavern.

Down and down, deeper and deeper they went. Where were they going? Papa spoke of how Hell and Satan existed in the mundane world. Hell wasn't pitchforks and wicked women carrying chalices of their excrements. It was idle gossip, rivalry, and unkind thoughts. Agnes clearly was from the strange outskirt of Hell. Supernatural, pagan and somewhat feral rather than outright malevolent. Did the blue woman have a soul? Could she be saved? She seemed to have emerged from some pre-Christian period, when the ancient Celts spilled blood in honor of warlike deities.

Eventually, though, Agnes stopped walking, having come to a dwelling place of some kind. One wall of the cave was covered in rough jagged crystals, clear stones with a violet tinge. The floor was worn smooth by a thousand years of foot traffic. Emily saw a bed of sorts, a pallet of cowhide and straw. A stone "desk" sat in the center of the crystal room, made of boulders with flattened surfaces. Agnes flung the dripping haunch on the top. She spoke a word that made Emily think of the howling winter wind out on the moors as it combed through frosted vegetation. It was a lonely sound, redolent of death and endless fields of white. And out of the whiteness, there was a spark.

And then there was light in the cave. No visible fire or particular source; it was as if the shadows had been shredded. Emily saw the crude furniture—a couple of chairs made of what looked like petrified wood, and a shelf against a bare stone wall, filled with—

"Oh," said Emily. "Oh, how marvelous!"

There were sculptures on the shelf, maybe thirty or so. They were lacy and porous chimerical creatures, perhaps three apples high. Emily saw that they were made of bone—tiny mouse, bird, and badger skulls perched atop things with bizarre anatomies—winged voles with spiny vertebrae, creeping cats that wore necklaces of bird skulls. The eye sockets were decorated with stones and crystals and the negative space between the bones were filled with dried flowers and entwined with bits of bracken. Emily prided herself on knowing the flora and fauna of her beloved moors. She saw rusty sheep's sorrel, white mouse ears, and yellow asphodel interlaced with fern leaves and rushes. It was such delicate and precise work, one that only could have been done with a poet's soul and a saint's patience.

"You like them, sylph?" croaked the blue hag with iron thorns on the end of her hand.

"Indeed, I do," Emily replied.

Black Agnes cackled, a surprisingly endearing sound. "Would you like to see them dance?" she asked, and flicked her wrist and whispered a word in the language of the moors.

The strange sculptures began to move. Not in disjointed ways, but with a silky, fluid grace. Winged things took to the air while lizards made of bone slid up and down the walls and the earthbound creatures slinked around the stone cave.

Keeper comically barked at the advancing bone fauna and cowered away.

"My mother and my father are the land itself," Black Agnes said between bites of the meat. Bits of gristle and sinew flew as she ate. "It reared me. Was my nursemaid and my teacher."

Emily felt kinship with this creature. Both were daughters and caretakers of a beautiful and often cruel landscape. Emily sat on one of the crude chairs, away from the witch and her gory mastication How could something so brutish create something so beautiful?

One of the animated figures approached her. It had the legs of a deer, the wings of a jackdaw and the skull of a human child. Tiny moths fluttered throughout its stout ribcage.

It was undoubtedly a human skull. The head of a child of seven or so. Agnes had decorated the eye sockets with milky blue chalcedony. They stared up at her, imploringly.

It was Heath Linton's skull. It all came back, the reason for her journey underground. Had Agnes enchanted her somehow, made her forget her quest? She remembered the boy's shade, filled in with the flora of the moors. It came flooding back. A child with the voice of an angel. That angelic voice floating about, hanging from the rafters. His small hands, held out for Keeper to sniff and lick. The games Emily and he would play, darting among shrubs, hiding behind the stones. His bright voice, calling her name. The time they waited out a sudden storm in the ruins of a barn, and the stories she told him to pass the time. The boy made of flowers and moths, that appeared outside of her window, the coolness of his ghostly grasp.

Was this Heath Linton's fate—to end up in the belly of a pagan witch and have his bones be desecrated? Emily could sense him, his spirit, somewhere in this cave beneath the sea of grass. He filled her brain with images and sensations. The rending of his flesh by iron-clawed nails. The cracking of his bones, the roasting of his flesh. Emily could taste his meat, tender as veal, tough as venison. She heard the pop of gristle, the grit of bone. The taste of the organ meat, all liver-flavored, the metallic gush of blood.

I've lost my way, he'd told the ancient witch that day, years ago. Heath had been incapable of understanding evil. His young mind thought that Black Agnes was some kindly old woman, an eccentric lady who dyed her skin blue. The sheer terror he must have felt when she dragged him fathoms beneath the earth to feast upon his flesh.

Her infatuation with Black Agnes came to a sudden end.

I have to kill her, Emily thought. She knew that it was a rash decision. She didn't want to die in some demon's lair. But she couldn't allow such a horrible presence such as Black Agnes or Annis or whatever she called herself to live. She had to do it for poor Heath's honor. She thought about the pain and fear he must have felt.

A tide of rage washed through her body, as red as the blood of Christ that hung in Papa's church. She could take her walking stick and brandish it like a weapon. But a quick glance at the iron claws of the ancient witch, blue as a harebell, made the tide subside. Could Black Agnes even actually die? She had lived through the ages, so what use would a tussle with a "sylph" like Emily have? Like the badgers, or pheasants, or the earth itself, Agnes was a product of the moors. Savagery had a place in the natural order of the world.

"You have been very kind to me," Emily said, standing. Her knuckles were white as she gripped the walking stick. "But I'm afraid that I must be off."

The witch held one of the bone creatures in her arm tenderly. She gave Emily a piercing stare. "You will forget me," she said. "For that is the way of things like myself. Your sojourn will be nothing more than a dream, if even that." There was a note of unbearable sadness in the blue woman's tone. "I see, in your eyes, your great love of this wilderness, sylph. No harm shall come to thee."

Emily was unsure of what to say to that. She wanted to embrace and to rend the crone in equal measure.

....A crack of thunder sounded, and she found herself at the mouth of a stony crevice in the earth, watching a storm. Keeper lay by her, resting at her feet. How long had she been here, watching the storm? It seemed that she couldn't recall. All was a blur of wet rain and grassy ground.

She waited until the last of the dark clouds blew over the sky, and patches of sunlight broke through.

Before she ventured out into the soggy landscape, Emily felt something in her hand.

It was a child's skull with two milky blue stones placed in the eye-holes. The teeth were entwined with harebell blossoms.

For one brief moment, Heath Linton stood in front of her, whole and unmarred. He grinned at her, his baby teeth gleaming like pearls. Then he faded from the air, like an afterimage. Emily stared at the spot where he'd stood for a good while.

She glanced back into the cave.

Then went on her way, eager to leave whatever slumbered there alone.

Craig Laurance Gidney writes both contemporary and genre fiction. He is the author of the collections *Sea, Swallow Me & Other Stories* (Lethe Press, 2008), *Skin Deep Magic* (Rebel Satori Press, 2014), *Bereft* (Tiny Satchel Press, 2013), and *A Spectral Hue* (Word Horde, 2019). He lives in Washington, DC.

HAMMERVILLE
By Bonnie Jo Stufflebeam

DRACULA

That which Dracula feared had arrived at last. When the vampire had been mortal, all those aching years ago, he had not feared death. Once he could never die, it was the only worry that dined on him in his dreams. It was like a husband who does not fear losing love until he holds his new wife in his arms, or a rich man who did not fear being poor until he possessed too much gold to lose. Dracula enjoyed a wealth of wealth, a wealth of wives, a castle that bore his name, and a body that would exist until the end of days.

To die would not be miraculous. He had said this once—a few days ago—in an opera house to a young woman with blood so vibrant it shaded her grey cheeks. He had said it before, to other women, to many mortals, but he had claimed the phrase only in an effort to bring his victims closer to the idea of his fangs in their neck. Had he brought death upon himself, to repeat such an asinine phrase? Had the crucifix heard him and decided at last to take its vengeance? But never mind. It was no use speculating. He was dying. Trapped in the bed of his death, paralyzed in his daytime sleep, and listening to the footsteps of that great bore Professor Abraham Lee Vansing.

Dracula felt his coffin open. He felt the stale air against his cheeks.

He longed to move, to up and run, to aim his gaze at the professor and take the man into his thrall. Dracula longed to fly once more into the night. He wanted to scream, but the professor's stake settled into the center of his chest, and Lee Vansing drove it in, and Dracula faded into the nothing he thought he would never see.

Dracula woke. Above him, the grey of his castle was a sight for the sorest of gazes. He rose. "Thank you," he said out loud to the world that brought him back. "Oh, thank you." He would show his gratitude for this continued existence; he would seek out a beautiful victim. He gathered himself to fly, to become one with his favorite form, that black bat that so frightened. He spread his wings, but it was only a flapping of his arms that occurred. He tried again. He scowled. He must look a fool. He searched about the basement; the shadows moved differently than they had before. He crept through the darkness and up the stairs. He opened a door, and from within the castle, a bright golden light hit him. What mistake was this! He shrieked and threw his cape over his face, but he did not burn up. Slowly, he lowered it. The castle in which he had found himself was not his Transylvanian home at all; it was a place altogether different from anything he had seen before.

It was full of color. Tall light posts held flickering yellow flame that illuminated a great hall. Dracula walked along a stone floor and let the light cast shadows upon him. He held out his hand and ran it along the wall. Instead of stone, the wall was smooth and white and draped in vibrant red tapestries. In the middle of a room, upon a table carved from exquisite redwood, a feast had been laid out, but it was no feast for the likes of Dracula: a loaf of black bread with a little container of butter, a decanter full of deep red wine, and a dead chicken glazed and roasted and with half its neck still attached, limp at the edge of the serving platter.

Dracula's brides had not cooked this, no; they were far too hungry to remain long in the castle kitchens, and when they served the men and women who visited to conduct Dracula's affairs and eventually succumb to his kiss, Dracula's wives cooked stews of chewy beef and sprouted potatoes. They served cheap wine, but this wine smelled like the very vineyard from whence it came.

Dracula approached the table; upon it lay a letter addressed to a man whose name Dracula knew well: Mr. Harker. He had been one of the men present when Dracula died—but then Dracula was not dead after all. Dracula patted down his suit. He had indeed entered a world of color. He touched each white button of his vest, each black button of his suit jacket, then ran his hand along the red silk inner fabric of his long cape. Oh, how pale he looked against the red!

"Mr. Harker," a man said from the top of a long stairwell. Trombones swelled as Dracula turned. Dracula pushed his hands over his ears, but the sound pervaded. At the top of the stairs stood the man who had spoken, a man who descended in a sweep of long legs. He wore a plain suit and a plain cape that settled still as the man reached the bottom of the stairs. "You aren't Mr. Harker." His grey hair was slicked back, and his long horse face was pale as Dracula's.

"I am Count Dracula," Dracula said.

"I'm Count Dracula," the man said.

Dracula laughed. "You mimic me, but you know not what I am."

The man opened wide his mouth; two bright fangs grew from his teeth. He hissed. "You threaten me," he said. "You don't know what I am!"

"Like me." Dracula stepped back. "Why have you come here?"

"You're an imposter," the man said. "What have you done with Mr. Harker?"

"What has Mr. Harker done with me?" Dracula said. "Are you in league with Professor Lee Vansing? Are you in league with Jonathan Harker? What have you done to my castle? What have you done to

Mina? She was mine. She had my scent all over her. Surely even a fraud such as yourself recognizes first rights?"

"You know Professor Lee Vansing?" the man said, advancing.

"He is my enemy!" Dracula said.

The man's face calmed. "He is mine as well." The man stepped to the table and fell back into one of its chairs. He sighed. "Mr. Harker isn't coming, is he?"

"I do not know," Dracula said. "He was here but a minute ago, right before they put the stake—" Dracula scowled. He pressed his hand to his chest, where his suit was unmarred. Had it been but a dream? Somehow, he had wound up in some other man's castle. Dracula joined the man at the table. "I do not know where we are, or why I am here, but I am not lying to you when I say that my name is Count Dracula. What is yours? Speak the truth to me."

"I'm called by that name also," the man said. "But I suspect you are some sort of trick, some distraction sent to me by Professor Lee Vansing. We do this song and dance, he and I. We repeat these scenes. We repeat these lines. Or at least we used to. It has been a while, I admit. I set this nightly meal for Mr. Harker, in the hopes that we will begin again, but Mr. Harker never comes. Perhaps I should not have turned him, the last time."

"You turned Jonathan Harker?" Dracula felt a lightness in his belly, like the buzz after a particularly innocent woman. "I do not care what your name is. I am happy to hear it!"

"I turned him." The man took a sip of wine then spit it back into the glass. "Then Lee Vansing killed him. He's such a bore."

"He is indeed," Dracula said. The two men chuckled half-heartedly.

"You are welcome in my castle," the man said. "But perhaps you should call me Master, to avoid confusion."

"I will call you no such name," Dracula said.

"Fine," the man said. "Then you shall be Dracula the Old, since you look like one of my ancient paintings of fools in your bright cape. You can call me Young Dracula, as my skin is less like ash than yours. You look, Dracula the Old, like you are still in the process of dying, after all."

"You mock me still," Dracula the Old said. "You will regret it."

"Do a dance for me, you fool of a man," Young Dracula said.

Dracula the Old met Young Dracula's gaze and dug into the man as deep as he could go but hunched against the table, exhausted and unsuccessful.

"You cannot thrall Dracula," Young Dracula said. "Or did you forget, with your rotting brain?"

"I shall see your death," Dracula the Old said, but he craved not death for this new enemy at the moment, only a rest in the dirt from his homeland. Only sleep.

Young Dracula stood from the table with a flourish. "We have the same enemy. We have the same name. Perhaps, you're the visitor I most needed after all. But you are correct, slumped there against the table as though withering away. Sunlight is near. It is time to sleep. You're a lucky fool. I have an extra coffin."

Dracula the Old had not the energy to fight; in fact, he swelled with gratitude for Young Dracula's offer. He stood from the table, and together, they swept through the halls of the strange new technicolor world as a damned saxophone wailed in the background. It was loud, this place, and it contained a Dracula too many for his discerning taste.

THE GORGON

Lee Vansing chased them into the catacombs, the Monsters Three. It was Medusa's favorite spot, with its skulls lining the walls and its musty stench and its stone statues of the dead. Roxanne, Dr. Hyde, and Medusa ran across the packed dirt, stirring up a cloud of dust in their wake. Behind them, Lee Vansing fell into a coughing fit.

Medusa paused to admire a skull with a seeming grimace. She was unsure if she had viewed this one before; it had such terrible teeth, crooked and worn. The sockets of its eyes were curiously round. She reached out to trace the eyeholes. Unlike her companions, she was unused to skulls. Her own victims lost their bones to stone. Bone was fascinating to her; she wanted to taste it, one swipe of her tongue up its cheek, but her sisters pulled her along.

"M, he will catch up to us, you know," Roxanne said.

"Not all of us are immortal," Dr. Hyde said. "Some of us die from perfectly normal afflictions."

"About that." Roxanne bared her fangs. "Whenever you're ready."

Medusa giggled. Dr. Hyde rolled their eyes, revealing for a moment the whites. It made them somewhat more grotesque, to see two white eyes in the midst of a face whose features were split down the middle: on one side, the femininely prominent cheekbones, delicate chin, arched eyebrows, round eyes, full lips red with lipstick; on the other, the masculine stony brow, square jaw, thin lips ripe for pursing. It was remarkable how cleanly the one side faded into the other.

Medusa moved forward three paces. She pushed at a skull that had long ago cracked in half, and a trap door opened beneath them. The three monsters fell in a heap upon the straw they'd placed strategically inside their lair. Dr. Hyde loved to call it that, *lair*, while Medusa and Roxanne found the description cliché. Dr. Hyde kept it to themselves now, but Medusa could almost hear Dr. Hyde giddily repeating the word.

Medusa stood and brushed herself off. Her sisters picked bits of straw from one another's hair. Lee Vansing had chased them through the catacombs on ten occasions at least and not yet discovered how they always got away. He was not brighter than they were, at any rate. What chance did a moldy professor have against them? They were old and brilliant and feral.

Roxanne lit the candles along the lair's back wall. They'd formed them from body parts farmed from Medusa's victims: stone hands that now did their eternal bidding, making sure the sisters could see in the dark. It had never been an issue for Roxanne; the darkness was her friend before these two monsters were, anyway. But she allowed them this in the place they had decided to call their shared home. Medusa appreciated Roxanne for giving up her own advantage; the light hurt Roxanne's eyes, and Medusa tried to remember that whenever Roxanne became testy.

"Everyone is satiated, I assume?" Dr. Hyde settled in at the lair's dining table, placed there by Dr. Hyde for Dr. Hyde's benefit alone. Dr. Hyde arranged a dinner for themselves: stale bread dipped in cold broth with a small glass of their remaining merlot. "I request a robbery for our next venture. I'm in need of sustenance too, you know." Medusa sat beside Dr. Hyde at the table. She liked to watch them eat.

Medusa was not much for robberies. They stank of desperation. But Roxanne fell back into the bed they shared and stretched upon its red silk sheets. "Someone glamorous," she said.

"She means female," Dr. Hyde said through a mouth of bread.

"She means young, and innocent, and probably in love with some fool of a boy." Medusa giggled again.

"What's wrong with that?" Roxanne said. Medusa understood the sacrifices that Roxanne made for the sake of their sisterhood: silk sheets were one of the luxuries they allowed her to indulge in. She craved more, but it was creaking mansions, the desire for fame, and high-profile marks that had put them in the most danger.

"You have a type," Dr. Hyde said. They laughed, two laughs that formed a harmony. "Don't we all?"

Medusa blushed and kept her eyes trained to the table's grain. Dr. Hyde elbowed her. "Even you."

"What's my type?" Medusa said.

"Virgin men," Dr. Hyde and Roxanne said together.

Medusa scoffed, but when she thought of the last man she turned to stone, her snakes stirred under her mass of tangled hair. His name was Raoul. He had a pretty face unmarred by pain. He had loved her. When she tried to love him back, he froze. She'd convinced her sisters to carry the statue to their old lair, but they had not been able to grab it or any of the others statues from the stone garden before they fled Lee Vansing's last fire. Medusa could not help but laugh, at herself, at her friends, at the glee they shared in their catacomb lair.

"Tomorrow, we'll do a robbery," Medusa said. "I wouldn't mind if we found a brother-sister pair. For both our sakes, Roxanne." Their revelry echoed off the catacomb walls.

When they first met, the Monsters Three had tried to kill one another. Dr. Hyde had wandered into Medusa's rundown mansion. They explained later, over a ritual bleeding, that they needed to extract women's pineal glands in order to survive. Dr. Hyde had been stalking Roxanne, who had been on the hunt herself on the streets of a quaint English town. Roxanne had led Dr. Hyde through those streets to the old mansion. Roxanne loved a good mansion, she told them later, over a ritual demon-raising. She loved to drain her victims dry as they played a game of maze and mouse within the mansion's intricate hallways. Medusa had sensed them both enter through her gardens and had followed them until they'd backed themselves into a corner. She grabbed Roxanne to gift her the stony gaze; her snakes broke free of her hair and waved about her head. Roxanne hissed, her fangs bared, and jumped back, knocking right into the now-cornered Dr. Hyde. Then she had smiled.

"Amazing," she cooed, reaching out to pet a snake. Medusa started to advise against it, but as the snake struck, Roxanne cackled. "A vicious garment."

"It's not a garment," Medusa said. "It's me."

Dr. Hyde stepped forth from the shadows. "What are you?" they said. "Both of you." A shaft of moonlight shone down from a hole in the ceiling, and it illuminated their half-and-half face. They held their blood-stained blade at their side.

"What are you?" Medusa said. She'd never seen a human such as them.

"I'm a doctor," they said, two voices blending into one.

"Me too," Roxanne said. "I'm a doctor too."

"You're a vampire," Medusa said. "I've been around long enough."

Later, around a ritual séance, Medusa tried to goad Roxanne into comparing ages. She would have won; she was as old as age itself. But Roxanne refused to play that game.

"A vampire!" Dr. Hyde said. "Fascinating. I'd love to get your cells under my microscope. Eternal life! What a gift."

"It's a curse as well," Medusa said.

Roxanne reached out her hand and cupped it over Medusa's mouth. Medusa's snakes cried out, snipping at her one after the other. "It is no such thing," Roxanne said.

"And what are you?" Dr. Hyde circled Medusa and Roxanne. "I have read many books from the Great Library of Evil, but I have not read of your kind."

"They call her kind gorgon," Roxanne said. When Medusa raised her eyebrows, Roxanne smirked. "You think I'm not well-traveled, pet?" Roxanne let go her hand and cradled the bleeding mess to her chest. The blood dripped down Roxanne's exposed neckline, past the edge of her dress that formed a **V** for her breasts. She let her fangs expire back into her mouth. "You'll do well not to underestimate me."

"I know what I seek," Dr. Hyde said. "I know what a vampire seeks. What does a gorgon seek?"

Medusa considered not answering—to do so would weaken her in the eyes of these strange creatures—but what did she stand to lose? "Friendship," she said.

They did not trust each other at first, these women who, like all women, were used to being hunted. For Dr. Hyde explained that, too, as the Monsters Three decorated their second lair beneath the catacombs, letting loose spiders to build their webs and placing a bowl of blood on a nightstand, for the smell. They were male and female, but they were woman too.

That night, at Medusa's creaking mansion, they stumbled upon the plan as a well-meaning trespasser stumbles upon a body. Defeat was inevitable if they worked forever alone; together, they might stand a chance against the hunters who wanted their bodies to lay unblinking.

DRACULA THE OLD

Dracula the Old woke starving from his slumber. When he slid the lid off his coffin, Young Dracula leaned against a nearby column watching him.

"Took you long enough," he said.

"A vampire's slumber is precious," Dracula the Old said. "It is not a thing to be rushed."

"You know what else isn't to be rushed?" Young Dracula said "Breakfast. Shall we?" He offered Dracula the Old his hand, but

Dracula the Old scoffed and rose alone. "Mr. Independent."

"Where shall we hunt?" Dracula the Old said.

"I know just the spot," Young Dracula said.

Young Dracula led Dracula the Old out into the night. The full moon cast its light upon the landscape, and what colors winked back at him! The jealous green of the grass! The quick grey blur of a rabbit bounding past as the vampires made their way out the castle doors and into Young Dracula's carriage. The crisp and endless black of the road ahead. Dracula the Old's body hummed with excitement; besides his wives, who despite their bloodlust did not make perfect partners for their uncanny ability to gang up against him, Dracula the Old had not hunted with another for a good, long while.

Dracula the Old's carriage was more impressive than Young Dracula's; his carriage men were shapeshifters, like Dracula the Old. They spooked Dracula the Old's passengers half-to-death, getting their blood pumping before they arrived at Dracula's door. Young Dracula's carriage man was a man, pure and simple, and Dracula the Old wondered how Young Dracula kept from ruining his appetite before the entrée.

The carriage pulled up to the local tavern. The carriage man let down the folding step, unrolled a strip of velvet, and lay the fabric in a line down the three stairs. Young Dracula extended his hand. "After you," he said.

Dracula the Old was seated on the inner side of the carriage. He frowned but crawled across Young Dracula, who leaned himself back into the carriage seat as far as he was able. Dracula the Old stumbled down the steps and caught himself right before he fell face-first into the dirt. Young Dracula glided down. "Clumsy old fool, aren't you?" he said.

Dracula the Old's belly boiled with hunger, with rage for this fellow creature of the night, a man who did not admire him the way he should admire him. Dracula the Old was no fool, but he was no undignified firebrand either. He would have his revenge when Young Dracula least expected it.

"This is your favorite hunting ground?" Dracula the Old asked. The establishment before them was small, built on the bottom floor of an inn. A wooden sign branded with two clinking mugs of ale swung above the door in the wind that seemed to accompany Young Dracula wherever he went. A pipe organ howled in the background, then was replaced with the chirp song of crickets.

"This is a small town," Young Dracula said. "This is one of the only hunting grounds."

Young Dracula moved to the alley, and together the vampires slunk down the darkened cobblestones to the back door. Two women stood smoking by the back entrance, their hair coming loose from the pins.

"Good evening, ladies," Young Dracula said. "May we sit and share cigarettes with you?"

The women looked up with annoyed expressions on their faces, but their eyes met the eyes of the double Draculas and took in the familiar clouded gaze.

"Absolutely," the brunette said. "Couple of gentlemen like you."

The Draculas traded grins and moved in. Their hands grasped hold of the women's arms, and Dracula the Old felt his woman's petticoats push against his body. These women were unlike the women upon which he typically fed; their necklines plunged, revealing heaving chests. It was improper. It was thrilling. He tore the skin of her neck with his half-sharpened teeth and watched as the blood dripped down her cleavage. He pulled back, alarmed with himself. He looked to Young Dracula to see if he had noticed his indiscretion, to look at a woman so, but when Young Dracula pulled back from his own victim, he had blood dripping all around his mouth. His eyes burned red. Dracula the Old gasped. How awful! How obscene!

"You dine like an animal," Dracula the Old said.

"We are animals," Young Dracula said. "Pure and simple."

Dracula the Old felt the woman's life surge through him. He felt drunk with it—or with the red wine she had downed before meeting him—or with the thrill of so much skin—or with the thrill of letting a small slip of blood dribble out of the corner of his mouth. He wiped it quickly away.

"Isn't it good, old man?" Young Dracula said. "To let loose a little?"

"Loose," Dracula the Old said. "Yes, that is the expression I would use to describe these women as well."

Young Dracula cackled as he let the woman's body fall to the floor. Dracula the Old did the same with his. The world before him was a blur. He felt giddy.

"Shall we drain another pair?" Young Dracula said, licking the blood from his fingers.

"I am feeling quite satiated," Dracula the Old said. "I feel like running, like flying."

"Shall we explore the town?" Young Dracula asked.

"Yes! Where shall we drag the bodies?"

"We'll leave them," Young Dracula said, "for Lee Vansing to find."

Dracula the Old frowned, but he walked beside Young Dracula as the vampire made his way down alleys. Light filtered out from the buildings they passed with the rancid smell of home-cooked dinners. Families had their windows open as though they did not fear the night.

"Do you hunt here often?" Dracula the Old slurred as they passed a butcher's shop, closed for the evening. The smells that wafted from within were more pleasing than those from the other buildings.

"To tell the truth, I haven't been out in some time." Young Dracula hiccupped. "I have a fair share of curious villagers arriving unannounced at my castle. And the out-of-towners who don't know better. The truth. Without Lee Vansing around to stir their fear, they come up with their own answers for disappearances."

"How long has it been, since Lee hunted you?" Dracula the Old tried not to let the spinning world knock him off balance.

Young Dracula sighed and collapsed upon the rim of a fountain in the deserted town square. "A long while. I try to do the things that called him forth before. I wait for Mr. Harker to arrive. I leave the bodies for him to find."

"But why do you want him to return?" Dracula the Old collapsed beside him. He clapped his hand upon Young Dracula's shoulder. "Seems as though you, sir, are in the clear! Free to hunt as you please. A whole town for the taking!"

"I feed," Young Dracula said. "I have fed for a long time. I am, as you said before, satiated. These townspeople," and as if on cue, a giggling couple emerged from the shadows of an alley and stumbled, arm in arm, across the square, "they're easy to kill." The couple passed into the safety of a nearby building. "Too easy."

"There are other towns," Dracula the Old said.

"There is the same town, over and over."

"Surely there are challenges that do not involve Professor Vansing."

"I fear, for the first time in my life, I fear," Young Dracula said.

Dracula the Old thought of himself in his coffin, listening to the sound of Lee Vansing's footsteps, awaiting the moment he would cease to be; he had feared too, and that fear—or something else entirely—had brought him here. Surely his being here had purpose of a kind. Surely he was not meant to be teased by this imposter.

"What do you fear?" Dracula the Old asked.

"I fear that Lee Vansing has found a new foe." Young Dracula cried a single blood tear. "That he has no use for me any longer."

Dracula the Old squeezed Young Dracula's shoulder then patted the fiend upon the back. It was not Dracula the Old who was the fool, for was a man not a fool who wished his enemy's return? Dracula the Old wished instead for the destruction of his enemies. He smiled with his teeth that were not as sharp to the naked eye as Young Dracula's teeth were. They tore skin just the same. He was not a fool; he knew the way forward, understood his purpose, had a plan. He would rid the world of his enemies. They would drain each other dry.

"We must find Professor Vansing," Dracula the Old said. "We must make you known to him once more!"

THE GORGON

He was her first.

The Monsters Three had decided on the location of the robbery after hearing a group of young women enthusing after the wealth of a man who lived several miles away, a castle on a hill in the country-side. Medusa hadn't heard of this castle in the country before, but it seemed as though new castles popped up every day. She wasn't complaining; she delighted at the idea of new hallways to explore, even if she'd given up on castle lairs for discretion's sake.

"I haven't eaten in ages," Roxanne said.

"You ate yesterday," Medusa said.

"I'm so hungry I could die," Roxanne said.

"You could not," Medusa said.

"What does happen if you don't feed?" Dr. Hyde asked.

"I turn into a man." Roxanne winked.

The passersby had spoken of the eccentric rich man's gold, how he hoarded it to himself. The man was said, according to the passersby between pleas for their lives, to be a developer of real estate. He had an affinity for jewels and entertained many women, many nights of the week.

Roxanne dressed in her finest red dress, while Medusa wrapped herself in her standard white cloth. Dr. Hyde wore their best suit and their best veil to hide their face. The Monsters Three hired a carriage driver to take them to the eccentric man's castle, and when they arrived, they knocked upon his door like ordinary guests.

Medusa kept her gaze averted from the man, but she scanned him from the mirror inside his front door; he wore his hair to his shoulders, and red curls spiraled around his big ears. He kept a clean face, but not well; it bore the shadow of the day. She could not get a good enough look at his eyes, but he wore a long tan coat and strange white boots.

"Good evening," he said when he saw them all there. "How may I help you?" His voice was soft and kind. Medusa felt as though he would not hurt a fly, nevertheless a snake. Beneath her hair, her snakes slept.

"We heard stories about a gentleman who likes to entertain pretty women," Roxanne said. "We came to see if he was real."

The man smiled gently. "I'm the gentleman," he said. "I'm real!"

"Better let us have a squeeze," Roxanne said, and she reached across the threshold and wrapped her hand around his arm. "Real indeed!" she said.

"Is it just you in this big old house?" Dr. Hyde said.

"My father's staying with me for a time," the man said. "He's sleeping upstairs. My sister is here for the evening as well. I'm not sure where she's run off to." He laughed. "That's probably who you heard about, in terms of pretty women. I don't see many women like you all. I'm too engaged in family business."

"A man who knows the importance of family." Roxanne winked; sometimes Medusa wondered if she'd taken acting lessons, but there was real delight in her now: a sister, her perfect kind of plaything. "Your sister sounds lovely."

"Excuse me," Medusa said, keeping her head down still. "We've had the most dreadful time making friends in town. We'd absolutely love to spend the evening with you and your family. I understand that it's bold of me to suggest—"

"No, no," the man said, moving aside. "Come in, please."

Medusa blushed. She followed the lead of her companions, who entered the house scanning the surroundings, formulating their plans. Medusa let the others plan; for her, she needed no plans. Her victims always sought her out, and she always stoned them, whether she intended to or not. They could not help but look her in her eyes.

"I've dined already, but I can have my sister fix something up for you." He motioned to a hall that surely led to a dining room.

"That would be much appreciated," Dr. Hyde said. "But perhaps you have a garden in which we could dine? My sisters here prefer the outdoors."

"But it's so dark, and I'm afraid my outdoor lanterns are out of gas."

"We don't mind the dark," Roxanne said.

"We appreciate the fresh air," Medusa said. The floor was slate grey stone.

"Absolutely," he said. "This way." The man led the Monsters Three across a sitting room and through two large double doors to a courtyard surrounded on all sides by flowering trees and rose bushes.

Medusa took in the smell. It was intoxicating.

"I'll speak with my sister," the man said. "Have a seat."

Dr. Hyde and Roxanne slid into patio chairs with a single harmonized sigh. They laughed at themselves.

"This, dear doctor, was a perfect idea," Roxanne said. Medusa examined the roses; there were roses of every color: red, pink, yellow, blue. The door to the patio opened, and out walked the gentleman and his sister. Medusa examined the man's sister; her own red hair flowed in waves past her narrow shoulders. Compared to this woman, Roxanne was a beast of a woman with her broad shoulders and wide hips. Plus the fangs. Roxanne watched the petite woman carry in her tray and smiled; she was exactly her type, which was female.

The man's sister set down her tray. Dr. Hyde leaned forward and sniffed the contents: stewed beef on a plate of potatoes with a hint of mustard somewhere in the concoction. Medusa could smell it from where she stood by the roses. It smelled horrific.

"Will you sit with us, sweet creature?" Roxanne asked the woman.

The woman giggled and slid into a chair. "If you insist."

"I am Roxanne," Roxanne said, her voice as near a purr as Medusa had ever heard.

"They call me Annabelle," the woman said.

"Annabelle! What a sweet little name!"

Dr. Hyde nearly snorted into their meal, but Roxanne shot them one look that shut them up. The gentleman moved from the hubbub to the roses and stood beside Medusa. "Your friend is quite the charmer," he said.

"She makes friends easily," Medusa said.

"I have never been so lucky." The man reached out and fingered a pink rose. "I had trouble speaking up in school."

Medusa's stomach twisted; her pulse quickened. He was making it too easy to dance her dance: fall in love, kill, fall in love, kill. It was always the same with her, and she wondered, even after when she stared in horror at the skin turned to stone of the men who would have been her lovers, if she enjoyed the process more than her heart let her think she did. The man smelled like sweat and leather.

"I haven't either. Before these two, I had no friends of whom to speak."

Medusa heard the man's smile in his words. "You seem lucky now, at least."

Medusa turned her head from the roses and looked over the scene: Roxanne leaning into the young woman, one hand on her knee. The young woman melting under Roxanne's gaze. What was it like, to look someone in the eye? To know them by a look that held in it all the kindness of their soul? Roxanne had spoken to Medusa about the power of a lover's eyes, how you could see in them that someone loved you. Roxanne had a way of making people love her—a thrall.

Medusa looked at Dr. Hyde, scarfing their dinner. Medusa was so outside this world she lived in; she did not drink, and she did not eat. Not even flesh, not even blood. Dr. Hyde tossed a bone into the grass and speared a potato. They closed their eyes as they chewed, but then they frowned and pulled from their mouth something white, like a pebble. They held the thing to their nose and sniffed. They moved the potatoes around on their plate until they uncovered a whole layer of the things. Medusa could smell it from where she stood: garlic. "Garlic," Dr. Hyde said simultaneously. And as they echoed one another, Medusa and Dr. Hyde, Roxanne's eyes grew wide then woozy. She hissed as she fell from the chair, knocking over the table with the tray.

"You took my bait beautifully," said a familiar voice from the door. Lee Vansing. Medusa had no problem looking him right on; she hoped he would return her gaze. She dared him to, if in her mind. Beside her, the gentleman had gone with a rustling of the bushes. Medusa stood on high alert, watching Lee Vansing. The professor wore his signature tan trench coat. Medusa had seen him fight enough times to know that under its cover, he kept a stake, a blade, and any number of crucifixes. Roxanne's palm bore the mark of one of Lee's hunts, before she knew who he was, before he understood who she was. It occurred to Medusa then that this trap had been set for them specifically.

Annabelle glided from her seat to stand beside her father. Dr. Hyde tossed the garlic-covered plate into the grass. Roxanne recovered from her semi-stupor. Hyde helped her stand. Medusa tried to rush to meet them, but a hand pulled her back into the bushes.

"Are you as evil as they are?" the man said.

Medusa looked at the ground. "I am," she said.

"Prove it," the man said. "Look me in the eye."

Medusa's chest ached. Like Dr. Hyde, she understood what it was to be pulled in two directions. Like Dr. Hyde, she wished sometimes that she could be one or the other: innocent or guilty. She wanted to see his eyes. It had been so long since she'd looked into a beautiful man's eyes. She met his gaze, and there in the shadows she saw inside him. His eyes were brown and beautiful, and there she was reflected in them, barely visible through the dappled light from the gas lanterns above. He smiled at her. "You're not," he said, but he did not turn to stone. "You're not evil at all."

Medusa's body throbbed. Why wasn't he turning to stone? She opened her mouth to speak, but the man reached out and caressed her cheek. His skin on her skin. She shivered. Her snakes slumbered. She felt full even as she realized she had not dined. That's what the others called it: feeding. She was unsure that her needs rivaled theirs, but the shorthand was the closest she had ever come to naming her needs. "You should run," he said. "You should never look back."

Outside the safety of the bushes, Medusa heard a woman scream; her snakes woke at the sound. She grabbed the man's hand and kissed the palm.

"My name is Christopher," he said, and Medusa dropped his hand and rushed from the bushes. The scene before her had changed; Roxanne had Annabelle by the neck, and Lee Vansing aimed a one-handed crossbow at the vampire's chest. Dr. Hyde stood on Lee's other side, with Lee Vansing's blade at their neck. Annabelle maneuvered her hand into her pocket and stealthily pulled free a cross. She pushed it at Roxanne's chest. Roxanne's skin steamed and caught fire. Roxanne screamed.Medusa's snakes moaned as she jumped in one fluid motion at Lee Vansing and knocked him over. His crossbow fired, the bolt lodging in his daughter's neck. Roxanne bent to taste the blood. The blade glanced off Dr. Hyde's shoulder, and Dr. Hyde scrambled to their feet. Medusa's snakes writhed around Lee Vansing's face. He screamed a garish scream. There was so much screaming.

"Let's go!" Medusa called as she sprang from Lee Vansing's body and tore into the night. Behind her, she heard the thump of Roxanne rolling out her fire, then footsteps, but she didn't know how many until the Monsters Three slid inside their carriage, disappearing into the night.

DRACULA THE OLD

If Lee Vansing did not come to them, they would go to Lee Vansing. The first trouble was that Young Dracula did not know where Lee Vansing resided, but Dracula the Old would not let that stop him; he had his ways of finding information. Dracula the Old instructed Young Dracula to pack his bags. Young Dracula scoffed at the suggestion that Dracula the Old could give him orders, but when Dracula the Old crept from his slumber the following evening, Young Dracula stood waiting with two faded leather suitcases.

"I don't have any clothes that would suit your," Young Dracula paused, waving a hand up and down before Dracula the Old, "style."

Dracula the Old's white shirt was streaked with the blood of harlots. "Your servants can take care of this for me."

"I have dismissed my servants." Young Dracula wiped at his mouth, where Dracula the Old spotted a drip of blood at the corner. "Except for the carriage driver, of course."

Dracula the Old shook his head. "No matter, then. I will clean it." Dracula the Old removed first his cape, then coat, then vest, then shirt, undressing himself like Young Dracula might undress a woman. He held his shirt but folded the rest, placing them gently upon the lid of his coffin. "Your wash basin?"

Young Dracula shrugged, and his cape whispered around his ankles. "Your body's pale as a ghost there, Drac," Young Dracula said as the carriage driver, a squat fellow in a brown suit, hustled into the basement and lifted Young Dracula's bags.

"Anything more, Master?" the carriage driver asked.

"Show my friend to the bathroom." Young Dracula stood taller, looking pleased with himself. "That will be all."

Dracula the Old followed the carriage driver to the bathroom. He did not have a bathroom in his own castle, but it appeared that

Young Dracula had renovated his old-fashioned home. How odd, when vampires did not need to use them! Dracula the Old stepped past the water closet, the door open to the toilet inside. He recalled the days of outhouses, a misty memory of human needs. Perhaps the bathroom was an attempt to remind Young Dracula of his once-held humanity. The floor was porcelain. It must be cold, but no colder than he. He turned the knob on the hand-painted sink and scrubbed the blood from his shirt. Young Dracula would likely leave it be, moving through society with a red stain. What a slob! Dracula the Old scrubbed with his long nails. The water ran over his hands. He thought the steam was from the water at first, but there would be no hot water here—gas pipes were too dangerous to house inside—and as he continued to scrub, he felt his hands burn. He pulled them back from the water. They were red and covered in boils. He hissed as he cradled them to his chest. He left the shirt in the running water and rushed through the hallway.

In the front entry, Young Dracula lounged in a red velvet chaise. "Are you ready yet?" he said.

"My hands!" Dracula the Old thrust his hands into the light.

"You used water?" Young Dracula said.

"How else does one wash a garment?" Dracula the Old said.

"I don't have any idea how one washes a garment," Young Dracula said.

"You use water!"

"Running water wounds us." Young Dracula stood and eyed his fellow. "Do you need a lesson in what kills us? Perhaps you're an imposter after all."

"Stakes through the heart. The sun. We fear the crucifix," Dracula the Old said. "Do not talk down to me. Our kind do not die by running water."

"They do," Young Dracula said. "They will. Now are you quite ready?"

"I don't have a shirt," Dracula the Old said.

Young Dracula heaved a heavy sigh then stormed from the room. When he returned, he held in his arms a clean shirt and Dracula the Old's folded garments. Dracula the Old slipped them on, and once he fastened his cloak, the pair walked side by side to the carriage waiting outside for them.

"You first this time," Dracula the Old said, and Young Dracula grinned as he acquiesced. Dracula the Old was not to be fooled more than once.

The carriage rolled through the countryside night. The sound of the horses' clacking hooves was a song that Dracula the Old enjoyed more than the constant background drone of horns and piano. Dracula the Old missed his thoughts, missed how they throbbed within his head. The music did not allow him to think as he once would have thought. He closed his eyes and let the hoofbeats soothe him. He remembered Mina's dark grey lips. How he would have liked to drain them pale! He would have dressed her in one of the bridal gowns he kept in his castle. He would have wed her in the company of his many wives. They would have been happy together, had it not been for Professor Lee Vansing. What a terrible man! Dracula the Old pressed his hand to the place where the man had staked him, but that reminded him of the wounds still healing on his hands. He shivered.

"Why do you have a bathroom?" he asked.

"For my visitors," Young Dracula said.

"Ah." Dracula the Old pursed his lips. "I thought perhaps you were nostalgic."

"For what?"

"For your humanity."

Young Dracula laughed. "Humanity was the curse, old fool."

But Dracula the Old remembered even if he did not long for it; the song of a heart that beat faster when he ran, and the warmth of a fireplace in winter, and the caress of sunshine through a window, and the itch of a rash, and the ringing of an ear, and the sting of a wasp, and the salt of the ocean in a wound, and the warm sugar smell of a fresh-baked cake. He was glad to be immortal, gladder still to have died twice and risen on both occasions. He remembered the world that he came from in all its grey. He remembered the women, how they hid their bodies from him. Black roses and black lips. How fuzzy everything seemed, compared to this world's crispness. Like being human, Dracula the Old had begun to love the old world without longing to be part of it again. There was excitement here, and he was unsure if he would ever be satisfied with blood that did not weep the brightest red he had ever seen.

The carriage pulled into the city an hour from sunrise. Young Dracula knew the city to contain Lee Vansing's place of residence, but he did not know in which building the vampire hunter resided. A challenge! Dracula the Old relished a challenge.

The carriage driver dropped them at an old insane asylum at the edge of town. "Tomorrow evening, we shall scour the library," Dracula the Old said to Young Dracula as they settled into the coffins that the carriage driver laid out for them. It was not Dracula the Old's preference to sleep in a room haunted by mad ghosts, but he would do what was asked of him by the creature he aimed to destroy. The walls were white tile, and the floor was white tile, and there was an old pair of handcuffs dangling from a nail in the wall. An old iron bed had been pushed against one wall, stripped of its sheets, mildewed by a leak in the ceiling. There were no windows.

"Fine, we shall scour the library," Young Dracula said. "Now let me sleep, old fool."

In his coffin, Dracula the Old dug his pointed nails into his palms as he faded into the half-death of sleep.

To enter the library, Dracula the Old placed his thrall upon the night watchman. Inside, they lit a candle and held it up to the books in the occult and mythology section until Dracula the Old found what he was looking for. If the Professor Lee Vansing of this world was anything like the Professor of his own world, the man would have done what he did in black and white: penned countless tomes full of lore. As Dracula the Old suspected, the L section was littered with the professor's words, book after book bearing his name on the spine. They all were dusty, which made Dracula the Old smile to himself. No one read the man's books here either. Dracula the Old understood his enemy: the professor longed to be remembered, and his years-long battle with Dracula was the only way the professor saw to make that happen.

Dracula the Old removed one of the books from the shelf. The book left a track in the dust below it. Dracula the Old cracked the book open and turned to the back page, where the man's biography took up all the blank space. There it was indeed: Doctor Lee Vansing lives in Flashing.

"Where is Flashing?" Dracula the Old asked his partner.

"It's a neighborhood," Young Dracula said, blowing out the candle now that they had the information they needed. "It's by the river."

"Take me there," Dracula the Old said.

"You do not order me," Young Dracula said. "But we will go there regardless."

Dracula the Old carried the book with them. As they passed the night guard, Young Dracula paused. "I don't usually feed on men," he said.

"I don't either," Dracula the Old said. "They do not taste as good."

Young Dracula cackled, and the night guard did not budge.

"Sometimes it is best not to be too picky." Young Dracula swept forward and captured the guard under his arm; he sank his teeth into the man's neck, and bright red blood gushed from the wound and spilled all over, pooling finally at the vampire's feet. Dracula the Old examined the waste. So much waste! Was this a world obsessed with waste? To cook countless meals for a man who never arrived. To build a bathroom for no one to use. To spill blood instead of letting it flow down the throat.

Dracula the Old snatched the night guard's body from the grasp of Young Dracula and sank his teeth into the other side of the man's thick neck.

THE GORGON

The Monsters Three took shelter not in their lair—for even if Lee Vansing had not yet located it, he knew generally where it might be—but in the apartment of a young married couple. Roxanne had restrained the young woman upon a gorgeous mustard yellow chaise, pinning the girl with one hand upon her exposed chest. Two bite marks marred her perfect breasts. Roxanne agreed to give Dr. Hyde the woman's pineal gland, once she was done with her, and the young man who cowered in the corner of the sitting room was to be Medusa's. But Medusa did not want him, not after she had felt the gaze of Christopher. Christopher Vansing? It could not be.

"She mopes," Roxanne said, wiping a spot of blood off her lips. Roxanne could hardly keep open her eyes, and her skin smelled like charred wood. The woman beside her whimpered. "She thinks she has fallen in love again."

"Speak for yourself," Medusa said, hunched over in a pale blue needlepoint chair. "Or were those not stars I witnessed in your eyes?"

"I know my way around lust," Roxanne said.

"He saw me," Medusa said. "No one has ever seen me before."

"No one?" Dr. Hyde stopped pacing the room and paused before Medusa. They settled their hands on their hips. "No one at all, Medusa?"

"Leave M alone," Roxanne said, stroking the poor woman's hair. "She can't think when she's mooning."

"Handsome or not, Christopher's last name *is* Vansing. He is the son of the man who has tried, on more than one occasion, to kill us." Dr. Hyde resumed their pacing, and Roxanne cupped her hand around the woman's mouth and sucked a bit more blood. "You cannot possibly be thinking of doing anything but slaughtering him."

"He won't hurt us," Medusa said. "I know it. If I can just find him. If I can just talk to him. He may be able to get Lee Vansing off our backs. He may be able to end this."

"Oh, he'll end it." Roxanne let go of the woman, and the woman's head thunked against the chaise's arm. Roxanne tried to stand, but even after draining the woman dry, she was weak. She touched the cross burned into her chest. Although her complexion had calmed, no longer scarred red, her eyes still looked sunken in their sockets.

Dr. Hyde lay their hand against the wound upon their neck. "He trapped us. Surely you don't believe the words of a man over his actions. I have news for you, dear friend: men are far from innocent." Dr. Hyde caressed the masculine side of their body. "Even if we may pretend."

Medusa stood, her body rested and, more importantly, invigorated with rage. "You don't know him."

"You do not know him," Dr. Hyde said.

"Know him or not," Roxanne said, "you're not to see him again until we've killed him."

Medusa stomped her foot, and the sound was loud as a stone falling from a great height. Her snakes burst free from her hair and flexed at their full length, fangs bared. She hissed, and the hiss traveled throughout the room. The man on the floor cried out, but Medusa paid him no heed; she did not need to feed on life when she felt this much anger filling her up. When she felt so much longing pulling her forward. "You are not a leader of me." Her shadow seemed to grow taller in the flickering gaslight. "I am history. I am myth. I am that which does not rot. But look at the both of you. Wounded and sore. Reeking of death."

Dr. Hyde shrank at Medusa's words, but Roxanne merely closed her eyes and leaned back against the back of the chaise. "You will do what you do, I imagine. Leave us alone. We're too tired to hold you back."

Medusa did not understand; she expected her sisters to fight, and when they did not, the power fled from her posture. "You'll see," she said, her snakes burrowing back into her hair. "You'll see I'm right."

Medusa unlatched one of the horses from the carriage and mounted. She rode with the creature between her legs and the creatures atop her head writhing in their respective sheaths: the horse its saddle, and the snakes their bed of mussed-up hair. As she rode through a night pricked with stars, she rocked with the horse's sway. By the time she arrived at the castle in the country, her cheeks were hot with thoughts of Christopher. His piercing eyes. She had perhaps loved men's bodies before, but never their eyes.

She did not need to knock upon his door, for he was expecting her and opened it the moment her feet touched down upon his doorstep.

"I was hoping you'd come," he said as he swept her into his arms. It seemed like he wanted her to burrow into his chest, but Medusa pushed away.

"What's the matter?" he asked.

She gazed into him. "Nothing is the matter. I just want to look into your eyes."

She had only studied diagrams of the human eye, so she understood that it was his iris that was brown. Iris like the flower, but she had never seen a flower burn as fiercely; inside that brown circle was a landscape, craters leading to the black hole at the center of the world. She wanted it to tear her apart. The sclera was white veined with red, and the lens was convex and captured a sheen of light from the fixtures. She saw her reflection in those eyes, and in that reflection, she might be an ordinary woman. It interested her to think about being an ordinary woman, even if she did not long for it on a common day.

Crust had formed at his eye's caruncle. She wiped it away with one swipe of her finger, brushing his eyelashes. His eyelashes were like spider legs.

"How do you do this?" she asked.

"How do I do what?" he asked.

"How do you see me?"

"I often see what others don't," he said. "I always love the unlovable."

His words struck her, but it was true; she had never been loved before, because of who she was, because of what she'd done. Her snakes settled deep into her hair, and she shivered as she came to believe his words as truth. She was unlovable. He loved her anyway. She gave in to him when he pulled her to him and pressed his lips against hers.

When they finally parted, he ran his hands through her now smooth hair. "I'm glad you chose me over them," he said.

She closed her eyes to the feel of his fingers. "Over them?" she murmured.

"You're not like them," he said. "They're monsters. They're terrible. They deserve what they're going to get—" He smiled. "Perhaps I should not have said that."

Her snakes woke as though from a nightmare, spitting and sprawling about her head. One struck his hand, burying its teeth into the first centimeter of his skin.

"Tell me what you're talking about," she said. "Those monsters are my friends."

DR. HYDE

Dr. Hyde continued their pacing as Roxanne wilted further upon the chaise. There were very few times that the noise in Dr. Hyde's head was not caused by their warring factions: both parts of them were opinionated and strong-willed and hungry. Both parts of them longed for full control. But in that pacing moment, Dr. Hyde did not argue with themselves; both parts of them shivered with the exact same fear.

"Where are we going to hide?" Dr. Hyde said. "It's only a matter of time before he finds us."

He always found them; it was what Professor Lee Vansing did best: find them.

"I can hardly think," Roxanne said. "I'm so hungry."

Dr. Hyde moved in front of the young woman and picked up her limp wrist. "No more life in this one." They motioned to the man in the corner. "How about it, Roxanne?"

Roxanne scrunched up her face. "I think I'd rather die."

That was the problem with Roxanne, a problem that neither half of Dr. Hyde shared: she was not logical. She would not do anything to survive.

Dr. Hyde had another name once, but it was difficult to pull from the fog of memory. Once Dr. Hyde had a face that made the woman next door blush every time she looked at them; it was one face all the way across, the face of a man. But Dr. Hyde was a scientist, and a good one, and he didn't care about the woman next door's affections. Dr. Hyde longed for one thing and one thing only: to discover the secret to immortality, and in so doing, to locate the cure for any disease.

It seemed silly now, to obsess so over saving others when they themselves were so much in the dark. For all their days were spent in the little lab in their apartment building, which was full of scientists and their families, and all their nights were spent hunched into their thoughts as they scarfed down what dinner they could scavenge. Sometimes the woman next door brought them hot meals, and these warmed their body enough to carry on longer in the little lab.

Sometimes, they realized that having a wife would bring them many benefits, and they considered her more closely for a couple of days before fading back into their typical habits.

The first serum, made from the pineal gland of a cadaver they were lucky enough to procure—some nameless beggar—tasted as bitter as green olives and shone as brightly as silver in a candle's light. They had never seen anything so brilliant, so bright. They took it down the throat like it was candy.

The other half that emerged was nothing like the woman next door; their gaze burned through whoever it touched, and they moved like a high-class prostitute, and they ate chicken legs in the tavern as though they were an animal and this their first meal in months. Meat fell from their mouth as they chewed. Men found them intoxicating. They didn't want men; they wanted more of this existence, for they were in full control of the body, with no knowledge of that other inhabitant outside the barest inkling.

When Dr. Hyde woke the next morning, they remembered nothing of the other half or the night they pursued, but they found a note upon their nightstand:

Thank you for the lovely evening. Let's do it again sometime.

Dr. Hyde wrinkled their forehead. Who had been inside their apartment, when all they recalled was blankness behind their eyes?

Still, they craved the serum. The next night they swallowed it and emerged as the woman who longed for nothing more than to live. They patted down the body cloaked in oversized trousers and an old coat and scowled. This would not do. They scavenged the closed down shops for something more fitting and came upon a sharp green dress, the color of their beloved serum, with a deep neckline and material so thin it showed the mole on the left side of Dr. Hyde's belly. The dress hung on a model in the window, and Dr. Hyde found, when they tried to work the lock, that they had uncommon strength; the knob cracked off the door.

The dress made them come alive, and when Dr. Hyde awoke in

their body as a man the very next morning, they ran their hands down the silk and remembered everything.

It wasn't long before Dr. Hyde the scientist regretted their creation, for they were no longer able to spend those long nights hunched over their experiments, and at night, they longed to roam the night streets until the end of time. Dr. Hyde was torn between two internal states: the desire for success and the desire to do away with success altogether. Dr. Hyde farmed more bodies and concocted more serum, until the morgues ran dry.

It would require a workaround to continue their dual existence. If one side of Dr. Hyde refused, the other half of them agreed to carry out the devilish deed. Sometimes, in the act, Dr. Hyde was not even sure which part of them was in charge. Sometimes they felt like both of them were.

Then, one night, as they plunged their blade through the heart of a young vagrant woman, and the bright red blood spilled out over their hand and pooled upon the alley cobblestones, and Dr. Hyde looked down in shock at how much the woman had shed, and there was a pool of water there, too, from the recent rainstorm, Dr. Hyde saw their reflection in the glittering surface and realized that they were both halves at once in body as well as mind.

Dr. Hyde pulled Roxanne from the chaise and set her beside the young man. "Drink up," Dr. Hyde said. "You need your strength."

The young man did not run, even though he was under no thrall, no paralysis. Instead he cowered as he had cowered while Roxanne murdered his wife. He seemed not to dare look at any of them. He studied the wood floor instead.

Roxanne crossed her arms across her chest, but the motion was slow. Her eyes half-closed, she looked drunk and damaged. Dr. Hyde had never seen her this way. They rolled their eyes. Nothing to be done now. Dr. Hyde needed their own mind sharp, to figure out a way to fix this, all of this. Dr. Hyde removed their scalpel from their pocket and crouched before the dead woman on the chaise. She had such beautiful gold hair. Dr. Hyde was going to cut it off her.

They grabbed the hair in one hand and pulled while drawing a line with the other. There was very little blood; Roxanne had seen to that, but a thin line of red formed where the scalpel met skin. Dr. Hyde removed the scalp. Now for the skull, which they usually removed using a saw. Desperate times. Dr. Hyde placed one hand on each side of the woman's skull and pressed until it broke. They picked pieces of skull and brain and tossed them on the floor until enough clear space remained for Dr. Hyde to pull the brain from its bone casing.

Dr. Hyde took their surgery to the dining table, where they cut the brain in half. What a beautiful spread. Dr. Hyde's hands and the table were covered in muck. Dr. Hyde wiped their hands on their clothes. With the scalpel, they pulled out the pineal gland.

Dr. Hyde no longer required the serum; they were both halves of themselves without any help from anyone or anything. But they craved it: the bitter taste, the bright green glow. Plus, it gave them a focus that had resulted in their best ideas. Dr. Hyde didn't have the other ingredients for their serum, but they had the gland. It would have to do. They opened their mouth and swallowed it whole.

The door caved in. Dr. Hyde sprang to their feet. Behind the shattered wood, Professor Lee Vansing held a sledgehammer in his hand.

"I already understand her weakness." He motioned to Roxanne and smirked. "And she looks like she will be no trouble tonight. But you. I was unsure of the best way to kill you. If it's your brain that powers you," he said, pointing with one long finger at Dr. Hyde, "I'll bash it in."

MEDUSA

Christopher screamed as the snake's fang sunk a deeper into the skin of his hand. "I didn't mean anything by it!" He tried to pull his hand away, but a second snake blocked its way. "I just meant—you're not like them—that's a good thing!"

"I'm like them," Medusa said, and as she said it, she realized it for perhaps the first time; she had never been like anyone before. Never mind that this man could look her in the eye; that didn't mean anything. They hadn't shared a lair. They hadn't shared their life stories. They had not murdered anyone together. If she chose the man over her friends, she would go her whole life never looking anyone but him in the eye ever again. "What have you done to them?"

Christopher grimaced. "It's not me!" he said. "It's my father!"

Medusa had no time to waste; she let her lover go and rode off into the night.

ROXANNE

The monster hunter was about to kill the monster, and wasn't that always how it went. You could prepare all you wanted. He would come for you anyway. You could hide anywhere. He would always find you. Roxanne laughed, slumped beside the young man who reeked of testosterone and bad humor, and neither the monster hunter nor Dr. Hyde so much as glanced her way. This is what she, a seducer of women, a drainer of life, had been reduced to. Her skin burned with the memory of fire.

Lee Vansing advanced on Dr. Hyde and lifted his sledgehammer. Dr. Hyde, her friend, her sister, caught the sledgehammer as it fell toward their face. They struggled to push it away, legs spread wide in a squat, arms quaking with the effort.

Roxanne closed her eyes partly to block out what was to come and partly because she could not hold them open any longer.

Roxanne had been sleeping before the mysterious aristocrat made her like him. Roxanne had made her entrance at the masquerade in a white gown that floated like a cloud across the checkered floor. Her mask was a white cat with long whiskers, and it glittered as she danced with every man at the party. Men loved her; they often proposed, claiming that they had always longed to love a pure creature like herself.

Roxanne only had eyes for one person, and that girl danced with her own fiancé across the room. If Roxanne were to ask her love to dance, the whole room would stop with shock. It would not do, and so Roxanne moved to the next man, an older gentleman in a long purple cloak. He stopped halfway through and held his heart.

"Oh, I'm out of breath," he said. "Would you accompany me outside for a spot of air?"

Panic seized Roxanne's chest. "Of course!" she said.

The man grasped at her arm, and she helped him hobble through the front doors, nodding to the doorman as they passed to signal that she was okay, that she was not in need of a chaperone. Once the night air hit them, Roxanne examined the man, who perked up suddenly under the moonlight.

"Are you sure you don't need—"

He grabbed her head and pushed it until the neck strained; she struggled but could not remove herself from his grasp. He'd fooled her. He sank his teeth into her skin, and she felt the blood leave her, a dizzying feeling that made the world spin around her. Until she fell. The last thing she felt was his hands picking her up. She was light. She was air.

She awoke the next evening at the center of a hedge maze, surrounded by evergreen bushes shaped into boxes. She lay upon black dirt, her hands crossed across her chest like the dead. She sat straight up. The man sat upon the closed lid of a casket.

"I have made you one of me," he said. "We will live forever together."

Roxanne lifted a finger and ran it across the pointed teeth that had grown overnight. Everyone knew about vampires; everyone half-believed they were real. It was hard not to, reading newspaper articles about dead bodies with holes in the neck or stumbling upon those bodies yourself while strolling through the woods. Living forever sounded like a glorious notion. Often, she pined at the passing of time. Many days she dreamed of yesterday, knowing that yesterday she was one day less close to death. She loved being young, even if the ones she loved did not love her back. She loved the look of her smooth skin in a mirror.

"I don't think so," she said. "I'll be fine on my own."

The man furrowed his brow and stood. "What?" he said, but Roxanne only shrugged. The man's body quaked. "I made you! Did you not hear me? You are mine."

Roxanne stood up and dusted the dirt off her clothes. She would need new ones, clean ones. Maybe something red. The man was pathetic. He angered so quickly, from a simple no. Men were too fragile. She had always known, but now she had the words for their condition. Everything felt clear.

"I'm not," she said. "Thank you for the immortality, but I have no interest in forever with you."

The man stepped toward her. She turned and ran, and she was quick; her body felt like a cloud. She closed a hand around a branch and snapped it off. She turned and held it out at him; it had a pointed end where it had broken.

"You think I don't know how to kill a vampire?" she said and plunged it into his heart with all her strength, which was significant. Blood gushed from the wound. His mouth opened in a silent O as his skin turned to ash before her eyes. His bones went next, collapsing in on themselves and cascading to the ground. It was quite beautiful to watch. She dropped the branch and stepped back from the pile of him. She wiped her bloody hand upon her dress; the red stained a large patch at her belly.

"Oh, that's lovely," she said.

She spent a whole evening finding her way through the maze and stumbled free from its green prison as the birds began chirping. Before her stood a mansion on a hill. She would come to realize, being a monster, that there were more mansions and castles on hills than ever she had imagined during her human life. She ran up the hill with the last of her strength and burst through the unlocked door. To her surprise, a maid was mopping the floors in the entrance.

"May I help you, miss?" the maid said. "The Stokers aren't awake quite yet."

Roxanne composed herself. "I'm supposed to meet them for breakfast."

"I'm afraid breakfast isn't for another couple of hours," the maid said. "Are you all right, miss?"

"Just... famished." Roxanne worried at her lip with her fang.

The maid leaned her mop against a wall. "Are you sure you're all right?"

Roxanne moved toward the woman. She was cute, round, and smelled of sweat and worry. Roxanne could tell that she had not slept much, had enjoyed too much wine with friends the night before and had lost track of time. Time meant little to Roxanne now. She took a step and slipped, and the maid rushed forward to keep her from hitting her head on the marble floor. Roxanne let herself be held by the girl.

"Thank you," she said. "A kiss on your cheek, for the trouble!"

The maid smiled. "Not necessary, miss," but she seemed flattered by the request.

"It's rude in my country to refuse," Roxanne said, and the maid nodded once then leaned down to accept the kiss. Roxanne grabbed the woman's face and kissed her neck, grazing the skin with her teeth. The maid giggled, but the way she was positioned, Roxanne saw down the dress she wore, into the cavern of her cleavage. In one fell swoop, Roxanne let go of the woman's face, grabbed hold of the edge of her neckline, yanked it down, and sank her teeth into the tender skin of her breast. The taste of blood was magnificent, better than any taste she had acquired during her time as a human. She let the blood flow over her tongue and down her throat. She let the blood warm her belly. The blood rushed from the wound so quickly that Roxanne could not capture it all in her mouth, and it gushed out and down her chin, dripping onto the top of her stained white dress. Roxanne pulled back and let the woman's body fall. She rubbed her hands across the stain, dyeing as much of the dress as she could. It wasn't enough blood, and Roxanne's eyes grew heavy, and the sun was beginning to peek in through the windows. Roxanne had very little time.

She climbed the stairs. She checked every room. When she found a sleeping body, she clamped her hand over its mouth and drained as much as was able, then moved the body to the edge of the bed and lay beneath it, letting the blood fall onto her dress. She killed a young man, a father, and a mother, but when she reached the daughter's room, she found a sleeping beauty so mesmerizing that she could not kill her. Instead, when the woman woke, Roxanne captured her in her thrall, and together they lay until morning.

Roxanne woke to the young woman's screams. She had padded down the hall, encountering the bloodied bodies of her family. Roxanne rolled her eyes and soothed the girl, and just when she seemed calmed, Roxanne finished her dress's transformation.

The mansion's stables were full of horses. Roxanne helped herself to one and rode back to the city she had once called home.

As she conquered the night in her red dress, Roxanne made herself a vow: she would find her best friend and give her the gift the old man had given Roxanne. Together, they would take whatever in the world they wanted. But something had happened during the brief few days Roxanne had been away. When Roxanne returned home, she found her best friend's family cloaked all in black. When she visited the cemetery, she knelt at the grave of the woman she was too late to make one of her own. She touched the gravestone—humans died so easily, threatened even by invisible particles in the air—and when her fingers neared the cross etched there, her hands smoked and burned. She pulled them back. Grief was for the living, and she was not living any longer.

Roxanne had not fed on a man since her first night of feeding. There, in the apartment of the married couple, with Professor Lee Vansing one right move away from murdering that great genius Dr. Hyde, Roxanne had no choice. She reached, eyes still closed, and found the man's trembling body beside her. Even his skin felt gross, clammy and rough, like he had never worn lotion or groomed a day in his life. She pulled herself to him. She clamped down on the first bare skin she felt. His blood tasted like steak and moldy potatoes, and she drank it down as though she had not eaten in an age.

She opened her eyes and pulled back from him; she had drained the man through his foot. She tried not to gag as his life transferred to her, as she absorbed his soul. That wasn't how it worked, but that's what she imagined when she drank.

She stood and steadied herself against the wall. "Stop!" she yelled. Lee Vansing faltered for a moment in his assault, and Dr. Hyde seized the advantage. They dodged their way out from beneath the sledgehammer, and Lee Vansing fell forward, losing his balance to the ground.

Dr. Hyde rushed to Roxanne and grabbed her hand. "Run," they said. They fled through the kitchen and wrenched open the back door. Medusa stood in all her monstrous glory on the other side.

THE MONSTERS THREE

We held hands, the three of us, as we mounted three horses and rode in sync. It was nearly daylight, but we rode quickly to reach our destination. Dr. Hyde formed an idea, one of their best; there had been monsters before us who survived, who thrived, outside Lee Vansing's shadow. We could not ask them directly, for we did not know where to find them, but we could read the words they had written. Their diaries were stored in the Great Library of Evil.

The living did not go near the Great Library of Evil, and so it held little use to monsters like ourselves. There were reasons that they did not go near it: it is hidden in the woods, it is guarded by wards placed by warlocks, and it is haunted. We rode past the edge of town and into the fierce thicket of trees. In the forest, the sun did not play by the rules. Sometimes day was a sudden surprise. Sometimes the night overstayed its welcome. For us, the dark was a comfort. It allowed us to reach the Great Library of Evil and dismount at its gates.

We took the path to the front doors by foot through a foggy cemetery. The fog tickled our ankles, and the ghosts climbed free of their graves and sniffed us out as we passed. We were no interest to them beyond their initial curiosity; they longed for their own fresh blood, fresh companions with whom to wile away their days.

It was blood, too, that the front door's wards were after. Medusa held her finger to her snakes and let them pierce her, then allowed ten drops to fall at the building's threshold. Dr. Hyde cut themself with a blade they kept in their pocket and did the same. Roxanne shoved two fingers down her throat and vomited enough blood that the doors creaked open, and we passed.

In the front room, a chandelier of bones hung from the ceiling. The building was empty but for the giant spiders spinning webs in every corner. There were six doorways barred by wrought-iron gates lining each wall, and the floor was dusty as we walked across it. Medusa stepped on the shed skin of a giant snake; she bent and pet the scales and smiled. We were home here. We were welcome. We were safe.

The gate squeaked as we opened it. Inside, the smell of old pages greeted us. Ordinarily, we did not enjoy the same smells that people enjoy, but the smell of books was different; it was death as well, the words scrawled upon the flesh of trees. We inhaled the smell gladly.

We searched the shelves until we found the diaries of the greatest monsters of our time, those creatures who never seemed to die: the man made from many men, the embalmed body come to life, and Dracula. We each took a tome and perused, and time passed without us realizing. When we woke upon the library floors, we found that we had slept away a day and passed once more into night. We continued reading.

In all three diaries, we found the same progression of events: live, fight, die. Live again, fight again, die again. Live again, live again. We had heard the stories of resurrection—of course we had—but here, in this context, they were a revelation: to die and rise, that was the secret to true immortality. That was the answer to the power that the other monsters held in their thick, manly claws.

DRACULA THE OLD

Dracula the Old and Young Dracula walked the Flashing streets, seeking out any hint of Lee Vansing's residence. Toward the end of the second street, they found it: a little house with a hundred crosses crowding the small yard.

"Bit obvious," Young Dracula said.

But Dracula the Old felt queasy in his belly. He turned away from the scene. "How can you look at it?" he said.

"It hurts," Young Dracula said. "But we are at a distance."

"How are we supposed to get in there?" Dracula the Old said.

"He's not there," Young Dracula said.

"How do you know?" Dracula the Old wheezed, his dead lungs constricting.

"He never is." Young Dracula turned away at last.

Across the street, an old woman leaned out her door. "He doesn't live there anymore," she called to them. "So you can get the hell out of our neighborhood, you fiends!"

Dracula the Old and Young Dracula shared a glance, then raced across the street and through the woman's yard, but she closed the door before they reached it. She knew her lore: she had left none of her windows open.

"Where now?" Young Dracula said.

"Surely Vansing will return home this evening," Dracula the Old said. "We wait."

"Old fool," Young Dracula said. "Professor Vansing is clever. He won't return home. This place is not his home any more. He moves. He leaves small traces. He misleads. It is his game. Did you think I hadn't looked for him before?"

Dracula the Old frowned. His own Vansing was not as clever. The puzzles that led his way were easy to solve, and the man's motivations were simple: to slay Dracula, to protect the world from vampires. This man who hid from his foe was not the same man Dracula had once fought.

"Come now." Young Dracula looped his arm through Dracula the Old's. "There's more books on our good man Vansing in the Great Library of Evil. Maybe you'll find something there that can help us."

Dracula the Old wrenched free of Young Dracula's grasp. "The what?" Rage boiled in his belly like hot blood. This brute claimed to long for a fight with Lee Vansing but withheld information that could help them. This beast called him "old fool." Dracula the Old hissed. "Why have you not told me about this place before?" His shadow stretched across the street; it looked as though it had wings then four legs then a tail. Young Dracula examined it but did not seem fearful of its strange transformations. "You will take me there at once, *young fool.*"

Young Dracula laughed. "Of course," he said. "Follow me."

The Great Library of Evil was like nothing Dracula the Old had ever seen. Inside its walls, Young Dracula pointed to one of the wrought iron gates guarding a doorway. "The section on monster hunters is right through there."

But Dracula the Old sensed a life in the place that was stronger than the spiders that crawled along its ceiling. "What is in that door?" He pointed.

Young Dracula puffed up. "That's the autobiographies," he said. "My diaries are in there, you know."

"How marvelous!" Dracula the Old said. "Show me your diaries!"

Inside the room, three creatures crowded around one single book. They resembled women, for the most part: a vampire in a red dress with black lace along the V-neck, a dapper gentleperson in a lab coat with a face that looked like two faces sewn together, and a snake-headed monster in a white long-sleeve gown that covered her every inch.

"Well, who do we have here?" Young Dracula strode right into the room and up to the trio. "Curling up with a good book, are we?" He grinned. "How do you like it?"

"Dracula," the vampire said. "Speak of the devil."

"And who is this?" the dapper one said, gesturing at Dracula the Old.

"Your grandfather?" The vampire smirked.

"This is Dracula II," Young Dracula said.

Dracula the Old took one tentative step. "Are you looking for Professor Vansing as well?"

The snakes atop the snake-headed monster's head lengthened and hissed. "Is he hunting you too?"

Young Dracula frowned. "Wait, it's you three?" He shook his head.

"Can't be. Why would he waste his time with three women?"

"Are we women?" the dapper one said. "Are you very sure?"

Young Dracula laughed. "Oh, Lee Vansing, you deluded idiot. Which one of you has stolen his heart?"

"Excuse me." The vampire's hand whipped out and closed around Young Dracula's neck. "You won't speak to us this way."

Young Dracula continued his terrible smile. "You can't possibly think you're a bigger threat than me."

"We are," the snake monster said. "You, sir, haven't been relevant for a very long time."

Dracula the Old felt light for the first time since he'd arrived, as though he might fly, if he could. They were interesting monsters, different than any he had before encountered. And how lovely! They were wedging themselves under Young Dracula's skin. Dracula the Old felt like laughing, like crying from joy, like dancing. He had not danced in so long! Perhaps one of the new monsters would dance with him. He could almost hear the music! But then—yes, he did hear music: a dramatic swell of music. It left in him a fear.

As the floor burst open no more than five feet in front of him, he jumped—and his wings flapped, kept him afloat. Lee Vansing sprung from the trap door, stake in hand, sword sheathed at his side. Dracula the Old flew into the rafters. He perched there; he was never one to miss a death scene.

THE MONSTERS, ONE AND ALL

Roxanne shoved Young Dracula toward Vansing, knocking them both to the ground. Vansing rolled atop the vampire and held the stake to his chest.

"Hammer, my dear," he called out, and a womanly hand reached out from the trap door. Lee Vansing snatched the short-handled sledgehammer from her grasp. Annabelle climbed out, her own stake in hand. She wore a bandage wrapped around her neck. Christopher emerged behind her.

Lee Vansing held the stake to Dracula's chest, and with his other hand, he hammered it in. Medusa gasped as blood oozed from the count and he transformed, layer by layer, into ash. Dracula was a legend. Medusa had heard stories of him, and Lee Vansing had just decimated him in less than a minute. They had read that the truest immortality came from death, but Medusa did not want to die. She had lived for so long. Medusa looked at Christopher, who was paused at the trap door, staring back at her. Could she do it? Could she let him kill her? Medusa dived beneath a nearby table and crawled into the shadows, where she belonged.

Roxanne had always known Dracula was weak, far weaker than she was, anyway. Even if he died and returned a thousand times, he would never match her. He did not deserve his own reputation; it was clear from how easily he had perished after Lee Vansing's arrival. To die so quickly; it was beneath immortals. She would not let Lee Vansing take her quickly. No, she would go down in the books as one who had dragged out her first deadly battle.

As for Dr. Hyde, they were afraid of death. They were human inside, full of human body parts that worked as human body parts worked. They might not come back like the rest of them. Though their words may live on—they kept their own diaries and experiment logs in a secure chest in the apartment they still shelled out money to rent—this body might be their last. They had agreed to go together, and they wouldn't break a promise, but the rational part of their mind said that they may be the only one of the three of them to stay buried in the ground.

In the eaves, Dracula the Old watched with interest, waiting for his time to make it out undead.

Christopher launched himself into the shadows, joining Medusa, seeking her out in the dark. Through the dark, she saw only his eyes. They danced their *pas de deux*. "I'm not here to hurt you," he said, and Medusa understood that he was lying.

Roxanne could not go down without a kiss, without one final

dastardly deed. She cast her thrall across the room, and Annabelle fell into it as easily as Dracula had left his body. Annabelle moved toward her as toward a shiny object.

Lee Vansing stood from the pile of dust that had been his kill. He scanned the room; Dr. Hyde it would be, for him, and how fitting.

They were both creatures of learning, after all. Dr. Hyde and the hunter advanced, one step at a time, until they met in the middle of the library. Lee Vansing held his sledgehammer across his chest. "Are you ready to die this night?"

"I am ready," Dr. Hyde said as they reached into their pocket, pulled out their knife, and stabbed their own heart. "No monster dead is dead forever." And they fell in a great thump to the ground. They yanked the blade from inside their skin and slid it across the room. It landed beneath the stacks.

"Well, that was easy," Lee Vansing said, frowning. He searched about the room once more; everyone was occupied, each foe spoken for. In the eaves, he heard the sound of someone laughing. When he looked up, there was nothing there. Roxanne pulled Annabelle close and stroked her face. Lee Vansing saw; he noticed; he realized with a start that his daughter did not, in fact, have the upper hand. He rushed across the room just in time to see the teeth as they sunk into Annabelle's neck. "No!" he cried, and the light left Annabelle's eyes.

Roxanne pulled away, her mouth ringed with the blood of Lee Vansing's child. He had not always known he had a daughter; she was new to him, delivered to his doorstep as an adult by her mother, a once-lover of times past. Vansing had hardly recognized the mother, but he recognized the daughter. She had his nose. "Annabelle!" he cried out, and Roxanne sprung onto a shelf, knocking a cascade of books across the room as she landed.

Inside the shadows, Medusa met her lover gaze-to-gaze. "Why can you see me?" she asked as he reached out for her. It was the only thing she wanted to know, before she decided if she would let him take her to hell.

"There's no reason," he said. "Perhaps my heart is already made of stone."

"I believe it," she said, and she grabbed hold of his face and snapped his neck. Her snakes struck all at once, to make sure the job was finished. One of their fangs broke off in his skin. When his body fell, the fang fell with it, tumbling beneath a shelf, into the place where sharp things waited to be reborn.

Medusa jumped from the shadows and onto the back of Lee Vansing. She let her snakes go wild. They twisted around him. He stumbled in a circle, his footing less sure by the second, and when he fell, he grabbed hold of one snake and tossed Medusa over his head. She landed upon her back. He straddled her and screamed as he pulled his blade from its sheath and cut her head clean from her body. When it rolled across the floor, it was stone. Her body was stone. Her eyes were stone.

Roxanne cried out. She had planned to die, but to watch her friends go, that was something dreadful. She could not help her feet; she ran away from him. She grabbed hold of a stone in the wall and climbed. Lee Vansing called after her: "Don't make this harder than it has to be!" But Roxanne burned with grief, for her first love, for her friends. She was a plague on this earth, and anyone who touched her perished. She loved it. She climbed the wall. It was a new feat, something she had not tried before. She climbed out onto the rafters on all fours, gripping the wooden beams with all her might. Her hand brushed against the bat, and he transformed into the other Dracula, that stranger she had not known when he entered the room.

"Can you transform?" he asked her. "We can escape here."

"Not into a bat, I can't."

"Then into what?"

"A cat," she said.

"Then do it! Let's go. We can escape him."

She thought for a moment; Lee Vansing didn't know she couldn't be a bat. There was so much that Lee Vansing did not know. Roxanne couldn't leave, not without the relics of her friends, not if leaving meant ensuring that Lee Vansing would never cease following her.

"You first," she said.

Dracula the Old grinned, then formed his wings. He hovered above the rafter. She reached out her hand and closed it around the bat, crushing its wings, then dropped it onto the ground.

"Ha!" Lee Vansing said, as he drove his stake into the dying bat's chest. "I've got you!"

DRACULA THE OLD

Dracula the Old heard the whispering music, like a gasp of last breath, before he even opened his eyes. He lay once more in a coffin. He rose. He took the stairs from the basement and found not his first home, not his second, but some new place. The walls were stone, and great cracked pillars lined one side of the open foyer as vast as any room Dracula the Old had ever seen. Off in the hall, a stone head stared out at him. A long stone table stretched across the room, and a portrait of a young warrior hung upon the wall.

Not again! Would this be his life forevermore, waking time and again in strange locations? The music whispered once more, and a man stepped from the shadows.

"Welcome to my home," he said. His skin was wrinkled and paler still than Dracula the Old's, his hair done up atop his head in two strange white buns on either side of his head. He wore a red silk robe, embroidered with gold. "You are not Mr. Harker," he said.

"I am Dracula," Dracula the Old said.

"Ah," said the man. "I understand the power of resurrection. For I am Dracula too."

ROXANNE

Lee Vansing gathered his weapons and left the Great Library of Evil, having come for three kills and managed four. He left the bodies of his children.

Roxanne jumped from the rafters. She searched the dusty floor until she came upon the relics of her fellow monsters' lives: the fang of a snake and a blade. She glanced about the room; surely there were books, somewhere in his place, on the art of resurrection. The library was not a bad lair, with a trap door in the floor and a tunnel that led to the forest outside. She would only travel into town to feed. Then she would return to read. This she would do until she brought back every creature she had ever loved.

"Welcome to your home," she whispered to herself as she opened her first tome. Outside, in the night, thunder cracked open the sky.

Bonnie Jo Stufflebeam's fiction and poetry has appeared in over 70 publications such as *Year's Best Dark Fantasy & Horror*, *Fairy Tale Review*, and *LeVar Burton Reads*, as well as in six languages. She has been a finalist for the Nebula Award and won the Grand Prize in the SyFy Channel's *Battle the Beast* contest; SyFy made and released an animated short of her short story "Party Tricks," set in the world of *The Magicians*. She curates the annual Art & Words Show in Fort Worth.

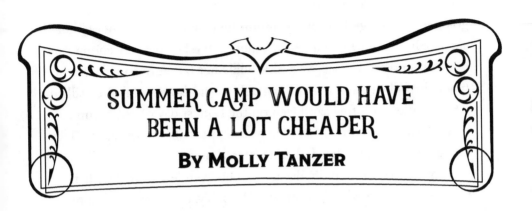

SUMMER CAMP WOULD HAVE BEEN A LOT CHEAPER

By Molly Tanzer

"LISTEN, FRED, I KNOW YOU think it's beneath you—but it means *two thousand bucks* in your pocket. Less my commission of course. Easy money for us both! Only a fool would turn it down. Are you a fool?"

They—Tilly Turner, her father Fred, and his agent Mr. Bernstein—were all having lunch at the counter of Eisenberg's, on 5th Avenue. It was July, and it was very hot. If the ceiling fans were doing anything other than ticking at slightly different intervals from one another, Tilly couldn't tell. There was no breeze whatsoever, no breath of air that didn't feel like it had come straight out of someone else's lungs.

Tilly had ordered an egg cream and, at the urging of her father, a reuben. He had ordered his usual, a liverwurst and onion. She could smell the onion in the heat of the deli and it made her want neither the egg cream nor the reuben.

What she really wanted to do was get out her book and read. She had just gotten to the part in *Atlas Shrugged* where Robert Stadler was going to try to seize control of the Xylophone, the big death ray that the bad guys had made based on his work on sonic physics. Exciting stuff.

But her father had forbidden her from reading at the table. Tilly didn't think that was fair. It was her summer vacation, after all, and she should be allowed to read if she wanted to, *especially* if she was going to get dragged to some crummy lunch meeting with her father's agent. She would be sixteen in January. If she was old enough to roam around the Upper West Side while her father brooded over his typewriter all day, she was old enough to stay home while he walked a few blocks for a free sandwich on the hottest day of the summer.

Well, two free sandwiches. That was it, probably—by making Tilly come along, he'd get her fed and watered on someone else's dime.

Tilly wanted her rapidly drying reuben even less now. The hypocrisy of it all turned her stomach. Probably her father was already gearing up to ask for a doggie bag for her leftovers!

"I dunno, Saul," said her father, through a mouthful of liverwurst.

Mr. Bernstein was only having coffee, black, and plenty of it. His turtleneck was black, too; she didn't know how he was enduring this heat. She was sweating through her tee shirt and shorts.

"You dunno *what?*" Mr. Bernstein talked faster than anyone Tilly had ever met, even here in New York City.

"Well it's just that I'm trying to finish up my edit on *The Chaff of Life* on time, and—"

Mr. Bernstein rolled his eyes, something Tilly was not allowed to do.

"*On time,*" he said. "Since when do *you* care about *on time?* And we both know what's gonna happen with that book of yours, no matter when you turn it in."

Tilly's father winced and dropped his sandwich crust down on his plate, but he did not protest either the aspersion upon his professional character, or the probable fate of his latest effort.

Alfred Turner's second novel, *Seven for a Secret*, had done pretty well. What that meant exactly, Tilly didn't really know. But she did know, from overhearing conversations like these, that none of his other books had done *as* well, or even "well" at all—and people were starting to wonder if Alfred Turner's "promise" had been merely that.

"Come on, Fred," said Mr. Bernstein, but his tone was gentler. "It's easy money, and quick too. They want it in a month. What's a month? You take that long to get contracts back to me."

"Yeah, well if it takes me that long to get a contract back to you, when will I have time to *write* it?"

"It doesn't have to be good. They just want *something*. This is a rush job. The first guy, my client Jake, he got two weeks in, and bailed."

"Why?"

"Said it was making him drink too much. But he got a few chapters done. I have them. You can take 'em or leave 'em. But you don't have to. They don't care."

"What *do* they care about?" asked her father.

"Making money, of course." Mr. Bernstein waved the waitress over and indicated she should refill his coffee. "That's what it's all about. This sort of book, it's a sure thing for publishers, no matter what it is. They know people will buy it because they liked the movie—why I can't imagine in this case, but there's no accounting for taste."

"What's the movie?"

"*Orchard of Sin*," said Mr. Bernstein. "Also being released as *The Apples of Sin are Sweet*, for the European market. It's a chiller. Schlocky stuff; Bayonet Productions is isn't known for their, ah, *subtlety*. They do a lot of historical stuff; they bought some farm in Maryland a while back, with a big old house and a barn, so most of their stuff is set in some time where you'd ride a horse to get around. I read the treatment, and this one's pretty much a Yankee Doodle-era soft-core *Invasion of the Body Snatchers*."

Tilly looked over at her father and found him looking sidelong at her, the lenses of his thick glasses flashing in the light. Mr. Bernstein coughed into his fist before extracting and lighting a cigarette, to cover the momentary awkwardness.

"And the advance is two thousand bucks?" said her father.

"Two thousand bucks for forty thousand words—*tops*. They made poor Jimmy Muir cut something like seven hundred lines from his novelization of *The Witching Year*—another one of these Bayonet turkeys—so that they could fit some ads in the back."

Tilly had learned to observe people very closely—she'd had to, to survive the upheavals of the past year. Her father was starting to consider the idea.

Mr. Bernstein saw it, too. "He blinks in the sunlight after being dragged from the cave!" he declared, pitching his voice a bit louder and gesturing to the other patrons of Eisenberg's with his cigarette.

No one looked up, not even any of the waitresses. New York City was really something. Back in Connecticut, that sort of behavior would be enough to get them thrown out into the street. Or the jail...

"All right, all right," said her father.

"You'll do it?"

"I dunno, Saul, I mean... what, they're gonna put *my* name on the cover? How will that help? Probably they'd be better off using a pen name."

"They *definitely* want a pen name." Mr. Bernstein smirked at her father's grimace. "Oh come on, Freddy! It can be open if you want, and anyways, everybody knows your style. It'll shine on through, like... I dunno, like the sun through clouds. Probably some lady fan of yours will see your truth through the charade and then, *bam*, you've got yourself a second wife."

"Better ask for more than two grand if that's how it's gonna be," said Tilly's father.

Tilly sighed into her egg cream. She didn't mean for it to be so loud.

"Poor kid," said Mr. Bernstein. "Sorry, Tilly. But the length of this lunch—it's all your father's fault, as I'm sure you've noticed. When he gives in and says *yes*, you can leave. Until then..." he shrugged. "If I'm going to buy two sandwiches and that egg cream, I need it to be worth my while."

Tilly had had enough. "Dad, can I please read at the table?"

"No, Tilly."

"Why not?" said Mr. Bernstein. He grinned at Tilly, but she didn't feel like smiling back. "Why shouldn't one of us have a good time? Whatcha reading, kid?"

Usually, Tilly would have a Philip K. Dick or Jack Vance paperback in her back pocket, but her latest obsession didn't fit.

Too big.

"*Atlas Shrugged,*" she said proudly.

"*Atlas Shrugged!*" Mr. Bernstein laughed, to her surprise. She had assumed he'd be impressed. "Jeepers, Fred. Do you need me to get her a copy of something more, I dunno... *wholesome? The Bell Jar,* maybe?"

Tilly bristled, but before she could reply, her father held out his hand, calling for quiet.

"Her mother gave it to her," he said to Mr. Bernstein, in a tone that made Tilly wonder if he knew it had actually been her mother's new boyfriend, Daniel, who'd passed it along. "Tilly's really enjoying it."

She was. She liked the *feel* of the book—all those people striding about, being brilliant inventors or executives, uttering only sharp, devastating rebukes or luscious speeches of praise. The moral ambiguities of her favorite paperbacks were nowhere to be found—black was black, white was white. Characters were either admirable or otherwise, which certainly made things less confusing.

"Enjoying Rand!" said Mr. Bernstein. "Well, I didn't even know such a thing was possible. What is it you enjoy?"

"Saul, she's just a—"

"I like that Rand writes about people not just as they are, but how they ought to be," said Tilly grandly.

Mr. Bernstein stared at her in apparent astonishment.

Hoping to further impress him, Tilly added, "Unlike so many writers these days, who seek to convey nothing with their art, she seeks to present the possibility of human perfection—perfection without compromise or apology. Humans without the worst of all traits, *hypocrisy.*"

That had been the thing Tilly had admired most in *Atlas Shrugged*—the active disgust for people who said one thing and did another. Tilly, too, shared this abhorrence, having witnessed enough of it to last a lifetime before, during, and still after her parents' divorce.

"Without hypocrisy, you say! That's quite an advertisement for anybody, but I'd say *especially* for Rand."

Mr. Bernstein was clearly skeptical. But Ayn Rand wouldn't back down in the face of skepticism, so neither would Tilly.

"I think it's sad that advocating for rational thought and objectivity is considered an advertisement," she said.

"Maybe, but her books all have flyers as the centerfold, don't they?"

Her father snorted, and Tilly got the sense she'd just embarrassed herself—but she wasn't quite sure how. She felt her face grow hot, and she decided it was time to study the remaining bubbles floating languidly across the surface of her tepid egg cream.

"Sorry," said Mr. Bernstein. "I was just surprised that someone so young had it all figured out already. Ayn would get a real kick out of you, I bet, Tilly. Maybe I can introduce you sometime."

Tilly found she was able to look up again.

"You know...?" Her heart was pounding. Her—meet Ayn Rand?

"Yeah, I know her," said Mr. Bernstein. "Stop looking at me like that, she's just a woman like any other. Isn't that what *she'd* say anyway?"

Tilly looked at her father hopefully.

"We've gotten pretty far away from *Orchard of Sin*," he said.

"If we need to get back on the subject at hand, does that mean you're taking the job?"

"All right," said her father. "I'll do it."

"Glad you've come to your senses." Mr. Bernstein slid a big envelope across the counter. "Here, this is the brief, the contract, and the treatment. There's no script. More freedom for you. Oh and you'll find the first few chapters of the previous attempt in there, too." He ground out the end of his cigarette in the ashtray the waitress had left with his latest coffee refill. "I hope it doesn't make *you* start drinking."

"Me too," said Tilly.

Mr. Bernstein made a sound somewhere in between a sigh and a groan as he signaled for the check.

"Don't you want to be a writer?" That's what Tilly's mother, Cecilia, had said, as she put in her earrings. Diamonds, given to her by Daniel. All her diamonds had been given to her by Daniel—save for the one she'd kept, from before, but never wore anymore. "Well here's your chance to really experience the sort of *lifestyle* you can expect from that particular career."

Cecilia had married for love only to discover she preferred comfort—or at least, comfort beyond what her own monthly allowance from her parents and Fred's advances provided. In the pursuit of such, Cecilia had taken herself and her monthly allowance to Connecticut, to be with oenophile, bon vivant, and notorious *Roué* magazine lifestyle columnist Daniel Murray, whom she had met at a party in the city while still—ostensibly—on her husband's arm.

While Cecilia's (and by extension, Tilly's) style of living had been significantly improved by this switch, Fred's had been reduced. He'd moved to the city, to a little apartment.

Before shipping her daughter to New York for the summer, Cecilia had taken a look at "Fred's flop" as Daniel called it, but ultimately deemed it "fine"; the worst part was how far away it was from anything interesting. Tilly would even have her own room, his father's little office. He'd move his typewriter into the kitchen. It would be "cozy."

Tilly had elected not to mention that coziness is what exactly *nobody* wanted in New York City, in summer.

Once she got there, Tilly had been fairly certain her mother's favorable description of the place had been influenced by her desire to spend the summer on Martha's Vineyard... without her fifteen-year-old daughter. Yet more hypocrisy from the queen of same! But to be fair, her father's place wasn't entirely squalid. It was small, and crowded with the detritus of their former family life out in Massapequa, but Amsterdam Avenue was home to an interesting mix of people: shop-keepers and artists and working families. Her father put no restraints on her beyond that she be home by eight, so Tilly was free to roam around as much as she liked when he was at his typewriter and mut-tering to himself. She became as frequent a patron of the Riverside Library as the creeps who went there to do whatever it was they did, saw Irish pubs where people drank after work, watched the construc-tion of some of the new high-rises going up. And above it all tow-ered the newly constructed Switching Center.

Tilly had walked to the Switching Center a few times, to stand in the sharp shadows of its stark lines stretching ever-upward into the sky. She tried to see it like Ayn Rand would—some sort of enthralling monument to man's genius and enterprise—but frankly, she thought it was pretty ugly. Maybe, she worried, that made her like the inferior people in *Atlas Shrugged*, the ones who would rather cherish an illu-sion than deal with the truth.

She sure hoped not.

Maybe she'd understand more once she read *The Fountainhead*. Or maybe it was that Rand's vision of a crumbling, dystopian New York looked a little different in Tilly's mind than the neighborhood where her father lived, in the noisyquiet Upper West Side. Maybe if she were looking down upon all of this from the glory of a penthouse apartment, or the executive suite of a skyscraper, she'd be better able to appreciate the Switching Center's Brutalist aesthetics as well as the ingenuity it could be said to represent.

Tilly's friends back in Greenwich hadn't been able to comprehend her lack of enthusiasm for visiting her father in the city. But that was because they didn't know her father, or the city. Cecilia had been right: Tilly wanted to be a writer when she grew up—but of a different sort than her father. She wasn't going to live in some crummy apartment that somehow managed to be both in the most interesting city in the world and in the middle of nowhere. She wasn't going to be pushed around by her agent. And she definitely wasn't going to waste half her days smoking cigarettes while sitting around half-dressed, and then waste the other half anxiously complaining about getting nothing done.

Tilly didn't think Ayn Rand would approve of this moody noodling. Writing was a job, and jobs were for doing. She, Tilly, was writing when it wasn't even her job—in the notebook she'd bought when her father had taken her on a little pilgrimage to the Strand. She'd filled nearly half of it with a story about a brilliant and brave librarian in a near-future world where books were a thing of the past. The librarian fell in love with a guy because he could reason perfectly; he turned out to be a cyborg. Tilly wasn't sure if the librarian would also be a cyborg. Maybe he would turn her into one after a terrible accident... or maybe she was a cyborg all along and didn't know it. Tilly couldn't decide, but when she'd asked her father his professional advice it hadn't gone exactly as she'd hoped.

"Why are either of them cyborgs?" he'd asked, as they ate chow mien and dumplings delivered to their apartment by a boy on a bicycle. "Why does it have to be the future? Why not write something set today, about real people doing things that could actually happen?"

Tilly hadn't expected this question, so she popped a dumpling into her mouth, whole, to give herself time.

"Would you eat like that in front of your mother?"

Tilly shrugged as she chewed messily. She didn't feel she had to answer questions about what things were like with her mother and Daniel.

Anyway they both knew the answer was *no*.

"Things that could actually happen could actually happen to a cyborg," said Tilly, before wiping her mouth with her napkin.

"What even is a cyborg? Like a robot? Because nothing that could actually happen could happen to a robot."

Tilly didn't just love to read science fiction, she loved to watch it too—shows like *Buck Rogers*, *Flash Gordon*, *The Outer Limits*.

She had been really excited when the death ray had appeared in *Atlas Shrugged*. That was much more her area of interest than capitalism.

"Cyborgs aren't robots, not really," she said. "They're more like humans, but enhanced with robot parts."

Her father did not share her interest in the speculative.

"Seems unlikely to me, given the cost of a new pair of glasses." They both self-consciously pushed theirs up the bridge of their noses as he said this. "What's so wrong with a real librarian, and a real guy?"

"Nothing's wrong with them, but how are they interesting?" muttered Tilly.

Her father cocked an eyebrow at her. She'd earned that—she'd read a few of her father's novels, and they were all the sort of books where an unhappy librarian would talk to some nervous wreck for a while, and then he'd do something crazy because he was sad. Tilly honestly didn't understand why anyone would read a story like that when there were plenty about going to outer space and meeting aliens, or what to do when a wizard makes an evil duplicate of you while you're unconscious.

"You should learn to write about real things and real people instead of getting hung up on all this sci-fi junk," said her father. "The point of art is to teach us about ourselves—get to know ourselves better. How does a story about a cyborg do that?"

"How does *Orchard of Sin*?" Tilly wasn't even sure she agreed with him about *the point of art*, but her dander was up.

They both knew that a week after their luncheon at Eisenberg's, the envelope from Mr. Bernstein remained untouched where her father had tossed it the moment they'd walked through the door. That meant he now only had three weeks to do it, which Tilly thought was a worryingly brief amount of time to write a book, even if it also seemed to her like an eternity. In three weeks she'd be packing up to go home, and it definitely felt like forever away.

Cheeks flushed from more than the hot mustard, Tilly's father dished himself out the last of the noodles. "*Orchard of Sin* proves my point exactly," he said, not backing down.

"How's that?"

"*Orchard of Sin* ain't art. It's pulp."

Before her parents' divorce, Tilly and her father had enjoyed the occasional verbal tussle. Arguing in the humid heat of a summer's night…it felt like old times. But also, her pride was at stake.

"Some people would say Rand is pulp," said Tilly, "but—*what?*"

Her father's derisive snort made Tilly's blood boil. She'd thought over her interaction with Mr. Bernstein a few times since it had happened, and his reaction still puzzled her. Rand was a philosopher, a best-seller; she was a controversial yet celebrated public intellectual. But in spite of that, Mr. Bernstein, and now her father, seemed to view Rand with little more than scorn.

"Look, Tilly, I know you're inclined to believe what Rand says about herself, but the truth is, didactic art is nothing more than propaganda." He wiped his mouth with a greasy napkin. "Only children and savages require moral instruction in their fiction."

"Didn't you *just* say the point of art was to *teach* us about ourselves?" Her father stiffened, and Tilly sensed she'd gone too far. "All I mean is that I bet with the right writer, a book about a cyborg, or even *Orchard of Sin*, could teach people about themselves."

"The right writer, huh? Who would that be? Ayn Rand, probably?"

Tilly had indeed been about to invoke Rand, but in her panicked need to save face she realized what she had to do. She tried to channel her inner Dagny Taggart as she sat up straight and looked her father in the eye.

"*Me,*" she said. "I could do it."

Her father laughed.

"You think so, huh?" He did not sound convinced.

"I do," said Tilly. "Why not? You told me once that the real purpose of a first draft is to convince editors you've been doing something with your time. If it's crummy, you can fix it when I'm back with Mom and you're done revising your novel."

In truth, Tilly wasn't quite as confident as she claimed. But she couldn't back down now, not after her father had laughed at her.

Tilly saw a calculating gleam come into her father's eye.

"All right," he said. "After we clean up, I'll get my old typewriter out for you, so you can prove me wrong."

That evening, as her father put down old newspaper on the kitchen table so he could do things with oil and small tools, Tilly opened the envelope containing *Orchard of Sin.* There was the contract, which she abandoned quickly. Legalese made her eyes cross. Beneath it was a cover letter all about the job. She looked it over. By the first week of August she would need to deliver an adaptation of *Orchard of Sin,* of at least 150 manuscript pages, but no more than 170. There was "some leeway for changes," but Mr. Bernstein had underlined this in pencil and scrawled *I'm pretty sure "some leeway" means the book's so late they probably won't look at it before sending it to the printers!*

Tilly wondered just how many "changes" she'd need to make in order to prove that *Orchard of Sin* could teach people about themselves. Probably more than a few...

She set aside the chapters written by the previous author in favor of the document Mr. Bernstein had called "the treatment," which was just a detailed synopsis of the movie. The cover letter said it would come out in late October, to cash in on some Halloween enthusiasm.

By then, Tilly would be back in Greenwich. She wouldn't be sweating through shorts and a tee shirt, she'd be shivering in her awful school uniform, back at her awful school, learning awful geometry and history and chemistry and whatever else. She couldn't imagine her mother would let her go to see a movie called *Orchard of Sin.* In fact, Tilly had never seen what could be honestly classified as a horror movie, though the idea of them intrigued her. The closest she ever got was the time her father had taken her to a double feature of *Vertigo* and *Rear Window*, and for her mother to consider it, Tilly had had to swear that no matter what, she wouldn't demand expensive psychoanalysis to fix their awful parenting.

Orchard of Sin

Logline: The mysterious and handsome owner of Orchard House, Lucien, hosts a ball with the aim of finding a wife, but the girls he woos that night change darkly. A soft-core *Invasion of the Body Snatchers* with bodices.

Characters:

Evelyn Price: The eighteen-year-old daughter of the town blacksmith, Evelyn has a good heart but few dreams beyond marrying and a starting a family. Definitely a blonde.

Prudence Browne: Evelyn's childhood friend, Prudence is a beautiful and lively prankster, who often drags Evelyn into her mischief. Preferably brunette.

Katherine Edwards: The mayor's daughter. Katherine's life of privilege has made her an arch and competitive young woman. She has the best of everything but still wants more. Redhead.

Lucien Dawning: The owner of Orchard House, Lucien is wealthy, cultured, stylish, and devilishly handsome. In fact, he has made a deal with the devil and is looking to pay off the debt with the souls of young girls.

Phoebe Dawning: Lucien's sister, Phoebe is also handsome and cultured. She's in on her brother's scheme and helps him out of a depraved sense of loyalty, and perhaps to save her own soul.

Reverend Perry: A man of God, and more than that, a good man, Reverend Perry is the foil for Lucien. He eschews vanity and excess for plain dress and clean living.

Opening Scene:

Orchard of Sin begins with Evelyn and Prudence clad only in their shifts as they make merry and splash each other in the creek. Their dresses lie abandoned on the bank. It is a scene that should feel innocent and sweet, but also shows off two good-looking girls having fun with each other. They eventually tire of this and collapse upon a blanket set in the shade under a sprawling tree. They tell each other of their dreams:

                    EVELYN

I wish afternoons like this could last
forever!

                    PRUDENCE

But they won't. We'll have to decide
soon what we want to do with our
lives...

                    EVELYN

Why, what do you mean, Prudence? We'll
marry, and have children, won't we? But
we'll always be friends.

                    PRUDENCE

Is that all you want, Evelyn? To be a
wife, and a mother?

                    EVELYN

What else is there?

                    PRUDENCE

That's the trouble, isn't it? We don't
know! Maybe I'll marry a rich man,
and he'll take me across the sea to
somewhere interesting! Not like here...

They curl together on the blanket, bosom to
bosom, as the sun gets low. Cut to them walking
home, both carrying their shoes, along a cart
path. They come upon a handsome young man in a
hay-cart heading out of the village who tells
them the news: The rich Dawning siblings have

returned from abroad, and they plan to throw a ball at Orchard House to celebrate. The idea of a ball excites the girls, and they grow even more excited when the boy shares the rumor that Lucien Dawning will be using the ball to look for a wife.

                          BOY
                      (earnestly)
        Will you be setting your cap for
        Lucien, Evelyn?

                        EVELYN
        My cap is not fine enough to interest
        the likes of Lucien Dawning, I'm sure!

Prudence then takes Evelyn's hand and leads her away. They giggle as they rush home.

Tilly pulled a face. This was pretty goopy stuff—nothing Rand would approve of. It seemed more like a simpering romance story than a horror movie. She turned the page, hoping something scary would happen soon.

                    Act One:

It is around the time of the American Revolution. Evelyn Price lives in a bustling if rural village. Gossip travels fast, and when the fashionable and wealthy Dawning siblings return from their time abroad, it is a major event. The ball they're throwing is the only

topic of conversation in town. It promises to
be quite an elaborate affair.

Evelyn is excited about the ball, but it is
Prudence who intends to snare the man in
question. In fact, it's all she can talk about.
She is still discussing it when they enter the
butcher's shop drawing the scorn of Katherine
Edwards, the haughty mayor's daughter, when she
overhears them.

When Lucien Dawning and his sister Phoebe walk
by in their finery, everyone gathers round to
watch them go by. It's obvious from the look
on Katherine's face that she will be trying to
snare Lucien for herself.

Lucien sees her, and bows. Phoebe, however,
only has eyes for the vivacious Prudence, whom
she acknowledges with a nod.

But just then, the butcher's faithful, gentle
dog escapes and goes running at Lucien, barking
madly. Lucien is furious when the dog will
not stop.

                    PHOEBE
    It's rabid!

                    LUCIEN
    Call it off! Won't somebody call off this
    dog!

                         PHOEBE
                        (terrified)
          Shoot it!

Lucien withdraws his pistol and shoots the dog
dead in the street. The butcher comes out and
asks what the devil Lucien means by murdering
his dog. Lucien replies that the butcher ought
to be fined for keeping such a savage beast. The
butcher calls him a bastard and a few other
choice things before Lucien gives him a look
that quells his rage.

The Dawning siblings walk on. Evelyn feels
unsettled. Just then, the customer ahead of
them in the butcher's shop declares the meat
she was buying to be spoiled. Evelyn and Phoebe
realize the shop smells terrible: all the meat
is rotten. They exit the shop hastily as the
butcher declares confusedly that the meat was
all good and fresh that morning.

Prudence's enthusiasm is undiminished by the
ugly scene, but Evelyn isn't quite sure about
Lucien or his sister. She still wants to go
to the ball, of course. But after Sunday
service, where Reverend Perry warns everyone
about giving in to vanity and carnal pleasure,
Evelyn's father forbids her to go. He relents
when her disappointment is so obvious, but
extracts from her a promise: that she will not
go anywhere alone with a man, nor let herself
be drawn into unbecoming entertainments.

The night of the ball, decked out in their
best, the two girls arrive arm-inarm at Orchard
House. It is lovely. There is wine, and punch,
and dancing, and a table laden with every good
thing to eat. Lucien Dawning is there, and
he is standing with Katherine. Katherine is
in a very revealing gown and they are clearly
flirting outrageously with one another.

                    PRUDENCE
    Why, that fast little... if she were to
    throw herself at him any harder, she'd
    need a cannon!

                    EVELYN
        (doubtfully, but hopefully)
    Perhaps it was love at first sight...

Just then, Phoebe Dawning approaches the girls.
She is all elegance, and bows. They answer
clumsily, but Phoebe does not scoff at them.
Instead, she leans in conspiratorially.

                    PHOEBE
    I saw you noticing the palaver over
    there...

                    EVELYN
            (nervously)
    No, ma'am. We were simply admiring the
    party.

PRUDENCE
And marveling at some of its attendees.

PHOEBE
(with comic relief)
Oh good, I thought I was the only one.

Phoebe and Prudence exchange cutting remarks
about Katherine. Evelyn doesn't like it, so
when the young man from the hay cart asks her
to dance, she accepts. The last thing Evelyn
sees is Phoebe taking Prudence's arm and them
going off together.

Evelyn and her young man dance, and afterwards
he takes her into the gardens to get some air.
Other couples are milling about, and in the
distance they see Lucien leading Katherine into
a little wooded area. The young man, with
mischief clearly in mind, urges Evelyn to come
along and follow them, and she reluctantly
agrees after making a token protest about
having promised her father she wouldn't.

Evelyn was right to be concerned: when they get
in the shadows, the young man starts pawing at
her, mussing her when she resists.

Tilly perked up at last. While she enjoyed the speculative and dystopian elements of *Atlas Shrugged*, what had really caught her eye was all the sex.

She hadn't known it was a sexy book when she started reading it. Daniel had given it to her after she'd come home from school one day, very upset after having her work critiqued harshly in her creative writing club. But the worst part of it had come after, when her teacher had kept Tilly back to tell her if she couldn't accept criticism, she'd never really be a writer.

Daniel had actually been pretty cool about it; he'd told her, "writer to writer," that "eating a serving or two from the shit buffet is all part of it." He advised her to listen to her critics, but also that the truth was, if she really wanted to be a writer, she was going to have to decide when to listen to other people, and when to decide she was right.

A few days later he'd handed her *Atlas Shrugged*. "Here's a book about sticking to your guns, if you're up for the challenge," he'd said.

The story had hooked her immediately. And then there had been all the sex. At first, Tilly hadn't known what to make of Rand's predilection for what seemed like strangely violent lovemaking, but at the same time, those scenes felt enthrallingly transgressive. Never had Tilly read anything so steamy as Hank Rearden's speech to Dagny after their first time doing it, where instead of telling her he loved her, he told her he felt nothing but contempt for her—that he was disappointed to find out that she was a vile, sensation-seeking animal. That he wanted her like a whore, not an equal. Something about that exchange, and Dagny's amused, almost bratty, reaction stirred something deep within Tilly that she hadn't known was there; like she was first hearing the ringing of a small and distant bell.

Sadly, *Orchard of Sin* did not prove quite as titillating.

```
Evelyn resists, but her would-be lover becomes
angrily insistent. At last Evelyn breaks
away to flee deeper into the wood. There, she
stumbles upon a strange scene: Lucien ushering
Katherine into a little grove. Evelyn crouches
down, hiding as her young man searches for her.
As she hides, she watches, and sees Lucien help
Katherine to sit on a bench beneath a beautiful
```

apple tree absolutely laden with bloodred
apples. Lucien picks one and hands it to
Katherine. Evelyn watches as she takes a bite.
The juice runs down her chin and Lucien laughs
as a bolt of lightning and clap of thunder tear
through the night.

Tilly read the treatment all the way through, then got into bed and
read it again, staying up later than she was technically allowed. But she
had never read anything like *Orchard of Sin*, and she liked it. She was
fascinated by the predictable and yet agonizing decline of Katherine,
who after her night with Lucien becomes an unscrupulous tart, and
then goes mad. She felt Evelyn's horror when Prudence, as Phoebe's
new favorite, becomes Lucien's next target.

Eventually, it comes out that the apple tree in the Dawning's grove
was grown from a cutting from the original Tree of Knowledge, and
that Dawning is using the apples to steal girls' souls to pay back a
debt to the devil. The pure and good Evelyn offers herself as bait,
at the behest of the stalwart Reverend Perry, and together they bring
down the Dawning siblings… even if, regrettably, they could not save
Phoebe from madness.

Tilly's window was open to the urban symphony of the sweltering
Upper West Side—small scurries, loud thumps, and the occasional
wail of a siren—but she dreamed of a deep cool forest. A forest
that was a city, thick with living skyscrapers stretching so tall their
branches seemed to brush the swollen moon hanging low in the sky.

Wizards lived in the city—they had grown it long ago, with seeds
mutated by deep magics plundered from the ruins of a yet more
ancient world. But the trees were not the only ones changed by magic;
the wizards were, as well. Each had a luminous third eye in the center
of their brow, which allowed them to see in the perpetual gloam-
ing of the city. There they lived a comfortable life, but one despised
by those who dwelt beyond the borders of the wood.

Tilly didn't live in the forest; it seemed an inaccessible wonderland to her as she gazed upon it from her rude hut in the hinterlands, where life was keeping the fire lit and bellies filled.

But one day, Tilly crept to the border of the forest, where the trees began to swell, and peered within the darkness. A man was there. A man with a third eye, bright as a star in the night sky. When Tilly worked up the nerve to speak to him, he asked if she would like to join them. Tilly thought she would, but before she could reply, he told her that to do so, she would need a third eye of her own. None of them were born with the organ; they had to acquire it for themselves, through study and intent.

"Does it hurt?" she asked him.

"Of course." Tilly felt her will falter, but then the man added, "but it is worth it."

When Tilly awoke, early, in the already warm pre-dawn of a city decidedly not full of wizards, the dream still clung to her like a sweaty sheet, and she tried to go back to sleep to re-enter it. When she awoke again, she was annoyed that she could remember only the city-forest, and the man's question to her: *What would you regret more—changing, or staying the same?*

The feelings of desire and uncertainty stayed with Tilly until they were halfway to Barney Greengrass so that Tilly could get a bialy with cream cheese, and her father a rye bagel heaped with vile-smelling sturgeon. Tilly, anticipating a long day of writing, ordered coffee for the first time in her life, nervously. Her father smiled down at the table, but he didn't make a comment, thank goodness.

She was also grateful when he didn't remark on her using a lot of cream and sugar after tasting it, either.

Tilly's cyborg story had flowed out of her, pouring itself from her mind through her pen onto the page. She'd seen the shape of it before she began it, and until the conundrum over the librarian, it had been going swimmingly.

It never occurred to her that *Orchard of Sin* wouldn't be the same.

In order to write a manuscript of the requested length by the first week in August, Tilly would need to produce six-and-a-half typed pages a day. She'd decided to just go for seven. This seemed pretty simple—three and a half before lunch, three and a half after, though "after lunch" of course extended into the evening.

Her father tended to do a session in the morning—early, before Tilly got up, he'd be hunched over his typewriter, smoking cigarette after cigarette, all before the heat of the day set in. She usually awoke to a kitchen wreathed in haze like the moors in the Basil Rathbone *The Hound of the Baskervilles*. She'd open the windows to air the place out, and that was it. Her father would not get back to work—not sincerely, anyway—until after dinner.

But that first morning Tilly didn't even get one page. Jittery from the coffee and her nerves, she stared at the blank piece of paper for hours after they got back from breakfast, unable to come up with even the first sentence. She sat there, still as a statue, while her father puttered around the apartment, doing dishes, paying a few bills, and sometimes returning to his manuscript.

It wasn't that she had forgotten the plot. She knew what the story was to be. She just didn't know how to write it—nor did she know how to write it in a way that would teach people about themselves.

She was doomed.

When lunchtime rolled around, Tilly pushed back from the table with a disgusted sigh. Her father had the decency not to ask how it was going—he could simply peer over her shoulder to see the vast white expanse of paper, after all. But after they had a little smorgasbord of fridge items—some cheese, a few cold slices of pizza, bites of a shared apple—Tilly returned not to her typewriter, but to the chapters Mr. Bernstein had provided her father, hoping to see if maybe she could find some clues for how to proceed.

Orchard of Sin

by

Jake Bradshaw

Evelyn Price looked at her reflection in the slow-moving water of the river. It was a face familiar to her, but also not. She'd always had a cascade of blonde hair, skyblue eyes, and fair features, but she still didn't know what to make of her breasts. Large but firm, they strained her dresses these days.

One such dress lay abandoned on the riverbank. She had shed it so she could bathe in the shadows of the willows, far from prying eyes.

She put her hand beneath one breast, just to feel its weight, and watched the way it swayed when she released it. Then two hands were on her breasts, and she squealed at the feeling of being held--but it was only her friend Prudence.

"Tis good you care nothing for the whistles of the boys," said Prudence, a mischievous glint in her dark eyes. "Had I your figure, surely I should be married--or sorely regretting that I wasn't!"

Tilly set the chapters aside. She did not think they would prove helpful. This was decidedly not the direction in which she wanted to take *Orchard of Sin*, even if she hoped to work in a few juicy sex scenes, like Rand would.

Like Rand would...

And just like that, Tilly knew what she had to do.

What would you regret more—changing, or staying the same?

"So how's it going?" asked her father, as Tilly once again sat before her typewriter. He was at the table, too, paying bills.

She smiled to herself. The blank page no longer frightened her. Instead, it seemed as full of potential as it was empty of words.

"It's going *great*," she said, as her fingers hit the keys.

She'd been thinking about it all wrong. *Orchard of Sin*, as it stood, had limited potential to show people something fundamental about themselves. Tilly would need to remedy that. She'd change the thrust of the story; make some revisions to the conclusion. The cover letter had said there was some leeway for changes.

Some leeway...

Surely that meant she could change a bit about the setting, too, as well as the plot. If the characters remained the same—mostly—it still counted as an adaptation.

Orchard of Sin
by
T.A. Lathe

The steaming water of the bathing pool had been softened with rare salts and perfumed with oils, and the bath-chamber was crowded with precious plants working hard to purify the air, but even so, Evie Price pouted as she soaked. It was an unexpectedly overcast day. The thick and churning clouds gave a sickly yellow cast to everything. She had wanted to take the sol-boat, to go and pay a visit to her dear friend Prue, in Southampton, but clouds like these meant there would be higher than normal radiation levels. Too high even for the brand new, cherry-red, top-of-the-line rad-suit

Evie's father had gotten her as a gift for her eighteenth birthday.

She would just have to stay inside, where it was safe. Or at least *safer*, with all the plants, and the radiation scrubbers, and the treated glass windows. Anything to protect the fragile human body from the harshness of the world beyond--the world other humans had made, long before Evie, or even Evie's grandmother, had been born. A world where the slime-creeps would grab you and suck you down into the poison soil, and things that were not birds flew through the sky, casting large and jagged shadows that made every living creature in their path fall silent and shiver in fear.

Evie was a very lucky girl. There were plenty of people living without scrubbers and rad-suits and the filtration systems that purified the water in her bathing-pool--at least, that's what she'd heard. But here on the East End of Long Island, everybody lived pretty comfortably.

But there wasn't anything anybody could do about the weather.

Evelyn picked up her hothouse loofa and set to work scrubbing any rough bits from her skin. It was an activity that had a function beyond vanity: it gave her the opportunity to look for any new moles or sores that might indicate corruption from the fallout. The responsibility to selfinspect was drilled into every child, no matter if they lived on the East End or in what remained of the Lower East Side. The body might fail in so very many ways, and early detection saved lives--sometimes, one's own; sometimes, those of others.

That was just the way of it. Buildings could be fortified with the fruits of man's ingenuity, but the body could not. That was the Prohibition, for that had been the cause of the Sundering...

A chime distracted Evie from her task. The vid-o-phone was ringing, and through her personal channel.

It was Prue! Evie switched it on. She felt no need to cover herself--she and Prue were like sisters. They'd grown up together.

"What are you doing in the tub?" said Prue. She was certainly dressed already, in a white gown as light as a cloud. Exactly the sort of thing for a hot day in late summer.

At least, that's what Evie had been told. She had never felt the seasons change; never felt the cool damp whisper of an autumn breeze, or the kiss of spring sunshine upon her skin. Her knowledge was purely hypothetical, passed down through story and tradition. She was always in a rad-suit when she was outside, and those were temperature-controlled; inside, climates were even more meticulously curated.

"I can't come over," said Evie. "Radiation levels are too high. I was going to call you when I was done with my bath, but this works just as well."

"What a drag," said Prue. "I wanted to be there when I told you the news."

"What's the news?"

"Lucien Dawning is back from Europe--and he's throwing a party next week!"

The Dawnings of Sagaponack had lived on the East End since the States were still United; before that, even. But they were as eccentric as they were old and wealthy. Lucien, especially, had a reputation. He had been a brilliant boy, sensitive and intelligent, but after being expelled--under uncertain circumstances--from the Northeastern Alliance's premier medical college in New Providence, Lucien had shed his promise like a caterpillar shedding its chrysalis. But what had emerged was no refined thing. No; instead, Lucien Dawning's disgrace had turned him into a cad and a wastrel. He and his sister Phoebe did nothing but take their sol-boat out for cruises, visit the most fashionable of local restaurants and bars, and host parties and attend them.

But then the Dawning siblings had surprised them all by using their wealth and influence to obtain a special visa to the European Consortium. And so they went abroad, to enjoy the pleasures of the world beyond the borders of the Northeastern Alliance; beyond the shores of North America--something unthinkable to most people. The Price family was well-off-- safe, comfortable, protected as much as anyone could be from the sun, and the air, and the earth--and yet Evie could not fathom how Lucien had managed it. It was almost impossible to cross the border into New Liberia, much less leave one continent for another.

"How did you find out about the party?" asked Evie.

"My father saw Lucien at the Night Market, and he said we are all to come up to Sagaponack, to Orchard House. He's bringing in *three bands* for the occasion!"

"Three bands!"

"Tilly, it's almost eleven."

Tilly looked up from her typewriter in surprise. They'd taken a break for dinner, but she hadn't realized how late it had gotten since then. She'd generated more than six typed pages; a fine first day's work, despite her late start.

"Seems like you really figured some things out," said her father, after Tilly closed up shop for the night, and emerged from the bathroom to pace around while brushing her teeth.

She nodded, saying around the brush and foam, "Yeah."

She went into the bathroom and spat. When she came back out, her father was looking at one of the pages, a curious expression on his face.

"Hey!" she cried. "What are you doing?"

"It's not bad," he said. "In fact, in spite of all the weird stuff about rad-suits, it's pretty good."

"Gimme that!" Tilly snatched the paper out of his hand. She'd known other people would read her book—that was the point, after all—but she wanted to be in control of when.

"All right all right." Her father smirked at her as he sat back down at his own typewriter. "Really though, you should be proud. I figured it'd be just some Randian garbage, but—"

Randian garbage! Tilly crossed her arms and fixed him with what she hoped was an uncompromising stare.

"Since *you* brought up Rand," she said, "perhaps it's time to talk about what *I'll* be paid for my labor here. Surely you weren't going to let me do all this for free."

Tilly, keen observer that she was, noticed the quick wince before the reassuring smile. "Of course not," he said. "You'll be the same as any writer—paid on delivery of the manuscript. Except that in your case, it'll go straight into your college savings account."

"*What* college savings account?"

"The one I'll open with your cut of the profits," said her father.

"What kind of cut are we talking—"

"Good night, Tilly."

"I ought to ask for a contract," she said over her shoulder, as she headed into her bedroom.

"That reminds me, I ought to sign and return the one for *Orchard of Sin.*"

"Shouldn't *I* be signing it?"

"Good night, Tilly!"

Tilly went to bed pleased feeling exceptionally pleased with herself.

They quickly settled into a pleasant routine. Their preferred writing schedules were just different enough that they started trading off chores and errands. Tilly ran out first thing to get them breakfast, coffee, and sometimes groceries, which gave her father a few more productive minutes at his typewriter in the mornings. In the evenings, when Tilly was always really cranking it out, her father would cook them omelets for dinner, or a steak, or trot up to Sal's for pizza. Dishes, dusting, whatever—by mutual unspoken accord they both did whatever needed doing whenever they were stuck, or were taking a break.

Tilly's summer vacation was turning out to be a heck of a lot more fun than she had anticipated, actually.

When Tilly's mother called, an event almost as rare as Halley's Comet, she seemed surprised by her daughter's cheeriness. This annoyed Tilly deeply; her mother could have at least pretended she'd been assuming Tilly would have a nice time.

"So, have you found some rational way to occupy yourself?" she'd asked.

"Sure," Tilly said. "I'm writing a novel."

"Is that so?" Adults never sounded as *impressed* as Tilly wanted them to. "What does that involve?"

"Well, *writing*, mostly."

"Boy are you a smart aleck," said her mother. "Put your father on."

Fred took the phone, clearly curious about his daughter's suddenly stormy expression. "Hmm? Of course we're getting out," he said. "We went to the Met just a few days ago, didn't we Tilly?" They had, but she wasn't sure what her unseen agreement would add to the conversation her father and mother were sharing, so she just shrugged. Her father waved her off with an annoyed look that his ex-wife also could not see. "A novel? Yeah she's been talking about it." Tilly's heart began to beat a little faster—but surely her mother could not take this away from her? "Oh come on, Cecilia. No. No! Well, if you feel that way, maybe that boyfriend of yours will send her to summer camp next year." Tilly shook her head vehemently *No*. Her father winked. "Yeah well all I'm saying is that visiting museums and writing her first novel ain't a bad way for our kid to spend a summer."

Her first novel!

There was something thrilling about the way he said it. As much as her father's novels failed to appeal to her, he was a real novelist, with half a dozen books to his name. And he thought she had the stuff.

"It's not bad at all," she said, after he hung up the phone.

"Eh?"

"Not a bad way for me spend my summer," she said.

"You'd better get back to work," he said, pointing at her typewriter. "You have a deadline."

Remember who you are.

That's what the sheriff had said, and her father, when they'd talked about sending Evie to Orchard House. Lucien Dawning's recent attentions had made her the ideal candidate to find out just what he'd done to Kitty, and to poor Prue.

At the time, Evie had wondered why they thought Lucien might tempt her to some transgression, rather than uncovering what he had done to those girls to drive them mad. But now, as they sat together in the early evening on a carven marble bench in the cool quiet of the grove within his astonishingly lush vivarium, Evie understood the danger. Lucien was handsome--distractingly so. But it was not his patrician features, nor was it the way his slender body seemed to fall as elegantly as synth-o-silk from his shoulders, that made her doubt her resolve. No, it was his calm demeanor, his gentlemanly manners, and the reasonable way he spoke to her. Like she was his equal. Like she was someone who deserved to be taken seriously.

Nobody had ever spoken to her like that before, and it did indeed make her heart beat a little faster.

"Evie, I know why you are here," he said. "And I know it is not because you were flattered by my invitation."

Evie stiffened up, alarmed. She had worried that Lucien would suspect her, given that everybody knew she and Prue were the best of

friends--or rather, had been. No way could Prue
still be alive. It had been three days since
she had stolen her father's sol-boat and sailed
away to no one knew where, without her rad-
suit to protect her. And everybody knew only
a few hours of exposure were enough to kill
someone...

Kitty had taken her father's glider and
escaped into the unknown, also without her
rad-suit.

And of course, that had been after she'd gone
into the orchard with Lucien Dawning...

Evie tried to hold herself very still, but
she was frightened. If she believed all they
said about Lucien, then he was a maniac; an
unscrupulous rake who had gone away to deflower
the European Consortium's virgins after they'd
become thin on the ground on Long Island.

"You have played your role admirably," he
continued, when it became evident that Evie
would not speak. "You could not have done it
better. There have been moments when--when I
let myself half-believe..."

He trailed off, and Evie saw a blush coloring
his pale cheek as he sat almost tentatively
beside her.

Could it be? Surely she could not have made
an impression upon Lucien Dawning...

"It is no matter," he said, with a smile that
was almost sad. All his years in the European
Consortium had given an elegance to his speech,
not just his manners. "Please, Evie. Do not be
afraid of me."

"I'm not afraid of you," she said.

"Oh but you are," he said. "I know it, because I can *smell* it on you."

Evie pulled away from him, half-getting to her feet, but he caught her hand.

"I do not mean to be impolite," said Lucien, squeezing her hand gently. "Please sit down. The scent of your hair, of your skin... it is intoxicating, as I have ever found it. But you see, Evie, I can smell what other men cannot--fear, deceit... lust. In fact, I can do many things other men cannot. I can see objects miles away as if they were as close to me as you are now. My hearing is also much improved. And I am stronger..." He cast about for a moment, searching; he picked up a rock, and before her eyes, crushed it to dust in his palm.

She gasped. She couldn't help it.

"But Evie--you must listen to me very carefully now. It is not that I am special. I am not. I am just a man. The power to do everything I can do is within you. Or, rather, it could be, if you wanted it."

Evie wondered if this was what he had told Kitty, and Prue--if they had heard a similar speech before going mad. But even so, there was a question on the tip of her tongue. And while it was not what she had come here to ask, she knew it was the question she wanted to ask, for herself. The need to know burned within her like an ember.

"How?" she asked. "How is it done?"

His smile lost its shyness. "Oh Evie! I knew you were the sort of girl I liked."

"Is there any sort you don't?" Evie blushed--it was never her way to be arch, but thankfully Lucien seemed amused rather than offended.

"I suppose I deserve that! My reputation is of my own design, after all."

"Design?"

Lucien stood then, and offered her his hand. "Come with me," he said. "I promise I will tell you *how*, my dear, but first, come walk with me while I tell you a story."

She took his hand, and allowed herself to be led deeper into the grove.

"I know you've been told I'm a dangerous man," he said. "Well, Evie, I am--but not because I'm a threat to your virtue. No; it is your mind to which I pose a risk! You see, I was expelled from medical school for my belief that we ought to augment our bodies to better survive the world."

Evie gasped.

"Yes yes, the Prohibition," he said dismissively, to her increasing astonishment. "It is archaic, it needs to be revised. It is hindering our evolution! You know as well as I do that the population of the Northeastern Alliance dwindles. We are dying out! The Prohibition was created to force mankind to retain its humanity. But what humanity is preserved if we're all dead in the ground?

"I felt there had to be a better way, and for that the state medical college turned me out into the street and forced me to give up my formal education! And not only that, but I knew my expulsion meant I had also given up my privacy. They would have their eyes upon me; their ears to my ground. I'd never work in their town again, so to speak, but the town was the entire Northeastern Alliance. And you know as well as I do that the Northeastern Alliance may as well be the whole world, for as easy as it is to leave it.

"I nearly went mad with grief at the prospect of a life without purpose, but it was then that my sister suggested a plan. I truly believe she saved my life that day, for I was close to despair. She declared that I would *not* give up my work--I would delay it! I knew well enough that even days are precious time to waste with the future of so many at stake, but I would have to. I would live a lie so convincingly that my watchers would believe I no longer needed watching; so that when someone asked, *Is that Lucien Dawning?* that the only possible reply could be, *It used to be.*

"When I had established myself as a waste of promise, then I applied for my visa. But I tell you, Evie, I did not flee to the European Consortium for pleasure. No, I went there to *learn.* Across the sea, and indeed even south of us, in New Libera, there is no Prohibition. Instead, they have chosen to walk a middle path. Advances for the human body are permitted if they are researched thoroughly and approached sensibly.

"And because of it, they thrive! They do not cower in their little terrariums, clinging to the past--they live in the world, in the present.

"If we are going to preserve humanity, we must consider *humanity*! To refuse to do so is the ultimate hypocrisy. I for one do not think we were meant to live this way--in these elaborate fishbowls where all we do is swim round and round! We were meant to feel the wind on our skin; the earth beneath our fingertips. If we change a little in the service of getting back something so fundamental, is that not an acceptable sacrifice?"

Evie did not know what to think or feel after this extraordinary speech, which came to a conclusion when they reached a glass air-lock in a glass wall. The vivarium was not a dome; it was a doughnut, and the hole in the center was open to the world, to the fallout that degraded the flesh, and the rain that burned it.

And yet, incredibly, planted at the center of the circular expanse was a single tree: an apple tree, the most beautiful Evie had ever seen. It was small, no taller than she was, and yet it was laden with the most perfect apples imaginable, bright green-gold even in the sickly orange light of the charred sky.

Evie looked up at Lucien, but she did not have to speak the question aloud. He knew what she wanted to know.

"You asked me *how*, Evelyn. *That* is how. It is my invention, based on much I learned whilst traveling. To eat the fruit of the tree is to begin to change. It will nourish you with more than vitamins. You will no longer be in danger from the sky, from the air. You could drink water right from a stream, from your cupped bare hand."

"Or steal your father's boat, and sail to..."

"To *anywhere*."

Evie's heart trembled like some caged thing trying to stretch its wings.

"Does it hurt?" she whispered.

Lucien leaned down and bit her ear--gently, but enough to make her whimper from pain that was too close to pleasure to know the difference.

"Not all things that hurt are bad," he said softly.

Lucien stepped back, took her hands in his and kissed them. The feel of his mouth on her skin sent ripples of sensation up her arms.

"You must open the door, Evie. You must step into the air beyond, quickly pick yourself an apple, and eat it. You'll be perfectly safe. Here, I'll show you."

He returned her hands to her, and opened the air-lock, shutting it carefully behind him. And then, to Evie's horror and fascination, he stepped into the open air beyond. He turned and smiled to her, and waved, and then went to pluck an apple from the tree. She could almost taste it in her mouth when he bit into what looked like crisp, juicy flesh.

Evie, tempted, considered all she had heard in the last hour, against all she had heard her entire life. A decision like this meant being certain.

What would she regret more--changing, or staying the same?

Tilly Turner finally typed "The End" the day before she was to take the train back home to Connecticut. When she handed the completed manuscript to her father, he didn't read it. He put it down on the table and gave her a huge hug, and then called for a reservation at her favorite place in the city, a tiny sushi restaurant that had bright pink ginger and a pickled garlic roll that Tilly thought was swell even if her father made exaggerated gagging noises every time she suggested it.

"So do you like it?" he asked, as he poked at his salmon sashimi. "The book I mean; you obviously like whatever it is we've ordered tonight."

"I do," said Tilly. "But whether it teaches people about themselves..."

"I'll read it tonight and tell you what I think," he said.

Her father was strangely quiet the next morning, as they rushed about to make it to the train. Tilly didn't want to ask if he'd gotten a chance to take a look, even if she was desperate to know. Probably it was the last thing on his mind, what with making sure she was all packed up.

Probably he was thinking about how nice it would be to have his apartment to himself again, after weeks of close quarters.

Tilly had a lot on her mind, too. Her summer in New York City was over. It was back to real life with her mother, and Daniel, and her friends, and the phonies at school. Back in Greenwich, she wouldn't be a novelist. She'd just be plain old Tilly Turner, pulling at the knee socks of her school uniform and swapping lunch items with her friends.

Then Tilly's train pulled up, and her father cleared his throat.

"The book, it's pretty good."

"You read it?" She broke out in a sweat, her heart beating a tattoo inside her ribs.

"Of course I read it. It's great. You win the bet." But any tears of joy Tilly might have shed dried up as he smirked down at her. "And don't worry, *Ayn*, I'll make sure you're fairly compensated for your labor."

"Dad!"

"Keep your hair on, you'll miss your train."

Tilly didn't know what to say, so she grabbed her suitcase.It felt strange to have no words after producing so many for so long.

"Think about coming back next summer," said her father. "I mean, if you want."

"Talk to Mr. Bernstein about another contract and maybe I'll consider it."

"Your mother was right. You really are a smart aleck, you know that?"

"At least I come by it honestly."

As the train pulled away from the station, Tilly vowed to herself that she wouldn't forget how she felt at that moment. She wouldn't forget who she was; or rather, who she had become. She was returning from her summer vacation a novelist.

But once Tilly was back in her room full of her stuff, around people who didn't know—or care—what she'd been doing all summer, she lost that sense of significance; of accomplishment.

More than that, even. She didn't know how to be herself anymore.

Not even reading *The Fountainhead* helped. She didn't care much about the plot, or the characters. Howard Roark seemed like kind of a psycho; Dominique a moody twit. She liked the villainous art critic, though. He seemed like a mensch.

If Tilly had changed, she figured she'd changed back.

But not entirely. The feeling of having written *Orchard of Sin* wasn't like a secret; something small and exciting she carried with her. Instead, it was like a worry, pressing on her whenever she thought about it, which was constantly. When she'd asked her father if he'd gotten edits, he kept saying he expected them "soon." But as September's showy leaves were blown away by the October wind, Tilly assumed the worst. The book must have been so crummy they rejected it.

This lessened the pressure she felt weighing on her in some ways and increased it in others. Would her father not get paid now? What would happen? But whenever he called, she couldn't bring herself to ask.

It wasn't until the Halloween-week issue of *The New Yorker* arrived at their house—Daniel subscribed—that Tilly got her answer. She always paged through it, for the cartoons, and sometimes for the fiction, but mostly to feel sophisticated. But this time, it was the table of contents that caught her eye:

TRICK OR TREAT
Edmund Wilson reviews Orchard of Sin

Magazine clutched in her hands, Tilly ran to her room as hard as she could pelt, prompting her mother to shout at her to stop stomping around so much.

"Mail's here!" Tilly announced, and slammed the door to her room—another defiance—before flinging herself down on her bed.

She knew it might be a review of the film. It had come out—just not in any cinemas close to Greenwich. Tilly didn't even get the chance to test her theory that she wouldn't be allowed to see it. Anyway, she suspected the review would be about the book.

Her book.

She also suspected it would not be a kind review. Wilson was a notorious crank who hated horror and fantasy. He'd called Tolkien "balderdash" and Lovecraft "undistinguished," so Tilly braced herself for his opinions about her freshman effort.

Two paragraphs in, she declared aloud, "I need a drink!" like her mother would at the end of an evening spent playing bridge, or raising money for a charity:

> It was twenty years ago that I wrote "A Treatise on Tales of Horror." Since then, I have been asked countless times if I would ever go back and read more. My response has ever been to shudder, but not out of any trepidation. No, it is the prospect of once again subjecting myself to the amateur stylings of the scaremongers that makes my skin crawl.
>
> And really, where would I even begin, if I'd wanted to? How could I go into a bookshop and ask for a volume that summed up two decades of so-called artistic production? No, that would be impossible, and too subjective. So when my editor demanded this piece of me, for the Halloween issue, I decided I would select a title scheduled to come out this month. And that is the horror story of how I ended up the victim of the crime that is *Orchard of Sin*.
>
> *Orchard of Sin* is, allegedly, an adaptation of a picture currently running in the less prestigious movie houses. I watched it for the purposes of comparison. It was a very bosomy sort of film, where innocent, buxom girls are menaced by a leering, apple-bearing Satanist hell-bent (so to speak) on making them fall, Eve-like. (The heroine's name is Evelyn, in case the apple and the sinning were not clues enough.)
>
> So, *Orchard of Sin*, the novel. Or "novelization" as it calls itself, though the book has precious little to do with the film. One might assume this to be a good thing,

but the writer of this, "T.A. Lathe," goes off script almost immediately. Instead of setting the book in an unpromising schoolchild's imagining of the colonial era, it is set in some far-flung future, where everyone's nuclear anxieties, from *Godzilla* to *Dr. Strangelove*, have come true. Evie Price, who in the film is a dim but wellmeaning blacksmith's daughter, is in this version a spoiled post-apocalyptic socialite. And instead of being tempted to fall by a lecherous aristocrat, Evie is bewitched by a hero styled in a mode reminiscent of the uniquely excitable prose of Ayn Rand. (Piercing gaze; refusal to compromise; speech-making). He tempts Evie not with the promise of pleasure, but of knowledge and reason— two things that horrible woman claims to respect.

Whoever "T.A. Lathe" is, he or she clearly admires Rand, aesthetically and philosophically—but due to that, the novel's condemnation of hypocrisy seems more far-fetched than its setting or its plot. Rand, that famous advocate of individual liberty who once denounced her Hollywood colleagues as card-carrying communists before the House Un-American Activities Committee, would surely be every bit as flattered as those of us who possess a different opinion of her ideas are amused.

The review went on from there.

Tilly read it all, twice, before setting aside the magazine. Daniel had told her that eating a few servings from the shit buffet was all part of it...

And really, as curmudgeonly as Wilson was, she found some encouraging words as well as harsh ones. Or at least things she chose to consider encouraging, such as Wilson's remark that "the horror of the novel ends up being the devastating consequences of man's resistance to change, which is at least a more realistic menace than the voluminously but ineffectively described creations of H.P. Lovecraft, or the 'ham' Satanists of the original." His concluding line could also be taken as a compliment, sort of: "I do hope the author of the novel was well paid for this waste of what talent he or she may possess, but so say I of most horror novelists—and novelizationists."

No, what really bothered her was the attack on Ayn Rand. Tilly hadn't known that Rand had testified before the HUAC. It seemed shockingly hypocritical of her. As far as Tilly figured it, snitching to the feds was pretty much the opposite of respecting private citizens' freedom.

"Tilly!"

Tilly chose to ignore her mother. She'd just say she hadn't heard her.

Maybe there was more to it. Maybe—but probably not. Rand stood upon her own scrupulousness. She said she didn't let her feelings get in the way of her reason. But what, other than hatred, could have inspire her to tell the government anything?

"Tilly Turner!"

Her mother was in her doorway, hands on her hips.

"Oh, hi Mom."

"Didn't you hear me calling you?"

"No, sorry."

Her mother looked skeptical. "Come downstairs. There's something I want to talk to you about."

"Now?"

"Yes, now."

Tilly followed her mother down the front stairs and into the solarium. It was nice and warm in there, from the abundant autumn sunshine pouring in, but the bare trees beyond seemed to shiver in a breeze that kicked up the fallen leaves about their roots. The little table in the warmest part of the room was her mother's favorite area for opening the mail; the day's letters lay there currently, along with her little mahogany letter opener, her current half-empty pack of Camels, and her Zippo.

Her mother sat, and lit up a cigarette. After exhaling, she slid a letter over to Tilly.

"What do you make of this, I wonder?"

Tilly opened it. It was a letter from her father, telling her mother that he had opened a college savings account for Tilly with $1700 of seed money in it. Also included in the letter was all the paperwork.

"Well?" said her mother, as Tilly struggled to regain her composure.

"He's fairly compensating me for my labor."

This time, she was the one smirking as she said it.

Her mother shook her head in exasperation. "You'd better telephone him and thank him."

When Tilly's father picked up, Tilly really let him have it.

"I thought they'd rejected the manuscript!" she said. "I thought you might be in violation of contract! You should have told me!"

"Jeez, and here I thought it would be a nicer surprise this way," he said, but he sounded amused on the other end of the crackling line. "Sorry. I should have known you'd already seen too much of the inner workings of the sausage factory."

Tilly wondered if he'd seen Wilson's review—if that was the source of his generosity. She decided not to ask. Her mother had come into the room, and she still hadn't told Cecilia the whole story. She would, one day. Just not yet.

"So," she said. "Have you seen it? How does it look?"

"Sure I've seen it; I have your ten author copies here at the apartment. I'd mail them but I figured you could get them the next time you came up here. Speaking of... you should come up soon, if your mother will let you. Saul—Saul Bernstein, you remember my agent, right?—Saul knew Ayn Rand was going to be at this party, I guess, and he told her all about you. Tilly, she wants to meet you!"

Tilly's stomach turned. After months of being away from the world of lunch meetings and late-night words, these thoughts and choices, everything was happening so fast.

The feeling was back—the feeling of being a novelist.

But that sensation had returned while she was reading Wilson's hatchet job in the *New Yorker*. It did not originate with this offer of an audience with a queen Tilly wasn't so sure she wanted to serve.

"That's nice of him," said Tilly, "but I think I'd rather just have lunch with you."

Her father paused. "What, really?"

"Yes really. Why not?"

"If that's how you feel about it… sure. Put your mother on, and we'll work out the details."

"Okay, see you then," said Tilly, and handed over the phone.

Molly Tanzer is the author of the Diabolist's Library trilogy: *Creatures of Will and Temper*, the Locus Award-nominated *Creatures of Want and Ruin*, and *Creatures of Charm and Hunger*. She is also the author of the weird western *Vermilion*, an io9 and NPR "Best Book" of 2015, and the British Fantasy Award-nominated collection, *A Pretty Mouth*, as well as many critically acclaimed short stories. Follow her adventures at @molly_tanzer on Instagram or @molly_the_tanz on Twitter. She lives outside of Boulder, CO with her cat, Toad.

THE THUNDER, PERFECT MIND
NICK MAMATAS

GERALD WALLACE WAS GETTING OLD. A decade of being an understudy to the famous Mr. Poole, portraying ——— in London, in Paris, in Munich, and now back around home. It was a good thing that ——— had no lines, as Gerald had no French or German. But a decade was a long time for so physical a role. What he did to his body to portray ——— necessarily limited his ability to play lead roles on the legitimate stage. Mr. Poole had not faced a similar problem, with his good looks and strong baritone voice. Gerald's joints ached, always. The grey leotard he wore, and this must have been the fiftieth he'd had to have prepared at his own expense, could barely make it over the swell of his belly these days.

Gerald's calisthenics routine, his planches, his endless swinging of his Indian clubs both in private and before paying audiences—nothing could stop time. He still did a good-enough job as ———, but not good enough for the London stage any longer, even as an understudy. So a Western tour of Wales it was.

And Gerald Wallace did have Welsh! But no lines. He was the star of the show, finally, but no hero. He played a being that had returned from the dead, but age was catching up to him, inexorably and inevitably. He groaned at the uncomfortable fit of his leotard, but the groan wasn't his.

It was ———'s.

Gerald didn't crowd the mirror with Dr. Frankenstein, Clerval, Fritz, and the other men. He knew how to apply his paints without reference. He also didn't want to look at himself anymore. They were down to one mirror on this tour of the West. Heavens, they'd cut little William's role to an off-stage scream, and were down to a single singing, dancing "gypsy" as well! And as far as gypsies went, Thomas Morris wasn't much of one; he had to darken his face and paste on a mustache every night. Man couldn't even grow his own whiskers, yet he had lines. Man looked his part not at all, and he got to *alter* his lines—the lines of *Presumption, or The Fate of Frankenstein*, that famed play by Richard Brinsley Peake, based on the even more famed novel by Mrs. Shelley! "Hilliho!—what tall bully's that?" he'd say as ——— made his entrance. "The steeple of Ingoldstadt taking a walk. See yonder, comrades!" And Morris changed the line to "The steeple of Wrexham" to get a laugh! But "See yonder, comrades," *that* he kept intact, despite the gypsy comrades having been cut for budgetary reasons.

Wrexham didn't even have a steeple, it had a tower. Gerald clenched and unclenched his hands. He could strangle a body. But instead he decided that he would finally speak to the management.

Carolinia Hewett was dressed for an audience. An intimate audience. Hair up high in curls, décolletage like a great glacier that the doctor would chase ——— across in the pages of the novel, face painted as eagerly as an understudy's when the lead develops a sudden palsy. She was cleaning her pepperbox pistol atop the steamer trunk she used as a desk and did not stop when Gerald walked into the small backstage area she used as an office.

"Good afternoon, Wallace," she said, sparing him a glance. Gerald was about to explain to Miss Hewett that she shouldn't be working with oil in such an outfit, but then he reminded himself that Miss Hewett was his employer, had taken the role of Elizabeth Frankenstein and thus clearly thought highly of herself, was the only person who could grant him the boon he craved, and was currently armed.

"Miss Hewett, thank you," he said. "Pardon me for disturbing your task."

"You look good tonight," Hewett said. She appraised him a moment longer, put her gun down. "Suck in the gut, please." Gerald complied. "Moan," she said. "Moan like the demon torn from the warm bosom of hell and poured against his will into the twisted patchwork body of a man." Gerald complied with that as well, or hoped he did. Hewett wasn't usually so focused on directing her actors; she hired him thanks to his experience with the role.

"One more time, indulge me please, Wallace."

"Uurrugh," Wallace moaned. His little trick was to push the air out of first his left nostril, then his right, and rumble both his throat and diaphragm at once. He'd always imagined ———— with the lungs of two different men, and the sinuses and nose of a third. A trade secret to bring verisimilitude to his role.

"Now in Welsh."

"Excuse me?"

"Moan in Welsh."

Moaning in Welsh was a little different—it had been different in French and German as well, as the tsk-tsking directors had explained at length through repetition and gesture. So Gerald moaned his well-practiced moan, but also imitated his grandfather's, who had always been complaining about something or other in the few years he lived during Gerald's childhood.

"You're a wonder, Wallace," Hewett said. "The girls can't sing, Clerval keeps stepping on Frankenstein's lines, the flutist is at death's door with a cold. It's up to you, O Demon, to save us all."

"I want a line."

"Pardon me?"

"I want a line of dialogue," Gerald said plainly.

Hewett laughed. She was an actress too, and her laughter was pulled from her storage house of humiliations. "You want to change the play? What would Mr. Peake say?"

"You changed the play. It's nearly fifteen minutes shorter and with a cast a third of the size demanded by the script," Gerald said. He was a monster, an unfeeling demon. He would not be defeated by the well-tempered laughter of a woman.

"I did *not* change the play, sir," Hewett said. She gestured as grandly as the confining corner to the small backstage area allowed. "The public changed the play. The fellows who constructed this theater changed the play. The play as written could not be performed here; no-one would attend at the price we'd need to set, and the only venue I could rent in this far-off country is…" Another gesture, her arms a pair of swans bowing their necks in defeat, completed the thought.

"The playwright changed the book," Gerald said. "The creature learns to read, he philosophizes!"

"Nobody is going to pay to watch you read with your lips moving for a quarter of an hour, Mr. Wallace," said Hewett. "The play could use a few more cuts, truth be told. You've played this role for years. Why do you want a line *now*?"

"Because I have played this role for years. Mr. Peake's play has been very good to me; too good, one might say. It's been years since I trod upon a stage and said something, or huddled with my comrades working over the script in the hours before a show. Miss Hewett, I often find myself in make-up and leotard in my dreams, playing my greatest role. Do you understand?"

"Even in your dreams, you don't speak?" she asked.

"Nor am I spoken to," he answered. "If I have other dreams, I don't recall them upon waking."

"Well then, Mr. Wallace, what would you like to say, on stage, tonight, in character, as the demon?" She steepled her fingers and peered up Wallace. Despite being two heads taller than Hewett, and that was when she was standing, somehow Hewett loomed over him now. Was it the lantern throwing shadows through the ropes and rigging of the backstage area, Hewett's waxen good looks, or the sheer fact that Wallace's costume looked and felt more than a little ridiculous when he wasn't on stage…when he was speaking.

"I… perhaps a line of dialogue from the novel," he said.

"Such as?"

"If you have a copy I might borrow, I'll peruse it and get back to you. I want a line of dialogue, but it need not be tonight. I'd want to rehearse it with whomever I was delivering it."

"Of course," Hewett said. "I am afraid I don't carry a copy of the novel with me. It differs greatly from the play."

"I imagine there are many fewer singing and dancing gypsies," said Gerald.

"Have you not read it at all?"

"It's…been some time."

"Perhaps you'll dream of a line of dialogue after tonight's performance."

Gerald practiced many obscure, even occult breathing methods, as part of both his physical and thespic regimes. He used them all now to swallow *If I were to dream a line of dialogue tonight, I wouldn't need to say it on the bloody stage, would I, you beautiful, bewitching, beguiling nitwit?!* before the sentiment pushed itself out of his lungs and throat.

"I suppose it was just a whim," he said instead.

"If I didn't know better, Mr. Wallace, I'd think that your request for a script change was just a ploy to spend a bit of time with me, alone," Hewett said. She winked at him, picked up her gun, and slid it off the trunk and onto, Wallace presumed, as peering over the edge would be uncouth, her lap.

"Good afternoon, ma'am," he said. "My interests are purely professional, I promise you."

Hewett didn't say anything to dismiss him; her nod and smirk were sufficient.

The performance went well enough, despite the small stage, the cuts, and the audience perhaps not as proficient in English as need be to truly appreciate Mr. Peake's dialogue. In England, ———'s entrance was most often preceded by red and blue lights signaling the alchemical science that would galvanize and reanimate a ragdoll corpse.

——— was then to break through a railing, leap upon the laboratory table, and then land upon the stage! In Wales, a black curtain was quickly dropped, and after two beats, just before the dimmest groundling could shout "What!" or *"Beth!"*, it would be quickly jerked and there, arms wide and head thrown back, would be Gerald centerstage, taking up as much space as he could, and howling from the depths of his diaphragm. Shrieks of horror and joy, applause and yelping, that narcotic moment of attention. Wallace was a god and the devil, a glowing star and a humble craftsman, manifesting the utterly unique and just hitting his marks as he had done over and over again for years.

And ——— moaned and howled and loomed over the lip of the stage, and the audience was aflame! Awe and the sublime, horror and revulsion. And then, the tedium of drama. Frankenstein shrieking, "The demon corpse to which I have given life!" which Gerald always found bizarrely maternal spilling from the lips of a man, not to mention the bizarre triple identity as newborn, dead man, and immortal spirit. "Its unearthly ugliness renders it too horrible for human eyes!"

That line would have stung, except that Burton wasn't cast as Frankenstein for his looks, or for his skill in stage combat, both of which were lacking. In England, there would have been a trick sword for Gerald to snap in two. Then Frankenstein falls into a swoon. Thunder booms and lightning dazzles the eye! But here in Wales, there was one sword, and so the only way to thrill the audience was for ——— to muster up to his terrified creator and with a great backhand send the sword flying out of Frankenstein's hand and skittering off the apron onto the floor.

Thus ended Act I of *Presumption*. A stagehand collected the sword in the dark, and even a Welsh audience knew to pretend that they saw nothing, perceived nothing at all but the passage of a dozen days and nights in a twinkling.

Were ——— to say something, this climactic moment would be as good a time as any. Perhaps when handing flowers to De Lacey in Act II, Scene 3, but no…that would ruin the pathos of the blind man greeting the mute demon so warmly. Perhaps it wasn't just the experience of creation that rendered ——— mute, but the rejection of the father, the violence of the sword, that made speech superfluous. After all, what is there to say in a world that did not mold you from its wonders and love, but from its rotting detritus and ambition?

Or maybe Act III, Scene 1, when ——— snatches up young Master Frankenstein. It's a bit of mimery, as there is no William in the cast. In that moment, ——— having something to say could thicken the plot; the creation was more than a demon, he was in fact an illgrown nephew to little Uncle William.

But that fact, remarked upon explicitly, could be cause for scandal, and the narrative had been scandal enough since 1818 when Mrs. Shelley saw it published.

And ——— would certainly have nothing to say when the avalanche took him at the play's end, if only because Burton would then demand a dying line of his own, and two actors shouting to be heard over the effects of the rifle report and the falling mountain—nothing more than a firecracker, bass drums, and papier-mâché boulders in this run—would render the katabasis absurd.

The truth was clear as a church bell; Gerald Wallace was an actor, not a playwright. And for that matter, he was a man of the body rather than, strictly speaking, the mind. Gerald was smart enough to know that he got work into his later forties thanks to his physique. In his youth, he was at least handsome, and could dance a bit—his baritone was passable. Now he was just large.

But of course he could read. Clearly, what he needed was a copy of *Frankenstein*. Not to read in-depth, but to skim. Or, really, what he needed was someone who had read *Frankenstein* to tell him all about the creature, to point out choice passages from which he could crib a profound line.

Miray, who played Safie, perhaps. Usually, after an opening night, the director and stage manager would give the cast a party, but not this director, and not this opening night. Hewett had all the charm of a clerk poring over a ledger once the curtain dropped. She didn't even want to make a grand turn and take in the applause of her cast and crew, not when there were shillings to stack. So Gerald would have to move fast, before Safie returned to the boarding house with the other actresses and shut themselves to do whatever it is women do with one another at night. Perhaps they read the book to one another, and chuckled at Gerald's ignorance, his oafishness, just as they did onstage.

He didn't take off his make-up or change out of his leotard, though a single run or tear would mean a tongue-lashing and his pay packet encumbered. He nearly caught himself lumbering in the manner of ———— but resumed his normal gait, long strides, arms swinging like a pugilist's, chin up, and then slowed down so as not to seem too keen to reach the knot of actresses of which Miray was a part.

"Miray—Miss Saatchi!" he called out. All the women turned to him as one, and not one of them offered a smile. "Evening, ladies. Miss Saatchi, so sorry to keep you, but may we speak privately for a moment?"

"Why Mr. Wallace!" Miray said theatrically, hand to her heart. "I'm sure we cannot, but we can all spare a moment for you, right ladies?" The others—the younger girl who played Elizabeth, beauteous Agatha, and the older woman who played Madame Ninon—nodded, shot him looks ranging from curious to dubious. They were all one another's chaperones, as Hewett couldn't be bothered to either hire an old woman or shepherd her actresses around herself.

Gerald nodded once, acting. "Of course. I just mean to inquire— you've read Mrs. Shelley's book? I heard you speak of it once, with Mr. Morris."

"You have prodigious ears, sir," said Miray. "Morris—oh, he merely pretended to have read the novel, so as to strike up a conversation with me." Her face betrayed no emotion, but the other girls' expressions lit up and old Madame Ninon clucked her tongue.

"I am Mr. Morris's opposite number."

"So you don't wish a conversation with Miray?" asked the woman who played Ninon. She hadn't removed her stage make-up as of yet, so her arched eyebrow wasn't just waspish, but outright malevolent.

Gerald controlled his expression—he knew he looked horrific regardless—"No. What I mean to say is that I've not read *Frankenstein*, but would like to. May I borrow your volumes?"

Ninon scoffed. "You want to read the book? Why now? You've been playing the role for a decade!"

"Mrs. Shelley has even issued a new edition," said little Agatha. None of them had undone their make-up. It was as though they were still all in the play, acting out a secret scene. Gerald wondered if they were thinking of him as ———, in the same way he heard the voice of the woman speaking to him and thought *Agatha De Lacey*.

"Yes," Gerald said. He thought for a moment whether he should say more, explain his desires. Would he be mocked, as Hewett had mocked him? Dismissed as actresses often dismissed attention from actors—though the reasoning was sound. There were no roles for women visibly with child, and that was leaving aside all the other complications of procreation.

It didn't matter; Miray answered presently. "I'm sorry, Mr. Wallace. I didn't pack *Frankenstein* with me for this tour. It's dreadful, deliciously so! But the play is as frightening, even though I watch most of it from the wings and can recite every line in my sleep. It's your performance, Mr. Wallace, that makes it so. So primal, utterly daemonic."

"In both senses of the word," said Madam Ninon. "Bravo, sir. But now I must get the girls to our rooms. Excuse us, and good evening."

The women could leave in full make-up, if they stuck together in a group and ostentatiously discussed the night's performance. The men who played Frankenstein and Clerval would probably accompany them as well, to keep them from being accosted by members of the lower social orders. Members of the lower social orders who didn't work in theater that was. But Gerald had to return to the dressing room and remove his make-up and leotard. It wouldn't do to go about in public and ruin the great reveal of the demon's form for free, not when his appearance was all he had to offer in exchange for a wage.

When Gerald returned to the dressing area, Morris was already nearly done removing his own burnt cork make-up. He met Gerald's gaze in his small mirror and smirked. "You should have removed your costume first, before chatting up that girl. Bellowing for her like she was an hen escaped from the coop."

"I wasn't chatting her up," Gerald said as he took a seat and leaned in to see himself in Morris's mirror. Morris obliged and said, "Oh, I wasn't either, and won't be tomorrow night, friend." He handed Gerald the mirror, reached into his pocket, withdrew a Châtelleraul, flicked the blade open as he stood up. From over Gerald's shoulder he peered into the mirror and cut away at the few whiskers under his nose. The knife was sharp enough that Morris need not even flex his lip. He put his other hand on Gerald's shoulder. "Neither of us will be chatting Miray Saatchi, that little songbird, up."

Gerald didn't move to reach for rag to remove his own makeup—a mix of red brick dust and carpenter's blue chalk—caked on thick and now dripping horrifically from his sudden, renewed sweat. He glanced at Morris's reflection for a moment, then back to his own filthy face.

Gerald could have used a line here as well.

"Don't worry, I know that the show must go on," Morris said. "The creature is meant to have stitches up and down his body, no? And your neck, it's not covered by the leotard."

"I might play other roles," Gerald said slowly, trying to keep his hand from shaking. "In the future."

"I think we both know this is your swansong, ol' Jerry. You'll be lumbering off into the darkened wings after this run ends. Just be happy you ain't got nothing to memorize." Morris smiled, picked the gap between his two front teeth with the point of the blade, then straightened himself up, folded the knife, and wished Gerald *noswaith dda.* "Picked that up, just from keeping my ears open, I did!" he explained as he slipped out.

Noswaith dda. But no, it had not been a very good evening, and the night to come wasn't shaping up to be very good either. Gerald didn't like being taunted by a small man, but that knife would make a fight more than even. He wasn't ———; he couldn't simply snap a sword in two with his giant hand. Gerald took off his make-up quickly and leaving behind a smudged, smoky mirror and a messy dressing table.

Gerald did not sleep that night, and not only because Burton snored, and Mr. Curry, who played Clerval, frequently got up to use the pot. Morris was in the other men's bunk, with the fellows who portrayed the male De Laceys. The smartest thing to do, or the smartest thing Gerald could think of to do, was to cross the hall, enter the room, and strangle Morris as he slept. No knifeplay then. But that would be murder, there would be witnesses, and press harsher than middling theatrical reviews. He could see the headline in *The True Sun* now: MONSTER DESCENDS FROM PROSCENIUM TO COMMIT HORRIBLE MURDER.

And yet, horrible murder was still the smartest thing Gerald could think to do. Informing on Morris to Hewett would be both humiliating and unlikely to lead to Morris's sacking. The show must go on, it's true, and it is not as though Hewett could disarm a man. If anything, she would turn to Gerald in case of any problem among the actors, but Gerald was the problem.

And he didn't even fancy Miray Saatchi; he just wanted to borrow the book!

No, that wasn't so either. He just wanted a line of dialogue for
————. The book was a means to an end. That means not only
failed, but led him afoul of Morris and his wicked French blade.

And now he didn't know what to say at all. Gerald didn't sleep
that night, but he did dream, after a fashion. The room was nearly
pitch black, but very occasionally when the wind blew the right way,
a sliver of moonbeam would penetrate the darkness and light would
play upon the walls. Once or twice, someone took a candle down the
hallway, and marched a puddle of illumination across the floor. And
there were sounds as well, snoring and other more noisesome exhala-
tions, and the creak of bed planks. It was a brilliant dark, a discordant
silence.

The human mind will come up with something when greeted by
nothing, Gerald knew that much. He tried to push away the thought
of the knife against his neck, of Morris's rotten-tooth breath. Focus
on the dark, focus on the silence. He began to experience lights that
weren't the distant moon or a wandering candle, sounds other than
weight on wood or air leaving bodies.

A sudden flash, and it was a woman. She was Hewett, but also Miray,
and also his mother, and also the Virgin Mary, and the girl Sioned who
first let him in, his old gran, his niece that he held once in his thick
arms when she was but a babe, and many more than that besides.

The woman told him many things. Most of them about herself—
her*selves*. She was famed and obscure, a whore and a saint, a virgin
and a wife, the mother of her own father and sister of her husband
to whom she had also given birth, the victim of lies from the tellers
of truths but it's those who seek to defame her with lies who speak
the facts of her existence. She was weak and powerful and all sorts
of other contradictions that Gerald could scarcely keep track of for
all the breasts. With every utterance, the women shifted and spiraled,
like shards of light in a kaleidoscope. Their meins and voices varied
widely, but there were commonalities—Roman noses, expressive
brows, and full ripe breasts with plum-like nipples, the flesh free of

any blemish whether it was milky white or slightly swarthy. The walls of the room fell away and the inky black of night filled with breasts, floating like nebulae in the sky. Truly, a milky way.

He wanted to suckle on every tit—the engorged and deflated, the breast that looked like fried eggs on a plate, the breast that reminded him of udders brushing over a meadow's grass. Gerald wanted them all; the young and the old, the civilized and the barbaric, the living and the dead. No, wait, that wasn't right... none of these women were dead, even the most ancient of crones had a strange unearthly vitality about them. They were for him, even Hewett and Miray who were certainly not for him in the idle daylight hours or the working evenings.

He wanted to ask, "Who are you?" but she had already answered that, exhaustively if not entirely comprehensibly. How humiliating it was, to time and again want to speak, to say something, and finding it impossible. Then he realized what he could ask of this assemblage of apparitions.

"Why me? Who am I to see this?" he said.

And they told him, this woman who was endless contradictory women. That he was alive and yet dead, articulate and mute, philosophical and simple, he had been threatened yet had shown mercy. He was the one who hated her, and the one who loved her, who had known her seeming but was ignorant of her appearance.

"I... don't know what to say," said Gerald. "I don't understand."

The woman, all of them, smiled and nodded at that, and said a thousand other sayings, as one and as many. Gerald's mind, no, his physical brain, was filled with what the woman told him. Gerald had eaten plenty of *cervelle de veau* during his French tour, and knew brain to be mushy, spongelike on the tongue. The way a beef brain absorbed the flavor of capers and butter, his, physically, absorbed what the community of women had told him. It was a bit like God, who was Three Persons and also One, but the women were myriad, and their reason for coming to him were myriad as well.

Gerald slept at dawn, hard but briefly.

It wouldn't do to tell Hewett, or the women of the troupe, about his experience of the night prior. The sheer number of bosoms that had somehow been on display in what was otherwise a dark room precluded that. And he could not tell the men of the troupe about Morris's threat. Gerald was the hard man of the theater, muscled and fearless. That's how all his fellows thought of him, or at least, he realized, as he struggled sleepily with his dressing gown in the late morning, how he thought all his fellows thought of him. How he hoped they all thought of him. Perhaps he truly was a mark to be intimidated and mocked, less actor than freak. Clearly Morris was not intimidated in the slightest. He ruminated for a moment, then the answer came to him. He would tell the men about his vision, the women about Morris and the knife. But who first? He'd missed the breakfast the landlord had prepared for the boarders already, and could scarcely get a cup of tea from him. It was to the theater then; Hewett was to pay per diems from last night's take, though Gerald had little idea where he could go to buy a roll in town. So to the theater it was.

Burton wasn't a great actor, but there was an aura of cagey intellect about him—he was just good enough for the role of Dr. Frankenstein, and he had toured the continent, and even the Americas once, performing bowlderized Shakespeare in saloons and haciendas. Further, perhaps he had heard something in his sleep, or dreamt of the Milky Way.

He was already at the theater, sitting on the stage, script pages on his lap. Gerald begged for a moment of Burton's time and told him of the... Gerald quickly decided on the word "visitation" though it wasn't quite accurate. Better than "waking dream, despite an absence of absinthe," which Gerald had briefly considered while walking over.

"Midnight visitation? Did you wake up a bit moist, then, Gerald?" Burton asked with a laugh. His voice was wine-sweet, though it was not yet noon. "I kid, I kid. I'm sorry, friend. You said you weren't dreaming at all? Was it strong drink or rich food—if so, you mustn't hold out on me. After all, I am your creator, and your executioner!"

"You sound like her now," Gerald said.

"Aye," he said. "Perhaps it's the play. There's alchemy in it, transmutations, and an absent woman."

"Oh?"

"Think of it, Wallace. In the book, the demon craves a wife. Mr. Peake did away with that plot, and inserted dancing gypsies. You've read the book, of course."

"Oh yes," Gerald said. "Of course." He licked his lips. "I was just thinking of the many things the play excises. The creature's dialogues, for instance."

Burton shrugged. "Perhaps. Some might say that the play is already overstuffed. A typical production, that is. What our dramaturge and director did…" Burton waved a hand, dismissing the very idea of Hewett and the entire production. "Forget a line, friend. You should get a wife, consummate the marriage on stage."

"I need a line of dialogue, Burton. I've been playing a lumbering beast for so long."

"Hmm," Burton said. "I am an unfortunate creature, deserted by all. If I fail here, I am an outcast in the world forever. Or something along those lines. I read the book of course, and some moving exchanges stayed with me, but I'm no sage or scholar. But the creature says that to old blind De Lacey, and I recall finding it touching."

"I was thinking of something for the end of the first act," said Gerald.

"Won't work, friend. As you know, the creature only learns human speech after he escapes. He's no more born with an adult mind than you were."

"Or *you* were," said Gerald. "Or is it so? The creature ambulates, wears a chiton and doesn't shit all over it, and performs many other tasks, save speech. He does have an adult brain, in an adult skull."

"It's just a story, Gerald," said Burton, "you cannot expect a logical explanation for every little circumstance. Theater is about spectacle, not rigor."

"Then the demon can speak immediately after his creation!"

"What would he even have to say, fresh from the slab?" asked Burton. "Standing agog before his maker?" He gestured grandly at himself and winked, then laughed. Gerald had to laugh as well.

"What would we say before God?" Gerald asked, but it was a general question, not one for Burton.

"Ah, I'd spit in the old bastard's eye for everything He's done to me here on Earth. The hard nights, poor dead Liza, every cold winter. You know I've got eight toes, Gerald? Wish I could pluck a pair from a corpse and get them sewn on, livin' and wigglin'."

"You're drunk already, and it's not even the afternoon," said Gerald.

"Not already—this is still last night's liquor loosening my tongue," said Burton. "Anyhoo, Gerald. It's not what you say to God when you meet Him the second time, but what you might say if you could see your mother and have a chat with her the moment you uhrm... issued forth and such."

"Thank you," said Gerald.

"I was thinking 'Damn you,' " said Burton.

"No, I was thanking you, sir," said Gerald. "That really is the core of it. What the demon should say at the end of Act I, and for that matter, about what I saw in our room last night. What might one say to God as a fresh-born babe, and wouldn't in our ignorance believe that our mother, the life-giver and love-giver, was God. I've much to think about."

"If it keeps your mind off trying to upstage me even more than you do with your grand entrance and strongman physique, I'm pleased to be of service," said Burton. "And with that, I must urinate, so I bid you adieu."

Burton took the contemplative mood, and the strange aura of confidence, with him when he left. There was something about actors; they could make the absurd seem reasonable with inflection, tone, and an impression of real interest. In a novel, one need only describe a hulking form loping across a glacier, its features obscured by wind so strong the snow seems to whip across the world from horizon to horizon rather than falling from the sky, and the reader *will* see it. An actor is even more powerful—he can gesture at a backdrop and transform it into that same desolate tundra despite it clearly being nothing more than paint and fabric, he can twist his face into a rictus of rage and confusion and transform himself into a dozen dead men stitched together and brought back to a shambling mockery of life.

All without a word. *Before* the word.

The very thought, which Gerald could comprehend but not articulate, gave him a headache. A knife to his throat was easier to contemplate. Death was as existential as a conversation between an infant and the Lord, but there was something prosaic about it. All men die, and some die of misadventure or like animals being butchered. That he could articulate, and he would, to Hewett, if he could find her.

There wasn't much business to do in the theater in the morning. This run of *Presumption* did away with all the theatrical effects—the light-splattered creation of the demon, the flaming cottage, a real rifle firing a blank cartridge, the fall of the avalanche—that had made the original London production so popular, and expensive. Hewett may well have been napping back at the boarding house, or even wandering the streets *sans* chaperone. She would scandalize half of Wales by curtain.

Even as Gerald stood, he heard Hewett castigating Burton outside. He'd apparently chosen to piss against the theater's rear entrance door. Another voice joined Hewett's, in near-perfect harmony, and then laughter. Gerald need only run his hands down the front of his coat and adjust his collar and strike a pose in which to be nonchalantly discovered.

He was fumbling with that last step, first his right hand on the stage, then both hands behind his back, when Hewett and the entire female cast of *Presumption* walked in. Miray's face was flushed, perhaps from her encounter with Burton.

"Good morning, Mr. Wallace," said Hewett.

"Good morning, ladies," said Gerald. "Ma'am, if it would not be too much bother, I would very much like to speak to you alone."

"Ah, you must have written a line for yourself! Well, there's no reason for us to skulk in the shadows; tell us all what it is. If it's any good, we'll all need to learn how to integrate it into tonight's performance," said Hewett.

Miray said, "Perhaps I let slip that you had asked after a copy of *Frankenstein* that you thought I might have carried." She offered Gerald a smile. He felt Morris's blade on his neck again. It had been warm, not *cold steel*, the phrase he had heard so often in his life.

"Perhaps it's been the singular topic of conversation all evening, and even unto the morning," said the woman who played Madame Ninon. "Maybe these little birds have been squawking about, begging for some fleshy worm to be regurgitated into tiny beaks, for an age!" For a moment Gerald wanted to reach out to her, trace the wrinkle on her cheek with the edge of his thumb, and explain that he understood. She truly was Ninon, a woman who calls out *Fritz! Fritz! Where is my stupid husband?* and then boxes his ears, and who then weeps for a poor dead child. She was cast for her mien and bearing just as Gerald had been cast for his musculature and grimace.

All these women were truly something. No wonder when he dreamed without sleeping, he saw women much like them.

"Well?" asked Hewett.

"A knife…" said Gerald.

"Hmph," said Madame Ninon.

"It's not about the line," said Gerald. "I wished to keep this between you and me, Mrs. Hewett, but perhaps it is best for everyone to know that last night, after the final curtain, Mr. Morris brandished a knife and threatened to murder me."

Miray and the girl who played Agatha gasped, and Ninon paled. Hewett made a contemplative sound in her throat. "I see. And whatever was the matter?"

"The matter? A knife, to my throat! That's the matter!"

Hewett held up a hand. "Do not raise your voice to me, Mr. Wallace. Save your beastliness for the performance. No human action is arbitrary; even a madman has a reason for things, if only a brain lesion. What precipitated this threat?"

Gerald sighed and exchanged a glance with Miray. Her face betrayed no trace of guile, but she was an actress.

"Mr. Morris has, it appears, taken a fancy to Miss Saatchi, and he got it into his head that my interest in reading the novel I asked after was a ruse to get close to her. As he himself fancies Miss Saatchi, he warned me away from her with a blade to my throat. A nasty little swinger of a blade too. The French type." Gerald drew a thumb across his own neck and snorted in what they'd all understand was a Gallic manner.

"Melodrama," said Madame Ninon. "What a rascallion."

"We're booked here through the end of next week. We have no understudies, and I would shudder to think of who we might find if we put out a call for local actors," Hewett began.

"Welsh accents!" Madame Ninon interrupted.

"Ahem," said Gerald.

"He's meant to be foreign anyway," said the girl who played Agatha. "Perhaps instead of an Egyptian gypsy, it can be implied that the character is a tinker, some sort of Celtic traveler." Then she turned to Gerald. "Would that be all right?"

Gerald opened his mouth to agree but Ninon's tongue was sharper and faster. "You're casting the play, and rewriting it! Carolinia, you must do something about these girls! Tinkers!" Miray raised a finger at Ninon. She was a Turk on her father's side—what would her objection be, and to whom?

"Excuse me," Hewett said. The other women froze in place. "I will speak with Thomas Morris. Mr. Wallace, Gerald, I presume you can keep your head attached to your neck until seven o'clock?"

"Yes," Gerald said. He was sure he could keep his head about him, but didn't know what Hewett confronting Morris would do for his reputation among the cast. The women, all of them turning their gazes from Hewett to him suggested nothing good. Men, actors, are hardly more merciful than women. Who knew if Morris was in a nearby pub now, plying all the boys except perhaps Burton with alcohol and rallying them in common cause?

"Very well," said Hewett. "I'll have everyone's per diems for luncheon ready in an hour." She exited and the assembled knew not to follow her and try to continue any conversation that they might have been hoping to pursue.

It was Gerald and the women. Agatha smiled. She wasn't acting. "I'm sorry Mr. Morris has proven to be so awful," she said.

"Yes," of course Miray said. "I'll have all of you know I have no interest in Mr. Morris or any other actor as a suitor. Of course, I mean no offense Mr. Wallace."

"Here's a line for you, Mr. Wallace," said Madam Ninon. "Just as you emerge from the laboratory, and Frankenstein brandishes a sword at the creature, you should say..." She quickly adopted an exaggerated pose, one hand held straight out, palm up, her other upon her breast, head thrown back, eyes wide and wild. Then, her voice low and mannish, she wailed, "Please, do not kill me! I am an innocent in this world, a mewling babe in the shape of a man!" The two girls began to giggle, but quickly swallowed what mirth they could.

"You know, Mr. Burton had broadly similar advice," said Gerald. "But his suggestion was superior. He's an intelligent man, an experienced thespian. No wonder he's playing the titular role. If you'll excuse me, ladies, I have to begin my exercises. I'm sure you all must prepare too." Then he smiled broadly at Ninon. "You have two scenes, ma'am. Such hard work, two scenes. You're a woman of uncommon vigor, if you'll forgive my observation—most your age would barely be able to hobble upon a stage at all, much less for two whole scenes. So I will leave you to your considerable making-up." He nodded to the two younger women, both of whom were now as pale as their dresses. "Ladies."

Gerald loved exercise, though his joints protested, and his eyes and mouth quickly filled with cups of salty sweat. Counting wasn't quite thinking, exertion less than cogitation, but also more. He wasn't just a brain in a body, but a body that was itself a brain. He did press-ups, deep knee bends, held himself straight like a plank, and when his arms were exhausted, only then did he appropriate several sandbags from the rigging to curl and swing. Gerald's muscles were on fire. It felt like both giving birth and being born, a body coming into being and a body being sundered. That's how he liked it.

Yelps and hallos from the male members of the cast filled the wings as they entered en masse. Gerald, on his knees now, sought a rag with which to wipe his brow, and when he had finished cleaning his face and looked up to it, he found Morris towering over him.

There was something in the man's pocket as well.

"Heya, Wallace," he said. "Tired yourself out, did you?"

"No," said Gerald as he got to his feet. Now he stood over Morris. "Physical culture is invigorating, not depleting."

"They say that about many activities," said Morris. "You're a degenerate, you know. Burton told me all about your little dream. We all have such dreams, but to share them, that's repulsive, sir."

"You've had the same dream! But it was not a dream... an experience, a vision! Did you have the same one? Last night?"

Morris took a step back, as though pushed by a strong wind. Gerald filled the space, asked again. "Did you?"

Morris held up his hands, palms out. "Easy, friend! It's not like that."

"We're not friends," said Gerald, bringing his chest up to Morris's chin.

Morris reached into his pocket. "No, I did not spend the night contemplating a veritable oceans of tits. I am not a perverted monster, obsessed with bodies, as you are!"

"Is that the voice of Mr. Morris I hear?" queried Hewett from the back office. "Come here please, immediately!"

"Women," Morris said quietly. "You and I will finish up our conversation this evening."

"I have nothing to say to you, Mr. Morris," said Gerald. Morris had nothing to say to that, and retreated when Hewett called for him again.

Truth was that Gerald could barely lift his arms after his routine. Was that what Morris was prepared to do? Goad Gerald into a confrontation, stab him to death, and make an appeal for self-defense? And all for a woman who didn't even fancy him, and whom Gerald did not fancy?

Fucking actors, Gerald thought. He stepped quietly to the flimsy door. There was no need to press his ear against it; Hewett knew how to project, and was indeed addressing the entire cast.

"And do not think, even for a moment, that I could not get a stagehand to play your role!" she announced. "Or his!" Who was this other man whose role was in danger? "That hunchback who brings in the kerosene for the lamps would do as well for our mute creature!" Ah, that explained that.

"Stare all you like! See what it contains!" Gerald could only imagine Hewett withdrawing her dainty pistol from within her décolletage. Was Morris mad enough to draw his weapon, sharp and pointed, from his pants?

Were sex and death always so tightly entwined, like twin strands of jute worked together to make strong rope?

That was an odd thought to have suddenly surface in his mind, Gerald realized, apropos as it was.

He was amazed that Morris had nothing to say in return. Perhaps Hewett had pulled the gun on him. Regardless, the man would be in a rage, so Gerald, still weak from his exertions thought it best to clear away until after luncheon. He turned and there was Miray, listening as attentively to Hewett's harangue as he had just been.

"He wants a woman," said Miray.

"He wants you," said Gerald. "Carolinia Hewett, I'm sure he could do without."

"No, Mr. Wallace. The creature you portray—in Mrs. Shelley's novel, his motivation is to be made whole by being given a bride. His crimes and infamies are largely oriented toward that end. He bids Dr. Frankenstein to construct for him a mate. I recall a line; it made me shiver when I read it. 'I demand a creature of another sex, but as hideous as myself!' " Miray didn't alter her voice when reciting the snippet of text, not in tone or intensity, but there was something to her presentation that struck Gerald in his heart.

Not "the opposite sex" or "the other sex," but "another sex." And Miray had said that phrase as casually as the rest of her utterance, passing over it as though it were unremarkable. And yet, she was so sure that she had remembered the line, not like Burton, who had covered up a weak memory with manufactured gravitas.

"Mr. Wallace!" Miray said, bringing Gerald out of his contemplations. "I believe Miss Hewett is about done lashing Mr. Morris with her tongue—oh, that sounds bawdy. But perhaps we should both find ourselves elsewhere, and different elsewheres at that. I must dress anyway. I hope you find my remarks in re the creature's motivation helpful! If I'm honest I'll say that without that desire for a companion on the part of the demon, *Presumption* scarcely makes sense." She put her finger to her lips, winked once, and ran off on her toes.

Gerald was no longer sweating from his prior exercises, nor did the heart buried in his barrel chest beat hard as it had when he was eavesdropping on Hewett browbeating Morris. He was entirely at peace with himself, with his role as ———, with the rubbish theater and the unsophisticated audience he was to perform for, with the end of his career no longer a distant point on a crepuscular horizon but simply a date, a week hence, as printed on the playbills hanging from every post and plank in town.

He had a line.

Theater was born of ritual. In ancient times, the priestly class were the actors; candles, icons, and statuary the set; the temple—designed with acoustics and the sweep of majesty in mind—the theater. And what ritual was for, what it did to the worshipper and the performers, was a type of magic. Ritual, theater, alters the mind of every participant.

The public cults were designed to protect the status quo. Fast and ration; consume your harvest but not your seed. Couple only on certain dates to keep careful track of your progeny and your property. Keep clean and respect the quarantine. But in every culture, there are transgressors. There are those who dare to violate the laws of God.

And these transgressors have rituals too. Where cathedrals soared, they met in the caves. When good families journeyed to hear their liturgies at dawn, or bowed their heads to the carpet at dusk, these twisted groups met under the full moon to howl in the fog-shrouded woods, or whirled under the yellow sky of blasted deserts. These rituals too were theater, and these rituals too altered minds. Inspired them, warped them.

And slowly but surely, ritual became entertainment and faith a thing of the inner secret heart. The public cults persisted, but as empty spectacle. No matter how incredible the architecture, faith was frozen in stone and steel. For a true experience with the great unknowable, the naming of the unnamed thing, one needed to find the ritual underground.

And there, in Greece, and Egypt, and even among the barbarians of the north, there was a certain cult. Some called her Sophia, or

Wisdom. For others, she was the Fourth Person of the Godhead, suppressed by the patriarchs to preserve their own power. But none of the small sects that venerated this woman could quite agree on what she was—a virgin or a whore, fertile or barren, beautiful or horror or beyond all visual perception, constructed of lies or a manifestation utter mind-shattering truth? Virgin Mary, Theotokos the God-Bearer, Isis, Hekate? And thus she was all of these things, and all who contemplated her were changed by her.

And there was a poem in the form of a riddle written about her, to be recited on stage. And it was suppressed. And the extant copies destroyed. And those who had memorized the poem were mutilated—tongues and fingers ruined.

Millennia later, the poem was rediscovered by a farmer in Egypt, who unearthed a clay jar full of Gnostic texts, the remnants of a dozen alternative Christianities, while plowing a field.

Millennia later, many an old text, many an old script, were recreated and captured forever on horse's hooves and precious metals—endless looping strips of gelatin seasoned with silver salts.

It was not uncommon in certain of these films for the captured, ossified, ritual to be recontextualized and made immediately apprehendable via monologue by an older man with an upper-caste accent. In this, the films called back to the most ancient of rituals—the patriarch explaining the theme and the plot of the very world to children huddled in the mostly dark, with some small flickering of light playing across their faces.

This segment of our tale is that explanation. Cast the actor of your choice, or construct one in your mind's eye. Are his cheekbones high, or brow low? Is this utterance bellowed at you, his eyes blazing? Or whispered, in stereo, by full lips under a flaring nose?

The poem was rediscovered in 1945, 111 years after the performance of *Presumption*. And yet the poem was real, and was also lies. And the figure it described in its organization of contradictions and riddles is real, and so despite the fact that *The Thunder, Perfect*

Mind was unknown to all people living, Gerald Wallace *did* know and experience the woman described in the poem. It was like a stroke of thunder, the sudden enlightenment, alighting upon a very imperfect mind.

Why him? He played the living, and the dead. He was the speak-maker rendered speechless, and the one who could communicate with silences. He lacked the perfect mind, but possessed the perfect body. He was birthed by lightning, which always precedes the thunder. He was always of two natures, as actors must be, and that made him a singular being. Unconsciously, though studiously, he led himself through the rigors of gnostic enlightenment, and at the cusp of it, his lips on the cup of it, he asked for still more. A single line. Something to say.

And this is what happened to him after.

The intermission is over. Raise the curtain, change the reel. The act that is both first and final begins, and is about to end.

There was no reason to clear the line with Hewett, Gerald decided. Surely she would be in a sour mood after having to discipline Morris, and just as surely she would have very little goodwill left for him. The hunchback stagehand, replacing the famous Gerald Wallace? He'd like to see that. Or rather, nobody would like to see that. His was the image on the colorful posters wheat-pasted all over Paris, his was the name on all the lips in London, and even here in distant, cold Wales, he was the hometown boy. Gerald Wallace was *Presumption* and he would be presumptuous for once.

The first act played out with an excruciating slowness. Fritz, the shambling assistant to Dr. Frankenstein, going on about how comely his sister Elizabeth is, and then speaking to Clerval about how desperate the scientist was. Why tell, when one could show, through proper performance and dialogue? No wonder Mr. Peake did away with all the speeches of ———, that Gerald had been told were depicted in the novel. There was no room for yet another major speaking role in this chaotic mess! Ah, and then there were the songs. Carolinia Hewett was a fair singer, but the musicians were little more than schoolboys. The most creative thing about them was the manner in which they tuned their instruments. A masque of anarchy! The highlight of Act I, Scene 2 was the opening number, sung by Hewett. Or rather, it was during the second stanza, when she sang:

Seems sympathy's voice to the ear of despair;
And the dew-drops like tears shed by angels of heaven,
Revive the frail hopes in the bosom of care.

She caressed her own bosom in a way better suited for a music hall than the proper stage. Gerald's countrymen hooted their appreciation and stomped their feet, despite the religious fervor of the country-side. Something about God brings out the Devil in a man. It's why Morris's line about Wrexham played so well.

Then came Scene Three. The demon stands revealed. Mr. Peake was clever enough here; no matter how tall Wallace was, nor how diligently he practiced physical culture, nor how enthusiastically he plied chalk and brick-dust upon his face, he was still but a man. The audience needed to be primed. Burton did a fine enough job describing Frankenstein's creation. "It lives! I saw the dull yellow eye of the creature open, it breathed hard, and a convulsive motion agitated its limbs. What a wretch have I formed. His legs are in proportion and I had selected his features as beautiful—beautiful! Ah, horror! his cadaverous skin scarcely covers the work of muscles and arteries beneath, his hair lustrous, black, and flowing—his teeth of pearly whiteness—but these luxuriances only form more horrible contrasts with the deformities of the Demon."

That was Gerald's cue. No sorrowful blue limelight turning fiery red in this small theater, no smoke and shattered balustrade here—it was all in how Gerald walked, how his muscles rolled, how he found a man and a woman in the audience and glared at them specifically.

——— would *eat* that woman, and then kill the sobbing, defeated man! Finding that couple every night and privately terrorizing them in public was key to capturing the audience, sparking a subtle miasmic panic that swept over the crowd, then weighed upon them all night.

And all the next night, and the next after that.

Gerald had pretty good teeth too.

He emerged from the behind the black curtain and loped onto the stage, and threw wide his arms and howled in the Welsh fashion, and the audience gasped as one, shocked into recognition. Were they in Wales after all and not Ingoldstadt as they had been promised, under the shadow of the tower of Wrexham? Was it them up on the stage, every being in their seats from the boxes to the ground having been liberated of an organ, a digit, a limb, a spoonful of sweetmeats plopped into a bowl of bone?

And Frankenstein said his line: "The demon corpse to which I have given life!"

And then ——— reached out, seeking the warmth of human society and fellow-feeling, as described in Mr. Peake's script. Frankenstein recoiled, and announced, "Its unearthly ugliness renders it too horrible for human eyes!"

Over the years, Gerald Wallace had many Frankensteins to play against, and many choices to make in this ever-repeating nightly moment. Should ——— take his creator's disgust and antipathy as an insult, and stalk over to the man, threat and bloodlust obvious in his gait? Should he approach uncomprehendingly, like a babe being cooed at by a parent? Directors always had ideas of their own, but in the moment, the decision was ultimately his own.

No wonder, he realized now, that this was the best possible moment for ——— to speak. And so Gerald intoned his line, or began to.

"Woman!"

There was more to say. Woman the virgin, woman the wife, woman the crone. The creature wanted all of them. A companion, both deathless and dead, just as he was. An eternal wife, who was ever a virgin, and whose body was ungainly like a crone's. That is what ———— wanted. What ———— would call down from the heavens, and summon up from the pit. Just a few more words, an incantation...

Burton was put off by *ad libitum*. "Are you mad!" he cried, instead of the usual dialogue, and he waved the prop sword more menacingly than he had the night before. Gerald took a hard swing at it to be sure to knock the false blade, which was still heavy wood, from his hand. The curtain fell to murmurs, scattered applause, and confused hooting. Then, that subpar music again.

"Woman!" Burton's howl was hollow, an angry whisper. "What the hell is that supposed to mean? I'm a woman? You're a woman? You want a woman? Calling for your mother! A sea of tits? No, a universe of them! Get a hold of yourself, Gerald!" Hewett, ready to enter Act II Scene I was Elizabeth, stormed up on both of them and said simply, "Marks. Now," as she passed.

Burton gave Gerald a conciliatory wink. "Speaking of a sea of tits!" he hissed. "Don't speak again!"

When the curtain rose for Act II of *Presumption*, the ad libitum continued. Though now in the home of Elizabeth, Dr. Frankenstein carried his sword. Burton must have snatched it up from the stagehand. He stuck to the script otherwise, however, and Hewett had another musical number. Thinking of Clerval, Elizabeth Frankenstein sang:

Ah whither shall my heart then turn,
To what sweet refuge flee?
With passion's fire then shall burn
And throb with love and thee.

And indeed, Hewett played up the final two lines with a nearly burlesque roll of the hips and stroking of her curves. There was hooting at the climax of this scene as well, but it was not confused.

Scene II was Morris and Gerald. Mr. Peake's play called for a trio of "gypsies" but all those characters had been cut save for the comical figure portrayed by Morris. His attitude was anything but comical that night. When he espied the demon, rather than cowering and running, he pulled his Châtelleraul—it was no prop. "Yer after me porridge, are ye?" he declared, instead of fleeing and leaving the food and the small campfire for ———— to explore.

Gerald didn't fear the knife, not in that moment. He walked up to the fire, took a big piece of kindling, weighed it in his hand—it was heavy, thick—then brandished it at Morris. It felt good; there was even a curve to it, and it was really warm, as though it had just been scorched by the propmaster this evening. If there was real blood to be spilled on stage this night, it would be the blood of Gerald Wallace and Thomas Morris co-mingled. It took a long moment of silent acting, but Morris slinked away, walking backward into the wings. Peering past Morris, Gerald saw Hewett fuming, and the two actors who played Agatha and Felix De Lacey standing near, confused and wondering how to enter the scene. Gerald quickly dropped the stick, clutched at his hand as if it had been burned by a phantom fire, and took up his mark downstage, in the shadows. As Agatha sang and Felix played the flute, ———— played the fool, seeking to capture the music flitting through the air as though each note was a night moth compelled to orbit the fire.

Gerald didn't leave the stage when the scene shifted to the De Lacey cottage, with the old blind father of the young De Laceys, and Miray as Safie choosing a humble life as a Christian wife over the harems of Arabia. There was a bit of business with flower baskets, and a pile of leaves—borderline comical on most nights, as huge Gerald constantly ducked away when any of the sighted characters entered the scene to check in on De Lacey, but tonight nobody laughed. There was a sense of some new motif being played out. *We are all blind.* The world swims with unfathomable beings—demons we may call them, in our ignorance!—who exist just out of our sight. Life itself, the everyday struggle to shit and eat and sleep and fuck, is organized by forces beyond our ken, just to keep our gazes from ever landing upon the dark wisdom of these creatures from realms beyond heaven and hell.

That's what was on Gerald's mind anyway, and embedded within the subtle changes in his performance: the scowl he wore instead of the stupefied face preferred by Hewett and other directors, the tension in his limbs as he teased discovery by slowly withdrawing, menacing Miray like the shadow of the worse angel of her nature, rather than scuttling away on hands and knees like a dog in a skirt as he had for the past decade.

Miray caught Gerald's gaze once, though Safie did not meet the eyes of the nameless demon in that same moment. She mouthed the words *You are bringing ruin!* at him. But one can read lips in many a fashion. *You are being human!* Gerald contemplated that for a moment. In Mr. Peake's script, his character is called a demon and a creature; in the cast of characters he is listed simply as ————. But is he not human? Is he not a child who quickly becomes a man, not through the mechanisms of maturity and family life, but through alienation and blood?

Something was terribly wrong with this play.

Act II, Scene 5.

———— tries, so hard, every night. In London, in Paris, and Munich, in theaters with the money to construct actual sets, Agatha De Lacey runs from the demon and falls into a rivulet. ———— saves her! He saves the girl, and places her, still in her swoon, next to her blind father. And then brother Felix, armed, and Frankenstein appear.

————, confused and frightened, is shot and wounded In his rage, he picks up a burning brand and lights the De Lacey cottage aflame!

Of course, this night, there is no rivulet, just a blue light, and no burning brand, just a stick painted red, and the thatch-roof through which the demon bursts is just a scattering of hay over a frame, and there are other differences too. Frankenstein still carries his sword, and the lone gypsy of what script demands be a group has a gravity knife in his hand. Morris sings:

Beware! Beware!
The hideous glare,
The fiend of Sin
With ghastly grin –
Behold the cottage firing.

And the demon runs off with Agatha De Lacey.

Thus ended Act II.

The fiend of Sin! Morris is the fiend of sin, Gerald thought as he carried the girl playing Agatha backstage. They passed Hewett again, who was about to take her mark for the big Act III opener between Elizabeth and Clerval. This time she smiled at Gerald, more warmly and authentically than Carolinia Hewett had ever smiled at anyone, as best he can recall. He was too stunned to react, but little Agatha blew a kiss.

"You may put me down now, Mr. Wallace," Agatha said. "I'm due back on stage in a moment."

"Ah yes, of course," Gerald said, placing her gently onto her feet.

"It's an odd evening," she said, casually calling damnation down onto the whole of the proceedings.

"Mmm," said Gerald, like the demon contemplating a spark of flame would have.

"I look forward to you murdering me," she said.

"Uhm…"

"I tease, sir."

Miray and Madame Ninon made their way to the wings from backstage and both nodded, smiling, at Agatha, and giving Gerald the cut. Gerald was only in the way, but something made him linger. Frankenstein retained his sword, still, which made little sense as in this scene he was meant to brandish a pistol. And indeed, Burton did produce a pistol.

A familiar one.

Hewett's.

An authentic pepperbox pistol, not the clumsy wooden prop used the night before.

The kindling in his hand from when he sought to defend himself from Morris in the scene by the fire. *That* had been the prop pistol, carved to resemble the long muzzle-loaded single-shot firearms of the prior century, and then appropriated and ruined by someone, and hidden in the kindling.

Morris! Or Burton! Or even Hewett herself! Just to get a real pistol on stage.

They were going to kill him. No, Hewett wouldn't—that was madness to contemplate. And Burton was simply too much of a drunk to make a plan, even if he were drunk enough to manufacture some grudge against Gerald.

Morris. Morris was insane, and had threatened him once, and had already carried one weapon on his person and even upon the stage.

At the climax of *Presumption,* the women are all gone. William Frankenstein, not yet a man, and in this production not even embodied by anything but a woman's far-off voice, is murdered by the demon. Frankenstein, Clerval, Felix De Lacy, and the gypsy pursue the demon into the blinding snow. Frankenstein levels a rifle at the demon, the gypsy warns that the report from so powerful a weapon could bring down an avalanche, but in his anger and self-loathing Frankenstein fires anyway, killing himself and his creation both.

What would Morris do? Change a line, the little bastard. "Hold, master! If the gun is fired, it will bring down a mountain of snow!" all he need say is, "Hold, master! Use your pistol, for your rifle will bring down a mountain of snow!" Would Burton actually withdraw the pistol and fire? No. But Morris could grab the pistol from Burton's belt and shoot. The report from the pepperbox would be drowned out by the percussion of the orchestra "trap" effects meant to signify the sounds of the rifle and subsequent avalanche.

Gerald should run. He could live in the woods, camp as he did as a child, make his way back to England on the goodwill of his fellow Welshman, or even just stay here and hire himself out as a docker.

But no. The show *must* go on.

It was time. He walked upon the stage, had his little scene with Agatha, who squeaked when she died, and then with Ninon and the phantom Master William Frankenstein. It was Miray who voiced that murder, and her scream was especially blood-curdling that night, as if a warning, or a summoning.

Act III, Scene V.

Frankenstein and his men pursue ———— to the snowy reaches of the lake's border. "Agatha! William! You shall be avenged!" Frankenstein cries out.

Morris doesn't bother to change his line, or speak it. He just grabs Hewett's pepperbox pistol from the belt of Burton's costume and levels it at Gerald's chest, then fires.

When Gerald awakened, he was surrounded by women. They were leaning over him. Despite the pain in his chest, which felt as though it had been cracked open like a nut, he could not help but notice first their bosoms. Hewett's prodigious chest, Miray's sandy flesh, young Agatha and old Ninon with their distinct charms of shape and contour.

"Physical culture," said Ninon. "A lifetime of press-ups saved your life, Mr. Wallace."

"What…"

Ninon held up a lead pellet. "Pulled this right out of your sternum. I was raised by Hospital Sisters; I know a thing or two about nursing a wound. Don't move, overmuch. I'm not much of a seamstress, and the theater's costumer fainted dead away at the state of you."

"Mr. Morris, whom the men tackled and bound, right on the stage, has been taken away by the watch," Hewett explained. "He took my pistol, and somehow convinced Burton to use it as a replacement when the prop went missing."

"I'm dreadfully sorry, Mr. Wallace," said Miray. Her voice was wet with tears. "I did nothing to excite Mr. Morris. There was just a demon of some sort in him; just pure wicked impery!"

"I'm glad you've not been murdered," offered Agatha.

"Yes…I agree, miss," said Gerald. He was ashamed not to remember her true name.

"The play…"

"Our run is over," said Hewett. "Though this night's ovation was stunning, I must say."

"Legendary!" said Ninon.

"Thank you, ma'am, for saving me," Gerald told her. "I know we've not gotten on well."

"If the arts of healing were preserved only for the good-hearted, the army of the dead would by far overwhelm the world of the living," she said.

"I feel…delirious…" Why would Ninon have said such a thing; it conjured up an image that would have been well-suited for Mrs. Shelley's novel. All these women were acting so strangely. They loomed over him, the quartet, like in that waking dream he'd had only one day before. The universe of women, the universal woman, manifesting before the last man.

And how had that dream that was not a dream ended? With a promise, Gerald remembered now.

"Your hand is growing cold, Mr. Wallace," Miray said. He could scarcely feel her small fingers clutching at his great paw.

"But his brow is warm!" said Agatha, stroking away the sweat from his hair.

What was that promise?

"Oh dear," said Ninon. "Have I let too much blood?"

And Hewett just looked at him, and she was different now. Not just a director of plays, but of all things. She was the size of the world; her breast was a great and frozen sea, like the dark places between the stars. And she knew her lines. She recalled the promise she had made to all men, and she spoke it to Gerald now.

> For I am the one who alone exists,
> and I have no one who will judge me.
> For many are the pleasant forms which exist in
> numerous sins,
> and incontinences,
> and disgraceful passions,
> and fleeting pleasures,
> which men embrace until they become sober
> and go up to their resting place.
> And they will find me there,
> and they will live,
> and they will not die again.

CPSIA information can be obtained
at www.ICGtesting.com
Printed in the USA
FSHW021254121020
74740FS

9 781952 283031